THE TWILIGHT BOX

Tales of Terre II

NOVELS BY TROON HARRISON

Millie: Dandelion Days, 2007

The Twilight Box
(Second Book of the Tales of Terre series), 2007

The Separated
(First Book of the Tales of Terre series), 2006

Millie: The Star Supper, 2006

Millie: The Button Necklace, 2005

Storm Lion of Penzance, 2005

Millie: Ride the River, 2004

Eye of the Wolf, 2003

Goodbye to Atlantis, 2001

A Bushel of Light, 2000

THE TWILIGHT BOX

by Troon Harrison

Second book of the TALES OF TERRE

Brown Barn Books
Weston, Connecticut

Brown Barn Books
A division of Pictures of Record, Inc.
119 Kettle Creek Road, Weston, CT 06883, U.S.A.

The Twilight Box
Copyright © 2007 by Troon Harrison

Original paperback edition

Library of Congress Cataloging-in-Publication Data

Harrison, Troon.
  The Twilight box / by Troon Harrison.
    p. cm. — (Tales of Terre ; 2)
  Summary: As they search for their identities, two very different teenagers living in a world of ancient magic join forces to save their land from the forces of evil.
  ISBN-13: 978-0-9768126-7-8 (alk. paper)
  ISBN-10: 0-9768126-7-3 (alk. paper)
  [1. Identity—Fiction. 2. Fantasy.] I. Title. II. Series.

PZ7.H25616Tw 2007
[Fic]—dc22

                                          2007015829

PRAISE FOR THE SEPARATED, THE FIRST TALE OF TERRE

"Vivid details create a lush and believable world of great beauty and even greater suspense."

—*AMAZON.COM EDITOR REVIEW*

Finalist, *Foreword Magazine Book of the Year Award 2007*

"In this tale of dragons, evil lords and majestic animals, three teenagers must learn that the world is not as they first thought, and that they themselves are not who they think they are. The author writes in such a way that you can actually envision what is happening, and the story will come alive as you read it. I'm looking forward to any future installments."

—*READER VIEWS, FEBRUARY, 2007*

"A skillfully crafted novel of fantasy action/adventure, *The Separated* is very highly recommended for its creative and magical world and tangible vivid descriptions."

—*MIDWEST BOOK REVIEW, JUNE, 2006*

"A rollicking fantasy adventure featuring three brave adventurers facing off against evil."

—*YOUNG ADULT BOOKS CENTRAL BLOG*

"*The Separated* is a wonderful fantasy adventure. Creatures of all kinds are here to be discovered. Troon Harrison is one of the most pleasantly descriptive authors I have had the pleasure of reviewing. While *The Separated* might have been written for an audience of youth, it will certainly appeal to adults as well."

—*CURLED UP WITH A GOOD BOOK, JANUARY, 2007*

Listed for Children's Book Council Summer Reading Extravaganza 2006

To Trevor

with deep appreciation for our wonderful love

CHAPTER ONE

THE BIANCO, THAT COOL NORTH WIND from the mountains of Bossano, had been blowing for three days, whipping the Golfo de Levanto's bright water into curling waves with foamy crests and hearts like green glass fishing floats. For three days, the migrating pelicans had floated in sheltered coves around the twenty-two scattered islands of the pirati archipelago, waiting for the wind to die so that they could continue their spring migration northward. Now, as evening approached, the wind was changing at last.

Resting his elbows on the gunwale of the rowing boat, Ambro the sea urchin scanned the horizon with his spyglass, one of his only two possessions, and saw the sea witch riding toward the islands with her black cape swirling around her stern narrow face. Her mount, a sea horse with pale green skin marked with orange patterns like coral, plunged swiftly through the cresting waves, its sea grass mane whipping in the erratic winds. Ambro suspected that the witch had something to do with the changing weather, for it was her task to look after the creatures of the sea, and the pelicans could not migrate until the Bianco had blown itself out.

It was said that the witch had power with the wind and the water, as well as with their creatures.

Watching the witch, Ambro felt the new wind out of the south licking with warm breath against the shaggy golden hair at the back of his neck. As the cool Bianco and the warm southern air met, clouds swirled and the waves, which had been running all in one direction, became choppy and confused, running at cross currents to one another and rearing up to slap with angry power against the rocky cliffs of the islands.

"Storm's brewing," said the sea urchin seated beside Ambro, sounding anxious.

"Come on, Ambro, we best run for shore," chimed in another voice.

"In a minute," Ambro said. He swung the spyglass around, following the dashing course of the witch as she headed home to her own island, where she lived alone in a round house of silver driftwood built beneath a giant salt pine on the point. Once she'd had a daughter who lived with her, but it was said the girl had gone away to live in one of the mainland villages to be a healer. As the witch neared shore, the pelicans lifted into the air and began to beat heavily northward.

Ambro smiled in satisfaction and swung the spyglass up the channel, watching the birds with their orange feet tucked into their snowy bellies, and their sagging beaks tucked into their breasts. They were magnificent, he thought, like galleons in full sail, like the trading ships that skimmed along the horizons of his life and that he loved to watch yet on board of which he had never been.

"Come on," urged the boy at Ambro's shoulder again and he sighed and was just about to remove the spyglass from his squinting right eye when something to the north caught his attention.

"Wait one minute," he said. "A ship's coming, a trading ship!"

The vessel, as though summoned by Ambro's thoughts of pelicans and ships, was tacking into the strengthening southern wind, the racing seas smacking its bow of fragranti wood from one direction and then another so that it plunged and slewed around like a frightened horse. Against the scudding clouds, dark lavender in the evening light, its sails were pale and taut. The topgallant and foresails were furled, the mainsails were reefed to reduce the amount of canvas. The ship lay low in the water, with little free-board, and Ambro guessed that her holds were filled with trading goods from the delta to the north: casks of fine dry wine, barrels of porcelain packed in straw, sacks bulging with wheat from the fertile fields of inland Verde, the green land.

"Let me look," demanded Pietro, the boy jostling against Ambro's elbow, and Ambro handed him the spy glass and squinted northward without it, his tawny eyes narrowed to slits. The trading vessel was close enough now that he and the other sea urchins crowded into their rowing boat could all see her clearly, even without the spyglass. The tiny figures of sailors scaled the rigging and more pale ochre sail was dragged in, cracking in the wind, to be lashed along polished spars. Tossing and twisting, her shining decks awash with waves, the ship beat an erratic course toward the pirati archipelago where the sea urchins balanced in their rowing boat, sheltered within the arms of a cove, their tat-tered clothes and rough hair flapping in the swirling gusts.

"She's going to go aground on the reef!" shrieked a small girl, crouching in the bottom of the rowing boat and resting her bony elbows on a thwart.

The sea urchins jostled against one another as the rowing boat bucked and tugged against her anchor. Like a pack of ragged animals they huddled together and stared at the ship sweeping toward their island.

"She's looking for shelter!" cried Belinda, an older girl.

Ambro gestured for his spyglass with impatient excitement and Pietro handed it back. Now, with the glass, Ambro could see the figures of men standing in the forecastle, pacing the deck and star-ing through glasses similar to his own. Their brass tubes glittered in the watery rays of the sun, as it sank into the heaving horizon of the Middle Sea which lay to the west. The men's faces appeared worried, creased with frowns. Arms pointed, orders were hurled into the wind and torn away from open mouths.

"We must help them into the bay!" Ambro announced suddenly, folding his spyglass up and sliding it into a pocket. The sea urchins gaped at him.

"But Ambro—"

"Pull the anchor!" he shouted. "They have no pilot. We must guide them around the point, out past the reef, and into the bay before the ship is lost. They cannot tack into this wind."

Even as he gave orders, Ambro was moving, hauling the anchor in hand over hand, the sea cold on his thin, sinewy arms, making his golden skin shine.

"Pietro!" he shouted. "You row beside me. Belinda, you row with Tessa. Nino and Mia, take an oar together. Umberto and Franco, row beside each other!"

The sea urchins scrambled to obey Ambro's commands, dragging worn oars from the bottom of the boat and sliding them into squeaking oarlocks. Heavily, the blunt bow of the old boat turned toward the mouth of the cove and breasted the dark swells. The sun fell into the sea and Ambro glimpsed the evening star winking intermittently between tattered purple clouds. Behind the urchins' straining backs, the moon rose over the mountains of Verde like a silver coin, and laid a path of fish scales between the rowing boat and the trading vessel.

"Light the lantern!" Ambro cried, and the smallest urchin, the only one not rowing, fumbled in the bottom of the boat with the tinder box. Inside the lantern, the wick burst into a petal of flame and Ambro stood up for a moment, balancing in the leaping boat with slender, wiry legs, and lashed the lantern to the mast, where no sail hung because the children didn't have one.

Slowly, like a tiny beetle, the rowing boat surfed out to meet the trading vessel where she labored dangerously closer and closer to the reef's dark, hidden teeth.

"Ahoy! Ahoy!" Ambro yelled, and the other sea urchins shouted with him until finally their voices and their lantern attracted attention on the merchant ship's decks. As the sea urchins rowed on, straining at the cumbersome oars, their boat creaking in protest as waves smacked her. A small boat was lowered down the side of the trading vessel and tossed across the water to meet them, its oars sweeping in rhythm.

"What do you want?" cried the man at the helm of the boat, and although he spoke the language of Verde, his speech was heavily accented and Ambro knew that he came from some foreign land.

"You're too close to the reef! The reef!" Ambro shouted, his hands cupped around his mouth. The faces in the other boat turned toward him, pale with wind and fear.

"You must make around the point into the next bay. You can drop your anchor safely there!"

"Can you take us around, boy? Do you know these waters?"

"Yes!" Ambro shouted back.

There was a brief consultation in the other boat as men bent their heads together and muttered. Then, on a curt command, the boat was rowed forward again.

"Ship your port oars; hold her steady on starboard!" a foreign voice rang across the water, and the sea urchins obeyed, struggling to hold steady with their thin wrists and their thin bent backs, while their eyes filled with salty spray and their mouths filled with the witch's southern wind. Closer and closer the two boats tossed until suddenly, for a fraction of time, their gunwales rested beside each other, almost touching, and Ambro leapt over the crack of dark water and landed with a thump—that knocked the air from his lungs—upon the ribs in the bottom of the other boat. Immediately the rowers dipped their long oars and the boat swirled away from the sea urchins and began pulling back toward the merchant ship.

"Row for shore!" shouted Ambro to the urchins, and watched while they turned their boat and it surfed away over the pale crests of the waves, heading back to the cove. There, he knew, they would run it up on the sandy beach and tumble out of it, roping it tightly to the roots of salt pine trees high above the tide line. Then they themselves would scramble around the point to where there was a fissure in the rocks, with a floor of sand and pale broken shells, and they would follow each other down the fissure into their cave. They'd light a fire of driftwood that snapped and burned blue and green with salt, and they'd roast a fish for supper and curl up to sleep on beds of dried seaweed, with the waves roaring far off in their dreams.

Ambro turned his back on them and stared ahead to where the merchant ship loomed, a vast hulk of creaking wood and snapping sails against the bruised sky and faint rash of stars. Ropes swung downward, whipped away by the wind, and the men in the rowing boat strained to catch them. Finally, they were attached to the davits and the boat was hauled up the ship's rolling sides until the men could clamber out onto the deck. A strong hand gripped Ambro by his collar, and steered him toward the forecastle where the captain stood with braced legs, peering anxiously into the night.

"Says he'll pilot us in, Sir!" the sailor roared, and thrust Ambro forward so that he stumbled and almost fell at the captain's feet. Quickly he regained his balance and drew himself up tall before the captain, jerking his collar back into place around his throat. The ghost of a smile passed through the captain's eyes as he stared at Ambro's squared shoulders and raised chin, at his torn and patched clothes and the proud brightness of his eyes glimpsed through ragged hair.

Then the captain's face became stern again, his hawk nose casting shadow across his wide, thin lips. "Who are you?" he demanded.

"Ambro d' Monti. I'm a sea urchin. I know every rock, every reef. Sir, you must bear out past this point that lies ahead for the rocks run out from it two fathoms below the surface. You will tear the belly from your ship on your present course. If you clear the point, you can drop your anchor in the next bay and be sheltered there. The water in the bay is seven fathoms where I'll show you."

The captain studied Ambro's face for a moment longer, as if fearing a trick, but then, perhaps liking what he saw or perhaps remembering that even the pirati of the archipelago had forsaken their evil ways and no longer plundered the merchant ships, decided to trust him.

"Where must we bear?" he asked.

Ambro stretched out an arm. "Line your bowsprit with the eye in the constellation of the cormorant," he directed. "Hold that bearing until we clear the point. We will be outside the reef then."

"Follow the bearing!" the captain barked, and the helmsman swung the great wheel of mandolo wood over, slewing the bow toward open sea. The masts creaked and groaned overhead and Ambro stared upward along their dizzying heights. Their tips seemed to rake amongst the fleeing stars. Sails snapped and billowed like thunderheads; ropes moaned and the wind played through them like the fingers of a giant hand thrumming an instrument. Ambro felt the thrumming in his own body and smiled with excitement and delight, standing where he had never been before on the deck of a trading vessel, right beside the captain in his blowing robe of bright fabric, and his high boots with rolled tops of fleece that shone pale in the gloom.

"Never seen it change so fast," the captain muttered. "I thought the Bianco was going to chase us all the way. But she died as this southern wind sprang up."

Ambro thought of the witch galloping home, her silver earrings shaped like shells, and her silver bracelets twined around her wrists like seaweed, all glinting in the blowing spray. He said nothing of this to the captain.

Slowly, slowly, the ship swung through the surging water, rounding the point, and slipped at last into the shelter of the bay where the sounding line with its lead weight was lowered over the side to measure the depth. "Eight at the mark!" the sailor shouted. "Seven fathoms!"

The helmsman held the great wheel steady, watching Ambro's outstretched arm.

"Drop your anchor!" Ambro said.

"Let her go!" the captain shouted, and the great anchor fell into the water with a splash and the chain ran out after it, crashing and grinding in the sudden silence for they were sheltered now from the boisterous southern wind. In the bay's calm the ship came to rest, rocking rhythmically, the barrels and casks and sacks safe in her hold.

The captain clapped Ambro's back with one hand. "Well done!" he roared. "You must come below and be fed supper, a fit reward for your evening's work! My fool of a navigator lost our chart for the Golfo."

Ambro followed the man's long stride down a flight of steps, and blinked in the sudden golden warmth of lamplight in a cabin ribbed with pale wood, gleaming with polish, and draped with bright tapestries.

"Sit!" The captain gestured with a sweep of his arm. In wonder Ambro crossed the floor, his feet sinking into the intricate twined flowers of the rug, to perch on a bench heaped with cushions of golden fabric shot through with green and red threads, and embroidered with strange, foreign patterns. Two other men, dressed like the captain in long robes, and wearing tall supple boots with rolled tops lined with fleece, entered the cabin and sat around the table.

"My companions and trading partners," the captain said. "May I introduce Lord Tafari, and Markos Dula. I myself am Captain Hakim."

Ambro stood, and shook hands with each man in turn, noticing the gem stones that sparkled on their fingers, and the golden hoops in their ears, and the tight fine weave of their brilliantly colored robes embroidered around the collars with a pattern of paw prints and grass. Lord Tafari was young, only a few years older than Ambro, with a slender, tightly muscled body and an arrogant, graceful way of moving; but Markos Dula was middle-aged and plump, with pudgy fingers. The captain himself was the oldest of the three, his face seamed with years of sun and wind.

All three spoke the language of Verde with a strange harsh accent, the familiar words changing shape on their tongues.

"This is Ambro d'Monti," the Captain announced to the other men, and the traders regarded Ambro intently while a servant bustled in and began to lay food on the polished table: a loaf of bread, olives swimming in fine oil, a wheel of cheese, a steaming stew of tomatoes and conger eel, and an almond cake. Ambro's mouth watered; he couldn't remember the last time he'd eaten. Nor had he ever seen food this fine and he stared at it all with longing.

"Ambro d'Monti. A strange name, even for a young man of Verde," mused Lord Tafari, his aristocratic cheeks creasing as his very white teeth crunched into the bread's crust. "How did you come by such a name?"

"I have never known my parents," Ambro explained. "I have been a sea urchin all my life."

"They are the orphans and outcasts of Verde's coastline," the captain explained to the other traders. "They live in caves and little boats. Am I right?"

Ambro nodded. "I was orphaned very young, in a shipwreck they said, the older urchins. But I don't remember any of that. When the urchins found me, I was strapped to a spar and washed up on a beach. I had two things with me, in my clothes."

Proudly, he drew his spyglass, tarnished with salt, from one pocket and held it out for the men to see. Lord Tafari took it in his slender fingers and examined it closely, rolling the brass barrel as though it held secrets. Ambro reached inside his shirt and, from the inner pocket of the tight vest he wore beneath, removed another object and held it out. "My name is written on this," he said. "That's how I know."

Captain Hakim reached out for the burnished wooden flute that Ambro held into the lamplight, and with one finger traced the faded lettering that was painted, with fine gold lines, along the underside of the instrument. "Ambro d'Monti," he said slowly. "As you said, your name, or your father's."

The trader called Markos Dula looked up sharply, his eyes narrowed. "That is not the name of the flute's owner," he said, "but of its maker. In Genovera—do you know Genovera?"

Ambro shook his head, his mouth too full of saliva to speak. The steam rose from the eel and tomato stew in gentle curls that tickled his nose and slid down the back of his throat.

A glint of humor passed again through the captain's eyes. "Eat, young man," he commanded and slid a porcelain bowl—a foreign bowl with decorations of suns and strange looking trees—toward Ambro. He filled it with fat chunks of eel, with olives and tomatoes and herbs, and topped it off with a slice of warm cheese and crusty bread. Ambro bent his head over the bowl and began to eat, while the trader called Markos Dula talked on.

"Genovera lies in the north of Verde, on the bank of the great River Arnona that runs from the mountains down to the delta, where we moor our ships. In Genovera, twenty years ago, there was a master instrument maker by the name of Ambrosi d'Monticello. Surely, it is the remains of his name on your flute, for it is a fine instrument. See? Letters are missing, rubbed off with time. This is not your name at all."

Ambro's throat closed in a spasm around a chunk of eel, and he felt a burning behind his eyes.

"It is my name now, I have claimed it!" he cried. "It is the only one I have!"

His eyes glittered with defiance in the lamplight, as he stared at the traders perched around him like exotically plumaged birds.

Markos chuckled. "The cub roars."

"Well spoken," applauded Lord Tafari smoothly. "It is a fine name for you, even in its shortened form."

Ambro bent his head over the pungent cheese, while the ghost of his imagined father—a musician by the name of Ambro d'Monti—drifted away from him, leaving him alone as he had never been before, when he had at least a scrap of a dream to believe in, when it seemed as though he might once have had a family to call his own.

"And what is it like, being a sea urchin?" Lord Tafari asked. Ambro shrugged, his face impassive. "It is well enough," he said shortly. "We know the sea and the islands. We know where to keep dry in storms, where to fish."

He bent back over his food, trying to cling to that ghost of a father that had kept him company for so long and that was fading now into emptiness. He clamped his jaw hard onto a piece of bread and kept his eyes averted from the traders. Tomorrow, *they* would be gone, with their schemes for making gold, with their accounts in long columns on scrolls of parchment and their swinging scales, with their full bellies. And tomorrow, *he* would still be here, chilly in his ragged shirt, belonging to no one, living by his wits and filling his belly with limpets scraped from the rocks, with stews of sea grass boiled over a beach fire. He wouldn't let them take away his name when they left.

"How old are you?" Markos Dula asked.

"They said I was about two years old when they found me on the beach. That was fourteen summers ago."

Markos Dula leaned across the table, his eyes over his plump cheeks alert and intent, as though he were an animal hunting something. "Fourteen years since the wreck that cast you here. And did no one else survive?"

"Not that I ever heard of."

Markos turned toward the other traders. "Do you not remember?" he asked. "The loss of the *Jaffa Queen* with all hands, fourteen years ago on the eve of the spring solstice, in that great storm that blew for two weeks?"

The other traders looked at Markos intently, and then turned their gazes to Ambro. He met them without flinching, daring them to show pity.

"There was a child on board the *Jaffa Queen* when she went down; surely he was the son of a kinsman of Ayan Kalif, who lives in Jaffa and owns three salt caravans."

Captain Hakim and Lord Tafari continued to stare at Ambro.

"Look at his eyes," the captain muttered. "Look at his hair."

"He is a Kiffa-walker," pronounced Markos with grave solemnity. "Look at his skin color, his nose."

"Consider his arrogance." Lord Tafari sounded admiring.

Ambro pushed his hair back from his face and stared around in confusion.

"Boy," the captain said gently, "did you ever see yourself?"

"Only my reflection in tide pools."

The captain stood and opened a cupboard of fragranti wood, cunningly built into the wall of his cabin, and took out a mirror with a handle inlaid with mother of pearl from the islands of Lontano. "Look at yourself in this."

Obediently, Ambro curled his fingers around the slender handle and stared at his face in the mirror's burnished surface. The reflection there was much clearer than anything he'd seen in the stillest of tide pools. Golden skin, burned red on the high cheekbones by sun and wind and salt. Wild hair, beautiful hair—even he could see that—hair that was brown shading to pure blonde streaked with bright highlights, like old honey seen in sunshine. Beneath the slender aquiline hook of his nose, his eyes were the color of the cinni spice that came from Terre and that rich nobili of Verde imported and drank hot with cream.

"What about it?" he asked in his clear, cool voice, handing the mirror back and uneasily aware, with a prickle that ran up his spine, that the traders gathered around shared his own characteristics. How could he have failed to notice this before? He stared at them all as they studied him in return; he saw how Lord Tafari's golden moustache draped gracefully from the corners of his mouth, how Markos's tawny eyes gleamed in the lantern light, how the captain's hair fell to the collar of his robe in a sweep of dark honey and bright streaks only slightly dulled with grey.

"You are one of us," the captain said. "Did you never wonder why you were the only child with this coloring, these features?"

Ambro ran his mind's eye over the other sea urchins, over the knobs of their knees and elbows, over their scars and freckles that he knew as well as his own, over their heads of black hair and their deep brown eyes. They looked, he realized, the same as most of the other people who lived in the pirati archipelago and in the coastal villages of Verde. It was he who was different, despite his ragged clothes and prominent collar bones, despite the wind burn on his cheeks and the rope burns on his knuckles and his ability to read tides and waves like a map. In some recess of his mind, he must have known of his own difference, he must have noticed—but it had never mattered.

Until now.

Now, it seemed, the way he looked might be a faint trail, like footprints half-washed away by a rising tide—a trail that would lead him back through time to someone, somewhere, who had once known his father's true name, and the ship that his father traveled on, called the *Jaffa Queen*.

"Where are you from?" he asked the men hungrily, while the cabin rocked them and the crumbs rolled around on the table between the thin porcelain bowls with their foreign designs, and lamplight glittered off the men's robes and golden earrings.

"We are from Terre, and so are you," the captain pronounced. "Have you heard of Terre?"

Ambro nodded. "It's a desert land," he said. "It trades with other nations using its salt and gold. It lies to the south of here, in the latitudes of heat, below the Middle Sea."

Around the table, heads nodded.

"There are three fine cities in Terre," Markos Dula said. "We are sailing to Jaffa, the northern port. On the south coast lies the port of Shoa. Inland, at the edge of the great rift valley of Nini, is the city of Safala. She is the heart of Terre, a great trading city."

A sigh of admiration and longing escaped from Lord Tafari and he smiled dreamily at Ambro.

"She is the most beautiful city on earth," he said. "Imagine—" his slender hands waved in the air, as though a vision of his city might appear before them all in the cabin's dim interior. "She is a city as old as time, built into the rocks of the plateau where it rises from the valley of Nini. A city lapped by wheat fields and held, like a jewel, in the midst of the caravan routes. Her buildings, her palaces and stairways and aqueducts, are carved out of solid rock; she shines in the sun's heat like a rose. Her towers are fretted in pale pink; her treasury is carved from strata of gold-stone; her Kiffa temple is ruby when the setting sun touches it. Ah, Ambro, you have not lived until you have seen Safala and walked in her cool shadows while desert hawks wheel overhead in cracks of azure sky."

Languidly, Lord Tafari's voice trailed off but Ambro continued to stare at his slender profile, as though seeing right through it to the city of rosy stone.

"Where was my father from?" he asked.

Lord Tafari shrugged. "Not from Jaffa, I think. Perhaps from Safala herself?"

"I thought the kinsmen of Ayan Kalif were from Kalli," suggested the captain. "It is a small town, on the caravan route to the gold mines south of Safala."

"No, I think they came from Safala," Lord Tafari said. "You had better come home with us," he announced with sudden energy. "Terre is growing rich and powerful; she will subdue all nations soon. Her gold and her salt mines grow deeper by the hour; her caravans groan laden to the ports. All the goods of the world come to her doors. You can come and fight in our army, if you wish."

"Whose army?" Ambro asked.

"That of the Kiffa-walkers, of course." The captain laughed. "Drive those Wind-wanderers down into the mines where they belong, the scum."

"Wind-wanderers?"

"Dust-eaters is a better name," scoffed Markos Dula. "They are the other ancient tribe of people in Terre," he confided, leaning across the table toward Ambro, his plump cheeks pursed and his voice sinking low. "They wander in the desert like riff-raff. They have no culture, no learning! They form outlaw groups, bandits, and attack us as we ply our honest trade along the caravan routes. They are without mercy or justice!"

"They live in hairy tents, and herd shugras," the captain said.

"Shugras?"

"A woolly animal; they drink its milk, tan its hide, weave with its fleece. Even their children and wives smell like shugras!" Lord Tafari laughed mockingly.

"They won't bow to Kiffa, he who is mightiest of all gods!" Captain Hakim muttered in shocked tones. "They cling to some goddess, some outdated female deity."

"A moon goddess," said Markos Dula. "They pierce their belly buttons, every one of them—*fah!*—instead of their ear lobes, like civilized beings. They hang from the piercing a crescent moon. It sickens me to think of it." He lifted his wine glass and took a long draught, as though washing an unpleasant taste from his mouth.

"They must be subjugated. We, the Kiffa-walkers, are the true inheritors of Terre's wealth. We have temples and culture; we build while they roam, we civilize while they live with their animals," Lord Tafari explained. "We have nobility." He gazed down, as though in modesty, at his own slender and muscular limbs sprawled at the table's edge.

Markos leaned further over the table toward Ambro, his plump cheeks almost squeezing his eyes shut. "And, what do you think?" he hissed. "They have—I can hardly say the word." His two chins quivered. "They have—*webs*! Webs, between their toes!"

Lord Tafari's noble profile contorted with disgust, and the captain's eyes gleamed with arrogance. Markos shuddered fastidiously and made little motions with his plump fingers as if shedding something sticky and unpleasant. Ambro nodded gravely. Beneath the polished table and resting on the marvelous twined flowers of the thick rug, his own toes, hidden in a pair of worn rope shoes that he'd bargained for with a string of reef fish, curled protectively together. He cleared his throat, and after a moment the gaze that he fixed on the captain's face was steady.

"What time do you sail in the morning?" he asked.

"At first light, if the wind has dropped."

"I will give you my answer then, whether or not I will come with you to Terre."

"You can sleep in a hammock in our guest quarters," the captain said, and he rose, his head almost touching the ceiling, while the traders bowed themselves toward the door.

"Sleep soundly, Ambro d'Monti," Lord Tafari said. "Sleep soundly, young Kiffa-walker, and dream of Safala, the rose-red city."

CHAPTER TWO

WHEN AMBRO ROLLED FROM HIS hammock in the morning, with the pattern of its webbing imprinted in his back where the rug had slipped off, he padded silently in his rope shoes onto the deck. Outside the bay, the south wind was still whipping foam from the crests of the Golfo's green waves, but overhead the sky sang with a thin, clear blue and Ambro was sure that the captain would sail as soon as the sun rose fully over the mountains of Verde.

He leaned on the brass railing and stared toward the coast. Smudges of grey marked where the cooking fires of village homes sent smoke into the dawn air. Ambro imagined, as he often liked to do, how it would be to awake inside one of those tall, narrow village houses, with its blue shutters and stout walls of golden stone. He liked to linger, in his mind, over the details of a kitchen with a red-tiled floor, over bunches of herbs hanging to dry and releasing a sweet fragrance that mingled with the smell of breakfast cooking. He liked to imagine a bevy of children, his brothers and sisters, scrambling around the woman at the stove. His mother.

When she turned, she would smile at him, ask him how he had slept, offer him a bowl of mandolo nut porridge sweetened with honey and almonds. Her smile would linger on his bent head as he ate; her wide, dark, mysteriously beautiful smile…

Ambro gave his head a shake. For many years he had been dreaming about belonging somewhere, but he had never had a place to belong, here on Verde. The closest thing he had to a family was the bunch of sea urchins with whom he survived, shivering in chill caves in winter, growing burned and wind-swept in summer. Still, it was not such a bad life. He remembered fishing with a lantern at night, staring down through the clear water at the pink anemones flowering on the reef, at the tangles of golden seaweed streaming in the current, at the flash of spotted fish and the tentacles of squid. He remembered swimming on nights when the sky was a bowl of stars inverted overhead, and his limbs dripped with blue phosphorescence. No, it was not such a bad life but still…it was not belonging.

Gazing over the side of the merchant ship at its tight, calked timbers of gleaming fragranti, Ambro thought about sailing away southward toward the heat and the sand of Terre, toward an old thread of a tale about shipwreck, and a whole tribe of people with his own golden hair and tawny eyes. With them, he might belong. There, he might even—dare he think it?—find some kind of a family, perhaps some cousins, perhaps someone who could remember the brightness of his mother's smile in her dark face.

A sound on shore snagged in Ambro's thoughts and he stared toward the rocks as the sea urchins climbed around the point and ambled onto the beach, yawning and rubbing their eyes. They stooped to pick up the discards of the sea: a pale whelk shell, a piece of rope with a frayed end, logs to burn in the cave. At the water's edge, the children stood in their faded clothes and stared across at the ship, and waved to Ambro. He waved back, naming them each in his mind: skinny Nino with his sharp elbows, sad Umberto with his deep eyes, Pietro with pale, jagged scars on his arms. Only Mia appeared to be missing; she must be still curled up in her seaweed bed, beside her battered but precious hurdy-gurdy.

It seemed to Ambro that it would be hard to leave the urchins.

He turned at the soft pad of steps and saw Lord Tafari striding along the deck in his supple rolled boots, his azure robe blowing open and billowing like wings, tugging at its golden clasp. The sun struck sparks from the lord's hair and his drooping moustache, from the gold earring inlaid with amber that dangled from his right ear, and the metallic threads in his leggings. He strode loose limbed toward Ambro, a magnificent figure with long straight bones and taut muscles, and leaned beside him on the rail.

"Saying good-bye?" he asked.

"Yes," agreed Ambro, the word flying from his mouth as though it had ambushed him.

The lord nodded, seeming unsurprised. "It will be slow, tacking into this cursed wind," he judged, shading his eyes and staring out the mouth of the bay to the rollers creaming northward. "Still, in twelve days at most you will surely be home, Ambro. I am traveling from Jaffa on to Safala and you can join my caravan, if you wish."

Home.

Home! Ambro thought. Home, where my people are, my true family. Home, where I am a Kiffa-walker.

He drew himself up tall against the rail and nodded gravely. "I would be happy to come with you to Safala," he said, and the lord's lips twitched in admiration as he glanced at the sea urchin's profile.

"A man would be proud," he said, "to have such a son as you. Perhaps, in Terre, there might be an uncle. Come, there is time for breakfast before the anchor's hauled," and he turned away from the children gathered like spindly shore birds along the edge of the water.

Ambro hesitated, taking hold of his shirt and thinking that, instead of eating breakfast, he'd strip and swim ashore to say goodbye to the urchins. He could also fetch his worn cloak from the cave, and the necklace of sea glass that Belinda had made for him. He began to lift his shirt over his head; then he paused. He thought of his clothes lying on the deck of the merchant ship in a tattered heap, and of his tarnished spyglass and his flute with the faded lettering that gave him the name that was not his name, lying on top of the clothes; lastly, he thought of his worn rope shoes sitting on the deck boards beside everything else. At that thought, his fingers uncurled from the fabric of his shirt as if they'd been scorched, and his hands fell to his sides.

He leaned over the rail and waved to the children and pointed to the ridge of rock that ran out from the arm of the bay to plunge downward into the water like a crooked spine and become the reef. After a moment's uncertainty, the urchins seemed to understand his gesture and they ran nimble and barefoot along the rocks until they were standing as close to the merchant ship as they could. Ambro cupped his hands around his mouth and shouted.

"I'm going to Terre! I'm looking for my family! Goodbye!" His words rolled across the ripples and shivered in the morning air. The urchins' faces stiffened with surprise and shock. One by one, they took turns to balance out to the farthest rock, slippery with sea lettuce and salt sponge, and call their farewells to Ambro while, onboard the merchant ship, the sailors ran the sails up the masts and swarmed in the rigging, and bent to the capstan, hauling in the anchor. It came at last with a groan of chain, with a swing and a gurgle. The bow came around. Wind filled the sails, straining them taut, and the swell of the open sea lifted the boat.

Not until the sea urchins were tiny dots on the shoreline did Ambro leave the rail and go forward to stand in the bow, his face turned towards the southern horizon where, it seemed to him, the air was thick and white with heat, and let the southern wind rush through his hair. He stood there alone for a long time, letting the wind wash away his past and fill him with courage. He stood there until he had ceased, he thought, to be a sea urchin and had become instead a Kiffa-walker; had grown into the hook of his nose and the glint of his eyes and the pride of his birthright.

Lord Tafari had spoken the truth; as long as the wind blew from the south, it was a slow passage beating toward Terre, running across the wind and the seas, the ship heeling over and her timbers creaking as she ploughed through the heavy swells. On the second day, Markos approached Ambro on deck and slipped one hand into a pocket of his robe, then pulled out a small book with a smooth leather cover that he held out to Ambro. "Here, Ambro, I have had this copied for you. It has helped me when I'm trading and it might help you, too. If—can you read?"

Ambro nodded. "An older urchin taught me, who had some schooling."

Opening the book, Ambro saw lists of words in columns. One set, he realized, was written in his own language, the tongue of Verde, but the other was a list of foreign words.

"So you can learn our language in Terre," Markos explained.

"Yes!" Ambro exclaimed. "And I speak a little already! An old hermit, who has traveled the world and learned its tongues, lives in the pirati archipelago. We call him the reef-fish. I have passed winter storms in his cabin and he has taught me some of the speech of Terre."

"Ah!" Markos beamed. "You will not have any trouble with your mother tongue."

Ambro grinned, excitement bubbling up into his throat so that he could hardly speak his thanks. My *mother tongue*, he thought, and felt as though the language alone was already giving him a family and welcoming him in. He returned to the pile of rope where he'd been sitting, and pored over the lists of words.

At last, on the thirteenth day, the wind swung into the west and the ship's motion changed. Excitement grew in Ambro until it seemed like a water skin stuck in his chest, squeezing his heart and his lungs. The sailors began to chant the songs of Terre in their harsh foreign tongue, words that sounded like birds crying; Ambro strained his ears to recognize the words that he knew. He scanned the southern horizon restlessly and after some time, he was joined by Markos Dula in a robe of flowing ruby silk and stiff felt slippers with curled toes in place of his usual high boots.

"Are you traveling on to Safala?" Ambro asked.

"No, I am from Jaffa. I will supervise the unloading of the ship, and the delivery of our cargo to warehouses where our goods are stored. Lord Tafari will travel with the caravan to Safala. He has interests in the gold mines, you know. He is very rich as well as very noble. Still, I do not envy him his journey across the desert."

"Why not?" Ambro asked, staring curiously at the trader's pursed lips and grave frown.

"The Wind-wanderers, "he hissed. "They are growing bolder and more savage. They can run fast across the sand using their—their *disgusting*—toes, and they have fleet horses. They rob the caravans whenever they can. They slit the caravaners' throats with blades as sharp as vultures' talons."

Markos made a slicing motion beneath his double chins and his eyes rolled. A shiver passed down Ambro's back but he straightened it immediately. "I'm not afraid of some desert rabble," he said boldly and Markos clapped his smooth palms together.

"You're a Kiffa-walker," he applauded. "Never forget it. We will soon have those desert rats, those dust-eaters, below ground where they belong."

"Dead?"

"No, what good are they dead?" Markos asked petulantly. "In the mines, Ambro, working in the mines. Fetching out our gold and our salt, making us rich. We are building temples and palaces such as you have never seen. Our cities will be the most marvelous on earth. In Jaffa itself, they have begun building a Kiffa temple with towers of ivory stone, imported from the quarries of Mombasso, and inlaid with tiles of lapis lazuli and with—"

"Land! Land ho!" cried the voice of the lookout, and Markos and Ambro rushed to the bow and stared ahead, but saw only a smudge of cloud on the southern horizon over the limpid sea. "We will dock before dark," Markos breathed happily, while the great ship tacked closer and closer to the northern coast of Terre.

At sunset, it slipped amongst the three islands clustered around the mouth of the bay where Jaffa gleamed in the last light, a city of white stone. Ochre dust rose into the air above its streets, and across the golden glimmering water rang the rattle of chariot wheels, the shouts of street vendors, the tramp of feet. Braziers glowed like dull red eyes in the purple dusk and Ambro leaned on the ship's rail and breathed in the mingled smells of dank water and dust, animal dung and smoke, foreign spices and food grilling, and the dry grassy smell of the plains beyond the city. He even fancied he could smell the harsh, empty, mineral scent of the desert farther beyond yet, but it was probably his imagination.

Terre, he kept saying in his head and then, aloud, he spoke a word he had already learned in his mother tongue: *Etu*, home.

A tug on his sleeve made him turn.

"Mia! What are you—how did you—?"

The sea urchin stared up at him, her eyes beseeching dark pools in her brown face. "I swam out to the ship before it sailed from Verde," she confessed, "and climbed up the anchor chain and slipped inside and hid."

Ambro shook his head in amazement; only Mia could have managed such a feat. A scrap of an eleven year old, she had joined the sea urchins the previous winter after running away from a troupe of traveling players. She could juggle smooth beach pebbles until they spun in a continuous blurred circle; turn back flips or tuck her toes behind her ears as though she possessed seaweed for a spine; play her hurdy-gurdy and dance at the same time. Indeed, she carried this instrument still, fastened to her back with a worn strap of green leather and wrapped in a casing of waterproof fish skin.

For one moment, Ambro felt delight at seeing a familiar face, but this feeling was swiftly replaced with apprehension. How would his Kiffa-walker relatives receive him with this disheveled child in tow? What if Mia ruined his fine new chance of belonging somewhere?

"What are you going to do now? Why did you come?" he demanded.

"I'm tired of eating fish and being chilly," Mia said. "I thought I would come with you to Terre and be warm, and eat pomegranates instead." Her beseeching expression changed swiftly to one of gleeful anticipation.

"I didn't invite you to join me, "Ambro said stiffly. "I'm trying to find my family. Or I may join the army. What will you do then?" Mia's face changed again, becoming solemn. "You could say that I'm your sister," she said in a small voice, and her hand stole out again to touch Ambro's sleeve. When he remained silent, she hung her head and traced a crack in the decking boards with one dirty bare toe. "Please, Ambro," she whispered.

He flung back his hair in exasperation. "By Sirena's tail!" he cursed. "You don't know anything about Terre. How could you be my sister when I am a Kiffa-walker with golden hair and skin, and tawny eyes, like all the people of my tribe? Look at you—you're a child of Verde, with dark hair and brown eyes. No one would believe you're my sister."

Mia's chin slumped against her chest. "Fine," she muttered. "I shall find something of my own to do in Terre."

Ambro heard the desolation in her tone. "You can travel with me," he said more gently. "Look, here comes Captain Hakim. We can ask him what you might do."

The captain listened to Ambro's explanation for Mia's presence onboard his ship; and he stared from the top of her head to her grubby toes, and gave her a kind but absent-minded smile. "Perhaps they will have need of a serving girl in Ambro's family home in Safala," he suggested. "If not, you might call on a lady of my family who lives in that city. Her name is Asha and she lives in the Street of Cucumbers. I believe she is in need of a cook's helper."

Abruptly Captain Hakim swung away, shouting "Drop anchor!" and it rattled out to plunge into the limpid water of Jaffa's inner harbor amidst spreading concentric ripples.

As darkness fell like a cloak, suddenly they were rowed closer to the long fingers of the docks. The brazier lights along the harbor walls burned with fiercer brightness. The air was close and soft, pressing around Ambro, and thicker yet with the smells he'd inhaled while still onboard the ship. From a café door, light and strange wailing music spilled outward accompanied by the muffled beat of drums, and the ululation of a woman's voice. Ambro craned his head, trying to see through the darkness, to claim for his own this city that was foreign to him, even though he had once been rowed across this very water to embark on a voyage from which he would not return for fourteen years, and from which his father would never return at all.

"My mother," he whispered suddenly into the darkness. "Was she on the *Jaffa Queen?*"

"Yes," Captain Hakim nodded after a moment's reflection, "I believe that she too was lost."

Ambro bowed his head over the pain, and barely noticed the comforting warmth of Mia's shoulders, pressed against his legs where she sat in the bottom of the boat. For a moment, crossing the inner water of the harbor toward the smoke and music and commotion of Jaffa's stony streets, Ambro thought once more of his mother as he always thought of her: a dark face, a flashing mysterious smile. Then he raised his head, letting her go in peace. He knew now that he would never see her.

"Nearly there, nearly home," Markos Dula said with weary satisfaction, and Ambro shook off his momentary sadness and felt in the pockets of the silk robe he'd been loaned by Lord Tafari to put over his tattered clothes, to make sure that they still contained his spyglass and his worn flute. His fingers slid along their smooth lengths, as they had done so many times before, and he felt the faint scratches on the spyglass and the holes carved in the flute and was comforted and eager again to reach shore.

Lord Tafari was met with a chariot; in the light of flaring torches, Ambro saw how the spokes gleamed and the golden bits glittered in the horses' mouths. He stepped back as the horses swung restlessly in the traces, their hooves striking sparks from the cobbles, and at his shoulder Captain Hakim chuckled. "That's right, boy, keep your wits around these horses. Sons of the desert, they are, the oldest bloodlines in Terre. Pure fire."

Ambro stared at the team; they were perfectly matched, standing shoulder to shoulder, their huge dark eyes reflecting the torchlight, their nostrils soft and lined with deep pink. They had long, scooped, arrogant faces and their manes cascaded to a great length, reaching from the crest of their curved necks to the tops of their slender legs. They were pale ivory all over their bodies, except for on their hindquarters, where they were patterned with soft, golden stripes. Ambro drew a deep breath and fell in love with them in an instant; he had never seen anything that combined such fiery power and beauty.

"Goodbye and good luck! If you can't find an uncle, join the army!" Markos advised cheerily, drawing Ambro's attention away from the horses as he pumped his hand. "They'll feed you and welcome your strength! You can route out the desert scum!"

"Be safe, and call on me in Jaffa if you need anything," advised Captain Hakim more quietly, taking Ambro's hand in turn. "Beware of the webbies."

"Webbies?"

"The Wind-wanderers, Ambro."

"Climb up!" shouted Lord Tafari and he reached out and caught at Ambro, swinging him aboard the chariot as it leapt forward, the horses charging into the crowd around the dock which scattered at their approach.

"Wait!" Ambro shouted. "Wait for Mia!" but she was already speeding after them, light footed and agile. With one dexterous leap she jumped, caught hold of the chariot's rim, and swung herself onboard.

"By the Kiffa's paw!" exclaimed Lord Tafari in surprise, but when Ambro hauled Mia to her full but insignificant height and introduced her, Lord Tafari merely flicked her with a disinterested glance and ignored her thereafter. They plunged on through the city; the horses' hooves rang in silvery rhythm against the pale stone walls of Jaffa's buildings, the facades of her soaring temples, the studded doors of her treasuries.

Ambro rocked in the chariot with exhaustion, and gripped its rim of beaten metal while below him the haunches of the desert horses sped forward, their stripes of gold rippling like seaweed in a fast current. Ambro felt light-headed with fatigue and disbelief and excitement.

CHAPTER THREE

AMBRO SLEPT, THAT FIRST NIGHT in Terre, in one of Lord Tafari's palaces in the heart of Jaffa, in a bed strewn with soft cushions of Mombasso silk. He awoke to the smell of incense and the patter of servants' feet on marble floors and, with wide eyes, wandered through the palace's courtyards and along its shining corridors. Mia was in one courtyard, turning cartwheels for an assemblage of serving girls, and she gave Ambro a jaunty wave but otherwise ignored him.

All that day, and in the ones that followed, while Lord Tafari conducted business at his warehouses, Ambro explored the streets and listened to the language of Terre as it poured, strident and melodic by turns, from the mouths of laundry women at wells and children playing in alleys and men conducting business at stalls and fishermen mending nets along the harbor. He craned his head and stared, dazzled, at the temple towers as straight and slender as spears, and ran his hands over the smooth expanses of walls tiled in golden and purple ceramic. He bought unknown foods from vendors with coins Lord Tafari had given him and held them on his tongue, absorbing the spices, their fire and strangeness, their hint of the dark.

Sometimes, giddy with the smells of incense and the throbbing of drums, he would retreat to Lord Tafari's courtyard and, seated beside a tinkling fountain, he'd memorize words from the list given to him by Markos. At times, he thought of the sea urchins and wondered what they were doing at that moment on a beach or in an old boat. He played plaintive tunes on his flute—tunes that were like wind calling in salt pines, and light sparkling in channels of water when the tide ran fast in the pirati archipelago, and tunes he'd composed to lull younger urchins to sleep. After the chaos and clamor of the streets, the tunes calmed him and reminded him that Kiffa-walkers were men of courage. Mia, hearing the tunes from where she played cat's cradle and starburst in the servant's quarters, came light-footed across the tiles in her ragged green dress, and sat beside him and hummed his tunes in a husky, sweet voice.

Each evening, when Lord Tafari returned from his business, Ambro would sit with him to eat fresh figs and wheaten cakes filled with dates, and drink a spicy wine made from the sap of the nuga palms that grew in the desert oases.

"I have spoken to Ayan Kalif," Lord Tafari announced one evening. "I met him today in the treasury. He remembers your father and the ship *Jaffa Queen.*"

Ambro felt himself go very still. Clearly, in that long moment of stillness, he heard the trilling notes of a bird in the pomegranate tree growing by the fountain.

"What was my father's name?" he whispered into the bird's song.

"He was a very minor, very distant kinsman of Kalif's only," the lord replied. "Kalif thought that his name was Dawit and that his family name, his own father's name, might have been Jaser. But he was not sure on that point. And it seems also that there was some shame hanging over his name. Kalif advises you to travel to Safala, where you might indeed find someone of your father's family, but not to expect to be welcomed."

Ambro sprang to his feet, his eyes blazing.

"I don't believe him!" he cried. "There would not be shame linked to my father's name!"

Lord Tafari shrugged gracefully and arched his aristocratic eyebrows, plucked that morning by his body servant into perfect crescents.

"Be seated, Ambro. It may be a rumor only. Kalif is an old man now, with a memory that wanders in all matters except those concerning money. He muttered something about your father's unsuitable marriage."

Ambro paced the courtyard, around the pomegranate tree where the bird had fallen silent, and felt something clenched in his chest like an angry fist.

"Take me to the treasury tomorrow!" he demanded. "I will speak to Kalif myself!"

"He has left tonight with a trading ship."

"Old fool," Ambro muttered, and Lord Tafari laughed indulgently.

Later, alone in his room with its heaped cushions, while incense curled from a brazier and wafted amongst the shadows, Ambro bent his head over his book of words and ran his finger down their long straight columns. "*Jaser*: fearless," he muttered. "*Dawit*: beloved."

He lay on his back and closed his eyes, and waited for the fist to unclench in his chest, and fell asleep at last thinking of a tall man in a billowing robe who strode the deck with swinging strides, and whose eyes watched with bold courage as the equinoctial storm swirled over the horizon of the Middle Sea to engulf the doomed *Jaffa Queen*.

On the eighth morning, Lord Tafari prepared to cross the desert to Safala. Ambro dressed at dawn with care, in the clothes the lord had provided for him: leggings of finest leather dyed pale red, high boots with rolled fleecy tops, a robe of shimmering light blue that fastened at his chest with a golden clasp. When he strode into the courtyard, past the beds of exotic lilies shaped like bird beaks and the trickling music of the fountain, the lord flashed a glance over him and smiled.

"Now," he said, "*now* an uncle would recognize you for what you are. Maybe an uncle can get you some rings."

Ambro flushed with pleasure—he *would* be welcomed in Safala, he promised himself, despite rumors of family shame—and strode from the courtyard in the lord's wake, his head high. His legs felt longer and stronger in soft leggings, and his shoulders seemed broader, like a man's, inside the swinging robe. In the high boots, his toes were protected and hidden, and he had forgotten all about them. He felt like a lord.

Before setting out, they bowed themselves into Lord Tafari's private temple erected to Kiffa, the Mighty Protector, He Who Shall be Given Glory. Lord Tafari prostrated himself on the cool amber tiles inlaid with a design of paw prints and grass, before the golden statue of the kiffa god with its man's face and its body like a huge cat. Its whiskers were crafted from golden wire, and its eyes inlaid with precious amber. Its body, with elegant spine and strong haunches, was of burnished red wood inlaid with bandings of ebony around its legs and eyes. Lord Tafari muttered prayers for a safe desert journey. Ambro pressed his forehead to the smooth ceramic and waited, thinking about the real kiffas which Lord Tafari had told him lived in the desert. He wondered if he'd see one soon, and tried to feel as powerful and courageous as one himself. If there was shame awaiting him in Safala, he would fight it; he would avenge his father. When he glanced up at the statue, the god's brilliant eyes seemed to shine encouragement at him, as though aware that he was newly come to his birthright as a Kiffa-walker, and in need of welcome.

In Lord Tafari's chariot, Ambro rode to the edge of the city where the caravan was assembled in the dust beneath scattered palm trees that cast a ragged shade. Ambro stared in amazement at the commotion before him. Hundreds of shaggy creatures, with black and grey plumage, weaving necks and enormously long pink legs lay on the ground with knees folded, or staggered to their feet to swing their serrated beaks at the drivers and handlers who dodged amongst them. The creatures' stout bodies were loaded heavily with bales and boxes of trade goods, strapped on with the tough rope made from the corda tree, and their musky stench and shrieking cries filled Ambro's head.

"Are they—birds?" he asked, for their plumage appeared to be feather-like in texture, forming a mane around the back of the creatures' necks. Yet no wings were visible, and they were bigger than any bird Ambro had seen before.

"They are doda, the ships of the desert. Flightless but immensely strong in the leg. Watch out for their beaks."

"These are all yours?"

Lord Tafari smiled, showing his very white teeth. "They are a few of my many doda and men," he said. "I have other caravans working at the salt and gold mines. Come, we will go ahead out of the dust and stink," and he cantered the chariot team in a wide circle, around the trees and the watering holes, to the edge of the desert itself. Ambro stared ahead eagerly, drawing the clear harsh air deep into his lungs.

As the sun lifted from the horizon, they set out southward with the long columns of doda falling into place behind them, flanked with household guards that moved up and down along the caravan in chariots drawn by tough brown ponies, while a dozen more formed a cluster directly behind Lord Tafari, where he led the column. The doda themselves moved at a stately but swift pace, their pink legs reaching in long strides and their beaked heads bobbing. They were roped together by leashes fastened to neck collars, and each group of twelve was led by a human handler. Mia followed somewhere in the caravan, for Lord Tafari had arranged for her to travel with the servant women who alternately walked and rode, swaying high above the sand, on a doda's red tasseled blanket.

It became hotter as the sun rose, bleaching the sky to white, and stiller. The shuffling, marching sounds of the doda train, and the occasional voice or bellow, shrank in the vast stillness into sounds so insignificant that Ambro barely noticed them. The desert reached farther than he had imagined; its great expanses of ground littered with pale rocks, unbroken by any vegetation save thorny ankle-high shrubs, and its distant swells of rippled dunes all reminded him of the ocean. There was the same sense of apparent emptiness that was not empty, of power held in reserve, of a living presence that breathed down the nape of his neck and watched him.

"It is Kiffa you feel," Lord Tafari muttered. "He who watches all."

Still the sun rose, bleaching color from sand and stone, and sweat gathered beneath the collar of Ambro's robe and trickled down his legs inside the light boots. Ahead of them, the hindquarters of the desert horses grew dark with sweat, while the red tassels on their harness swung and the golden hammered decorations glittered in the light. Ambro watched them with admiration; they were infinitely more beautiful than the ponies driven by the guards, for they were an unvaried brown all over and had thin short tails and short manes that stuck straight up in wiry bristles.

"What are their names?" Ambro asked.

Lord Tafari indicated the right hand horse with the tip of his whip. "This is the stallion, Sun Runner; this is the mare, Dune Dancer. They are from my stables in Engedi, south of Safala, where the pure bloodlines of the desert horses were preserved in an ancient book. These two can trace their parentage for forty generations, and every one has been fleet of foot and sound of limb; every one has had the scooped face and slender cannon bones of their race."

"Why don't your guards drive desert horses in their chariots?'

"They are rare, Ambro. Only rich men drive them."

"And are they all this color?" Ambro asked.

"They are ivory, or cinnamon brown, or golden like amber, or pale yellow like fine sand, or they are white, or lilac grey. Very rarely, one will be born that is a smoky, palest pink like a dawn sky. They are all the color of desert. And they are each patterned over their quarters with zigzag stripes in another color. It is to remind them that the kiffa is king in the desert, and to be humble before his might."

"Tell me about it," asked Ambro, for he had learned already that Lord Tafari loved to tell stories. He settled himself more comfortably against the chariot's sides and watched Lord Tafari's face as he continued.

"This is a tale of the far-off days, when the kiffa and the horse and the other desert creatures had scarcely any form or shape, when they were not as they appear now, when they were weak and dusty creatures just beginning to be formed by the Great Kiffa. In those days, there was a horse, which did not look much the way a horse looks today but more like a cloud of soft desert dust blowing in the wind. This horse, who was arrogant and foolish, came down to drink at a watering hole early in the morning, when the kiffa was there drinking. Now the kiffa did not look as he looks today either, but was a small thin creature, like the shadow of a thorn bush. The kiffa, disturbed as he drank, looked up to see the horse trotting closer, kicking up sprays of sand in the morning sun. The horse kicked sand into the kiffa's face, and it stung his eyes and blew up his nose, and he snarled at the horse. 'You must wait your turn,' he told it. 'I am the king here, and no animal may drink in the mornings before I do.' The horse tossed its head proudly, and rolled its wild eyes. 'I shall do as I like,' it said. 'I shall drink whenever I want.'

"Hearing these words, the kiffa sprang at the horse to drive it away and teach it a lesson. So it began. The kiffa chased the horse through morning's calm, through afternoon's deep heat, through evening's lilac shadows. He chased the horse up the sides of sand dunes and over rippled plains; he chased it amongst jumbled rocks and past salt licks and through scattering antelope. He twisted after the horse amongst the tough trunks of corda trees, and galloped across pans of cracked mud, and splashed through water holes and mirages of water holes and the smell of minerals. The chase continued through the desert for many, many days.

"As they ran, the kiffa's thin legs thickened and strengthened. His teeth grew longer, sharpening themselves on his anger and his hunger, and his skinny chest swelled around his new and mighty lungs as he sucked in air. His heart grew larger, a huge muscle pumping in his new chest. Yet always the horse ran just ahead, out of reach.

"So the chase continued. The kiffa chased the horse over brittle salt pans and over sheets of polished amber, through sword grass and groves of bay trees, through sunrise and sunset. As he ran, the kiffa grew still stronger, mighty and powerful; he caught the noon sun is his eyes and they glowed with fire; he absorbed its rays into his coat and became burnished like red stone. He laid his footprints on all the sand in the desert and claimed it as his kingdom. He roared and his voice filled the sky, and all the other animals bowed to him as he ran past.

"At last, with a mighty spring, the kiffa flung himself off a rock and onto the horse. His sharp claws scored across the horse's hind quarters. Then the horse lay down in fright, and cried, 'Spare me, oh mighty king of the desert. I have been proud and foolish, but from henceforth I shall be humble. I shall wait until you have drunk from the water hole at dawn. I shall be careful where my hooves kick up sand. I shall teach my children's children to bow to you.'

"The kiffa was merciful. 'I shall spare your life,' he said, 'but where my claws have touched you, you and your children's children shall bear the marks, to remind them that I am king, and they are but shadows, running in the desert wind.'

"And so, Ambro, from that day to this, the desert horses are striped on their hindquarters with the marks of the kiffa's claws, whether their coats be ivory or amber, cinnamon or lilac gray. And when the kiffa roars at night, Sun Runner and Dune Dancer tremble in their thin skins, and bow their heads in submission."

Ambro listened with eyes half-closed, his body swinging to the chariot's rhythm, and smiled.

On the first evening, after they pitched camp, Lord Tafari took Ambro out into the desert and taught him to shoot targets with a bow and arrow. As the sun set, it siphoned all the heat from the air; Ambro was surprised by how cold the desert nights were, and wrapped himself from head to toe in a cloak that Lord Tafari gave him. It was lined with a soft brown wool, but when Ambro asked what animal the wool came from, the lord ignored him and threw more twigs onto the fire. Outside Lord Tafari's tent, a servant built a fire which flared brightly as Ambro and the lord walked toward it. Sitting by the blaze, watching sparks soar into the indigo sky like fiery insects, Ambro sighed with satisfaction. Already, he loved the desert: its vastness, its long swells of sandy dunes, its plains of shining stones, the sound of its breath in his ear. The desert was just another sea, he thought, and he had lived with the sea all his life. He lay back on a roll of pillows in the doorway of Lord Tafari's red silk tent, with the taste of the gazelle's sweet flesh still in his mouth.

"How long until we reach Safala?" he asked.

"Another three days," Lord Tafari replied. "It is five days from Jaffa to Safala, and tomorrow we cross through the dunes of Enlon. It is a bad place for the caravans."

"Why?"

"The dunes provide the dust-eater bandits with ambush sites. For this reason, I keep guards posted along the length of the caravan. Here, Ambro, arm yourself with this."

Lord Tafari rummaged in a pile of baggage and presently sent something spinning across the campfire to Ambro. It was a small knife with a straight blade that whispered from its scabbard of leather and inlaid metals when Ambro pulled it out, entranced with the feel of its hilt, delighted with the way in which it fit into his palm as perfectly as though it had been forged for him alone. The blade's polished edge glittered in the lamplight. Ambro barely touched a finger to it, and drops of blood spattered onto the sand.

"Be careful. It is very sharp," Lord Tafari said belatedly, and Ambro slid the blue shine of the blade back into the scabbard and knotted it around his waist with leather thongs.

"In the morning, I'll teach you to fight," the lord said, peeling a tangerine and letting juice run down his chin. "Perhaps we'll be lucky this time, and the webbies will be too busy with their stinking shugras and stinking wives to bother us. Do you know, Ambro, they all dress alike in breeches; the men and the women? It's indecent; you cannot even tell the difference between some lawless bandit and his own wife. Ah, the Wind-wanderer women are not like the women of our tribe. Kiffa women are without compare, Ambro. They sit beside the pools of Safala like drifts of flowers; they twine their hair with beads of pearls and lapis lazuli; they sing like birds. Soon we shall be in Safala, and you shall meet my beautiful new wife with creamy cheeks like a desert dawn. And you shall find yourself a dancing girl, or an uncle, or a place in the army."

Lord Tafari's face grew dreamy and abstracted in the fire's glow, and Ambro left him to himself and slipped his worn flute from a pocket. Setting it to his lips, he began to play, slowly and softly at first: notes that fell into the evening silence like the first drops of rain before a shower. Faster and louder the notes fell, a torrent of sound filled with shimmering threads. The music seemed to encompass the desert within itself; at one moment it sighed like wind blown sand, at another it soared high as the vault of open sky. Lord Tafari leaned on an elbow, his expression rapt as he listened. Suddenly, Ambro saw the lord's eyes widen with amazement. "Name of Kiffa!" he breathed.

Ambro did not stop playing, but he twisted a little so that he might look over his left shoulder, to where the first dune receded from the firelight to rise darkly against the early stars. A tiny striped antelope, with tapering horns, stamped its delicate hooves at the edge of the dune. In a flurry of air, a hawk descended to the dune's crest, folding its huge wings as it landed. Three yellow lizards, striped with lilac, scuttled over the sand and became still; their eyes, black as onyx pebbles, shone in the faint light from Lord Tafari's fire. The bulk of two wild dodas rose over the dune; they snorted and lowered their shaggy heads to listen to Ambro's flute; presently they were joined by a family of dune partridge, their rosy breasts glowing. Two more antelope, of a different kind than the first arrival, trotted into view; they were tall and brown with twisted horns.

Then, miraculously, a kiffa padded into view on huge paws tipped with six sharp claws. It was lithe and elegantly powerful. Its svelte red coat burned in the light, unmarked except by black lines around its tawny almond-shaped eyes, and black bandings on its long legs. Red tufts rose to points on each large, upright ear. It sat on its haunches, and fixed Ambro with a mesmerizing stare. Lord Tafari's eyes bulged. A thrill of awe tingled through Ambro. What a magnificent animal the kiffa was! How clean and spare its form, how beautiful its triangular face, how piercing its eyes surrounded by sweeping black lines! No wonder the Kiffa-walkers revered it; it was the power of the desert personified! Ambro played until he could play no more; until the song of the desert sweeping through him, moving his fingers to its rhythm, fell into silence. Then he lowered his flute to his lap, and heard the rustle of the animals as they slipped away. The kiffa melted into the darkness with a swing of its long smooth tail. Ambro stared at the place where it had sat, and at the great paw prints that remained. Pride coursed through him. Surely he would do anything to be associated with the Great Kiffa!

"What manner of magic is this?" Lord Tafari croaked in astonishment.

Ambro shrugged. "I don't really know," he admitted. "The animals of Verde also loved my flute and came to listen."

"I did not need to teach you the use of a bow to hunt with. You can simply draw the antelope into the supper pan with your music."

Ambro shook his tousled honey-colored hair. "They will not come if I play with hunger and greed in my thoughts," he explained.

"Your tunes spoke of the desert," Lord Tafari mused, "yet you learned to play in Verde."

"I do not really think that I make up the tunes," Ambro said modestly. "It is the land playing its music through my fingers."

Lord Tafari contemplated this in silence as the fire sank into glowing embers and as Ambro yawned and lay down on his bedroll, still swaddled in his fur-lined cloak, to fall asleep before he had counted more than a handful of stars.

In the morning, true to his word, Lord Tafari gave Ambro lessons in how to fight with a straight blade, while behind them the pulsing sun tipped itself over the horizon like a pool of molten gold, and lilac shadows grew shorter, and small blue lizards basked on pale rocks. Ambro thrust and parried, agile on his feet, determined to hold his own, even audacious enough to press an attack. Lord Tafari backed away at last, laughing. "Ai, ai, you are truly a Kiffa-walker," he said. "Though raised in another land, your heart has not forgotten its bold birthright. Enough now. Learn to temper your impulsive courage with cunning."

He turned away to organize his guards who waited, drawn around his tent in a semi-circle of stamping ponies and glinting chariot wheels, while for half a mile behind them the doda cara-van prepared for the day amidst clouds of dust and flies, curses and the crack of whips. Ambro watched with a grin, feeling the tip of his knife touching his thigh, and the blood surging through his arm muscles. *Yes!* he thought. This is right, to be here. This is who I am, a fighter for the Kiffa, and this desert is my true home. The joy of this thought, the sense of belonging, filled him with a hot, surging energy.

They rode out soon afterward, heading southeast now, their shadows keeping step beneath their feet. Ahead, Ambro could see the horizon lifting and swelling; it was like watching a motionless storm at sea, where the waves hung suspended and never crested or broke. Lord Tafari pointed. "The dunes of Enlon. Keep your eyes open."

Ambro rested his hand on the hilt of his blade, braced his feet more firmly against the jolting floor of the chariot, and scanned the horizon. Gradually, as hours passed, his eyes filled with dust and heat haze. The dazzle of the sun seemed to be burning holes in his forehead. He poured water from a skin over his face but Lord Tafari scowled and told him to preserve it for drinking, because they wouldn't reach the next water hole until noon tomorrow. Time seemed to stand still, with the sun high overhead, shadows fore-shortened, and even the dodas silent, plodding stoically beneath their heavy loads. Ambro's chin nudged against his chest and he struggled to hold his head up and keep his eyes wide open.

Ahead, the patterns on the horses' quarters seemed to swim and wander across his vision, while to each side the massive dunes, pale golden sand rippled with wind, hung over them and gathered heat in their bellies. At last, there came an imperceptible cooling in the air, and long shadows began to slip down the dunes. The first star twinkled high overhead and Ambro felt tension easing in his chest, and lifted his palm from the hilt of his blade to flex his stiff fingers. The day was ending, and away to the southeast he could see where the last of the dunes swept down to join the flat plain again and where, tomorrow, they would make faster progress toward Safala.

He fumbled for his water skin, and raised it to his lips. As he took the first tepid gulp, the air was riven with blood curdling cries. They echoed between the dunes, rending the evening stillness like the cut of a knife.

Lord Tafari lashed the horses into a gallop with such suddenness that the water skin flew from Ambro's hands and he lost his footing and fell to the floor. He scrambled across its smooth, jolting surface, felt the crash as the off-side wheel hit a rock, felt the floor tip to slide him to the edge. His hands flailed, desperately seeking something to grasp hold of. His knees slid over the back of the chariot and banged across it so that sharp pain shot up both legs. The chariot, scraping free of the rock, surged forward with Lord Tafari still yelling at the horses and lashing them with a black whip. Ambro slid completely off the chariot and hit the sand with a thud that knocked the air from his lungs.

He sprang to his feet, his hand already drawing his blade singing from its sheath, and Lord Tafari's chariot already too far away for him to reach. Other chariots milled around him as the guards formed into a battle position, and Ambro dodged amongst flailing hooves and the rolling, wild eyes of brown ponies. Beyond, dodas roared as drivers beat them forward into a circle. Sand sprayed from their feet; ropes swung, men cursed and shouted orders. Mia was nowhere in sight.

The webbie bandits poured over the nearest dune like a wave of sand. Hoof beats thundered like an incoming tide. Wild voices cried in a savage tumult. Riders crouched over the necks of their horses, brandishing glinting blades.

Ambro stood his ground with legs braced and tawny eyes gleaming. Though his heart was deafening him, his knife was steady in his grasp.

CHAPTER FOUR

NOLEENA CROSSED THE FORECOURT of the temple, its cracked tiles scorching beneath the tough soles of her bare feet, and stooped with her bucket of tanned shugra skin over the central pool. The water in the pool was so clear that she could see tiny flecks of red dust that had fallen in and sunk to the bottom to lie like freckles on the blue and white mosaic. When she dipped the pail in, the water lapped warmly against her arms; it bubbled up from deep fissures in the barren, rocky cliffs surrounding the city of Safala, and was always warm. It was said that the fires in the earth's heart warmed it, and that no man knew its source, though it seeped and bubbled from the rocks in a dozen places throughout the city, and flowed along channels hewn from the stone to fill pools and bathhouses.

Smelling harshly of minerals, a smell that Noleena associated with a shade of blue in evening skies, the warm water could not be drunk. Instead, drinking water for the city of Safala was collected from the sparse rainfalls, and conserved in reservoirs carved into the cliffs above the city. Other water flowed to Safala, along aqueducts and through culverts, from the Moon Mountains that lay to the east, lifting their shaggy peaks into a shawl of mist. Sometimes, drowsing in the heat of mid-afternoon and surrounded on all sides by looming cliffs of rock, Noleena would dream about the cool, blue-green Moon Mountains and wonder with a tickle of fear and daring if she would ever see them. It seemed unlikely. For most of her fifteen years she had lived within the confines of the temple, deep in the heart of Safala's twisting alleys and chasms of stone, like a little animal hiding in its place of safety.

It was said that men who wandered into the Moon Mountains might never return, and that the mountain flanks were thick with immense and majestic rhododendrons lifting blooms twenty feet into the air to be pollinated by brilliantly plumaged birds with crested heads. It was said that rain fell in the mountains every afternoon, and that ferns, delicate orchids with pale blooms, and lush moss grew on the trees themselves. Long ago, it was said, the moon goddess had lived there with mythical beasts called the Corno d'Oro, from whose foreheads sprang single horns of whorled gold. Sometimes, thinking about this, Noleena imagined that she could smell the pure fragrance of the lilies that were said to have grown wherever the Corno d'Oro lay in the flowering grasses. She wished that she knew more about all this but the priestess, who had shared what she knew, had said that the ancient stories of those far-off days were fragmented and forgotten, shrouded in mystery like the peaks of the mountains themselves.

The shugra hide pail was full. Noleena lifted it from the pool and carried it back across the temple forecourt, noticing a blue lizard that ran ahead of her like a tiny bolt of lightning to disappear into a crack at the base of the courtyard's outer wall. Noleena waited until the lizard was safely in its hiding place before sluicing her water over the tiles. Their surfaces, faded in the heat, transformed suddenly into a vivid, aquamarine blue as the water touched them. Taking a broom that leaned in a corner, Noleena began to sweep the tiles clean, pushing tattered scraps of apricot and pomegranate blooms, spindly broken twigs, dead flies, shards of pink and golden rock, and even the discarded skin of a lizard, ahead of the bristles. She worked hardest where the tiles were cracked with age and neglect, digging debris out from the cracks and sluicing more water from her pail.

Slowly, as she worked, the narrow blade of the sun crept across the courtyard, cleaving the shadows cast by the red cliffs overhead. Occasionally, Noleena rested from her sweeping to lean on her broom and stare upward to the ribbon of sky enclosed between those red cliffs lined with strata of pink and ochre. The white doves, which nested in the rocks, wheeled like petals against the blueness and the sun's hot eye.

"It is the hour of heat and dreams, child," said a voice, and Noleena turned.

The priestess had stepped out of the cool, dark recesses of the temple onto the steps, between the smooth pillars of white marble, and regarded her with silvery blue eyes. Noleena leaned her broom in the corner with the pail beside it, and trailed across the courtyard to the steps where she sat down at the priestess's feet and rested her chin in her hands. "I'm too hungry to sleep." She sighed, feeling her stomach pinching beneath the sash of her gown.

With a whisper of fabric, the priestess sat beside Noleena on the step. Her pale blue robe, though made from the finest of Barbari silks shot through with silver threads and embroidered with patterns of leaping dolphins, was faded. Here and there, repairs to holes and tears marred the fabric's flawless weave, and the hems of the flaring sleeves were fuzzy with broken threads. Noleena's own gown was in a similar state of wear: the blue silk pooled between her skinny legs was worn thin with age, and the hem at her ankles was stained pink with Safala's dust.

"I am hungry, too," the priestess admitted in her silvery voice that was like small waves running up a beach and sinking into the sand.

"Tell me how it used to be here, when I was first brought to you," Noleena asked wistfully. "I don't think that we were always hungry and alone here. I remember things used to be different."

Not really expecting an answer, she stared into the priestess's narrow face, her soft skin scored with a hundred fine lines.

The priestess's eyes took on a faraway look, and she nodded. "It is time that I told you what has been happening in the city," she agreed. "I have kept you hidden here like a caged bird, for your own safety, and hoped that the tides of men's affairs would change again. But I think now it is too late for hope. I must tell you what I know."

Noleena's thin frame went rigid with expectation. It was rare that the priestess shared news with her, although at night she stood on the temple steps and talked with the Wind-wanderers in hushed words that Noleena, lying on her mat near the altar, strained without success to hear clearly.

"When I was a younger woman in the temple," the priestess began, "the Wind-wanderers filled the forecourt daily to wait, with silent dignity in their cinnamon and ochre tunics, for their turn to worship. In those days, their horses filled the passageway outside with their heads hanging in the shade, and the zigzagged patterns on their hindquarters quivering as flies landed. In those days there were four priestesses in the temple instead of only me, with one acolyte called Noleena for company."

Here the priestess smiled at Noleena, her thin mouth stretching her dusky cheeks.

"In those days, there was plenty of food; the Wind-wanderers brought us purple grapes with the bloom of the desert sun on them, and honey cakes stuffed with nuga paste, and pomegranates filled with seeds as red as rubies."

Noleena's mouth watered.

"What happened to the other priestesses?" she asked. "I can hardly remember them."

"They went home to their families."

"Even when I was first brought here, when I was three years old, things weren't as bad as they are now, were they?" Noleena said. "Even a few years ago, the Wind-wanderers used to come every day."

The priestess sighed, a long sound like wind slipping over dunes.

"Yes," she said. "In five years, terrible changes have occurred in Terre. Now it is dangerous for the Wind-wanderers to enter Safala as they used to, to barter and trade and enjoy the city. It is dangerous to visit us here in the temple."

Noleena nodded, thinking of how those Wind-wanderers who still came arrived in the courtyard after dark, pressing themselves against the cliff walls and shifting like shadows on the rocks. With grave dignity they bowed on the blue tiles and begged the goddess for safe passage across the sea of desert that lapped at Safala's hard, red feet. Then they slipped away into the night, walking now that it was no longer safe to bring their desert horses into the city, and using the constellations to guide themselves, as though the sky were a map.

"Why are things changing?" Noleena asked. "What is happening?"

"Over the sea to the north lies Verde," the priestess explained. "Verde and Terre have long been trading partners. For many years, Verde was ruled by Lord Maldici, a cruel hard man with darkness and a lust for power burning in him. He found a black book, in the forgotten library of his ancestor Lord Morte, the first great sorcerer of Verde, and he set about mastering the darkness of that book for he planned to subdue the world and bring its princes crawling to his feet. Five years ago—you were still only a child of ten—there was a great battle and Lord Maldici was killed when the mountains fell upon him. The Corno d'Oro, taken captive into Verde after our moon goddess returned to the stars, appeared on the field of battle and turned the tide of evil with their power."

"So if the battle was won," Noleena mused, "what has gone amiss in Terre?"

"Ah," the priestess continued, "the sorcerer's daughter, Princess Maldici, escaped. They say she has a dangerous beauty, with wild red hair that sparks in the dark, and pouting red lips, and she is as filled with cruel greed as her father before her.

"She fled to Terre aboard a trading ship, with her assassini guards and their brutti dogs. She came here to Safala, the rose-red city, and captured the heart of Prince Mhadi, son of the Kiffa-walker king. They were married. The prince is young and weak, and Princess Maldici has poisoned his thoughts with greed for power, and has used her father's book of dark arts to gain control over him and the land of Terre. Her spells and powers have set our tribes apart, for we used to be neighbors and friends, the Kiffa-walkers and the Wind-wanderers, with no struggle between us. Now, the princess has poisoned Prince Mhadi's heart against us, and he herds the Wind-wanderers in from the desert as if they were shugra, and sends them down into the black depths of Terre, to labor and die in the mines for salt and gold. In his ports of Jaffa to the north and Shoa to the south, he builds a great fleet of ships with the profit from the gold, and dreams of setting sail with his armies to conquer the islands of Lontano."

"But why doesn't the king stop this?" Noleena asked.

"He died in the year of the royal marriage; there were rumors of poison and unnatural pain at his deathbed. Then, three years ago, a child was born to the Princess Maldici; a son. He has been named Kebi which in the ancient tongue of Terre means 'god of the earth.' Doubtless his mother has great plans for this young prince: that he will rule all earth like an emperor once she has taken possession of it through warfare and treachery."

The priestess fell silent, her face creased into downward lines, and Noleena leaned against the pillar of white marble veined with blue, and carved with leaping dolphins, and felt the sadness of the temple's silent forecourt fill her empty stomach and press upon her heart.

"We are abandoned here, in the middle of Safala," she said. "Soon, people will forget we are here at all. Then what shall we eat, and what shall we do?"

"We shall serve the goddess," the priestess replied, folding her lips together so that Noleena was afraid to ask anything else. Already, she had learned far more than when she had previously asked questions; usually, the priestess told her that her task was to serve in the temple and that knowledge of the world was unimportant.

After a long silence, the priestess sighed and shifted her position before muttering wistfully, "If only Luna, our moon goddess, might give us a sign...surely there is an ancient wisdom in this land that has been lost, and we are too blind to find it. The memory of the star gate has faded into ignorance."

"The star gate?" Noleena asked, leaning forward with curiosity.

"In the high and far-off days, Luna was a queen in the Moon Mountains, and the Corno d'Oro trod upon the high peaks, the fragrant star lilies springing up where they had touched the grasses. But when Luna's time on earth ended, she returned to the stars to become the moon goddess...you know all this, Noleena. You have heard it many times."

"The star gate," Noleena reminded the priestess. "I don't know about it."

"It was through the star gate that Luna returned to the heavens...no one knows now where it might be, hidden and forgotten, high and deep in the Moon Mountains far to the east of Safala. I have heard that the power of the star gate can only be accessed on the thirteenth moon—but what it looks like, I do not know. It was once a place of great power, though whether this holds true I do not know either."

Noleena pondered this, watching the shadows of doves sweep across the courtyard tiles. "Do you know anything else about the star gate?"

"Only a verse in the old tongue, taught to me when I came to the temple as a child, when the oldest priestess was alive. It was she who taught me, in the week before she died.

Over its mountains the Blue Moon
Hangs like a baited hook;
At the moment that the great fish leaps
Stand in the sacred gate and look
For Luna's wisdom that will safely keep
A balance in the tides of Terre."

Noleena had not realized that she was holding her breath but now, as the last words of the verse died in the heat, air eddied from her lips. While the priestess had spoken, Noleena had felt time suspended—for those moments, the shadows had remained still under the walls, the doves had fallen silent, the lizards lain motionless. A tingle had run through Noleena, a sense of urgency and expectation as cool and sharp as the touch of an evening breeze off the desert. She shivered as the tingle passed through her.

"What is the great fish?" she asked. "And what do tides have to do with mountains and with us, so far from the sea?"

"The ancient wisdom is lost," the priestess repeated. "I cannot answer your questions nor tell you any more, Noleena."

She sighed again and lapsed back into silence, and after some time Noleena rose to her feet and fetched her broom and, as the long afternoon trickled past, she swept the temple from the front steps—where the priestess seemed to have fallen asleep, her back slumped in its silvery-blue robe—to the base of the alter. As Noleena swept, she listened to the little shushing noises of the bristles against the blue marble tiles, and the cries of the doves that circled, free and untroubled, far overheard in the crack of sky. She felt the afternoon's heat pool in the small of her back, against the pinching hunger pains in her stomach. The air seemed to grow more still and thicker as she worked, so that she felt as though she were drowning in it and sudden panic shot through her, although she had never felt this way in the temple before. Since she had been brought here as a young child, she had always felt safe, hidden from the desert's hot breath.

Reaching the altar, she swept around its base, and then pressed her face against the carved marble hem of the goddess's robe, where it mingled with the carved foaming waves. The stone was cool against her flushed cheeks, and she closed her eyes and tried to remember the time before the night when she had been brought here to the temple—but could remember nothing. Her earliest memory was, as always, of a nightmare: blackness filled with screams of terror and the flare of torches, hoof beats galloping over hard packed sand, stars wheeling westward, a night rent with her own sobs. Out of this terror she had been given into the priestess's arms to stare up at the marble face above her: the face of the goddess crowned with stars, her slender hand holding a staff tipped with the crescent moon, all blurred and swimming in Noleena's tears.

"Hush, hush, you are safe here now, with the goddess," the priestess had told her, and gradually her sobs had subsided and she had eaten wheaten cakes and crawled onto a mat to sleep where she could see the starlight sliding between the pillars to touch the base of the alter. In all the years since, she had remained here, ignorant of events both inside and outside of Safala, and without family save for the priestess—but content because she felt enclosed and safe.

A hawk cried, wheeling above the craggy red cliffs, and Noleena straightened from the carved toes of the goddess and wandered outside, past the priestess who was still asleep. The sun was sinking into the western sky, and the light touched Safala's facades carved from the rock itself, and kindled them to gold and rosy pink and glowing red. Now the city shone more brightly than the sky, which the heat had leached of color so that the crying hawk wheeled against a backdrop like parchment. The doves had taken refuge in the cliffs.

Noleena wandered across the tiles of the forecourt, long since dry after the cleaning she'd given them, and down the crumbling steps into the passageway that led from the temple out to join other, busier streets in Safala. A wide crevice, the passage twisted and angled between walls of red striated stone, worn smooth with thousands of years of wind and dust. Its floor was of fine, dusty sand and desiccated pebbles that had rolled down the rock faces above. Noleena stared down the passageway into lavender shadows, wishing she might see a Wind-wanderer pacing silently toward her with his cinnamon tunic falling to the thighs of his creamy breeches, and his grave dark face breaking into a smile at the sight of her. The way was empty, with one exception.

A hundred yards from where Noleena lingered on the steps, on the left-hand side of the passage, an alcove was carved into the cliff and contained the hunched figure of the beggar man seated motionless in it, as he often was. Noleena padded toward him, the pigeons that had been strutting in the alley whirling upward into the air as she approached. Amongst their drab forms, Noleena noticed the bright flash of several rock-roses with rich pink bodies and wings, and heads and breasts barred with gold. When all the birds were aloft, Noleena approached closer to the beggar, noticing that his begging bowl lay empty at his feet, and cleared her throat.

His face, with its blind eye sockets covered by a strip of grubby leather, turned toward her.

"Noleena," he said in his surprisingly deep, strong voice, for he never failed to recognize the pad of her footsteps.

"I'm here," she replied. "Has anyone been past today?"

The old man shook his head. His cheeks, darkened with sun and wind, were as fissured as the cliff at his back, with deep lines running from the corners of his eyes to touch the corners of his lips; in the ruin of his face his lips were two firm, proud lines. The black hair that fell to his shoulders, and the beard that flowed over his chest to his belt, were grizzled with silver. He fumbled in the folds of his tattered robe, that perhaps had once been yellow or brown and that now hung faded and stained over his shrunken chest, and pulled one dried date from a pocket. He handed it to Noleena, his hands veined with blue and trembling slightly.

"Take it," he said. "You're hungry."

The date was very sweet and hard. Noleena's mouth filled with saliva around it and she pressed it against her back teeth and willed herself not to bite down on it, just to suck it until it softened and the juice ran down the back of her throat into her aching stomach.

"Can you remember when they brought me here?" she asked suddenly.

The beggar man bowed his head as if in thought, and Noleena waited a long time for an answer. She began to suspect that the old man was falling into a doze, but finally he lifted his head.

"You were a beautiful child," he said hoarsely. "You had skin as soft as the inside of a shugra's ear; you had laughter like bird song in palm trees."

"Could you see me?" Noleena asked.

"In the days when you were a baby, I had my sight," the beggar man explained with dignity.

"But who brought me here? The priestess says she doesn't know."

"You came on the back of a desert horse, rushing through the streets of Safala at night, scattering sand and people and shards of rock to either side. You came with a young man of your tribe wild-eyed with fear. You were sobbing in his arms."

"Why?" Noleena asked. "What had happened? Where were my parents?"

The beggar man's bearded chin sank to his chest while Noleena waited impatiently for his answer, sucking on her date and wondering why it had never before occurred to her to ask these questions, for the old man had begged in this alcove for as long as she could remember.

"Don't you know—?" she began at last, when the date was a soft blob of golden fiber on her tongue, but she broke off suddenly. The evening's quietness was changing. Overhead, the doves stopped cooing in the fissures of rock. Surging up the passageway, at first like a distant echo and then increasing in strength until it reverberated from the rock walls and filled the passage with a confused roar, came the sound of a crowd shouting and banging skin drums.

Noleena stiffened and the old man's head jerked off his chest and he turned as though to stare down the passage with his sightless eyes.

Now Noleena could make out individual voices and even words.

"—webbies—!"

"Drive them out!"

"—underground—"

Two hundred yards away, the mob broke like an incoming wave around a rocky corner of cliff, and at that moment the beggar man grabbed Noleena by one arm and yanked her into his alcove with a strength that amazed her. He flung a tattered robe across her and across his lap, and under the robe's cover Noleena lay with her cheek pressed into the sand and her eyes filled with dust while the voice of the mob surged into her ears. She heard a deep baying sound that she couldn't identify, and the crackle of torches; their ragged light shone through the loose fibers of the old man's rug.

"Stay still," he hissed, but she was already frozen in place, her mind whirling with the remembered sound of hoof beats and a woman's scream and the roar of a mob on the night she'd been brought here. Her heart felt weak and fluttering.

She wanted to ask the beggar what was happening, but her jaw was clamped shut and her tongue seemed glued to the roof of her mouth; and in some part of her mind she knew the answer already. They had remembered, the Kiffa-walkers, about the Wind-wanderer temple still standing, nearly abandoned, in the midst of their city and they had come to wreak havoc in it.

"The priestess!" Noleena whispered, but the old man's bony hand closed around her wrist, under the blanket, with a fierce grip.

"Be silent," he hissed.

For endless time, Noleena lay under the blanket, inhaling its dusty smell of dried grass and sand and horses, straining to hear every sound in the chaos that wailed near her. Tiles shattered. There was a shriek of laughter, the splash of water, curses, and then the voice of the priestess, terrible in its calm resolve, soaring above the din.

"This is a holy place," she cried. "Consider what you do! You were our brothers not so long ago! Your hearts have been turned to darkness by the foreign princess; you have become like brutti dogs that run without thought to her whistle. Where is your dignity, your courage, Kiffa-walkers? Where—"

But then her voice was cut off by the renewed shouting and cursing of the crowd, and something shattered with a crash that made Noleena jerk and quiver beneath the blanket, so that the old man tightened his grip on her wrist again. After that, the mob roared back up the passageway, one or two throwing jeers at the blind beggar man or poking him with the tip of a spear but most of them not even noticing him where he sat, still as the rock from which his alcove had been hewn. His empty bowl was picked up and flung high overhead, spinning against the sky, before falling with a ringing crash against the rocks and into the sand, where feet kicked it aside. The mob passed, their torch light leaping.

The dust settled. After some time, the doves commenced cooing in their roosts, and the sky flamed golden and crimson in the crack overhead. Stiffly, the old man moved his knees and the blanket slipped off Noleena's shoulders so that the fiery light fell across her dark cheeks and wide blue eyes. Her teeth chattered with fear.

Gently the beggar man lifted her to a sitting position. "They have taken the priestess away," he said. "They dragged her with her wrists chained."

"Where?" Noleena cried wildly. "Where will they take her?"

"To the mines," the old man said grimly. "Underground, where all Wind-wanderers are taken, to slave and die. To slave and die for the greed of the Kiffa-walkers, for the beauty of their palaces and the might of their ships! They are jackals and black of heart! They betray us!"

His voice had risen to a cry and he thumped his long staff of corda wood upon the sand, so that the doves fluttered in alarm, and his shoulders shook with emotion. Noleena had never seen him so agitated; usually he was dignified and grave in his tattered robes, holding his spine straight and his head high and graceful through the longest and hottest of afternoons, the hungriest of mornings. He had remained calm and polite in all the years that she had lived in the temple.

"What will happen now?" she whispered, and shivered in the evening's chill that fell down the cliffs to wash purple shadow across her shoulders.

"You must return to the desert," the old man said. "You will die here like a gazelle trapped by kiffas at the end of a canyon."

Noleena shook her head in desolation. "I don't know where I came from. And I'm afraid of the desert."

Her head swam with hunger and her earliest nightmare memories.

"You must return," the old man repeated. "You cannot stay alone in the temple and starve."

"I should have helped the priestess!" she cried, tears of shock making rivulets in the dust on her cheeks. "I shouldn't have lain here hiding. I've spent my whole life hiding!"

"It has kept you alive," the old man said. "But the time for hiding has reached its end. You will have to leave soon."

CHAPTER FIVE

SPEWING OVER THE FACE OF THE DUNE, the bandits curled around the doda caravan and forced Lord Tafari to swing his team of desert horses brutally about, the chariot briefly tipping onto one wheel. As the team thundered past Ambro, standing with legs braced before the onslaught and his knife steady in his clenched hand, he leaped and grasped the rim of the chariot. He swung there wildly, his palms tearing on the metal edge, his ribs pounding against the side and his legs dangling perilously close to the spinning wheels, but eventually he managed to haul himself inside to land at the toes of Lord Tafari's boots.

Struggling to his feet, Ambro saw that Lord Tafari's chariot had now joined the ring of guards' chariots that were trying to encircle the panicking doda and their wildly shouting drivers, while the bandits swept closer in thunderous attack. A swift volley of arrows flew from the taut bow strings of Lords Tafari's archers, to rain down on the bandit ranks that flowed on unchecked toward them. Now the riders were so close that Ambro could see the wild blue eyes of the leader, his teeth bared in a snarl, the rippled patterns of blue mineral paste on his dusky cheeks, and his long black hair braided into a single plait and wrapped around the crown of his head, gleaming iridescent in the evening light. The man crouched low over the neck of his horse and Ambro saw that it was a desert stallion, an aristocratic, powerful horse with a scooped face and a coat of pale gold that shimmered in the long light, and that its haunches were striped with cinnamon patterns. Straight toward Lord Tafari's chariot the rider galloped, the horse's golden mane blown back like a billow of sand onto the orange tunic of the rider. Ambro saw the sword raised in the bandit's lean hand, and felt outrage tighten his heart.

"He's attacking us!" he shouted but already Lord Tafari was drawing his own sword and to Ambro's astonishment he leaped over the front of his chariot and ran out along the single shaft, between the curved backs of his horses and their tossing heads, and balanced there with his green robe flowing open from the golden clasp and his sword raised in silhouette against the horizon of glimmering clouds. Breathlessly, Ambro watched as the bandit leader surged closer, while all around guards notched arrows to bow strings, horses neighed in terror and doda leaped under their heavy loads. From the corner of his eye, Ambro saw a box slip from its corda ropes and fall from a doda, spilling a cascade of golden coins into the sand.

Now the bandits were upon them, and Lord Tafari's guards abandoned their bows and drew their swords, the ring of the blades mingling with the bandits' wild cries and the outraged screams of the doda. The bandit leader reached Lord Tafari's team and swept past at a gallop, crouching flat against his mount's neck and slashing at the harness of the nearest chariot horse as he passed. Lord Tafari swung his sword but it was impossible to tell whether the point had touched the bandit, slicing through the orange of his tunic and into the dark skin of his shoulders, or not.

"Stand and fight!" Ambro yelled in frustration and saw, swiveling his head, his eyes filling with the clash and blur of battle—the tumble of falling men, the rhythm of horses' running legs, the bright fabric on arms raising swords, the clouds of flung sand and the dancing purple shadows—the bandit leader reining his horse in a tight circle. Unscathed, he galloped back through scattering guards, his horse never faltering or swerving, and headed for the other side of Lord Tafari's chariot.

With impetuous courage, Ambro flung himself over its side and leaped toward the bandit, his knife raised in his hand. He saw the gleam of light on the bandit's smooth young cheeks and the wisps of hair that had escaped from his braid and mingled with the flying golden mane of the stallion. With all his strength Ambro leaped forward, swinging his knife, but on an unseen command the horse reared up, his great hooves swinging over Ambro's head, pawing at the sinking sun. A foreleg crashed against Ambro's chest, the long straight cannon bone smashing across his ribs and knocking all the air from his lungs so that blackness and stars filled his eyes and he reeled on the trampled sand.

With a leap the horse passed him, and dimly Ambro heard Lord Tafari's shout of alarm. Seconds later, strong arms grabbed him as he staggered in circles and he felt himself being hauled across the ground and then onto the floor of a chariot. The roar of the battle filled his head, and a surge of sickness swept through him so that he clenched his teeth and collapsed, fighting for air, on the chariot's hard floor. It was impossible to know how long he lay there; perhaps it was only for seconds although it felt far longer, and when he opened his eyes and hauled himself, retching, to his feet he saw that the shaft of Lord Tafari's chariot rested, empty, upon the ground.

The bandits were retreating, streaming away over the dunes into the fiery setting sun, horses' manes and tails billowing like filament against the light, their riders dark huddles on their backs. Loose amongst the bandits ran Lord Tafari's horses, Dune Dancer and Sun Runner, their severed harnesses trailing behind them in thin dark lines, their wide nostrils rimmed with hot pink as they ran straight into the sun and disappeared over the horizon.

Lord Tafari stood by his empty chariot and cursed.

"Sons of jackal bitches! Desert rats! Spawn of *frogs!* May shame take you by the throat, may your children die with sand in their mouths and your mothers' corpses feed the vultures! May your names go into the dark!"

Ambro stared around in dismay. Guards were sheathing swords, and tending to the slumped figures of the wounded. The sand settled slowly, drifting down in shimmering curtains to net the caravaners' hair and the wrinkles in their tunics with gold. Doda and men coughed harshly. From out of the dust a slender, sprightly figure in brilliant, tattered clothing ran toward Ambro and flung herself against him.

"You're safe!" Mia yelled, and Ambro drew himself tall with wounded pride.

"There was nothing to fear from them," he said stiffly. "They are only webbies," but he could hardly bear to look at where Lord Tafari stood by the empty chariot shaft, his sword hanging from one hand with its bright point buried in sand and his shoulders slumped.

"They have taken trade goods from the doda," Mia said. "They have stolen beautiful woven carpets and flagons of oil and—"

"Stop chattering," Ambro commanded. "This was not street entertainment, Mia! They have taken our best horses!"

"Ours?" she asked slowly.

"You forget, I am not a sea urchin anymore, but a Kiffa-walker."

She stared after Ambro as he stalked off to stand at Lord Tafari's side; then, with a graceful shrug, she twirled on her toes and moved away.

Ambro risked a glance into the lord's face as they stood together in the eerie silence that had settled over the caravan, and saw the anger that smoldered in his narrowed tawny eyes. "They shall pay," he declared vehemently, turning to Ambro. "They shall pay for this with their sisters and sons, their wives and cousins. How dare they, *how dare they* steal my horses! I shall grind them into the sand!"

Ambro stared at the horizon, where nothing now remained of the sun but a slender crescent of pure gold, and at the vast desert sky filled with pearly clouds, and felt within himself the desolation and loss of those two beautiful horses running away with the bandits, while the lord's chariot shaft lay motionless in the sand, and the shadows of the dunes of Enlon fell like a cloak upon the looted caravan.

"I will help you be avenged," Ambro muttered, "since we are of the same tribe," but Lord Tafari ignored him and turned on his heel, ramming his sword back into its sheath, and shouted for guards to bring him other horses.

It was a still faintly subdued caravan that wound toward the valley of Nini three days later, and Lord Tafari was silent, plunged into a haughty melancholy by the loss of Dune Dancer and Sun Runner. Ambro swayed high above the sand, wedged in front of a bale of trade goods on the back of a doda and feeling as though he were adrift in a rocking boat. How far away Verde's coastline seemed now, its familiar world of tides and water! The continent of Terre lay shimmering in the heat in every direction, its ochre and golden sands so vast and absolute that Ambro's memories of water seemed as remote as a dream.

Around noon, the caravan halted and Ambo saw that they'd arrived at the top of a great cliff, below which the rift valley of Nini ran from north to south, angling through the heart of Terre, its fields and terraces glowing an impossible shade of green. A stir of activity ran through the caravan as loads were shifted for balance, chariot brakes were tested, and straps restraining boxes and bales were tightened on protesting doda. Men dismounted to lead impatient animals that could smell water and knew their homes were not far off, and gradually the whole caravan sorted itself into a single file of people and animals that stepped over the lip of the cliff and began a tortuous descent on the narrow, rocky path. Ambro, on the doda, swayed at one moment inward against the cliff wall, with its striations of fossils and crushed shell, and at the next seemed to hang suspended over the valley of Nini itself, seven hundred feet below.

"Is there a river? Why is the valley so fertile?" he asked the trader who walked at the doda's side.

"It is watered by springs that emerge along the base of the cliff," the man replied, "and also by water carried in aqueducts from the rivers of the plateau lands that lie to the east. They are carved by canyons which bring water from the Moon Mountains. And look! There lies Safala!"

Ambro followed the man's out-flung arm with his gaze and saw indeed that, as they had rounded a slope of scree, the farther reaches of the valley had come into view and that, on the far side, it was now possible to see Safala, the rose-red city. Ambro gazed at it in fascination as the caravan descended to the valley floor and began to cross it, winding between terraced fields of grain, irrigation pools reflecting the cloudless blue of the afternoon sky, and clusters of nuga palms that cast deep shadow. Small villages were tucked amongst the terraces, their stone houses blending into the landscape, but Ambro's attention remained riveted on the view ahead as the city of Safala grew larger. It rose up the cliff; its columns and facades, its towers and porticoes—all carved from the solid rock itself—glowing rosy and golden in the heat. It was beyond anything that Ambro had imagined and, as the caravan approached closer yet, he craned his neck to stare up at the walls and aqueducts, the slitted windows and hanging terraces, the carvings of kiffas and horses and gazelles and lizards that decorated cornices and overhangs.

Home, Ambro thought; this might be my home. Even now, at this moment, members of my father's family might be inside those walls, not knowing that I am here, coming closer—coming to join them. He stared at the city so hard that spots began to dance before his eyes, and a giddy sense of hope made his heartbeat quicken.

The caravan arrived at last at the city gate: a massive door covered in beaten metal that, when closed, sealed off a cleft that angled into the city's heart between two towering flanks of solid rock. However, the gate was open and a steady stream of people wound their way through it and into the purple shadow that lay beyond. Doda and jennets—those sturdy, round bellied beasts of burden that Ambro had seen in Verde—accompanied the people. The shadow fell across Ambro as his mount stepped through the gate, passing the guards who stood on either side in tunics of pale red overlaid by leather breastplates carved with the face of a snarling kiffa, and with their long spears held upright. Even the shafts of the spears, beneath the tips, were decorated with the kiffa's head, Ambro noticed as he stared sideways at the men, at their drooping golden moustaches and their fierce tawny eyes that stared back at him without a flicker. Ambro remembered what he'd been told of the Kiffa-walker army, which would drive the desert bandits underground and subdue them, and he straightened his spine on the doda's broad back and saluted the men. Perhaps, after finding his family, he would join the army; perhaps he too would stand erect behind the kiffa's snarl, would heft the kiffa spear in his hands.

The doda swayed through the cleft of the rock and Ambro saw that it was like a long passageway, with sand underfoot, that split the solid rock in two. High overhead, wheeling doves flashed in a sliver of brilliant sky. Around Ambro, the tunnel echoed with the voices of travelers and traders, but the tramping feet of people and animals were silent, muffled by the sand. Presently the entryway to the city opened out into a great square, walled around with sheer faces of rosy rock, carved with towers and doorways, and filled with market stalls where trays of flat bread roasted in clay ovens, and chicken morsels sizzled on sticks; where lengths of brilliantly colored fabrics hung in the still heat and trays of rings glittered in the sunlight; where men and woman bartered for pale green melons, pyramids of juicy oranges, and long twisted gourds. Contained by the solid stillness of Safala's cliffs, its market pulsed with heat and color like a flow of lava.

Ambro stared around in fascination, and was just in time to glimpse Mia slipping into the crowd in a flicker of motion, her hurdy-gurdy still strapped to her back. "Mia!" he shouted urgently but she had already disappeared behind a stall. Ambro frowned.

He felt responsible for her. She was such a skinny little thing; how would she survive in this strange, harsh land without his protection? He had promised, on the journey across the desert, that she could help him to find his family and that perhaps they would have room for her. At that moment he caught another glimpse of her as the crowds parted; she had positioned herself between two stalls and spread her shawl on the ground. Already a small cluster of people was gathering around it as Mia juggled fruit in a spinning wheel of bright orange motion. Ambro's frown relaxed into a rueful grin. Mia was perfectly able to live by her wits, and would find whatever it was she had come looking for in Terre: adventure perhaps, or people to listen to her music and watch her dancing, to throw coins into her shawl. Anyway, it would be easier for him to join his Kiffa-walker family without such a waif in tow...

Someone shouted his name and Ambro turned his attention back to Lord Tafari's caravan. Shrieking doda were being led off in various directions. Women, holding wide-eyed children by the hands, came forward to meet the traders, and passersby called greetings. Lord Tafari strode toward Ambro and smiled for the first time since the desert ambush.

"Safala!" he exclaimed with a wave of one hand, as though presenting Ambro with a gift. "Come, we will dine in style tonight!"

Stiffly, Ambro slid down the doda's side, brushing against its black and grey plumage and feeling his knees shake with fatigue. Lord Tafari clapped him on one shoulder and plunged off through the crowd, with Ambro straining to keep up, passing through arched doorways of golden and pink stone and down long sandy streets walled with rock, and up through the city's heart on sweeping stairways carved from the face of the cliff until coming to a halt at last before an imposing door flush with the rock face. The guard standing outside saluted and Lord Tafari swung the door open and strode through with Ambro silent at his heels. The air inside was cool, and silent but for the trickling of water flowing into a pool where fish swam languidly. Ambro glanced around at hallways and stairways, at marble tiles and plants with long red petals hanging in the beams of sun beneath skylights carved far overhead, at walls covered with brilliant hanging tapestries.

"Come, my love, I am home!" Lord Tafari shouted and down a hallway, her footsteps silent in slippers of pale green leather, came the most elegant woman Ambro had ever seen: Lord Tafari's wife. He tried not to stare at her flowing green robe, at the tiers of gold rings encircling her slender neck from collarbone to ears; at the bracelets chiming on her arms, the jewel in her nose and the winged tips of her arched eyebrows. Her slanting eyes were encircled with painted golden lines, and a golden circle was painted at the outer apex of each cheekbone. She embraced Lord Tafari and then looked questioningly at Ambro.

"We have a guest?"

"Ambro d'Monti," he replied, aware of the dust on his feet and the sand in his hair, and the smell of sweat and doda that clung to his clothes. He raised his chin. "I am a Kiffa-walker, come to seek my family in Safala," he announced, his clear tones ringing off the walls.

"You are a Kiffa-walker indeed," the lady replied gravely, meeting the bright pride of his glance.

After Lord Tafari and Ambro had washed, they ate with Lady Tafari on a terrace of stone that radiated the day's warmth into the chill air, and with the towers and rooftops of Safala falling away below the balustrade. Farther below and away yet, the valley of Nini lay in darkness but for the twinkle of village cooking fires. Overhead, the first stars pricked pale green and yellow in the violet sky, and Ambro sighed with satisfaction. Perhaps at this very moment, on another terrace, members of his father's family were also dining, staring up at the same stars, unaware of him and of how soon he would join them. The knowledge of his presence in Safala seemed to him like a delicious secret, sweet with anticipation, sweet as a hidden fig ripening amongst the leaves.

CHAPTER SIX

ALTHOUGH AMBRO ROSE EARLY the next morning, he was disappointed to find that Lord Tafari had already left on his day's business, overseeing the distribution of goods from his caravan.

"I will explore the city," Ambro told the Lady Tafari and she nodded, making the glass and gold beads woven through her hair tinkle.

"Lord Tafari has asked that I instruct you daily in the language of Terre," she replied. "Let us set aside the hour after supper, beginning tomorrow."

All that day, and in the ones that followed, Ambro explored the city on foot, pacing its terraces and springing to the top of its many stairways hewn from the face of the cliffs: grand sweeping stairways and narrow twisting ones that seemed barely to cling to the rock faces and on which a misplaced step would have precipitated Ambro into thin air to fall into courtyards below. From eyries high in the rock, he studied the city through his spyglass, and watched the farmers toil amongst their crops in the valley of Nini. He grew accustomed to the fine pervasive dust that coated his hot cheeks, and the sounds of Safala became a familiar dull surf in his ears. Doda cried shrilly, traders haggled, doves cooed in their nests along rocky ledges until silenced by the sharp whistle of wheeling hawks. Everywhere, down twisting alleys and in broad squares, the Kiffa-walker people moved with graceful purpose in their brilliant robes. Treasury doors swung open and shut between soaring pillars of pale ivory stone. Scales both large and small tipped up and down, balancing profit and loss, on every street corner and in every square as caravans wound their way daily through the heart of Safala, the doda and jennets loaded with gold and salt, corda wood and spices, brilliantly woven carpets and a multitude of goods from other lands: coral and sea sapphires from the islands of Lontano, porcelain and wine from Verde, silk as smooth as skin from Mombasso, wool like thistledown from Angoli.

Foreign traders, translators, market vendors, fruit sellers, doda handlers, and playing children jostled for space between the granular walls of stone that bounded every open space. Men squatted over games of nam nam, transferring smooth glass balls from hollow to hollow on carved wooden boards. Women scooped cinni spice from pyramids spread on sacking, and stirred it into hot water inside silver urns, to percolate over slow fires and be drunk from tiny silver cups. Other women wove their way through the crowds with massive baskets balanced on their heads; Ambro marveled at their strength and poise. And daily the soldiers marched through Safala: raw recruits with sunburned necks, foreign mercenaries speaking guttural tongues, and older men with stern eyes; all clad in the leather breastplate embossed with a snarling kiffa.

Ambro would have been perfectly content to simply explore, except for the impatience that was mounting in him to find his family. Even Mia seemed to have found a niche for herself in Terre, for Ambro met her in a market square one afternoon in the company of a troupe of children doing acrobatics on rugs to the amusement of the crowd that had gathered. Ambro watched while Mia mimed jokes, turned somersaults in midair, juggled, and played her hurdy-gurdy while a skinny boy beat a drum made of a hollow gourd covered with skin. The other children danced to the rhythm, clapping their hands and shuffling their feet, setting their anklets of shells and nuts and coins ringing, and their brilliant clothes fluttering. One child held a small furry monkey on a leash and it too danced, its wizened face in strange contrast to its nimble legs. When Mia caught sight of Ambro, she danced across to him, her fingers still flying over the stained keys.

"Are you alright?" Ambro asked. "You can come to the lord's house with me if you wish, Mia. Are you eating—and where do you sleep?"

Mia executed a lively dance step and curtsied with mock solemnity. "My highest regards to Lady Tafari, but I decline her hospitality and the services of her body painter."

"But Mia—"

She danced away, her face gleaming with a mischievous smile and her slender feet stirring up dust. After a twirl, she returned to his side. "I am quite well, Ambro. I have joined the sand fleas of Terre; they are more fun than the sea urchins of Verde. I will see you again, young Kiffa-walker."

Before Ambro could reply, she had danced away again and was soon playing her hurdy-gurdy high above the crowd, balanced on a pyramid of children and with the monkey opening seeds on her back. Ambro shrugged and smiled, moving away across the square to continue his explorations of the city.

For days, Ambro saw little of Lord Tafari who was busy trading and did not return home until late at night, long after his lady had tutored Ambro in the language of Terre, her body servant painting golden lines on the palms of her hands and the soles of her feet as she and Ambro worked.

"You have the gift of a fine ear," she told him, but Ambro shook his head.

"This is my mother tongue," he declared confidently. "I am only remembering these words that I have known since a young child. Also, I have been taught some of this tongue in the pirati archipelago."

Each night, when Lord Tafari returned home at last, Ambro would stride to meet him and wait, in proud silence, for any news while the lord peeled off his soft leather boots with rolled tops, and sat down to eat roast meat and stewed figs and brilliant ruby pomegranates.

"In the marketplace today, I spoke with a distant cousin of Ayan Kalif, who may be a kinsman to you," Lord Tafari said one evening, after many weeks had passed. "He promised he would make enquiries on your behalf."

"Did he know my father?" Ambro asked eagerly.

"He did not know him, but he thought he had heard of him; he too recalled something about an unsuitable marriage. And he recalled the loss of the *Jaffa Queen* in the great equinoctial storm."

"How soon shall we hear from him again?" Ambro asked. "Does he know I am waiting?"

Lord Tafari bit into the succulent breast of a dune partridge and smiled indulgently at Ambro. "Patience, cub," he said. "The hunter is patient as well as bold."

It was hard to have patience, Ambro thought the next day as he explored deeper into the heart of Safala. He glanced hungrily into the faces of men as they passed, intent on their day's business, and wondered whether he would recognize uncles by some strange process of intuition—or whether he and they would simply pass, unaware of a shared lineage. He glanced at the girls of his own age, their eyes outlined with cinnamon-colored minerals and the spicy musk of their perfume drifting around them, and wondered if one might be a cousin or even—this thought took his breath away—a sister. Was he the only child of his parents or had there been others, left at home in Safala on that fateful journey to Verde, left to survive in safety?

Aware suddenly of the crowd jostling against him, moving him toward the side of the street, Ambro shook off his thoughts of family and glanced around. Ranks of soldiers were marching past, headed toward the end of the broad thoroughfare where a high red wall blocked the way; sheer and blank but for a great doorway through which the soldiers passed. Others issued out from the door and marched away. Ambro wandered closer; he had not been in this area of the city before nor seen this towering wall surmounted with terraces where sentries paced to and fro against the harsh blue sky, and with towers that seemed almost as high as the cliffs of Safala themselves.

"What is this place?" he asked a woman seated beside the road on a crimson rug and selling lemons in corda rope baskets.

"It's the palace!" she exclaimed. "You must be a stranger here. It is where our king and our queen live, long may they rule in health and harmony." The woman bent her head in a gesture of respect, then held out a lemon to Ambro. "Juicy and sweet," she wheedled. "Fresher than any others, picked this morning at dawn in a field by the city gates."

Ambro shook his head.

"The Kiffa-walker king and queen?" he asked, watching the soldiers as they passed, rank after rank in their high rolled boots and red tunics, their legs swinging in unison, their upright spears like a field of young grain.

"Of course, Kiffa-walkers," the woman agreed. "Our old king, long may he be at peace with his ancestors, died suddenly a few years ago." The woman shot Ambro a bright malicious glance and caught him by the wrist so that he had to bend over. "They say he died strangely," she whispered. "He was in perfect health, and then after a meal one evening he died in convulsions of great pain." Her voice sank lower and her grip tightened on Ambro's arm. "People spoke in the streets of poison," she hissed.

She released Ambro suddenly and shouted "Lemons! Fresh lemons from Nini, juicy and sweet!"

Ambro squatted beside her. "Who would have poisoned the king?" he asked, but the woman would no longer meet his gaze. "It was a rumor only," she said dismissively. "Perhaps a webbie plot was responsible for the death. But now all is well in Terre, all is prosperous and peaceful. The webbies are being driven underground, the gold flows across the land in the caravans. They say that a great navy is being built in Shoa, and that Terre has the largest army of any land now. They say that soon Terre will unleash its force upon all the lands around the Middle Sea. In Terre now, even a lemon seller can afford to wear jewels." She laughed sharply and shook her head, so that her dangling earrings, inlaid with bright stones, swung. "The prince, now King Mhadi—may he live in the kiffa's spirit—is a great ruler and his queen, from Verde, the most beautiful woman in the world."

"Verde!" Ambro exclaimed. "It is where I—" He stopped; he was a Kiffa-walker now and did not need to admit to strangers that he was from Verde. Still, he was curious about the queen.

"Who is she?" he asked.

"She fled here from Verde five years ago; her father had been defeated by his own brother in a great battle. Our king, before his death, gave her refuge and she stole the heart of the young prince Mhadi with her foreign, exotic beauty. Now she has become our queen. I myself saw her once in a procession—she has a great curtain of red hair, pale skin and brilliant green eyes. She wore a robe of azure blue and jewels on every finger and she rode a red horse, the color of the palace walls. They say that after four years of marriage, our young king is still bewitched by her; that foreign ambassadors weaken at the knees in her presence. And she has given birth to a son, named Kebi which means 'god of the earth.' They sing of him in the streets, that he shall be a mighty prince ruling all lands around the Middle Sea."

Ambro listened intently, the sun beating between his shoulder blades and the soldiers' booted legs swinging past in the periphery of his vision. Vaguely he remembered talk amongst the sea urchins of a great battle in Verde, when he had been a child. It had been around the same time that he had helped a pirati boy, Giovanni, vanquish the sea dragon from the pirati archipelago. The battle, he'd heard, had been won by Lord Verona, and the mythical beasts, the Corno d'Oro, had appeared on the battlefield and lent their power to the victorious army. Ambro had never seen the Corno d'Oro, nor traveled north to the delta of the Arnona, that great river on whose banks the battle had been fought. It must be this same battle of which the lemon seller now spoke, he thought. If a defeated princess of Verde could flee to Terre and become a queen, surely he too, Ambro d'Monti, might find a home in Terre and meet with success. He felt a surge of confidence and smiled broadly at the lemon seller, dropping a coin into her basket before selecting the largest, brightest fruit.

Then he rose and wandered across the expanse of red tiles that formed a plaza before the palace's looming walls and the great doorway that breached it. On either side of the door, ranks of soldiers stood guard and, coming closer, Ambro saw with horrified fascination that some of them were strange, deformed creatures and not Kiffa-walker men at all. Above these creatures' breastplates, their long, stretched ears hung to touch their shoulders, and every visible part of their bodies—bare arms, necks, legs between tunic hems and black boots, faces—were covered in wiry red hair. Approaching closer, hugging the street's wall of stone, Ambro stared, feeling prickles of cold fear run up his spine. Assassini, whispered a voice in his head. Assassini from Verde. He had never seen them before; only heard them spoken of with fear and loathing around campfires on the shingle at night; heard how they plundered the villages and how the land lay scorched and blackened in their wake as the grass and leaves died where the assassini had trampled them.

Now Ambro noticed the brutti, the dogs that milled around the assassini's feet, saw their harsh red coats gleaming in Terre's sunlight, saw their sharp teeth and the wrinkled skin of their muzzles as they snarled at passing soldiers. The hands that held the brutti leashes were deformed too, Ambro realized: the assassini did not have ordinary hands at all but digits missing or misshapen so as to grip weapons: the powerful crossbows and the serrated knives that the assassini used.

Suddenly a brutto sprang forward. A child, chasing a ball, had darted too close to the looming palace wall. In a flash, before Ambro could even move, the brutto was upon the child; the boy's small body spun through the air in a blur of motion. The brutto's snarl and the child's scream mingled. Ambro tried to leap forward to help but a jewelry seller grabbed his arm in a fierce grip and wrestled him to a standstill. "Don't interfere," the man hissed urgently. "Be inconspicuous."

The child landed face down, blood pouring from a ripped shoulder. There was a moment's terrible silence, followed by shuffling noises as street vendors and shoppers snatched up their wares and rushed away down the thoroughfare. The lemon seller, Ambro noticed, abandoned half her fruit in her hasty departure. Into the pool of silence surrounding the child's prostrate body rushed a woman, a bright flare of blue gown. Her scream, as she lifted the child and cradled him in her arms, chilled Ambro to the core of his bones. He shuddered. In Verde it was said that the saliva of the brutti was poisonous and brought a slow death.

The woman swaddled the child's bleeding shoulder in her shawl and hurried away across the plaza and into an alley; the sound of her keening cries died into the distance.

Ambro glanced around, realizing that he stood alone now on the expanse of red tiles before the palace's rearing walls; ranks of soldiers and assassini stared impassively into the heat haze, and overhead archers were silhouetted in the narrow windows of high towers. He quelled another shudder and reminded himself that he was a Kiffa-walker and that Terre was his birthright; he would not be frightened by these creatures from Verde. Mustering every fiber of his courage, he turned slowly on his heels and walked steadily across the vast expanse of tiles; between his shoulder blades he felt the narrowed gaze of spearmen and archers, the cruel watchfulness of brutti.

Reaching the far side of the plaza, he quickened his steps. Muscles quivered in his thighs. What were the assassini doing here? Ambro wondered as he headed back to Lord Tafari's house for his language lesson. Why did the courageous Kiffa-walkers tolerate this foreign intrusion? Surely their royal family didn't need such protection. But, he thought doubtfully, there were the webbies to contend with. He remembered the fierce glinting eyes of the bandits who had attacked Lord Tafari in the desert and stolen his horses. It would be necessary, he supposed, to muster unusual force against such an enemy. He would ask Lord Tafari about it that evening, he thought, but when he arrived at the lord's home he was met at the door by Lady Tafari, her beads chiming as she hurried forward.

"At last!" she said. "Make haste, Ambro. A guest awaits you on the terrace."

A surge of hope rose in Ambro, pushing all thoughts of his afternoon's experience from his mind. His heartbeat quickened; someone had come for him at last, to claim him and take him home to his family. He would leave behind forever that boy he had been, a sea urchin of Verde's shoreline, of her coves and caves and rough winds. He would be beloved, as his father had been; Dawit Jaser, his true father, and not the ghost he had believed in for so many years, the ghost of a flute maker in Genovera.

With rushing strides, Ambro leapt up the flight of marble stairs, veined with pink, and into the slanting sun of the terrace where a table was laid with grilled gazelle and honey cakes swimming in tangerine juice.

"Ambro!" Lord Tafari stepped forward, halting his impetuous rush with a hand on his shoulder. He turned toward a second man who leaned on the balustrade, his long white beard hanging from an austere face and down the front of a brilliantly colored tunic of fine Barbari silk fastened with clasps of coral.

"Allow me," said Lord Tafari. "This is the boy of whom I spoke, Ambro d'Monti, from Verde."

"But once from Terre," Ambro said firmly, returning the stranger's piercing gaze unflinchingly.

"So you like to believe," the guest replied. No trace of a smile softened his sharp gaze, beneath his pale plucked eyebrows, and Ambro felt his eagerness quail under such stern scrutiny.

"My Lord Kassa, pray be seated that we may eat and discuss this matter at leisure," Lord Tafari offered, gesturing at the table, but the older man waved one ringed hand dismissively.

"I have matters to attend to at home," he replied, his dry voice like sand blowing against rock faces.

"The boy—?"

Lord Kassa stroked his white beard and the sweeping moustache that almost concealed his chiseled lips, and straightened a coral clasp. The star sapphires hanging from his ears glittered in the long golden light.

"Ambro d'Monti," he said, and Ambro's hope surged within him once more. He stepped forward, listening intently.

"It is true that fourteen years ago, the *Jaffa Queen* set sail only to be wrecked in a great storm off the coast of Verde with all hands on board, with great loss of aged wine and fine porcelain and wheat. But there was no kinsman of Ayan Kalif on her, nor was there any child born into that family sixteen years ago. You are mistaken in your beliefs."

Lord Kassa turned away and began to move toward the terrace door, but Ambro leapt to stand before him and forced him to a halt.

"Look at me!" Ambro demanded fiercely. "I am a Kiffa-walker!"

"There are many trading nations in this world," Lord Kassa replied with asperity. "Who can say what your ancestry might be? For although it's true you have tawny eyes and golden hair, no man can boast of his birthright when he does not know the name of his own father. Let me pass."

Still Ambro stood motionless in the lord's path, his eyes blazing. "How do you know what children were born into the family of Ayan Kalif sixteen years ago?"

"I am Ayan's brother, and the keeper of the family records. You are no kin of ours, sea urchin." The lord's lips curled with contempt, and a terrible sense of loss cut into Ambro, deep and keen as the thrust of a sharp blade. With all his will, he forced himself to ignore it and to remain standing perfectly still and erect in the lord's path.

"You are mistaken," he argued, "for I do know my father's name; it is Dawit Jaser."

Something hot flared in Lord Kassa's gaze and was quickly extinguished; his voice when he replied was disinterested. "You may be right or wrong, urchin, but it is of no importance, for no such name is recorded in the bloodlines of Ayan Kalif and myself."

"Please," Ambro said and heard the quiver in his voice. He cleared his throat. "Please, my lord, can you not help me to find my family? May I look at the records you keep?"

"This insolence has continued long enough!" the lord exclaimed with sudden anger, and he shoved Ambro hard in the chest, spinning him sideways on his heels and then passing him with a swish of silk and the clink of the short knife—swinging at his belt—against stone. Briefly, at the door, the lord paused and directed his hard glance toward Lord Tafari who stood by the table where the gazelle meat had grown cool.

"Tomorrow in the treasury as agreed," he said. "I shall expect you before noon," and he strode beneath the rose-stone arch and onto the marble stairs. The rap of his heels receded into silence; the silence of Safala which was never the silence of the desert but a dull blended roar of trading and doda bellows, bird calls and music.

Ambro stood as though in a trance, deaf to the city's evening sounds, blind to the low sunlight that warmed his hair and kindled the floating dust into particles of gold, rigid with a disappointment that was swelling larger and larger in his stomach, rising up through his chest like a bitter bile. The sweet smell of the honey cakes and tangerines, uneaten on the table, seemed suddenly sickening. He unclenched his fists and tried to swallow his shame back into his stomach.

Lord Tafari stepped toward him, palms outspread in apology. "I invited him because I though he might help—" he began, but Ambro could no longer contain his pain and he jerked abruptly away.

"Leave me alone!" he shouted, rushing blindly through the doorway and down the stairs, careening past Lady Tafari's startled body servant holding a tray of mineral paints, past the languid fish and under the hanging flowers, to leap down the stairs in the mountain and plunge into the streets of Safala. Blindly, his eyes unfocused by tears, he thrust between laden jennets, merchants, street dancers in billowing pantaloons, and men playing nam nam, and began to run through the deep purple shadows of the streets, southward through the city until he was lost and gasping for breath. At last, still jogging tenaciously though his sides ached and his lungs burned, he staggered up a tiny alley between towering walls of red and ochre rock, and passed beneath the arched doorway at its farthest end. In the centre of a courtyard, paved with cracked tiles, he halted at last and stared around like one awakening from a nightmare. For long moments, as darkness deepened and the full moon rose to hang like a lantern in the branches of an apricot tree, Ambro panted for air. The hard pounding of his heart filled his ears but beyond that, he felt a great silence: the silence of the desert somehow contained in this sheltered, hidden courtyard, in its lingering warmth and stillness.

Ahead of him, he saw as he regained his composure, stood a building with ivory pillars, and walls tiled in pale blue ceramic that gleamed in the moonlight. He walked slowly forward and into the shadows behind the pillars. Deep inside, centred in a shaft of moonlight streaming through some aperture high overhead, a statue stood upon an altar. Ambro drew in his breath and let it out slowly in amazement. Sirena! he thought. Could it be? Sirena, the dolphin goddess of the pirati of Verde, landlocked here in the heart of the desert and far from her blue-green sea? To compound his surprise, a great wave of homesickness and longing washed through him and for a moment he imagined he could smell the salty air of the archipelago and hear the murmurous hush of small waves on a shingle beach.

Awestruck, still amazed by his strange discovery, he stared into the great vault of the temple, noticing the dolphins painted upon the tiles at his feet and upon the pale blue walls, and the pattern of wavelets that flowed around the perimeter of the room and receded into shadows. There were rayed suns and sickle moons painted on the tiles too, and some kind of flowering lily.

Ambro stared at the smooth marble of the statue gleaming in the moonlight. He saw how the light touched Sirena's crown of stars and sickle moon, and the curved backs of the dolphins frolicking at her feet, and the serene gentleness of her face: the marble eyes seemed to look directly at him. Slowly, his footsteps silent on the cool tiles, Ambro approached the altar. There appeared to be a smaller statue leaning against its base, but it was in shadow and Ambro could not see it clearly. He came within a few paces of the altar and craned his neck, staring up at the statue of the goddess, and stillness flowed down into him like sea water, replacing his misery and shame; replacing too the horror he had felt when the brutto attacked the child. For a long time he stood there while the light of the moon slipped across the tiles and the air grew cooler. Did the goddess have Sirena's tail? It was difficult to tell, for the folds of marble gown covered her to the base of the statue. Ambro reached out to touch the hem of the gown where sea stars twined in strands; as he did so his arm brushed against the other statue, the small leaning one in the deep shadow. It moved away from his touch and for an instant in time he thought it was toppling over. In another instant, he realized that it was moving of its own volition and he let out a startled shout.

Fleetingly, in the stark moonlight, he saw the girl's face: her dusky skin and the smooth curves of high cheekbones and sculpted lips, her cascade of straight hair—black but shining iridescent in the moonlight, threaded through with tiny white cowry shells—and her brilliant blue eyes. It seemed to him that the statue, in all its beauty, had kindled into life and that it was Sirena herself that faced him in the temple, as the ringing echoes of his shout died away. A tremble ran through him as he stared into her startled eyes.

"Who are you?" he whispered, but the girl turned and began to run, a blur of hair and diaphanous blue gown, across the temple floor and down its steps with the speed and grace of a gazelle.

"Wait!" Ambro called but already she had disappeared into the alley outside, and with sharp regret he sank at the base of the altar where the girl had been, probably asleep; and became aware of how tired he was himself and how alone. Everything today has gone wrong, he thought. Oh Sirena, help me; perhaps I should never have left Verde. How can I face Lord Tafari after such shame? And what will I do if I have no family here in Terre? Where shall I ever find a home?

CHAPTER SEVEN

For a moment, at the touch on her shoulder, Noleena thought sleepily that perhaps the sand fleas had returned to the temple for the evening, to light their small courtyard fire and cook whatever food they had scrounged during the day. It was the silence that alerted her to her mistake, for usually the sand fleas chattered like a flock of small birds.

Danger! her mind shouted in the silence. Danger!

She sprang up from the base of the altar and whirled to face the presence that was in the room, her skin prickling with fright. For a moment, in the brilliant moonlight, she stared at him: a tall, wiry boy with a thick tangle of honey-colored hair falling over a smooth, high forehead; with golden brows arched over startled tawny eyes; his wide mouth parted in surprise. He was dressed in an embroidered robe of pale green that fell to the top of his rolled boots, and at his waist a small knife glittered in the moonlight. Jade beads, strung on golden wire, encircled his strong wrists and upper arms.

Kiffa-walker!

Danger! her mind screamed again and, before even thinking clearly about the fact that he was alone and not with a party come to raid the temple and take her into slavery, she was racing away from him. She barely noticed the steps between the pillars and plunged down them without checking her pace, to flee across the courtyard and into the alley's gloom.

Luna, help me! she prayed. Let the beggar man be here tonight and not wandering through Safala.

She was sobbing for breath, her chest constricted with fear, as she leapt into the alcove in the rock where the beggar man often sat. As she collided with his reclining form, rolled in a tattered piece of leather as protection against the night chill, he let out a grunt of surprise and sat up with reflexes surprisingly fast in one so aged.

"It's me!" Noleena gasped, warding off the strong grip of an outflung hand, and felt the beggar's grip relax.

"What—"

"Hush," she pleaded urgently. "Be silent. Kiffa-walker."

She tried to stifle the rasp of her own breathing but even the pounding of her heart seemed loud enough to fill the whole alley with sound. She shuffled on her bottom into the very back of the alcove, tucking her toes away from a narrow wedge of moonlight, and pressing herself into the deep shadow at the base of the rock against which she leaned. The beggar man readjusted his leather wrapping and sat very still, so still in fact that Noleena had to keep straining her eyes to make sure that he was still there, a hunched form in the darkness. They waited. An eddy of air sighed through the alley, and a star winked into brightness high overhead, in the narrow crack of sky. Noleena could feel the day's warmth radiating from the cliff at her back, and smell the dusty alkaline scent of the rock itself.

Suddenly, she tensed. The beggar man reached out a restraining hand and caught hold of her ankle, giving it a warning squeeze.

The boy was walking slowly, as though very tired, his feet dragging in the sand with a soft shushing sound. He was alone, Noleena realized. What had he been doing in the temple; what had he wanted? Had he come to vandalize the building, to shatter the tiles into fragments, to scrawl on the walls and across the painted dolphins—*The Kiffa roars! Eat dust, webbies!*—or even to chip pieces from the statue of Luna herself? Had he been there the night that the mob dragged the priestess away, her fine silvery hair tangled in fists, her serene face contorted with anguish, the fine fabric of her pale gown torn, dolphins shredded into dangling threads? Had he laughed at the sport of it all, the giddy feel of power? Was he a boy who made games out of cruelty?

Noleena pressed her rigid shoulders hard against the cliff and prayed that the boy would not be able to see her; she felt like a tiny creature of the wild, frozen while a predator stalked nearby. Could he hear her hammering heartbeat as he slouched closer?

I hate them all, she thought, and the passion of this feeling disturbed her for she was usually a tranquil person. Now, as she watched the boy's tousled head moving through patches of moonlight, her thoughts swirled with cross currents of emotion. Grudgingly, she admitted that the boy was beautiful to look at. But, she thought, it was he and his people that were filling the city with danger, with hungry greed and haughty pride, and who had allowed the evil power of their queen, that Maldici from Verde, to poison their hearts...I hate them for turning the temple into a trap, she thought, and for destroying my contentment. They are the cause of my loneliness and hunger. They spoil everything!

She flinched as the boy's shadow fell across the lip of the alcove. At the same moment, the boy appeared to notice the beggar man for suddenly he flung up his head and swung to face the alcove with one hand on the hilt of his knife. He shifted uneasily, peering into the shadows and for a moment, as he moved and the moonlight fell across his cheek, Noleena noticed that his skin gleamed as though it were wet.

"This is a lonely spot to be waiting for your supper, old one."

"Lonely enough. And what do you look for here?"

"I'm just exploring," the boy said warily.

"It is late to be exploring. You must be newly arrived from another place?"

"Yes, recently."

"You speak like one not of Terre, but of Verde perhaps."

"I speak my mother tongue," the boy replied with a touch of hauteur. "I am a Kiffa-walker, though it is true that I spent my childhood years in Verde."

"Ah, Verde. A green land, where the Corno d'Oro live hidden in the mountains, healing the nation with their freedom and their beauty. I hear that all men are brothers in Verde now; that swords have been melted down and recast as ploughshares; that the star lilies carpet the high valleys and the grapes hang clustered on the vines."

What was the purpose of this, Noleena wondered. What dangerous game was the old man playing...was he grown addled with age and hunger? Did he expect some generous donation of coin from this insolent boy who had disturbed the evening's tranquility? She could have told the old man that the boy was empty-handed and dusty, but was afraid to speak and betray her presence.

She inched her toes farther in until her knees were pressed against her ribcage, within the tight embrace of her arms. The boy's eyes, staring into the shadows, made her heart race although reason told her that she must be invisible where she crouched at the very back of the alcove.

"And why would a cub spend his childhood in Verde?" the old man asked, leaning forward so that the moonlight cast the shadow of his nose over the thin curve of his lips and emphasized the deep seams of his face; his cheeks resembled desert sand patterned by wind.

"I was traveling with my family," the boy replied.

"Then you will have seen, when you returned home to Terre, how poison has entered our land; how the desert grows empty as the mouths of mine and smelter suck your brothers in, to chew them alive and spew them out dead."

The Kiffa-walker boy shrugged his shoulders, looking puzzled and uncomfortable.

"I have not spent time in the desert; I am told it is dangerous. The webbie bandits attack and pillage as they choose. We will subdue them though."

The beggar man shook his head slowly from side to side, his lips compressed and the corners turned down. "My little brother, no good can ever come of such an enmity. Did you not learn this in Verde?"

The boy gave another uncomfortable shrug, his eyes flicking uneasily from the ground at his boot toes to the old man's face, its blind eyes covered with a strip of soft leather. Suddenly he stuck one hand into a pocket and Noleena tensed, but he simply withdrew a roll of flatbread stuffed with dates that he laid in the beggar man's lap with one swift reach of his long arm. His jade bracelet, and the fine golden hairs on his arm, glinted in the light.

"Your supper," he said. "I know nothing of the doings of kings and queens nor have I ever seen the Corno d'Oro."

He spun away quickly, before the beggar could reply, and strode down the alley, his silk gown flickering between shadow and moonlight. Noleena stared after him until her eyes ached; she waited for him to return with a group of friends who'd been hiding around a corner, for them to pull the old man from his roost in the cliff and knock him down, for them to bind her wrists with corda rope and drag her through the city to the slave lines.

At last, she began to believe that the boy had truly gone and would not return.

"Why?" she asked the beggar man, her pent-up fear lending an edge to the usual softness of her voice. "Why did you place us in danger by talking to a Kiffa-Walker?"

"You are not harmed. He was only one boy, alone."

"But why?"

"In Safala, the walls of stone reach high, Noleena; some almost as high as the cliff top itself, but the highest wall of all is the wall of silence that has fallen between our tribes. Broken against this wall we die daily, Kiffa-walker and Wind-wanderer alike. I was but making a tiny window in the wall."

Noleena sighed again for the old man's philosophical musings seemed to have little to do with the fright she had received that evening, nor the submerged fear that was constantly present in her every day.

"He has given you a date roll." She shuffled forward to lift it from the old man's lap but suddenly there came a shout from farther down the alley and she stopped abruptly, holding her breath. After a moment she smiled and slid toward the lip of the alcove and jumped to the ground just as the sand fleas came into view in a ragged group, the monkey scampering ahead with a bunch of grapes held aloft in one paw.

"Noleena!" the children called. "Come with us!" "We have a whole quail for supper!" "And a cucumber!" "We will have salad with our stew!" "Watch me, Noleena! I can do a somersault backward in the air."

The troupe flowed around Noleena like a school of bright, darting fish and swept her along in their midst, under the arched courtyard gate and across the tiles to one corner. A boy threw down a bundle of sticks that he'd been carrying on his back and another child deftly arranged them and then sparked a flame beneath them. In a moment, another child had pulled a battered and blackened pot from a cloth bag and set it over the flames; a fourth child tipped water into it while a fifth sliced the pink carcass of the quail into pieces and dropped them into the water. A fine aromatic steam began to curl from the pot and into the moonlight as more ingredients were added by dusty fingers: a pinch of dried saffrona, a diced sour melon, a handful of green onions no larger than the marbles on a nam nam board.

The children squatted around the bubbling pot, their metal buttons and the bright metallic threads in their clothes gleaming, their dirty toes stretched to the warmth, their eyes alight with anticipation. A girl stitched up a rent in a jacket, her needle flashing along the seam, and a boy practiced a game of kiffa's hammock, his fingers fishing in and out of the nest of twine. Noleena sat amongst the children, with her back against the base of the apricot tree, and tried to breathe evenly and to feel safe. From the corner of her eye, she could see the entrance to the courtyard and she watched it for any hint of motion, for the wiry height of the Kiffa-walker boy. But what reason could there be for him to return to this forgotten, neglected place that most city dwellers—if they thought of it at all—must believe to be empty and abandoned? Surely he would not bother to bring his friends. Surely they would all have better things to do inside the cool splendor of their marble rooms hung with brilliant rugs. At this moment, the boy was probably sprawled at a supper table and stuffing himself with grilled goat and oven roasted yams, with little patties filled with chick peas, and marinated vegetables floating in bowls of delicate creamy sauce. No, he would not come here again tonight.

Into *my* sanctuary, she thought. The only place I have.

Still, she watched the gateway and so was the first to notice the blind beggar man shuffling toward them on his crooked legs, his long wooden staff thumping the tiles, and his head held to one side as he navigated by the murmur of their voices and the thin, sharp crackle of their fire. Noleena scrambled to her feet in surprise and, taking the old man by one elbow, guided him to her own seat beneath the apricot tree and settled him there with his staff laid across his knees. It was seldom indeed that he ever entered the temple's courtyard.

Gradually the stew cooked; the children's eyes grew heavy with sleepiness and the branches in the fire sank down into little heaps of fine ash that Noleena would sweep away in the morning when she cleaned the tiles with her broom. The children took turns leaning over the pot and scooping out the stew with a long-handled spoon; flat bread was torn into pieces and distributed; the monkey chewed its grapes and curled into a ball in a child's lap.

Noleena began to relax at last. She leaned against the beggar man's bony shoulder and chewed the piece of date roll that he had given her.

Soon, all the food was eaten and the children trailed away into the temple to unroll their leather mats on the floor and sleep in clusters, like drifts of fallen leaves, upon the dolphins and the rippled waves. Noleena shivered; the night wind from the desert was eddying through Safala, sighing against rock and sand, cleansing the air with its harsh clear scent. The moon, now directly overhead, filled the courtyard with light as though it were a pool brimming with water. The apricot tree cast a net of tangled shadow across the tiles; the moon, Noleena imagined, was also playing kiffa's hammock. The girl Mia, that scrawny dark child who spoke the language of Terre with a foreign accent, remained at the fireside, gazing into the sinking embers and humming in her sweet, husky voice.

"Noleena," the beggar man said suddenly, turning toward her. "I have told you before that this place is no longer safe for you. You must depart into the desert."

"I am frightened here, all the time," Noleena confessed reluctantly. "But I am more frightened yet of going into the desert."

"It was from the desert that you were brought here. It is time for you to return home."

"This is my home!" Her throat constricted with fear as the familiar yet confused memory of her arrival at the temple replayed itself in her thoughts: the flare of torches, hoof beats on hard packed sand, wheeling stars, screams of terror, the sobs of a very young child. And at last, the serenity of Luna's marble face, the soothing voice of the priestess as she took Noleena into the safety of her arms, as she carried her across the blue and green tiles and gave her sanctuary.

"I cannot return to the desert," Noleena whispered now to the beggar man.

The sand flea called Mia leaned forward and threw a few more sticks onto the fire so that it flared and sputtered; the child asleep with his head in her lap stirred and sighed; the monkey in his arms whimpered and curled its tail tighter around its haunches.

"The desert needs you," the old man said. "You are a child of the desert, Noleena, with webbed toes and blue eyes, with hair that shines iridescent in the moonlight. You are also an acolyte of our goddess, Luna, who guides us across the ocean of sand with her map of stars, who gives us safe passage on our voyage through life and into the dark currents beyond. You must intercede for the

Wanderers with your wisdom, Noleena, with what you have learned here in the safety of the temple. Your people need your help."

"I have no people, only the priestesses and they are all gone now."

"No, Noleena. The desert is filled with your people. They groan in the deep mines, in the darkness without stars. They bend their backs beneath the lash of whips, they are dragged behind doda, choking as their mouths fill with sand. They perish of starvation and cruelty, though they are a people long dedicated to peace. Children cry at firesides for mothers taken captive; sons have no fathers to teach them the language of hawk and gazelle, storm and desert dawn. At Engedi, our fleet horses are broken to chariots, to strain at the shafts like common ponies. In this hour, you must be of strong courage to bring aid to your people, to free them from tyranny."

Noleena shook her head, only dimly aware of the girl Mia watching with bright eyes or of the net of shadow from the apricot tree that had cast itself now across her own lap.

"I am no one. I cannot help the desert people. I just want to stay hidden somewhere, safe. That's all I ask."

"It is not your destiny to stay safe, but to seek the help of the goddess in her temple in the desert's empty quarter, in the flank of Mount Lalibela that has for generations been a sacred place for the Wanderers. There, within the temple, stands a statue of Luna. On the longest day of summer, at the moment of mid-day, she is touched by the light. In that moment, when the light of the desert unites with the power of the moon, it is said a Wind-wanderer princess may ask the goddess for help."

"I don't know any princesses."

"But you will know of one very soon, Noleena, for I will tell you a story never yet spoken. I have held it beneath my tongue for many cycles of moon and sun, through scorching heat and night's chill, in readiness for the right hour. It is a story about a princess."

The girl Mia's eyes widened; an owl hooted. Noleena stared at the beggar man, at his bony nose and craggy face, his long black hair and beard seamed with silver; the tendons in his neck. What story of a princess might he know, who had spent his years blind in the rocks of Safala?

"In the former days, when the Kiffa-walkers and the Wind-wanderers shared Terre in brotherhood and friendship, a young prince of the desert loved horses more than song or sunlight, more than wine or women, or the taste of pomegranates. For years, in the oasis of Engedi where the river runs and the pastures lie green under the harshest sun and the throstles and doves sing in the nuga palms, the prince worked and played and slept with the desert horses. He recorded their bloodlines in the ancient book of lineage, he rubbed dry the foals as they first balanced on their long legs, and he soothed skittish mares and calmed spirited stallions. He understood the language of the horses—of flickering ear and rolled eye, of lifted fetlock and bent neck—and he knew their every mood and need almost before they did themselves. For years, the prince wanted nothing more than the beauty of Engedi, its grass danced over by the horses, and so he grew of middle age without wife or children.

"But one day, a woman came to Engedi to buy a horse, and the prince fell in love with her and followed her back into the desert to marry her and live with her people in their shugra tents, and to tend their herds and horses.

"When at last the king of the Wind-wanderers died in peace at a venerable age, this prince who loved horses became the next king. King Lebna he was by name, and he ruled the Wind-wanderers by counsel and consent, not by harshness or law, for such has always been the way of ruling amongst those people. And he continued to live in his shugra tent, encamped in the desert and moving with the herds from grassy plain to thorny grove, for such has also been the manner of life amongst the Wind-wanderers from time before memory. From the door of his tent he watched many suns rise rosy in the east and sink golden in the west; saw the flight of the cranes as they returned to their nesting grounds; listened to the clatter of the loom as his beloved wove intricately patterned carpets. And in those years he thought himself the most blessed man on the face of the earth until, on the edge of his old age, he was given one more great blessing which eclipsed all blessings that had gone before. To him and his wife was born a daughter, a child he loved more than any other thing under the sun."

"More than the horses?" Mia asked.

"More than any horse that had ever been recorded in the ancient book of lineage," the beggar man confirmed. "More than the springs of Engedi and its tender pastures, more than the young moon or the taste of roasted nub nubs. This daughter was plump-cheeked and warbled sweetly like a moon wren. Her eyes were as blue as midday sky, her hair as black as a night without stars.

"But despite his great joy in his daughter, the king grew troubled for the tides of men's affairs were changing in Terre. A dark evil was percolating into the desert, as rain water seeps through sand, and it was flowing from the north, from Verde."

"The Princess Maldici," Noleena muttered, remembering what the priestess had told her, and the beggar man bowed his head in assent.

"The princess who eventually became queen of the Kiffawalkers, was at that time living still in Verde. Yet she was secretly corresponding with the Kiffa-walker prince, Mhadi, inciting him to greed and rashness and cruelty, turning him against his Windwanderer brothers in the deserts of Terre. As a man would crush an insect underfoot so did the Kiffa-walker prince, and the lords of high households, begin to treat their brothers. And as her influence over Mhadi and over the Kiffa-walker lords and in the land grew, the Princess Maldici began to fret about the Wind-wanderer king in the desert though he had offered her no insult nor any harm. She suspected that no people could be truly broken to servitude and slavery—for such were her plans—while their king lived unharmed amongst them.

"She persuaded the prince, without his father's knowledge, to dispatch an armed force across the sands; they came one night at a gallop in the dark of the moon, and fell upon the king's encampment, slaughtering his shugra, stealing his horses, and setting fire to his tents. The children were killed and left to lie amongst their games of Fox and Jackal, amongst their pet lizards and singing birds. The women were torn from their looms, their bright weavings, and the men from the herds; all were taken captive. The soldiers bound the captives together, neck to neck, and heated irons in the fires and branded them on their shoulders with an M for Mhadi or perhaps for Maldici; they were dragged, writhing in agony and terror, smelling of burned flesh, away into the salt mines of Shoa, the gold mines of Karifa."

The beggar man's voice broke on the harsh ridge of the story's pain, and faltered into silence.

Noleena put her arms around his neck and laid her head on his chest, against the hard curves of his protruding ribs and the dusty smell of his tattered robe.

"It was a long time ago," she comforted him. The man's chest heaved beneath her cheek and he began to speak again.

"After the prisoners were taken away, the Kiffa-walker troops divided the shugra carcasses into portions and roasted them on spits over the fires. They crucified King Lebna, joking and playing nam nam at his feet as they gnawed on their roasted meat and waited for his slow death to take him. Finally, in impatience, they put out his eyes and broke his legs, then left him blinded and hanging upon the corda wood, and they rode away to Safala with the desert horses whinnying and kicking on tight ropes behind their chariots."

"Did the king die?"

"He hung there against the sky until the stars were extinguished by the dawn sun and through the gathering heat of morning and the interminable shimmering hours of afternoon. Vultures wheeled overhead and he knew that they were waiting to tear him to shreds amongst themselves. He could not see them, for he was blind now, but he could hear their sharp keening cries and he pleaded for death to release him from the torture of his sorrow, loss and pain. But he was not released. At dusk, as the birds grew bolder, beating against his face with their long pinion feathers, a man of the desert ran over the sand dunes. The king heard his staggering pace for he had run many, many miles through heat and shadow, over cracked mineral pans and up stony valleys and through sword grass, to come to the king's aid. He had seen the people of the king's camp marching across the desert in the slave lines. He cut the king down, and carried him away on his shoulders to his own tent, and for many months the king lay there beneath the shugra skin, waiting as the balance trembled between life and death.

"But at last, a message came for the blind king: his precious daughter was not dead but had been saved by a young man riding a desert horse, and was hidden in the great temple of the moon goddess inside Safala. Then the king began to walk with a staff of corda wood for his legs had healed stiff and bent. Keeping the sun always on his right shoulder, he came southward into the valley of Nini and at last reached the winding alleys of Safala and an alcove in a wall. There he sat, a nameless beggar, keeping watch over his daughter as she grew within the sanctuary of the temple, a girl hidden from a world where she was commonly believed to be dead."

The beggar man stroked the back of Noleena's head tenderly, straightening the rows of cowry shells.

Noleena could barely breathe. She pressed her cheek harder and harder against the beggar man's bony ribs—against the ribs of her father who had been crucified in the desert and left, by those evil Kiffa-walkers, for hawks to devour. Who had sat all these years in the rock's hard cleft to be near to her.

"Why didn't you tell me before?" she whispered.

"It was safer that no one knew of this; that no rumor was let loose in Terre. Only one man alive knows of our connection, and that we both live. I wanted you safe, Noleena. I wanted you to have a sheltered life. It seemed all I had left in my power to give you—you, to whom I had thought to give the whole desert in all its fierce beauty, its great freedom."

"But this has been a terrible life for you, hiding here poor and alone!" she cried.

"No, no," her father mused. "Life is not terrible or wonderful either, Noleena. It is simply itself: a mysterious gift that we receive. It is like one of the carpets of Terre, woven of threads black as ebony wood from the Moon Mountains, and others as bright as a horse's tail. The threads are placed into our hands, to make of them what we will. Do not cry, child. I have not been miserable in my alcove; your laughter has been sweeter to me than the whinny of horses when they roamed at peace in Engedi. My life has been what it is, nothing more or less."

Noleena sat up, drew a long gasping breath and looked around for reassurance; the story had transported her so far from her familiar surroundings that she felt as though she might have lost them. Now she saw the ghostly gleam of the temple pillars, and the high dark wall that surrounded the courtyard, and the tiles, painted with rayed suns and sickle moons, where her toes rested. Across the fire, Mia's changeable face was cast in lines of contemplative sorrow; she appeared much older suddenly than her eleven years, and no hint of her mischievous urchin grin remained.

The owl hooted again, hunting in the streets of Safala for rodents foolish enough to stray into the moonlight.

Noleena wiped her eyes.

"What now—Fa-father?" she asked tremulously. The beggar man cupped her face in his hands and Noleena felt the strength of his great love.

"Now, you must be brave and go from this place on a Seeking. You must journey to Mount Lalibela to ask Luna for wisdom or a sign, for some way in which to counter this evil Queen Maldici and to set your people free from slavery and death."

"But I don't know the way to Mount Lalibela."

Her father reached inside his robe and pulled out a disc that shone silver in his lined palm. Noleena saw that the disc was embossed with a crescent moon on one side and a rayed sun on the other; she ran her fingertips over the raised decorations and was startled by the tingle of power that pulsed up her arm.

Perhaps her father sensed her movement as she snatched her fingers away, for he smiled. "The marks of the Corno d'Oro," he said with reverence. "Their power has not abated on this earth,

Noleena, though many moons have waxed and waned since Luna left them for the stars."

He fastened the silver chain, from which the disc hung, around Noleena's neck. "By this token, a young man who remains in the desert will recognize you for it has never before left my keeping. He will take you to Mount Lalibela; its location is known to all our people for it is our most sacred site."

"But how will I find this boy?" Noleena asked, as the disc slid over her collarbone, above the frightened patter of her heart.

"He is named Hasani, meaning joy, and he is the grandson of a man who was my closest childhood friend, and the son of Tekle. Tekle it was who ran over dune and through sharp sword-grass, to rescue me from my cross of corda wood. And Tekle's youngest brother it was, who brought you here."

"Where is Tekle now?"

"He is long lost to us, Noleena; not even the resting places of his bones are known for every one is scattered and bleached in the desert. He refused to give our ancient book, containing the lineage of our horses, to the Kiffa-walkers. They tied him behind a chariot and dragged him over rocky scree and through thorny scrub until his valiant spirit departed his battered body. And his brother was captured as he left Safala, on the night he brought you here; him they tied to a stake overnight and let the jackals devour."

Her father pressed the palm of one hand against the leather strip across his blind eyes, as though to hold back tears. Noleena bent her head and stared at her white knuckles.

After a moment, her father composed himself and continued in his normal voice. "I will ask Hasani to meet you in the valley of Gambela that lies to the southwest of the village of Omo."

Cold fear seized her at the realization of the distances she must travel; the unfamiliar territories that she could not begin to imagine. "This is too much, Father. I cannot go alone into the desert. Can't you come too?"

"My legs would never cover that distance, and I would be slow and useless."

"We will come," Mia said suddenly from across the embers. "You can travel with us, Noleena, disguised as a sand flea. We have freedom to roam where we wish; none question us or care. Can you juggle or do acrobatics?"

"No."

"Or play an instrument?"

"No."

Mia gave a shrug of resignation. "We will find something for you. You will be safe with us."

Noleena nodded uncertainly; when she thought of the Kiffa-walker soldiers, with their snarling breastplates and their long spears, a troupe of ragged children seemed little protection. Nonetheless, the thought of traveling with them was infinitively more appealing than the terrifying thought of traveling through distance and danger all alone.

"It is settled then," the blind king said. "Your Seeking will be to lead your people from their great anguish, from this evil that has overtaken them. It is for this high purpose that you have been preserved in safety."

"Yes," Noleena agreed in a small, trembling voice. She felt herself shrinking on the tiles; tinier and more vulnerable than she had ever realized, a pebble about to be catapulted against giants. She pressed her fingers to her lips, holding back a whimper of panic.

CHAPTER EIGHT

Hour after hour, as the full moon slipped from the apricot
tree and across the temple roof and over the rim of the cliffs of
Safala, Noleena lay awake on her leather bedroll at the feet of the
goddess. Around her in the darkness the sand fleas breathed softly
and evenly in their sleep or made muted rustling sounds as they
turned over. The light had moved on now from the statue of Luna,
and the white marble with its veining of blue was almost invisible;
Noleena sensed as much as saw the goddess's serene smile and
the fins on her frolicking dolphins.

Father, Noleena kept thinking. I have a father. It was difficult
and strange to accept the reality of this; to use the name "father"
in her thoughts when she imagined the blind beggar man in his
tattered robe of indiscriminate color and his leather bound eyes.
She felt humbled by the knowledge of all the years he had faithfully watched over her, and she wished she had gone into the
alley to visit him more often, given him the best of the food that
was brought to the temple by the Wind-wanderers in years past.
And what of the woman of the desert whom he had loved? My

mother, Noleena thought and again the words seemed strange in her mind. Once she whispered aloud, "Mother, Father," but the words felt foreign on her tongue.

And all night, as the moonlight slid away from the temple and it was plunged into the silent, impenetrable darkness before dawn, when nothing moved or made any sound but for cool eddies of wind sighing between the pillars, Noleena struggled in the grip of a cold, devouring fear. Mount Lalibela. Omo. Hasani. Names spun in her head. How could she face this journey, this task placed upon her? She wished only to find some tiny space, a burrow or a crevice, and curl herself into it unnoticed and safe like a gerbil or a roosting dove. Was it so much to ask?

Luna, help me! she prayed to the invisible statue. Give me courage and give me strength. But as the first cool light of dawn stained the eastern rim of cliff and slid, chilly and grey, across the tiles to the foot of the alter, Noleena felt no comfort, only an aching dread in her heart and bones. The face of the Kiffa-walker boy intruded into her thoughts, as though taunting her with its smooth high forehead, its wide generous mouth. She visualized him clearly: every strand of golden wire around jade beads, every golden eyelash around his startled tawny eyes. Also, the images of her father's friends battered to death and torn into strips by jackals while still alive, flashed across her mind with increasing intensity until, with a low cry of despair, she could endure them no longer and rose stiffly to her feet. Across the floor the girl Mia opened her dark eyes, and after a moment she sprang up, nimble and lithe, and paced after Noleena as she went down the steps.

"Let's get a fire going," she suggested and Noleena watched while Mia deftly lit a flame under a bundle of twigs and filled the battered pan with water. From one pocket she drew a pouch and sprinkled dried aloba leaves from it into the water; shortly, the tea had brewed and Mia poured it, green and bitter-fragrant, into the pale blue ceramic cup that Noleena held out. The remainder of the tea, Mia poured into her own tin mug and for a few minutes there was no sound but the girls blowing onto the tea's surface to cool it.

"Are you really leaving Safala to journey into the desert?" Noleena asked timidly at last.

"We blow where the wind drives." Mia's bony shoulder rose in a nonchalant shrug. "If you need us, we will go."

"I am not brave like you," Noleena confessed in a small voice. "I am so frightened, Mia. I can't go, I can't do this thing my father has laid upon me."

"If you don't do it, then all the years he has watched over you have been for nothing. Why waste time worrying about possible dangers? One moment is all we ever have. Right now, you are safe and drinking hot aloba; why spoil this moment?"

"I suppose so," Noleena said doubtfully, but privately she thought that while this philosophy was all very well for a sand flea, it did not become a princess who must live by strategy and who must steel herself to walk the path of her destiny. As though to emphasize her own point, Mia downed the last of her aloba tea with a loud gulp, licked her lips, winked at Noleena, and began to practice a tumbling routine across the tiles; her agile body twisted and turned in midair as the light warmed the cliffs above with a rosy glow.

With a final flip, Mia landed at Noleena's feet. "See, another moment has arrived," she said mischievously, "and you are still safe, princess."

Noleena nodded and, despite herself, smiled a grudging admiration for the girl's clever carelessness. "Yes," she agreed, "and I think it is a good moment to visit the begg—my father."

She rose and crossed the courtyard. The alley outside the gate was still in dusky shadow, but the cliff above was brightly lit by the rising sun, and glowed with an increasing intensity of color so that Noleena felt as though she were walking inside a flower or a seashell. Doves cooed throatily in crevices and the air grew warmer, although the sand beneath Noleena's bare feet still retained night's chill.

Her father was awake and sitting upright in the alcove; his head swiveled toward her and he smiled. "Daughter," he said and she felt suddenly shy, and paused a few paces away. How did a daughter behave toward her father?

"Come, be seated." He gestured toward the lip of the alcove and Noleena perched there and stared down the alley as it twisted away into deep shadows that were becoming suffused with amber light. She found that she could not look directly at her father; the knowledge of his overwhelming sorrow filled and humbled her and she was afraid that, through his heightened senses, the old man would know this although he could not see her troubled face.

"You are abroad early," he said. "You have lain awake all night at Luna's feet and implored her to remove this burden of knowledge from you, and pleaded for your fate to push and pull you along some other road."

"Yes," Noleena whispered, her chin sinking to her chest.

"Do not be ashamed, daughter. Your road requires great courage."

"My mother...what happened to her?"

"She was killed in the raid upon our encampment. I thank Luna that she was not taken captive but that she died quickly in the desert's open air, for she was a woman who hated confinement. She lived for the wind and stars, for sun upon her cheeks and kiffa's roar on distant hills at dusk, for the taste of spring water in oases and the long swell of open dunes. All that she loved awaits you, Noleena, on your journey. You are returning home; in the desert you will find the strength that is your birthright; you will love the desert as she did."

The light, growing stronger every minute, poured down the alley now like a flood of water and the rocks, saturated with it, reached their full intensity of color: rose and deep red, pale ochre, dusty amber, burnt orange. Seams of darker rock, rich brown, lay against layers of ancient shell sediment that barred the walls with palest cream. The light threw the cliff's texture into sharp relief, so that Noleena could see every pit and ridge on the surface. The sun spilled into her lap, warming her chilled legs, stiff and tight with tension and fear. She unknotted her fingers.

"Father, how could you talk to that boy last night, after what has happened to our family?"

"When I first lived, Noleena, after Tekle cut me from the cross and nursed me in his tent, my hatred for the Kiffa-walkers was like a wild beast within me. It tore me and burned me; it was savage and uncontrollable. I carried it with me to Safala and sat with it in this alcove; I walked with it through the streets of the city and begged with it in market squares. By night I lay down with it and let it rend me until it had devoured almost every shred of my spirit. And then one night, I realized that it was killing me slowly, more slowly than I would have died upon the cross—and I did not want to die, because I had a daughter to live for. And so, I began to send the animal of anger and hatred away. Otherwise, I was no different from the men who had tried to kill me; it was their animal that I was living with. If you wish to stay alive amongst your enemies, Noleena, you must be careful not to let their animal create a lair in your own heart. To keep the kiffa out—though he paces circles around me—I practice forgiveness in every moment."

Noleena stared thoughtfully at her dusty toes; her head ached and her eyes felt as though they'd been blown full of gritty sand. She admired her father's wisdom, but if the price of wisdom was being so broken by sorrow, then she did not wish for it. She would prefer to stay sheltered and ignorant, and for her life in the temple to continue from one placid untroubled day to the next. She did not wish for the kind of knowledge that her father had accrued.

"Watch," her father said suddenly, and he began to croon with the sound of a contented dove: a kind of running chuckle deep in his throat. Noleena stared around and then tilted her head back as she caught the whir of wings. Four rock-roses drifted down to alight beside her with a flutter of pink and gold barred feathers. The birds hopped on pink legs as thin as twigs, and cocked their smooth heads. Their dark bright eyes shone like water droplets. Noleena stared at them, entranced by the beauty of their plumage colors, like the rocks of Safala, and by their bold confidence.

Her father pulled a handful of millet seeds from one pocket and sprinkled them on the stone; the rock-roses pecked at them eagerly with curved golden beaks.

"Do you know about the magic of these birds and their Namer?"

"No, Father."

"The birds live throughout Terre but they are rare, and rarer still is the person who knows their magic. If you take a clutch of eggs from the nest of a rock-rose and hatch them yourself, you must make sure that your face is the first thing the chicks see when they clamber from the broken shells. Then you must speak your own name, over and over, as the chicks' fluff dries to golden down and as their eyes, dark as ebony beads, stare at you. You must hold each chick in your palm and speak your name to it under noon sun and midnight moon, for seven days and seven nights. When they are grown, the birds from that clutch of eggs will always fly to you when your name is spoken, even though you be a great distance away across sand or water or bay tree forest. No man understands the mystery of this, how the birds can fly unerringly to you, or how it is that these birds live to be as old as their Namer and then die in the moment that he dies, no matter whether they are with him or far away.

"The young man Hasani found a rock-rose's nest and he divided the eggs—creamy white speckled with pink and golden dots—into two baskets. One basket he sent here to me, in the city, and one he kept for himself. Both of us spoke our names to the chicks as they scrambled into the daylight, and then Hasani took my chicks into the desert and left his own chicks with me. These birds that you see here will always return to Hasani if I speak his name. Thus do we send messages to each other and thus I know that Hasani lives. Watch."

Noleena leaned forward in fascination as her father held out a lined palm and chirped. The closest rock-rose hopped nimbly onto his palm, and gently her father transferred the bird to his knee. Then he pulled a scrap of parchment from a pocket and curled it around one of the bird's legs. Noleena marveled at the sensitivity of her father's touch, that he could so deftly handle tiny things without seeing them. It was as though, she thought, he had developed the sense of sight in his fingertips. He secured the parchment to the bird's leg with a length of scarlet thread, then lifted the bird until it was on a level with his face. When he chirped again, the bird cocked its head and stared at him intently with its bright dark eyes. "Hasani, Hasani, Hasani," the old man crooned, deep in his throat as when he had called the birds down from their rocky roosts. After a moment the bird let out a liquid warble and suddenly launched itself into the air in a rosy flurry like a wind-torn flower. Noleena narrowed her eyes to watch; the bird ascended quickly into the gathering heat, into the bright dome of blue sky. In a moment, it was a speck moving southwestward; in another, it had vanished over the lip of the cliff.

Noleena sighed in admiring wonder. "Will it really fly to Hasani?"

"It is carrying him the message that you are coming to the valley of Gambela."

"But who wrote the message for you?"

"I have a friend who is a scribe; he is discreet and trustworthy. And my messages are in code. This message was scribed last night."

For a moment, a blade of fear tickled painfully under Noleena's ribs and her muscles tightened. But then she thought of that tiny bright bird winging faithfully over the valley of Nini, over the backs of farmers bent amongst their wheat and millet, over the shadows of nuga palms and out across the vast sea of desert; thought of it cleaving the afternoon's heat with its golden breast, to bring news of her to one who would await her. A warmth flowed into her at the thought, displacing her fear. She smiled down at the three remaining birds as they pecked millet.

"How will Hasani's bird return to you?"

"He will speak my name to one of my own birds, that is with him, and it will bring his bird back to me. The scribe will read aloud Hasani's message to me. And now that the message is sent, you should soon begin your journey."

"Yes," Noleena said and despite herself, her voice sank to a shaking whisper, and the image of the magic bird winging south faded in her mind. She slid down onto the sand. "You are welcome to join us for breakfast," she said, but her father shook his head.

"It is better that I stay outside the temple, as I usually do, lest any guess our story. I am going into the city to beg for more millet seed."

Noleena watched as the old man shifted stiffly across the alcove and moved away into the twisting crevice of the alley with his shuffling gait and his corda wood staff that thumped the ground ahead of him, being his eyes. A great sadness welled up in her as she contrasted his broken form, rounding a bend to disappear, with the vision of the man he'd once been: vigorous and free, a man who could swallow the horizon on the back of a running horse.

I must not throw away this suffering, she thought. I must play my part in saving the Wind-wanderers, his people and mine. Otherwise though I spend my whole life safe in hiding, I will never be able to hide from my own shame.

When she reached the temple, she found that the sand fleas had eaten their meager breakfast of chickpea gruel and rolled up their leather sleeping mats. Four girls danced in a circle, using bright streamers of silk that they waved in the air so that the fabric undulated like a snake. Mia was beneath the apricot tree, playing a sprightly tune while a small boy scrambled up the trunk, holding out a grape and trying to entice the monkey down from the highest branches where it clung, chittering stubbornly. At Noleena's entrance into the courtyard, Mia skipped across the tiles, still playing her hurdy-gurdy, the pale green leather of the baffles opening and closing along worn folds softened with age and use. She curtsied at Noleena's feet with mock formality, her face a smooth mask wiped clean of emotion.

"Good morning, Princess. Will you prance, will you dance? Will you tumble and flip? Will you a-play the monkey or the wise fool? How is it your pleasure to earn your keep on the road to Omo?"

"I can't do any of those things," Noleena confessed.

Mia executed a mournful jig in slow motion, her face contorted comically into a mask of dismay. "The princess cannot dance, cannot somersault!" she cried.

A twittering ripple of amusement eddied through the children who had gathered to watch but Noleena didn't mind; she detected nothing mean about their laughter and knew it was directed more toward Mia's antics than toward her.

"Can you sing?" piped a boy in baggy pantaloons that he hitched up around his skinny waist every few minutes.

"Can you sing?" Mia sang in her sweet husky voice. "When the hurdy-gurdy plays, can you sing? When the doves lay their eggs, can you sing? In the spring, can you sing? Can you make the desert ring?"

Now Noleena was laughing too as Mia capered, her bent arms still squeezing the hurdy-gurdy open and shut and her thin fingers dancing over the keyboard. She stopped suddenly before Noleena. "Well, can you?" she demanded.

Noleena looked shyly around at the listening children. The boy with the gourd drum stepped forward and sat beside Mia with the drum cradled between his legs; he began to beat a slow rhythm upon it with his palms and the sound thudded in the courtyard like a heartbeat.

"I don't know whether I can sing," Noleena confessed. "I could try."

"Listen," Mia commanded and she began to play a simple, haunting melody in a minor key and to sing, while the drumbeat continued its slow cadence.

"I sent my love a cooing dove,
I sent my love a kiffa cub,
I sent my love an evening star,
My only love, who roams so far,
So far, so far away across the sea of sand."

On the second playing, Noleena began to sing too, hesitatingly at first but then with more confidence, her sweet clear voice ringing off the walls and sending the doves wheeling overhead.

"I sent my love a lizard blue,
I sent to him my heart so true,
He caught it in a golden snare,
My only love, who roams so far,

So far, so far away across the sea of dreams."

When she and Mia had practiced each verse and then sung the entire song without a pause, the children burst into a flurry of clapping that surprised and then comforted Noleena. "Hurrah!" they cheered. "She can sing!"

"Only you cannot go dressed as a priestess," Mia decided, "with dolphins around your hemline and star lilies around your neckline," and she motioned to a small girl who scurried forward with a bulging cloth bag. From this, Mia dragged various garments and shoved them back in again until at last she found what she was searching for. "Change into this," she said, throwing a bundle of fabric toward Noleena who barely caught it to hold at arm's length: a patchwork of vivid colors—red with gold threads, blue with silver stars, green with bronze threads, patterns of birds and trees, dark velvet squares and triangles of yellow Barbari silk—all stitched together with a multicolored thread.

"Even in this, I will look like a Wind-wanderer," she said, suddenly aware of her fear—that the drumming and singing had dispelled—clutching her around the chest again and squeezing her breath out.

"Look at us," Mia said with a wave of one hand, and Noleena looked at the assembled children, at their eyes that were palest blue, dark blue, green, grey or amber in faces round or thin, freckled or smooth, dark brown or ivory beneath hair that was kinky or straight and that varied in color from almost white to pure black.

"We are the riff and raff of the earth," Mia said. "No one will notice you amongst us." And she tied a green ribbon around Noleena's forehead and threaded a spray of rock-stars, those tiny white flowers of the cliffs, through the ribbon.

"Now, you are ready. Tomorrow, we leave early. Today, I will teach you more songs."

The children scattered and reformed into a ragged group that streamed under the arched gate and away down the alley, their shrill cries receding into the distance, swallowed by Safala's massive rocks and impenetrable heat. Noleena went into her room in the temple and changed into the bright dress and then, feeling self-conscious in so much color after having worn only pale blue all her life, she joined Mia on the temple steps. Mia played the hurdy-gurdy and taught Noleena tunes. Then she sang and taught her words; by mid-afternoon when the fish were almost motionless in the pool, stunned into inactivity by the sun's bright eye, Noleena knew half a dozen.

"Tomorrow then," Mia said, "we go into the desert. But now, we go into Safala to sing for our supper."

"I'm not ready—I don't know the songs well enough yet. Please, Mia—I need one last afternoon in the temple before I leave."

Mia grimaced and shrugged. "As you wish." Then she was gone, light-footed, her shadow hopping at her side. The deep silence to which Noleena was accustomed welled into the courtyard and shimmered to its brim. A blue lizard crept out to bask in the sun. Noleena lay upon the low wall surrounding the pool, her back against the hot stones, the sun burning red inside her closed eyelids, and tried to imagine tomorrow. Maybe I won't go, she thought drowsily. Maybe I'll say I'm not ready...how can I leave this place? And will I find her again in Mount Lalibela: Luna with her stars and sickle moon? And what am I to do there; how do I find the wisdom and for what sign do I seek? How can I possibly turn aside the great and frightening powers of that evil Queen Maldici? Everything is changing too fast, before I am ready for it to change. Where is the priestess now?

A sudden shout from the direction of the doorway jolted Noleena from her musings; she sat up to see Mia racing toward her with the hurdy-gurdy bouncing on her back and her dress flapping against her shins. She caught hold of Noleena's wrist and tugged. "Come!" she panted. "Kiffa-walker boys are heading into the alley, looking for a place to fly their kites. They will be here very soon. Come with me!"

Hand in hand the girls ran across the courtyard and past the beggar's alcove where not even a trace of millet seed remained. A pink feather, barred with gold, fluttered to the ground as the girls rushed by.

"But—we will meet the boys coming this way!" Noleena cried, her heart drumming against her ribs.

"Follow!" was all that Mia answered, dragging her onward around twists and bends; she expected imminently to crash against a solid mass of boys carrying long-tailed kites shaped like eagles, hawks, and kiffas; those kites that she occasionally saw swooping above rooftops or climbing against Safala's red cliffs into open sky.

Suddenly Mia dodged to the right and leapt upward onto a tiny twisting stair that ascended the cliff. Noleena felt loose sand and flakes of pink rock slide beneath her feet, felt space dropping away on one side as she panted higher, felt her breath burning in her lungs. Faintly, far below, she heard the shouts of boys and sped upward against Mia's heels. She kept her gaze fixed on each step as it passed through her vision at eye level; each was rough hewn, the surface still bearing the mark of the mason's tools, the lip worn smooth by time and a thousand footsteps. One more. One more. Her lungs heaved and her heart seemed ready to burst from her chest. Ahead, Mia dislodged a pebble that bounced down between Noleena's legs to hurtle into the chasm that now yawned to their right; faintly Noleena heard it ricochet down and down into darkness. Higher they climbed. Still higher. The steps grew ever more narrow, hugging outcroppings of harder and darker rock, twisting around corners, skirting dry crevices.

From the corner of her eye, Noleena saw a hawk riding the thermals at her shoulder, climbing lazily and effortlessly beside her.

Abruptly the path ended on a massive flank of flattish rock, deep red in color, that sloped with gentle incline toward the chasm. Across this Mia scrambled, sure footed as a gazelle. Noleena stared after her in horror; if she slipped, she would roll right across the rock and plummet to her death. "Come on!" Mia yelled over one shoulder and Noleena took a hesitant step onto the slab, feeling its heat blast upward against her bent face and her legs, and began to cross the open space. Dizziness trembled through her and spots swung before her eyes. For a moment she faltered, off-balance, waving her arms and always aware, without looking toward it, of the sheer face down which she would tumble if she fell: a somersaulting princess after all.

"Come on!" Mia urged.

And in a sudden rush Noleena sprang across the space that remained between them and felt the tight grasp of Mia's hand for a brief moment before Mia turned to launch herself at the rock wall that blocked their progress. Her toes scrambled for purchase and Noleena saw the tendons strain tight in the backs of her hands as she hung against the rocks, clawing her way upward. At the top, she straddled the wall and reached down for Noleena. "Dig your toes in!" she commanded and Noleena found herself climbing, although she had never climbed a wall before; the fear of the boys with kites and of the empty yawning space at her back seemed to lend unusual strength to her arms and legs so that she was soon beside Mia. From this vantage point, she could see the terraces and balconies, the rooftops and towers of Safala clinging to the base of the cliff like a heap of fallen rock; could see beyond them to the valley of Nini, a slash of brilliant green, and farther still the opposite high cliff: a dull red ribbon of rock holding back the desert's hazy blue emptiness. Into her line of vision a fleck of color, as brilliant as a carpet, rose corkscrewing and fighting as the wind touched it: a kite above the temple courtyard.

She listened but there was no sound of any pursuit. She drew a long shaky breath and felt sweat beading between her shoulder blades. "Now where do we go? We can't go back the same way. Are we stuck here?"

"Don't worry, there's a way down." Mia's flushed face was alight with energy and her eyes gleamed; she was enjoying this, Noleena realized in amazement.

"Come on." Mia balanced along the wall, and Noleena noticed that, hugging its base on the far side, was a huge pipe constructed of small dark bricks. Onto the top of this pipe, Mia jumped to land lightly and run along its sloping surface as though she were in a street and not balanced precariously near the top of a mountain. Noleena swallowed hard and stared. "Come on!" Mia cried once more and Noleena readied herself to jump. In midair she knew that she had misjudged the distance; as she sprawled against the side of the pipe, bricks knocked the air from her chest and her head spun. She clung to the pipe's gentle curvature and waited for Mia to run back and haul her up.

"Please," she said shakily, "where are we going?"

But Mia was already running on. "Not far now!" she called back.

Noleena balanced cautiously down the pipe's gentle incline, testing every step before she rested her full weight upon it. Suddenly Mia stopped at a hole in the pipe, and lowered herself down through it to drop from view. When Noleena bent over the hole the smell of water filled her nostrils: a delicious freshness that seemed to sparkle and chuckle on her senses, obliterating the smells of dust and sweat, and that seemed to contain the aroma of mint leaves and dewdrop blossoms, of strange unknown ferns and leafy foliage. It was Moon Mountain water, Noleena realized. A shout from Mia bounced and echoed inside the darkness of the aqueduct. Noleena let herself down into the hole, the bricks scraping her armpits and terror lurching inside her, and landed with a splash in the cool shock of the running water that tugged at her thighs. Mia's slick wet hand gripped hers and propelled her forward.

They waded downhill for a long time, sliding their free hands against the smooth interior wall of the pipe and feeling the steady rushing pull of the water. It seemed to Noleena that they spent hours in the pipe, groping through impenetrable darkness. Suddenly the pitch changed. Mia whooped and their hands slipped apart. Noleena groped wildly in the darkness, her frightened shout bouncing off the walls and filling her head with ringing vibrations. The water's speed increased; it yanked her feet from under her and she screamed a high wail, her open mouth filling with water as she went under and was swept downhill, whirling and tumbling, bumping against the sides of the pipe, in a torrent of Moon Mountain water.

A hand grabbed her; legs blocked her way. Her head broke the surface and water streamed across her eyes. She gasped for air, pushing away the hair and cowry shells plastered to her cheeks, and saw that the pipe had leveled out again as well as grown smaller in diameter, and that daylight was falling onto her from a hole overhead. Around her the water was pure green where the light touched it, and splintered with fractures of silver.

"Breathe," Mia said, tugging her onto her feet and slapping her back. "We're safe now. Come on." She reached up to grasp the sides of the hole and haul herself through it. For a moment her body blocked the sunlight and darkness fell across Noleena where she stood alone in the water, and she had to bite back a cry of panic.

"Your turn!"

Noleena reached up and gripped the rim of the hole, then swung from it with bricks tearing at her palms and the water sucking her back. Wildly her legs kicked at air as she hung from the rim, while Mia tugged at her shoulders, bunching up handfuls of the sodden patchwork dress and sending rivulets of water running down the hot bricks to soak into the porous surface or evaporate before they had trickled more than a few yards. Finally, Noleena was out of the pipe. She sprawled on her back on top of the aqueduct, panting, shaking, feeling the wet fabric of her dress cling to her and seeing the sun sparkle in the water drops clustered thickly in her eyelashes. After a few minutes she sat up and looked around to find with astonishment that they were already outside the city and that the pipe was running through a field in the valley of Nini; the tender green of wheat waved around and below them in every direction. The cliffs across the valley, that had before been a faded ribbon against the skyline, now towered above her, solid and vividly colored. Behind her, when she swiveled around, she saw the facades of Safala blending with the rock.

"How did you know we wouldn't drown?" she asked.

Mia laughed. "I've done this before."

"Does nothing frighten you?"

The laughter died abruptly in Mia's eyes and her expressive face grew solemn; once more, she briefly appeared older than her eleven years. "I haven't met that thing that will frighten me yet—but doubtless I will."

"You are lucky," Noleena said shortly. It seemed unfair that this rag-tag street child should have such nonchalant courage while she herself, a princess of the Wind-wanderers, should have so little.

"I am sorry that I couldn't explain it to you, Noleena. There wasn't time. And it was my fault about the boys; I beat one of them at a game of Fox and Jackal and he got angry; they started to chase me and the alley was the only place I could run into. Sorry. You are good at running."

"Oh yes, I am very good at running and hiding," Noleena said with a depreciating scowl. "How will we get back into the city?"

"But we don't need to! We can set out into the desert this very afternoon."

Noleena's heart, that had been beating high in her throat ever since the chase began, now plummeted into her stomach and lay there like a fallen stone. "I'm not ready to leave," she mumbled.

"You will be just as frightened tomorrow."

"I haven't said goodbye to the—my father."

"He doesn't want your goodbyes; he just wants you to go."

"What about the sand fleas; aren't we traveling with them?"

"They are in the valley today, amusing the villagers. We will find them on the road and travel together. Come."

Mia rose and held out her hand; slowly, reluctantly, and wondering whether she had been tricked, Noleena rose to grasp it before they jumped together from the aqueduct to land amongst the swaying wheat. Mia picked a handful of milky kernels and began to push a path through the crop, eating her wheat, spitting out husks. Presently they reached a dusty road and Mia turned toward the cliffs that held back the desert and began to swing along it, occasionally executing a dance step. Noleena trudged alongside, feeling the city of Safala dwindling at her back; the familiar precincts of the temple farther and farther away with every step. It is my childhood I am leaving behind, forever, she thought. A great sense of loss swelled in her chest and tears pricked her eyes, but Mia appeared not to notice. Her husky voice broke into song and her flat sandals seemed to beat a rhythm on the road's rutted surface.

"I sent my love a rosy bird,
I sent my love a tender word,
I warned my true one to beware
Of wandering out so very far,
So far, so far away across the waves of sorrow."

Presently, Mia began to hum another song but Noleena was no longer listening. Her thoughts had drifted ahead, into the desert's frightening vastness. She tried to imagine how a rosy bird might navigate its way through this vast space to reach at last a valley south of Omo and the tent of a young man called Hasani. Would he smile or scowl, this stranger, unfurling a scrap of parchment to learn that she was coming—she was crossing the desert to join him? Would he welcome her for the sake of their families' friendship? Would he take her to Mount Lalibela? And would they find a sign there at the feet of Luna—or only meet with sorrow as had their fathers before them?

CHAPTER NINE

ON THE LIP OF THE CLIFF, up which the sand fleas had toiled on a tortuous path, Noleena paused and turned to stare back longingly at the valley of Nini with its sparkling irrigation canals and scattered stone villages. Safala was already lost to view. Home, my home, Noleena thought. When will I ever see it again? Her father had told her that the desert was her home but as she turned at last to trudge after the sand fleas along the route that led them into the desert, Noleena felt nothing but anguish. Safala was her home; the place where she had learned to run across the courtyard tiles on short legs, where the priestesses had sung to her and plaited cowry shells into her hair, where she had been safe and cherished. Safala was being torn out of her with every step that she took toward the sand.

The desert, as she began to traverse it, seemed to offer nothing but emptiness: mile after mile of fierce heat that reflected blindingly off sloping dunes and scoured rock; the sharp tear of thorny shrubs at her patchwork dress; the thin edges of sword grass cutting spidery lines across her shins. They dried so fast they couldn't bleed. Even the sand fleas grew silent as the afternoon progressed and the faint track wound on ahead of them toward a southern horizon that they never seemed to reach but only to toil endlessly toward as the sun, sinking lower, dazzled their eyes and evaporated the sweat from their foreheads.

At last, as the sun became a fiery ball rolling along the western rim of the world, and lilac shadows poured down the eastern slopes of hills and dunes, the sand fleas halted to build a fire. They unrolled their sleeping mats and began to extract the food, earned by their morning's work in the valley of Nini, from their travel-stained packs. In short time, a stew of leeks and fennel, radish, yellow-patch peas and sour melon, bubbled in the battered pot suspended over the flames. Noleena sank down by the fire, numb with sadness and fatigue. She was grateful for the children gathered around her, laughing softly, talking, telling jokes; beyond them, she was conscious of darkness creeping across the sand, filling the desert's emptiness with mystery and possible danger. She huddled closer to the fire and willed herself not to think of the miles of emptiness that surrounded them. Closer and closer the darkness came, growing thicker, until even the dune at their backs was obscured and their world shrank to a tiny pool of firelight. The darkness seemed to press at Noleena's shoulders so that her neck prickled uneasily and she tugged her shawl tighter.

After dividing the stew amongst themselves, the sand fleas lay down to sleep. Noleena unrolled her borrowed mat near the oldest of the troupe: twins, a boy and a girl who seemed close to her own age. Mia and another child took the first watch by the fire, keeping it alive with handfuls of prickly shrub that, despite the small size of its twigs, burned slowly. Noleena lay rigid in her shawl, feeling the night cold dropping from the huge bowl of sky to soak into her bones. She waited for some unknown danger—that she couldn't imagine but could only feel—to leap on her from the desert breathing at her back. For hours she was too frightened to sleep and lay with her eyes stretched wide and focused on the fire; its star of comfort. She must eventually have dropped into sleep because when she next looked, there were different children guarding the fire and Mia lay near her. Faintly, far off, she heard the yammering shrieks of jackals and she shivered and rolled closer to the twins to doze fitfully. When she next came fully awake, the air was still, silent and perfectly clear. A rosy flush of color stained the sand pink and the sky was suffused with rays of light shooting up from the eastern horizon.

The sand fleas reached a village that afternoon, its clay houses with thatched roofs packed inside a high wall painted with geometric designs in bright shades of red and yellow. They trailed through the open gate into the village square, where chickens scattered at their feet and goats stared at them, bleating forlornly. Brown pigs, spotted with white, grunted and squealed. Gradually, the villagers themselves became aware of the arrival of the sand flea troupe. Women ceased pounding millet in stone mortars; men squatting around nam nam games in the shade of acacia trees rose to wander into the square.

Who are these people; are they Kiffa-walkers or Wind-wanderers? Noleena wondered, watching the villagers fill the square. She could not be sure; Kiffa-like azure robes billowed over Wanderer-like breeches; some villagers wore grass skirts and others wore strange foreign clothes she didn't recognize. Bead necklaces hung on bare chests decorated with patterns of scars; dyed feathers were stuck in rows of tiny plaits; shawls of green and yellow were worn beneath conical straw hats, whilst other heads were crowned with turbans of various colors. Women wore massive circular collars of beads that stuck out around their shoulders on wire hoops.

The sand fleas began their entertainments; they juggled and danced and contorted their bodies in acrobatic displays. Noleena sang to the accompaniment of the drum and Mia's hurdy-gurdy. She felt naked and exposed before the villagers' curious eyes of many colors; as exposed and vulnerable as she had felt lying down in the desert to sleep. Her voice wavered through the first song, and quivers of nervousness shook her thighs.

"Forget about them—just sing!" Mia hissed between verses, and Noleena lifted her eyes and focused on a nuga palm planted across the village square. A flock of tiny rainbirds, that only nest after a storm, fluttered and preened in the palm, their plumage brilliant as star sapphires. As she watched the rainbirds, Noleena's voice grew stronger and she forgot about the staring villagers and let the melodies transport her away into their own world. When she had performed the six pieces that Mia had taught her, the villagers placed donations on the shawl by her feet: a soft yellow gourd, a hen's egg, a handful of chickpeas, a cup of goat's milk, a coin. She scooped it all up gratefully, conscious of a tiny flicker of confidence kindling into life; perhaps she was not as entirely helpless as she often felt.

Later, as the children divided up their food, Noleena whispered, "Who are these people?"

Mia shrugged. "I don't know. They are the same as the people in Safala; of all races and nations mixed together."

"But there are no Wanderers in Safala anymore."

"No. The ones that live here must be working for the Kiffas that are here, I suppose. Why worry about it? They are all the same under their skin."

No, they are not! Only the Kiffas would hunt me, Noleena wanted to protest, but she said nothing.

The children remained in the village overnight and Noleena slept more restfully with her back against the reassuring solidity of a mud wall. Yet the desert reached her even there, filling her nose with its particular scent, tickling her with its cold breath, sending chills running up her spine as she thought of its vast expanses where she knew nothing and no one, where she was like a newborn animal in need of constant protection. Predators, she knew, were able to smell that scent of weakness and would follow its track for miles, confident of an easy kill. She thought of the Kiffa-walker boy in the temple—his strong wrists and wiry shoulders, the lock of blonde-streaked hair that fell across his forehead—and shivered, pressing her shoulder blades harder against the wall at her back.

For eight days the sand fleas toiled southward, stopping to perform in scattered villages tucked into narrow rift valleys or in oases sheltered by high dunes. The twins wore gauzy pantaloons of vast proportions and danced energetically, leaping upward and spinning about, so that the pantaloons filled with air and ballooned around them in swirling curtains of brilliant pink. Their anklets of coins chimed as the dancers spun, a thin clear ringing sound. Mia danced with the monkey while the drummer drummed; she parodied the monkey's movements, her expressive face contorted into a wrinkled, old-man grimace like the monkey's face. The villagers hooted with laughter and afterward gave Mia dried figs and handfuls of dates and nuga fruit, which she and the monkey shared, chattering to each other softly.

Day after day, following the faint path southward across salt pan and patches of sword grass, over sliding dunes and between solitary bay trees, Noleena's sense of dread and desolation grew stronger. The desert is a terrible place, she thought. I do not love it as my mother did. My legs ache and my eyes hurt; I am always thirsty and tired; I am always frightened. At every moment, I expect the Kiffa-walkers to catch me, or for us to become lost and never seen again; for the jackals to hunt us or the kiffas to devour us. The desert is all my fears under one sky; I wish I was back in Safala. I wish I had never left.

On the evening of the eighth day, the weary band straggled into the village of Omo and lay down to sleep inside the walls; they were too tired to perform and did not even cook a meal but simply tore flat bread into strips and rolled them around chickpea paste seasoned with fennel, then filled the crannies in their stomachs with dried dates. For hours, as the moon rose and wind clattered softly amongst the fronds of nuga palms, Noleena lay on her back and stared up at wheeling stars. Tomorrow I will meet Hasani, if I am lucky, she thought. If he is in the valley of Gambela. If he is still alive. If the bird reached him, the rock-rose that he Named. But if not—then what? Shall I be a sand flea like these children? How will I help my people?

The whole notion of being able to help her people and turn back the great powers of the Queen Maldici, secure behind the towering red walls of her palace and protected by the cruel assassini, felt absurd. The more Noleena thought about it, the more absurd it seemed until the whole idea took on the dimensions of a bizarre dream. Hasani would take one look at her troubled face and frightened eyes, and would scoff at the very notion of her being able to help even one person taken into slavery. I am ignorant and useless, Noleena thought; I have less courage in my whole body than Mia has in a little finger. Tears of despair welled from her eyes, sparkling in the starlight, and she wiped them away with the sleeve of her patchwork dress.

In the morning, the children were awake early, as the first light touched the plastered mud walls of the village huts with their painted decorations of yellow and red geometric shapes. In no time at all, a fire was lit, the twins were dancing outside doorways for breakfast food, the monkey had scaled a palm and was hailing the children below with fruit, and laughter rang through the village. Noleena, slumped against a wall, watched the frolic with dull eyes. Presently, Mia came and sat beside her. "Cheer up! This is the day you've been waiting for!"

"What if Hasani isn't there or doesn't want to help me?"

"What if the sea was hard as rock; what if the stars flew in a flock?" Mia sang mockingly; then she hugged Noleena and slipped a soft orange nuga fruit into her hand. "Eat! We'll be walking again soon."

All morning, as the sun climbed overhead and heat rippled from rocks and baked minerals, the children trudged southward, searching for the valley of Gambela. There was no path to follow now but one of the boys had a compass and they followed the flickering swing of its needle south by southwest, as the villagers had told them to, across an expanse of bare rock scrubbed smooth by centuries of wind and sand. The children's feet slipped; they fell and scraped the skin from their knees and ankles. The heat sucked the breath from their lungs and the moisture from their mouths. Cacti speared their arms with twisted spines as fine as thread that burned as they entered. Silence fell over the children; without the sound of their usual chatter, Noleena felt the desert more keenly than ever. It is going to kill us all, she thought; we will bake to death on these rocks and our bones will slide down the crevices and never be seen again. The desert seemed to be moving in closer and closer, crowding her steps, pressing her down against the scoured brown surface of the rocks, making her acknowledge that she could not hope to escape from its mysterious power.

By late afternoon, the troupe had become a straggling line strung out across the floor of a dried lake, its surface a maze of cracks that spidered away in every direction. Each step dislodged clouds of choking alkaline dust. Children sneezed and coughed, but otherwise moved in exhausted silence. Their clothes and skin were coated with dust that stuck to sweaty skin and clung to hair and fabric so that the children became paler by the minute. Noleena thought they began to resemble a troupe of ghosts. On the far side of the lake, the sun was sinking behind a ridge of loose, flat rock. Noleena panted as they climbed it while evening nipped at their heels, driving them on. Rocks, dislodged by children above, skittered toward Noleena and threatened to dislodge her and send her tumbling back onto the lake bed. Sharp pains stabbed in her side, and her skin itched but when she rubbed she could not get rid of the mineral dust; only managed to smear it around as it mixed with her sweat and turned into a sticky paste. We will never reach this valley before darkness, she thought; we will not find Hasani. A chill shook her but at that moment, high above, the boy with the compass reached the ridgeline and let out a whoop, his body a silhouette against the darkening sky, before he plunged from view.

Noleena struggled on, holding her side, her breath coming in hard, short gasps. Suddenly, the ground fell away beneath her: rocky scree plunged down and down into a narrow cleft of valley hidden in the heart of the desert. The boy with the compass was leaping down the slope, dislodging flat rocks on which he balanced and rode briefly before leaping on again.

"A Wind-wanderer camp," Mia said at Noleena's shoulders and she stared farther, past the boy and into the bottom of the valley where the shadows were already deep and purple, to see a huddle of tents made of some dark brown, hairy material, and clustered together around a fire's bright eye.

"We've arrived! Get out the supper pot!" Mia yelled and she too plunged down the slope amongst the shouting children who slipped and leaped, and rode the flat sliding stones. Noleena watched, frozen with apprehension. In a few moments, if she moved, if she traversed the slope into the valley, she would be given new knowledge: the knowledge of her people, of Hasani. I don't know if I want it, she thought. After coming so far, I may be given knowledge that turns the world upside down, knowledge as large and frightening as the desert that makes me feel tiny and helpless.

At last, she realized that she was the only person remaining on the ridge. The twins, who had passed her a few minutes before, had almost reached the valley; they seemed to sail down the slope on the wide wings of their gauzy pink pantaloons. Noleena stepped onto the sliding rocks, almost lost her balance, windmilled her arms, and leaped farther down the slope. She discovered that it was possible to ride a single rock for several yards, then leap quickly to another one as the rock lost momentum and came to lodge against others. Leaping, dodging cacti and crevices, her ears filled with the rocks' harsh clatter, Noleena arrived at the bottom in a flurry of dust, gasping for breath and with her eyes covered by her hair.

"Welcome, traveler, welcome to our campfire, the shelter of our tents, the sustenance of our food, the comfort of our company."

Noleena jumped and flung up her head, pulling hair from her eyes at the sound of a deep voice, musical and dignified, speaking the formal welcome of the Wind-wanderer people. The speaker stood five paces away: a dark, burnished young man of perhaps eighteen, with blue eyes beneath long, iridescent black hair that was wound around his head in a single plait like a crown.

Words abandoned her. In their absence, she fumbled at her neck and drew out her father's medallion from where it hung beneath the fabric of her dress. She held it out to the Wanderer; with a sigh of admiration and wonder he bent over it and cradled it in his callused palms.

"The seal of King Lebna. And you—his daughter and our true princess. Welcome," he repeated, letting go of the medallion to take her hands in his own instead. He held them like small birds that needed protection. Noleena was still staring; she knew this, and felt humiliated by her rudeness and her tongue-tied silence, by the rents in her patchwork dress and the white dust smeared in her sweat, and the tangled disarray of her hair. Still she stared at him: his proud mouth, his high cheeks decorated with rippled lines of blue mineral paste, the crescent moons in his ears, the blue beads at his throat, the width of his chest beneath a tunic that was the dark orange of cayenne pepper, the length of his legs in cream breeches.

Childhood memories crowded into her mind: the Wind-wanderers slipped silently through the alleys of Safala, left their ivory and golden horses by the temple gates, strode inside as lithe as wild animals in their flowing tunics of orange, amber and ochre, their breeches of soft fabrics colored cream or brown. They carried baskets of grapes and pomegranates still warm from the sun which they set down on the steps. With sharp knives they split the red skin, then picked out the juicy seeds to feed to her, a favorite child. They filled the shadows with their lilting laughter and musical voices, with their blue, alkaline smell of wind and dust.

Now, beneath Noleena's stare, the young Wind-wanderer's lips twitched upward. Suddenly, startling herself, she stepped forward and wrapped her arms around him and pressed her face against his robe—its faint remembered smell of wind and dust and horses—and against the steady thump of his heartbeat. Heat flamed in her face. What would he think of her behavior? For a long moment, he held her. All the loneliness and fear she had experienced in the desert quivered through her muscles and he stroked her back with his long brown fingers, the way a person might gentle a nervous horse. "I thought we would never find you," she whispered.

"The rock-rose told me you were coming. I have waited for you."

"You truly are Hasani?"

"I am he, bandit and outlaw, son of Tekle."

"Bandit?" She drew away from him in amazement, searching his face to see if he was joking, but it held no hint of laughter.

"So the Kiffa-walkers call me, those horse thieves, those jackal dung. I spit on them!" His eyes blazed with a fierce light, blue as chips of mosaic in his dark face, and the muscles tightened in his arms.

"My father told me about your father...I am sorry," Noleena said softly and the fierceness died from Hasani's eyes.

"Yes, my father, may his spirit wander the wind in peace. May I have such a fine courageous heart." He bent his head and traced a circle in the sand with the toe of his boot. "But now Noleena, we must eat and you must rest briefly before we leave."

"Leave!" Dismay shot through her, and she looked longingly over Hasani's shoulder at the encampment with its sturdy tents around the fire that flared brightly in the falling darkness.

"I have been here too long already," Hasani explained. "I have no camp now, Noleena, no place to stay. I hunt the Kiffa-walkers and they hunt me; tonight we ride far from here before I bring the hunters down upon my family. Come, you must meet them before we go," and he took her by the hand and led her toward the tents, past a herd of shugras with long shaggy brown coats, curved horns, and mild eyes. They lowed in bell-like tones as Hasani and Noleena walked past, and briefly Noleena glimpsed a woman bent beside one of the beasts, milking it into a leather pail.

Then she was amongst the tents—they were made from shugra hides with the hair still on them, she realized—and then they arrived at the fire where the sand fleas were already spooning a thick broth of shugra milk and green onions into their hungry mouths and beginning to revive so that ripples of laughter and mischief circled the fire. Mixed amongst them, Noleena saw, were Wind-wanderer children in their desert-colored clothing, with their long black hair hanging in shining curtains. They became still momentarily as Hasani led her forward, turning their blue gazes on her, but just as quickly they turned their attention back to the fascination of the sand flea children and laughter spilled from their mouths.

As Noleena took a seat cross-legged in the sand, women emerged from the tents and came to be introduced to her; though they were old, they moved with strong confidence, Noleena noticed with admiration, loose limbed in tunics, breeches, and boots identical to those worn by the men except that their tunics were unbuttoned down the fronts. Beneath these they wore short blouses of pale ivory that left their stomachs bare. Their crescent moon amulets, hanging from their pierced belly buttons, glinted in the firelight. They squatted before Noleena to smile at her and kiss both her cheeks: a bewildering procession of old great-aunties and grandmothers with faces as cross-hatched as the face of her father. The women gripped her wrists tightly in their strong, twisted fingers and blessed her in the name of Luna. She quailed a little beneath the scrutiny of their wise gazes.

They are trying to see whether I am strong inside, as they are, she thought. Probably all they can see is how scared I am of riding off into the darkness with a boy for whom the Kiffa-walkers hunt.

"Eat," commanded an auntie, holding out a bowl brimming with shugra broth. Noleena took it gratefully and sipped at the hot liquid, feeling strength flow back into her tired muscles, and afterward she filled her mouth with honey cakes that crumbled into sweetness on her tongue.

Mia stood up and began to play her hurdy-gurdy and the Wind-wanderer children ran off to their tents and returned carrying little drums made of shugra bone and skin, and gourd rattles filled with dried yellow-patch peas that they bounced against the palms of their hands. The old aunties swayed to the music's rhythm, their eyes glinting slits in their creased faces and their thin lips smiling, and the blue eyed children clapped. A toddler began to dance on pudgy legs, her tiny toes sweeping patterns in the sand, and the aunties laughed appreciatively.

"A song!" cried a sand flea and the cry was taken up around the fire. Noleena rose to her feet, feeling suddenly shy, and Mia paused and then began to play the first song that she had taught to Noleena. Her face was solemn above the squeezing baffles of her instrument as the haunting tune, in a minor key, eddied into the still air. Noleena took a deep breath and began to sing and the Wind-wanderer children fell into an intense silence as they stared at her: at the perfectly symmetrical, smooth planes of her oval face, at her wide, wondering blue eyes. Her full lips parted around the song's words so that they were like shining birds that flew away from her to circle the fire and disappear into the darkness.

"*I sent my love a rosy bird,*" she sang. "*I sent my love a tender word.*"

Her gaze fell upon Hasani, seated on the other side of the fire with his legs crossed beneath him. His blue eyes shone in the light, above the rippled decorations of mineral paste along his cheekbones. The beads around his throat glinted like water droplets. A flush ran up Noleena's neck and over her face and she became acutely aware of the old aunties watching her. They know, she thought. They know already by some strange intuition that I love Hasani, that I loved him the moment I pulled my hair from my eyes and saw him standing there like a prince, like the desert given human form. "*I warned my dear one to beware, of roaming off so very far, so far, so far away across the sea of sorrow.*" She sank to her knees by the fire as the children clapped. "Sing some more!" they shouted but she shook her head, conscious of Hasani's steady gaze and her own burning cheeks.

"She is tired," an auntie intervened kindly. "Come with me, daughter. You will need other clothes than those if you wish to ride tonight."

Noleena followed the old woman into a tent and waited in the warm darkness, inhaling the musky scent of the shugra hide, while the woman rummaged around by feel and lit a small tallow lamp. The flame guttered, sending grotesque shadows sliding across the smooth leather of the tent's interior and across the brilliant carpets strewn on the floor. An upright wooden loom held the threads for another carpet; half-finished flowers bloomed along its edge. The auntie stooped to open a chest and then thrust a pile of folded clothing toward Noleena. "The one who made these will never wear them. They are yours. And these boots—you will need them.

I hope they'll fit. There's a bowl of water there to wash in. And a pack with food."

Then she was gone, her bent form slipping through the tent door—a triangle of darkness pierced with stars—and Noleena pulled the tattered patchwork dress over her flat stomach with its bellybutton pierced by a sickle moon, and over her narrow shoulders and her tousled hair, to drop onto the carpet's pattern of rainbirds and flying cranes and yellow blossoms. When she had washed, she unfolded the clothing and was delighted to find that it was identical to what the other women wore: a short top of pale ivory fabric, a loose tunic of burnt orange, a pair of breeches the warm brown color of the shugras. The tunic was embroidered around its hemline and neckline, in silver thread, with moons, stars and cranes, and all the fabrics felt tough yet soft to the touch. As she unfolded the clothing, something fell from it and landed against her bare foot: a small cloth pouch that she opened to pull out a comb of shugra bone, and a string of blue glass beads. In the centre of every bead, she saw as she examined them, was a tiny crescent moon, and every fourth bead lay next to a tiny silver one. She fastened the necklace at her throat and tugged the comb through her hair before pulling on the boots; the leather, expertly tanned and pale golden in color, felt as soft as the fabrics. Noleena stared down at herself with satisfaction; in these clothes, she felt strangely more competent, more at one with her surroundings. She picked up the leather pack, bulging with provisions, and slung it over one shoulder.

Ducking from the tent and walking self-consciously toward the gathering at the fire, she wondered what Hasani would think of her, now that she was clean and looked like his own people instead of like a street urchin of doubtful lineage. But Hasani had gone from his place, and the old aunties were clapping and swaying as the twins danced. Their gorgeous pantaloons flared in the firelight like exotic blossoms before being swallowed by darkness as the twins leaped away again. Noleena watched, smiling.

Someone touched her arm. She spun around, tense, startled, and Hasani's eyes glinted with amusement. "Are you ready?" he asked.

She nodded, but she did not feel ready. She wanted to linger, while the moon rose to shine down into the crack of hidden valley, while the music played and the twins danced, while the aunties' faces creased into a thousand lines of laughter. She wanted to feel safe for a few more moments.

"Come," Hasani urged gently and she had the feeling that he understood her reluctance. She turned in silence to follow him, and Mia danced into her path and curtsied with her hurdy-gurdy. "Fare you well, travel far, come again, don't be shy, off you fly," she sang mischievously with her urchin grin; but as Noleena bent to hug and kiss her goodbye, she thought for a fleeting moment that the girl's face changed, that a shadow of sadness flickered across it. Then Mia was dancing away, and Noleena followed Hasani past the tents, past the dark huddle of shugras clustered, stamping occasionally, in their own spicy-sweet scent.

"Where do you need to go?" Hasani asked. "Your father did not tell, only that you are embarked upon a Seeking."

"I am going to Mount Lalibela to implore help from the goddess. My father says that I must look for wisdom or a sign, to turn aside the tide of evil and the darkness of Queen Maldici."

She watched Hasani closely as she spoke, expecting and yet dreading to see his lips curl scornfully at the thought of her—a girl of not quite sixteen years, who had led a sheltered life and who jumped when touched in the dark—accepting this arduous challenge. But his lips did not curl and neither did any amusement shine in his eyes. Instead, he bowed his head with grave dignity. "I know of Mount Lalibela, though I have never been there. It lies to our north, in the empty quarter where no caravan routes pass. It will be an honor to take you there to the goddess, Princess Lebna."

Then he kissed the flat of his palm and pressed it to her forehead, as the Wind-wanderers used to do to the priestess in the temple when they took an oath dedicating themselves to a high Seeking.

"I swear by the breath of the desert, that is mother and father to us, and by the light of sun and moon; by the name of Luna and the power of the Corno d'Oro; and by the beating of my heart and the blood of my lineage, to dedicate myself to your Seeking."

His musical voice flowed in solemn cadence over the traditional words, and his palm was a steady warmth on her forehead. Noleena willed herself to stand perfectly still, though quivers shook her calf muscles. For a long moment, after he fell silent, they stared at one another. Then Noleena ducked her head in embarrassment, feeling deeply unworthy of such dedication.

"Thank you," she whispered.

Hasani turned and strode on into the valley, and Noleena saw that his pack was strapped around the small of his back and that higher, on his shoulders, he carried a wicker cage containing two rock-roses. The birds huddled into a nest of coarse hair—the long, thick hair that grew upon the neck of male shugras—and crooned sleepily to themselves. Hasani gave a low whistle; after a moment, Noleena heard hoof beats approaching carefully between the scattered rocks. She strained her eyes, then gasped in admiration. The horses were the most beautiful creatures she had ever seen, as beautiful and powerful as the Corno d'Oro had always been in her imagination. There were two of them, perfectly matched in height. Their huge dark eyes reflected the starlight; their nostrils were soft and lined with deep pink. They had long, scooped, arrogant faces and their manes cascaded to a great length, reaching from the crest of their curved necks to the tops of their slender legs. They were pale ivory all over their bodies, except for on their hindquarters where they were patterned with soft, golden stripes.

"Dune Dancer, Sun Runner," Hasani greeted them softly and they stepped in close, bending their heads down to blow on his palms.

"Can you ride?" he asked Noleena, but she shook her head, speechless with admiration and awe.

"These horses are pure children of the desert. They are brother and sister, from the most noble and ancient lineage written in the book that my father died protecting. About them is told a story, how their ancestors were touched by the Corno d'Oro in the high places, amongst the star lilies, and how the Corno d'Oro blessed them and breathed power into them. In every generation, horses of this line are fleeter of foot and more intelligent than any other horses. Sun Runner and Dune Dancer were stolen by the Kiffawalkers but now they are back with me again."

"How did they come back?"

"They were brought by a bandit." Hasani's tone held amusement but his eyes, in the starlight, shone again with a fierce and dangerous glint, and Noleena knew that it was himself that he spoke of, and that he would not boast to her of whatever bravery and skill it had taken to reclaim the mare and stallion.

"They wear no bridles or saddles," Noleena said.

"They need neither, for they have been mine since I was a tiny child; they know my voice, the touch of my knees on their sides and my hands on their necks. And because the Corno d'Oro blessed them with wisdom, they understand much more than any other horses. You cannot ride?"

"No, I have lived my whole life in the city."

"You will have to begin to learn."

Noleena's heart thumped in her chest for the horses seemed huge in the darkness, their coats a pale gleam like fine silk, their eyes dusky pools of banked fire.

"I can try," she said, and held out one hand with the palm open. The mare stepped closer, her hard hooves clattering on rocks, and Noleena again willed herself to stand very still. The mare's muzzle brushed her palm with a touch softer than the softest of Mombasso velvets, and her warm breath ran up Noleena's arm like strength. She touched her muzzle to Noleena's shoulder and forehead; then the stallion in turn stretched forward his neck and laid his muzzle upon Noleena's forehead. The horses' breath, scented like star lilies, flooded Noleena's whole being with a sense of beauty and certainty. In that moment, she loved Dune Dancer and Sun Runner in the same way that she loved Hasani, as though she had always known them and always loved them.

"They are pledging themselves to your Seeking," Hasani marveled.

Then the mare bent her knees before Noleena; her waterfall of golden and silvery mane fell from the curve of her neck onto the rocks as Hasani stared in amazement.

"Ai ai, you are your father's daughter, for it was said that the horses would dance in the pastures of Engedi for his pleasure. You had better mount; the moon rises."

Noleena laid her palm against the mare's smooth shoulder, still feeling the same sense of certainty—as though some knowledge, that she hadn't known she possessed, were waking inside her. She slipped onto the mare's back and twisted her hands through the long gleaming mane as the mare surged to her feet and the ground receded suddenly. Hasani mounted the stallion in one lithe spring and turned him around, heading south down the valley. All was silent but for the horses' hooves tapping against rocks. A pale ribbon of stars filled the crack of sky above the valley's steep dark rims.

"Hasani," Noleena asked when the horses walked side by side, "whose clothes am I wearing? The auntie said that the one who made them would never wear them."

"A young mother in my family. She is dead now, like many others."

A pang of sorrow seized Noleena, that she should be riding into the night on a fiery horse, while another young woman lay dead. She was aware with sudden intensity of how, as her father had said, life was simply itself: a beautiful gift. Gratefully, she listened to the horses' soft breathing; craned her neck to stare at the constellations overhead; felt the tough tangle of mane in her fists, and the presence of Hasani beside her.

"And where were the other young women of your family tonight?" she asked after a while.

Hasani tightened his lips. "You know the answer."

"Taken?" she asked in a small voice, and he nodded.

"The old aunties are left because they don't last long in a mine; they are more valuable as caregivers for the next generation of slaves."

Noleena thought of the children clustered around the fire, of their soft palms clapping together; of their plump bodies swaying to the rattle of the gourds and of their mischievous laughing eyes. Her hands gripped tighter in the mare's mane. They shall not be taken, she swore to herself. I will not let them be taken! But she didn't see how she could keep this promise; it was a feeling, she suspected, with no more power in it than a shadow that is crisp at noon but vanishes at dusk.

The stallion took the lead now as the valley narrowed, and presently the horses began to climb up a steep gulley filled with flowering cacti; the yellow and pink blooms glowed in the light of the rising moon and a great moth with silvery-blue wings and feathery antenna drifted past Noleena to swoop amongst them. The horses' hooves slipped and grated against the dark rocks and they snorted softly and bent their heads, their powerful hindquarters thrusting them upward until they reached the top of the cliff. Noleena saw the open desert stretching before them eerily silent and silver in the moonlight. The wind stirred in her hair and lifted the horses' tails out like pennants.

"Now!" said Hasani with a gleam in his eye. "Now, we ride!"

CHAPTER TEN

T HE HORSES SURGED FORWARD with sand spraying from their hooves and the moon floating tiny in their eyes; their flaring nostrils sucked at wind. Noleena crouched over Dune Dancer's neck, her face whipped by flying mane, and laughed aloud with exhilaration; the mare's ears flicked back to catch the sound before it was torn away. The drumming rhythm of hoof beats filled Noleena's head. For a moment she closed her eyes and felt darkness rushing past her, the world spinning beneath pounding hooves, stars wheeling overhead, and power coursing through the mare as she plunged swiftly into the desert's vast fields of sand. Noleena had never known such freedom, such powerful rushing joy

"Noleena!" Hasani shouted beside her, and she opened her eyes to see that they were riding knee to knee and that his face was alight with excitement. He caught her hand and for a few hundred yards they flew together across the light and shadows that patterned the desert, their bodies and the bodies of the horses all one united mass of muscle and movement. Then, at the touch of Hasani's legs, Sun Runner veered off and their joined hands parted.

All her life, Noleena would remember that night: the first time she ever rode a horse, and her first ride with Hasani. They backtracked on themselves, muddling their trail, and once they waded for miles up a narrow stream with water tugging at the horses' legs, so that they left no trace of their passing.

"Do you always travel this way?" Noleena asked, and Hasani smiled, his teeth glinting in his dark face.

"You are traveling with an outlaw," he reminded her.

"And do you always travel alone?"

"No."

She waited for him to say more but realized that he wouldn't; that he was protecting whoever rode with him in raids against the Kiffa-walkers.

At last, as the sun began to rise, they scaled a steep pinnacle of rock, the humans walking and the horses picking a careful path through sliding sand and loose shale. At the summit they slipped in amongst a jumble of boulders to be hidden from view. The horses cropped the wiry grass in the level spots between the rocks, and Hasani pulled cold roasted shugra meat, wrapped in leaves, from the pack he carried on his back and handed some to Noleena. She sank wearily against a rock as the sun touched it and kindled it into pinkness, and as the last darkness drained from the sky and it became saturated with brilliance. She ate the meat hungrily.

"What are the decorations on your face?" she asked Hasani as he returned from gazing over the desert.

"They are the marks of a Seeking."

"But you had them when I arrived and you had not yet dedicated yourself."

"I had a Seeking of my own, to bring back my horses from the grasp of jackal dung."

"Could I have some marks too?"

He nodded and chewed his meat before opening his flask to swallow a draught of tepid water. Then he reached into his pack and pulled out a small alabaster jar inlaid with dolphin patterns; when he unscrewed the lid, she saw that it was filled with blue mineral paste. "Hold still," he said, and taking her chin in one hand he dipped a finger into the paste.

"The pattern is different for women," he said, and he drew his finger first above her eyebrows in a curved line, and then painted one rippled line along the slanting angle of her cheekbones. Noleena could barely breathe as he leaned in close to her, his dark face intent and focused, and as his finger smoothed the paste onto her skin. She stared over his bent shoulders at a hawk wheeling lazy circles in the rising sun, its wings tipped with fire.

"There," Hasani said, smiling, when he had finished. "And you're not afraid anymore?"

"Not now," she agreed, but she knew even as she replied that her fear was not banished; that it would return in an hour or a day, and that she would feel vulnerable and defenseless again. She watched while Hasani recapped the jar of paste and spread out his bed roll. Sun Runner lay down beside it, and Hasani leaned against the stallion and closed his eyes. Noleena spread out her own roll beside the mare. Even in the shadow of the rocks, the heat was gathering and Noleena sank down into it.

"We are safe here," Hasani reassured her and she opened her eyes a crack to see his drowsy smile.

"I know," she murmured. She felt as sheltered as she had at home in the temple courtyard. Within moments she slept, surrounded by the bastion of rocks and with the sweet smell of grass and horses in her nostrils; her reclining form was a tiny speck in the hawk's keen eyes.

It was dusk when Noleena awoke. The horses were grazing again and Hasani stood behind a boulder to stare out across the landscape. She joined him and saw the desert spread below like a great sleeping animal striped with purple shadows. North, south, east and west Hasani stared, his eyes narrowed in concentration, but nothing moved below them except for the shadow of the rocky pinnacle itself. It stretched longer and longer until it was like a giant's finger laid across the sleeping animal of desert. Hasani pointed into the hazy distance. "That way, five night's ride, lies

Mount Lalibela. We will travel by the wind-ways. Are you ready to leave?"

Noleena nodded and Hasani turned away, whistling for the horses.

As they traveled, Hasani began to teach her the language of the desert. "Smell this," he said one morning, crushing the succulent leaves of a plant from beside a deserted well until a green paste coated his fingers. "You can spread this on the forehead for sunstroke." He taught her how to recognize the leathery leaves and thorny bush of wild aloba tea; they brewed it over a small smokeless fire and shared the amber, bitter-sweet liquid. Another time, he slid from the stallion's back to gather a handful of lichen growing on rocks. "For packing into wounds," he explained. He showed her the flickering movement of yellow lizards striped with lilac, and how to catch them through their own curiosity by making a tiny trap baited with a moth, and how to grill them skewered over hot embers in a pit of sand. He made her practice the skill of smelling fresh water in hidden oases from a mile out in the dunes. He gave her the name of the rock throstle so that she could recognize its liquid song. He pointed out the flight pattern of cranes, like fronds of fern against the sky. At night, as they rode, they shared with each other the constellations, for they both knew every one by name: the Gazelle Twins, the Sleeping Lizard, Old Woman's Knee, Eye of Falcon.

Once, in the darkness before dawn, a pair of great ivory colored antelopes with spiral horns, and liquid eyes in noble faces, appeared to leap alongside the horses. "Run, my brothers! Run, my sisters!" Hasani shouted, his face alight. Dune Dancer and Sun Runner spurted forward and they raced together, horses and antelopes, over miles of sword grass; it seemed to Noleena that they ran for the joy of it, for the wind on their elegant scooped faces and the blood surging through their hearts. At last, the antelope veered away and were lost to sight.

The desert no longer seemed to Noleena like a vast emptiness but a place filled with life and a harsh, majestic beauty. The desert was the gift that Hasani gave to her, and because of this she began to love it. She grew familiar with how wind ran through the sparse grasses in waves, and with the lacey shade cast by groves of corda trees, with their thin crooked trunks. She learned to recognize the ground-hugging leaves of the nub nub plant, and the dry scaly feel of the tubers buried beneath as she dug them up. Scraped with a knife and eaten raw, they were sweet and nutty in her mouth. According to Hasani, nub nub was the favorite food of the shugras, which dug for the tubers with their cleft front hooves.

Sometimes, as they rode, Hasani recounted stories from his childhood, but he never spoke of his father and Noleena never asked. And sometimes he asked Noleena to sing; she obliged with those tunes that Mia had taught her. Once, at night in a dry rift valley, she sang about sending her love a tender word, her love who roamed so far, so far away across the sea of sorrow. She kept her eyes averted as she sang; it was impossible to sing *my love* and to look Hasani in the face. The horses breathed gustily down her neck and stamped uneasily as she sang, and afterward Hasani was silent for a long while.

"Is something wrong?" she asked at last in a small voice.

"I once heard it sung in a slave line," he said in a low tone. "Our people were knotted neck to neck, behind a salt caravan returning from the port of Jaffa. The slaves plodded behind the doda, singing."

In all the time they rode together, they avoided tracks or villages. "We will travel by the wind-ways" Hasani had told her. When she questioned him about this, he explained that they were ancient pathways, often hidden by rock or dune, often buried in drifting sand, known only to a few Wanderers but to no Kiffa-walkers at all. "My horses know the wind-ways," he said with a trace of pride. "Where the ways exist, we can travel in safety."

On the fifth night, Hasani and Noleena camped amongst dark, jagged rocks that broke the surface of the desert like the protruding spine of a buried dragon. Hasani called to Noleena and she scrambled up to balance in the rocks at his side. "Look, there to the east, the plateau lands skirt the Moon Mountains," he said and she looked in the direction of his pointing arm and saw, on the rim of the world, a line of darker blue that seemed to hang, suspended like a motionless wave, above the sea of sand.

"And look, to the north, Mount Lalibela."

Noleena stared again and saw a jumbled spine of rock, much like the one they were encamped in but higher, and the steep mountain that erupted from it. The setting sun touched the mountain's flanks of smooth, wind polished rocks so that they glowed deep red above the purple shadows. "Into that mountain is cut the temple of Luna, hewn from solid rock."

"We do not need to be there for four days yet," Noleena said. "At the time when the sun is highest in the sky, on mid-summer's day, the light enters the temple through a skylight in the roof and touches the statue of Luna beneath. In that brief moment, a high priestess or a Wind-wanderer princess may entreat the goddess for a sign or special help in time of trouble."

"And you are both a princess and a priestess," Hasani said. "Who better than you to bring a Seeking to Mount Lalibela?"

He jumped to the ground below and strode away toward the horses. Noleena lingered on the rock, staring across hazy distances and wondering whether she had only imagined the admiration in Hasani's voice. Perhaps it had merely contained respect; even respect from Hasani would be something to cherish. She stared at Mount Lalibela and waited for her heartbeat to steady. She wondered if there was another girl, hidden somewhere in a shugra tent in a swell of desert, who waited for Hasani to ride over the dunes, who thought of him with love as she wove her bright carpets. But perhaps the girls whom Hasani had admired had all been taken into the darkness of the mines; perhaps he carried their names in his heart; names unspoken but yearned over in secret.

For four days they waited, hidden amongst the rocks while summer ripened toward the longest day, while heat shimmered over the land of Terre and fruit ripened in its vineyards and terraced gardens, and in its groves of nuga palm and pomegranate; while the water level sank in wells, and the rivers in rift valleys evaporated into the air as though they had never existed but had merely been blue mirages. In the desert the Wind-wanderers milked their shugras, moving constantly onward away from the Kiffa-walker soldiers who swept them across the desert as a broom sweeps sand. In the mines, the sounds of pickaxes filled the stale air while sweat dropped from bent backs and slaves groaned for mercy or for death beneath the overseer's lash. Doda caravans crisscrossed the country, walking on their own short shadows through the long hours of daylight, bearing panniers of salt; merchants' scales swung in warehouses and treasuries. In the port of Shoa, the great new ships of the king's navy roared down the greased slipways to wet their mighty keels in the motionless sea; in the port of Jaffa, stone masons raised the towers of the new Kiffa temple higher into the hazy sky. And in Safala, that beautiful rose-red city carved from solid rock, the assassini cracked their whips at soldiers and scrambling children outside the soaring walls and mighty door of the royal palace where the queen, the red haired sorceress, incited the powers of greed and darkness to snare the land of Terre in a tight-woven net—and then to fling her net wider, across all lands around the Middle Sea. On the rug at the queen's feet, the young Kebi sank his new teeth into a wooden rattle and yelled with pleasure, his future a gleaming assurance of power and victory, for had not his mother vowed he should be god of all the earth?

At an unnamed spine of rock in the empty quarter where caravans and nomads did not pass, Noleena knelt on the sand and prayed to Luna for succor in this time of desperation. She prayed that she would be stronger than she seemed, and braver than she felt; that she might be blessed with wisdom that she did not possess; that Luna would look on her—a child of sheltered safety—and grant her a sign so that she might aid her people.

This Seeking, she often felt, was doomed. It should have been someone else who had been preserved for this hour; an older, wiser, stronger person with more knowledge of the world, with more cunning and experience.

"No, no," Hasani reassured her when she shared her fears. "This Seeking belongs to you, Noleena. Surely the goddess will hear your prayers."

Noleena nodded but she did not feel reassured; perhaps Hasani was simply being kind to her and perhaps, behind his words, he hid grave doubts about her capabilities and her chances of success.

On the third afternoon, as Hasani groomed Sun Runner with a soft brush that he carried in his pack, Noleena clambered around in the rocks and found a spring of water that emptied into a pool; it was so clear that she could see down through it to every detail of the granular pink rocks below. She pulled off her tunic and rolled up her breeches before wading in; schools of tiny fish darted for sanctuary and the rippling water sent fractured lines of light running up her legs and splintering across her smiling face as she bent over it. She waded in deeper; although she could not swim, she was unafraid. Her bare toes gripped the rocks, and the water lapped against her and soaked up through her clothing, spreading a delicious coolness through her thirsty body. For a long time, while the heat intensified in the deep silence, she waded around in the protective embrace of the pink rocks. It was a time of perfect contentment.

Presently Hasani climbed over a rock; he stood on the top of it for a few minutes, watching her. Then in one motion he stripped off his tunic and leapt in, sending up a spray of water that splattered onto the hot rocks and dappled them with bright color, and that filled Noleena's vision with prisms. Hasani swam into deeper water and floated on his back and presently Noleena attempted to float too. Blue sky filled her eyes; sun beat upon her face and the water cradled her like loving hands.

Tomorrow is midsummer's day, she thought. And even if everything is dark and difficult from now on, at least I've had this one perfect afternoon in this beautiful place. With Hasani.

Now Hasani was pretending to be a dolphin; he plunged and leapt, caught her ankles and towed her along. Water sloshed into her mouth. She shrieked and splashed him. In a moment, they were flinging water at one another: sheets of water that sparkled as it fell over their dark wet heads and soaking shoulders. They filled the flying water with their shouts and laughter. And then, stillness fell around them; heat lapped the rocks. The water smoothed back into its pink reflections. Hasani took her by the shoulders and for a long moment their gazes met; then he bent and kissed her solemnly and gently at each corner of her lips.

When Hasani stepped away and turned to climb onto the rocks, Noleena lingered, feeling the light and the water's dance, and the ripple of his kisses, sink deeper and deeper into the heart of her being. Then she too climbed onto the rocks. They lay there until their clothes had dried, then Noleena picked feathery cress, growing in a damp crevice between pink boulders, to add to their supper of dried antelope and a handful of apricots. When they had eaten, Hasani unscrewed the lid on his alabaster jar and reapplied the blue decorations to Noleena's face. He worked with great concentration, smoothing the cool mineral paste above her eyebrows and along her cheekbones. She knew that he wanted the patterns to be perfect; that he was as conscious as she that tomorrow she would appear before Luna in a sacred place, with a great Seeking heavy on her shoulders and a great fear weighing down her heart.

"Thank you, Hasani," she said humbly when he had finished. "Thank you for everything on this journey."

He flashed her a grin. "It's been a pleasure to see whether a princess could ride a horse or not," he teased.

"And?"

"She rides well enough for a beginner; it must be to the credit of her horse."

They both laughed, for they both knew that Noleena had ridden all week like one born to it; after that first over-awed moment, she had ridden Dune Dancer with an easy confidence that was usually acquired only after long practice.

Hasani dipped his finger again into the paste and began to reapply the patterns, that had been washed away as he swam, to his own face; watching him, Noleena wanted to offer her help but she felt too shy and couldn't form the words.

Despite her apprehension about the next day, Noleena fell asleep easily beneath the protective spine of rocks, and soothed by the steady breathing of the horses. Morning seemed to arrive quickly; the early morning of mid-summer's day, and Noleena awoke thinking of her father alone and broken in his alcove, holding onto a slender thread of hope that was fastened to her, so many miles away. She felt how his blind eyes searched through time and distance for her, for the saving of his people.

"Hasani," she said, "can we send a bird to my father? He must be wondering what is happening. I would like him to know."

Hasani gave her a questioning glance. "Isn't it better to wait and send the bird later, afterward?"

"I want it to go now, in case anything happens...in case I fail."

"Have faith in yourself," he said with such kindness that she ducked her head. She searched in her pack for a piece of parchment and a sharp-pointed quill that she dipped into a tiny pot of the cayenne-colored ink made from the juice of the jobi shrub.

"We near the sacred place" she wrote; there was not room for anything more. Hasani opened the wicker cage, that he had carried on his shoulders for so many miles, and lifted the two birds out; one was his own and the other belonged to Noleena's father. He fastened the parchment to the leg of his bird.

"Watch," he told Noleena. He gently pulled one gold-barred feather from the breast of his own bird and wove it amongst the feathers of her father's bird. "The bird which lost a feather will follow the other bird where ever it flies," he explained. "This way, your father receives a bird of mine and his own bird back as well." Then he lifted her father's bird on the flat of his palm until it was at eye level, and chuckled to it deep in his throat. The bird cocked its smooth pink head and watched Hasani with its tiny dark eyes. "Lebna, Lebna, Lebna," Hasani crooned and suddenly the bird became airborne in a flurry of brightness. Instantly the other bird followed it and together they lifted into the pale, translucent yellow of the dawn and circled once, then began to move southward. They flew higher and higher, tiny specks against the blazing sky, until Noleena could not see them and her eyes filled with spots.

Hasani closed the door of the empty basket, and Noleena divided up a portion of food for their breakfast. As they ate, the sun seemed to rise with astonishing speed and heat flooded their hiding place amongst the rocks. The horses shone glossily and Noleena thought longingly of the secret pool of smooth cool water that lay nearby; there was no time now to play there. She felt her face settling into a kind of rigid sternness that masked her fear. Hasani too looked solemn and preoccupied, as though his powers of concentration were focused on the hours ahead.

As they swung their packs onto their backs, the horses snorted softly and came in close to them, touching them on their arms and shoulders with soft muzzles as though to impart strength and comfort. When they emerged from amongst the rocks, Mount Lalibela was a silhouette on the northern skyline but rapidly, as the sun rose higher, the details of the mountain were illuminated: the jumble of pink rock at its base lying in purple shadows, the smooth rounded dome of dark red rocks at its peak.

"I can't see the temple," Noleena said anxiously.

"It's hidden halfway up, carved down into the rock itself. When we get there, you will descend alone into the temple and I'll wait above with the horses."

"Please Hasani, can't you come with me? I don't know what I'm looking for. What if there's a sign and I miss it?" Her voice sounded thin and brittle with anxiety and she bent her head in shame, wishing she hadn't spoken.

Hasani shook his head. "You are the one," he said. "You will see whatever there is to see."

She didn't argue but a cold ripple of fear shivered through her although the sun burned on her back and sweat drenched her short top. Though she tried to recall the peaceful contentment she had felt the previous afternoon, she could not regain it; the afternoon seemed long ago and now her stomach churned hard and sour as though she had eaten unripe palm fruits.

The mare pranced skittishly under her and she tried to let her clenched legs hang loose. What if I fail? she thought. Who will help my people? And what if I succeed here in the temple? What great task will be laid upon me?

Now the rocky ridge was growing higher as they approached it and the sun, spinning upward like the wheel of a great golden chariot, beat upon it and bleached its colors so that rocks that had glowed fiery at dawn now appeared faded and dull.

"Will we reach it by noon?" Noleena asked. Hasani nodded, but the horses began to trot, their hoof beats drumming on the dried minerals of the plain as they dodged amongst spiny scrub. Sweat broke out on their haunches and chests; in the oppressive heat their tails and manes barely lifted. Noleena stared forward at the mountain; for a long time it seemed to remain the same size. She licked her lips, tasting salt; the light pounded on her forehead like hammer blows. Heat rose from the plain in wavering bands and the base of Mount Lalibela floated in a ribbon of shimmering water. Froth flew from the horses' mouths and flecked their riders' breeches.

Suddenly, Noleena realized that she had to crane her neck to look up at the peak. It soared above her: immense, implacable, etched with the thin hard lines of crevices and gullies. Striations of color banded the edges of the shadows: deep amber, bright pink, dark brown, purple. Sheets of flat rock shone blindingly like mirrors. Noleena tilted her head farther back to stare at the sky; surely, the sun was almost at its zenith. Panic flooded her and she nudged the mare into a canter, aware of the stallion springing forward on her right hand and of Hasani's dark face intent and focused, like the face of a hunter.

"There must be a path," Hasani said as they came to a panting halt against the jumble of fallen rock that buttressed the mountain's base. Even here, in the shadow, the heat seemed to suck away Noleena's breath. Hasani slid from the blowing stallion to walk along the base of the cliff, his eyes scanning it for any sign of a place they might climb upward. When he shouted, Noleena and the horses joined him to see a narrow, winding track that ascended steeply amongst hohoba shrubs. They began to climb, Hasani and Noleena walking, their feet grating on debris. The heat, reflecting from the rock faces to the side of the path, seemed to Noleena like a solid thing; a curtain that she had to push through. Her shadow shrank around her feet as she struggled upward, and her heart beat with a stacatto rhythm. What use would it be if she arrived too late, in the moment that the light slipped from the statue and fell away across the floor?

Finally, the path leveled off, following a broad ridgeline where grass grew scarce and yellow and a lone sand-pine leaned over the cliff's edge, its tortuous limbs forking skyward. Suddenly, the ground gave away beneath Noleena's feet and she reeled on the spot while Hasani bumped into her back and muttered in surprise. Below them, on the side of the ridge closest to the mountain itself, the ground had been cut away; beneath their feet a face of smooth rock fell sheer for fifty feet, and Noleena saw that indeed an entire rectangle had been cut into the mountain. In the centre of this, and also carved from the solid rock, stood the temple of Luna: a massive block with a sloping roof, and with pink columns supporting a portico above the darkness of the entrance.

"Look, there are steps," Hasani said. "You go down and I will stay here. May Luna speak to you for all our people, Noleena. May you find what we have come for."

"Yes," she whispered, staring into the grave concern of his blue eyes. She could feel his attention on her as she descended the narrow flight of steps carved into the rock face, and as she climbed the steps toward the pillars. They were fluted with narrow grooves, and stars were carved around their bases. For a moment, outside the yawning entrance, she paused and looked back to see the shapes of Hasani and the horses high overhead, sharp edged against the white-hot sky.

Then she stepped through into darkness, her heart hammering deafeningly in her ears, and paused again as her eyes adjusted. It's good that it's so dark inside, she thought. It means the sun has not entered yet and I am in time.

Slowly, details of the interior closest to where she stood became clear to her. The rock walls were painted all over with delicate brush strokes: panthers and moon wrens, wombos, dolphins, star lilies, sickle moons, and rayed suns. Relief filled her at the familiarity of these symbols, and her heartbeat steadied. Against her chest, the medallion that her father had given to her and that bore the marks of the Corno d'Oro, grew strangely warm and a faint tingling sensation radiated from it and across her skin. She kneeled on the floor's blue tiles painted with rippled waves and cool air stirred on the back of her neck. Pillars of rosy rock, fluted as were the exterior pillars, soared above her into the dim vault of ceiling; a sense of timelessness and ancient power seemed to fill the space. The base of the pillar closest to where Noleena kneeled was carved with small frolicking animals that she did not recognize; they were furry with extraordinary long whiskers, and amongst them was carved the word "mugwawa." Noleena read it several times, pondering it. The mugwawa, she had heard, was perhaps a mysterious being who lived at the feet of the Moon Mountains; or perhaps nothing more than a myth.

She peered into the darkness ahead of her, where the temple's spaces receded into shadow, and bent her head. "Luna," she prayed, "hear me in this hour. Show me your favor; grant me the wisdom to help your children rise from darkness, and break the chains of evil that bind them. Give me courage when I am frightened, strengthen me when I am weak, lead me when I am blind." Then she began to chant aloud the words of power in the old tongue that the priestess had taught her; the tongue of Luna in the days when she walked upon the Moon Mountains with the Corno d'Oro, when star lilies sprang up where they passed. Noleena's voice, low and timid at first, swelled in volume until she was aware of it echoing from the pillars and rising into the high vault of the roof. As she clutched her father's medallion in one hand, it seemed to pulse within her palm.

She opened her eyes to see whether sunlight had yet entered the temple, but the farther areas were still shrouded in deep shadow. Noleena supposed that the statue of the goddess must be there, deeper in, and she shuffled forward on her knees, straining to recognize Luna's serene expression and the backs of her frolicking dolphins, but it remained too dark for her to see anything. She tilted her head, scanning the soaring vault of ceiling, above the stone pillars polished smooth as marble, and saw the square of hot sky that pressed upon the skylight. She waited, barely breathing, unaware of the hard floor beneath her knees.

She thought fleetingly of the priestess from the temple in Safala, and wished that she was here with her silvery voice and wise gaze. Let her still be alive and safe, Noleena thought, trying to block out images of the priestess suffering in slavery.

Sunlight slid like a finger along the lip of the skylight. Her heart clenched. Now! she thought. This was the moment, the one moment on mid-summer's day in the sacred place, when a Wind-wanderer princess might bring her petition in desperate times.

The sun touched the ceiling beside the skylight, illuminating the stones' curvature and the paintings there.

Then with such suddenness that Noleena gave a startled lurch—though she had been waiting for it—a great shaft of golden light pierced the aperture and flooded the temple with brilliance. The colors on the tiles and in the wall paintings, and the stone of the pillars, assumed a dazzling brilliance. Noleena blinked and narrowed her eyes to peer into the farthest reaches of the room. And there was the altar, its base carved of golden stone with a filigree of leaves and star lilies, and a smooth polished surface and—

Noleena cried out in horror.

Upon the top of the altar the statue of Luna lay toppled. Her severed head had rolled several feet away to rest on the tiles; her nose was a rough, pale scar of smashed stone. Noleena scrambled to her feet and rushed forward; she saw that one arm was also broken off and lay in pieces upon the floor. She bent over the torso prone upon the altar, every muscle in her tense, and heard splinters of stone and dust from the shattered arm crunch beneath her boots. She saw that the goddess's face had been scored through with jagged lines incised with a sharp blade, and that along the remaining arm had been scored the words *Die, dust-eaters!*

Bile rose in her throat.

Even here—here!—in the most sacred of places, the Kiffa-walkers had brought their evil hatred, their violence and cruelty!

She traced her fingers gently over the goddess's face, over the harsh lines of desecration and the smooth curves of her smile and eyes, and over the words carved in the forearm. She kneeled amongst the sharp shards on the tiles and laid her forehead against the altar. Hot tears welled from her lids. She wept for the priestess taken captive, for her father blinded and eking out existence in the alleys of Safala, for her mother's bones strewn in the sand, for the slow deaths of Tekle and his brother. She wept for Hasani, who roamed like a hyena in the desert. She wept for herself, helpless to bring healing to her people.

The sun slipped across her shoulders and the marble folds in Luna's gown. For a moment, it hung beneath the skylight in a fading pillar of gold, then it grew fainter. The finger of light slid over the sill. The light vanished and the colors in the temple were quenched. Noleena rocked on her knees in the darkness. At last, she stood stiffly and trudged toward the bright square of the entrance. She toiled up the narrow steps in the rock wall to where Hasani waited with the horses.

"What happened?" he asked fiercely, seizing her by the arms, staring into her swimming eyes.

"She is destroyed, Hasani! The Kiffa-walkers have been here—they have knocked her over and carved her up and broken her!"

His arms dropped, rigid, at his sides and fury rose in his face. She saw him struggling to contain it; he walked to the edge of the rock face and stared down onto the temple roof. Behind him the sand-pine was perfectly still, its needles limp in the turgid heat. Silence fell. The horses stood with drooping heads.

"Was there nothing?" he asked beseechingly, returning to her side. "Nothing at all, Noleena?"

She shook her head, her mind wandering over the tiles, over the wall paintings, the carvings of stars on the pillars, the word "mugwawa." Why was it there? It seemed to tug at her.

"There was no sign," she said dully and Hasani balled his fists and swung impotently at the air.

Mugwawa, she thought again.

"Hasani, do you know anything of a being called a mugwawa?"

"Very little; the mugwawa is an ancient and magical being—an auntie told me about her. The mugwawa is the Keeper of Stories who lives in a secret canyon in the plateau lands and can speak to all animals. Why, Noleena?"

She shrugged. "I don't know...her name was on a pillar, that's all."

Together they stared disconsolately down into the rectangle carved out at their feet; at the sloping roof of the temple with its uneven tiles of pale pink stone, at the fluted pink pillars. Suddenly the horses sprang forward behind them in alarm, snorting and rolling their great dark eyes so that the whites showed.

Hasani spun on the balls of his feet, his head flung up.

"What is it?" Noleena asked nervously.

A magpie flew out from the branches of the leaning sand-pine; its black and white plumage flashed like a warning and its raucous cry was harsh in the silence. *One for sorrow; two for joy,* Noleena thought: the proverb spoken in Safala about magpies. She squinted toward the pine but no other bird appeared, and the first one flapped off around the shoulder of the mountain still crying harshly.

The horses gazed down onto the plain, skin quivering on their flanks, and Hasani moved over beside them, then shouted urgently.

"Kiffa-walkers! They will trap us up here! Fly, fly!"

He turned back to Noleena but already she was mounting, the mare barging into her in terror, sweat breaking out afresh on her chest. The stallion plunged into a trot, his hooves ringing on stone, but Hasani mounted him in one flying leap. Noleena clutched the mare's mane as she plunged down the precipitous path, stones tumbling over the edge and soaring into space or hitting the flanks of sheer rock with a harsh clatter. Staring outward, between streamers of mane, Noleena saw the tiny shapes of brown ponies galloping toward the base of the mountain with a golden chariot in their midst. Light glinted on the tips of spears.

She clung tighter to the mare who ran with her muzzle pressed against the stallion's haunches as he plunged ahead of them, sliding downward with his front legs braced and his hind quarters tucked under. Like one animal, the horses leaped over rocks, tendons straining in their legs, their hocks flexing as they took shortcuts across bends in the path. They jumped hohoba shrubs, their knees brushing through the topmost layers of spiky twigs. Gravel spurted from their pounding hooves. They snorted with exertion; their eyes rolled with fear. Once a black crevice flashed beneath Noleena as the mare leapt across it, and once the mare jumped up onto a flat boulder and then launched herself over the gulley that lay beyond. Her hind hooves barely cleared the edge as she landed; stones spun away beneath her to bounce down the mountainside.

Closer and closer the Kiffa-walkers thundered to the base of the mountain, trailing a plume of white dust that hung motionless in the intense heat.

And now, ahead, over the stallion's haunches and the bent shoulders of Hasani, Noleena saw the jumble of rocks at the base of the cliff, lying orange in their shadows; saw the white blinding sheet of mineral plain beyond; saw the snarling breastplates on the chests of the soldiers as they raced forward to block the mouth of the path.

Until the very last moment, she still believed that they might manage to reach the base of the mountain in time and might escape. But as the stallion surged forward between the rocks, Noleena saw that the soldiers had reached the far side and were forming a wall of ponies.

"Hasani!" she screamed but already he had plunged away from her into a maelstrom, trying to clear a path through the encircling troops. She saw the stallion rear, striking out with his forelegs—they gleamed in the harsh light like spears—and the crimson swirl of the soldiers' uniforms below their open mouths, and the spinning of the chariot spokes, a golden blur, as it shot forward. A confused roar of shouting filled her head along with the high, furious squealing of the desert horses. In one moment, she was watching Hasani and the stallion battling their way forward; in the next moment, Hasani had disappeared into the swirling tangle of spears and helmets, the thrashing bodies of the soldiers' small ponies.

"Hasani!" she screamed again, her voice ripping her heart from her chest.

CHAPTER ELEVEN

I SUPPOSE I MUST RETURN to Lord Tafari's house, Ambro thought as he trudged up the narrow alley that twisted between black walls of towering stone. Though surely the lord will not allow me to stay in his home now that I have been shamed before him by Lord Kassa; my birthright set at naught, my parentage scorned. Lord Tafari will wish that he had never brought me to Terre, like a useless stray dog, but had left me with the sea urchins on the windswept coast of Verde. He will tell his cooks not to make my favorite dish of chicken roasted with chickpeas and fennel anymore; he will tell his lady wife, with her slender neck encircled by golden rings, that I don't need to learn the tongue of Terre. My mother tongue; ha, there's a joke. Ambro's lips twisted in a scowl of scorn and anger, and he kicked at a loose shard of red rock so that it ricocheted harshly against the alley wall to his right. Then he wandered on, his hands shoved into the pockets of his green robe and his thoughts in dark turmoil.

What will I do? he wondered. Where shall I go?

The narrow alley spilled him out from its mouth into a broader street and he began to walk northward, uncertain of his exact whereabouts. Once he stopped to warm his hands at a brazier, for the night grew chill and the moon shone with a clear silver light high overhead, casting the harsh shadows of cliffs across the squares of Safala. At a corner, Ambro bought a steaming cup of cinni spice brewed in hot water over a silver urn; it trailed a sweet, fiery path into his belly. In a northward running street, he lingered for some time to watch a game of Fox and Jackal being played beneath a towering acacia tree, and in another street he stood in the shadows to watch two boys trying to catch a runaway jennet that lashed out with its hind feet and butted with its curly horns. Ambro did not offer to help the boys; he felt too weary and too lonely. Who would welcome help from him; an outcast from another land, an orphan without home or family—a boy who did not after all even know his father's name?

At least in Verde, he thought, I believed that I did know my father's name, before I found out that Ambrosi d'Monticello was a flute maker in Genovera and not my father. Now, I'm robbed even of that small comfort. I wish I had never tried to help that merchant ship as it careened closer and closer to the reef; I wish I had never boarded her and eaten supper with the Kiffa-walker merchants, or been dazzled by their tawny eyes and befuddled by their golden words. I wish that right at this moment I was back in Verde in a cave, smelling the salty tang of seaweed and being lulled to sleep by the roar of waves, with my urchin friends sleeping around me.

Except, he contradicted himself, I do love the desert with its heat and silence.

He trudged on, his shoulders sagging, and eventually came to a street that he recognized and made his way from there to the steps that ascended to Lord Tafari's massive door in the side of the cliff. He wondered, as he toiled up them, whether the guard would let him pass or whether perhaps he had been ordered to turn him away. His heart pounded but he set his face in bold stern lines, as he had seen Lord Tafari do. The man saluted and stepped aside, and Ambro gave an inward sigh of relief and pushed the door open. For one more night, at least, he had a place in which to sleep. The household seemed to be in bed, and Ambro was grateful not to meet anyone as he walked quietly past the fish in their pond, beneath the hanging tapestries' brilliant colors, and up the marble stairs to his bedroom. He stripped off his dusty clothes but was too tired to wash in the tiled bath; instead, he stretched out on the cool sheets beneath a tall, narrow window.

Moonlight inched across his pillow, touched his forearm and shone in its fine golden hairs, slid across his cheek. He thought about the statue of Sirena standing in the moonlight of the stone temple, hidden and deserted at the end of a tiny, twisting alleyway. How strange, he thought drowsily, to find such a blue and green place in the midst of Safala's red rocks and pink dust; how very strange that Sirena should be landlocked there with her leaping dolphins. He recalled the goddess's serene smile and the steady gaze of her pale marble eyes, and the hot churning misery inside him began to ease. He thought for a moment that he caught a whiff of salt-pine needles, a tang of seaweed drying in Verde's sunshine, and his scowl relaxed into smooth lines. As the moon lingered on his forehead, he slept to dream of swimming with the dolphins; of their shining fins and merry eyes as black as currants.

In the morning, Ambro awoke early. The sky was pale yellow in the narrow window and the air still felt cool and fresh. He stretched sleepily, relaxed and happy; then, suddenly, the events of the previous evening leapt into his mind with awful clarity, and all the pleasure disappeared from his awaking. He swung his feet over the side of the narrow bed, with its frame of mandolo wood and mattress of rope and Angoli wool, and stared disconsolately down at his dusty bare toes. I suppose I must join the army, he thought gloomily. I must go now and bid Lord and Lady Tafari goodbye. Somehow, the thought of becoming a soldier with a snarling leather breastplate and a light-tipped spear—that had seemed appealing and glorious before—did not bring him any pleasure now. I expected to make an uncle proud when I enlisted, he thought. I hoped for a girl cousin to cheer as I marched past.

But now, no one will care whether I march or simply juggle on street corners like an urchin. No one will notice. I am more alone than I have ever been.

He sighed and rose to his feet, pulling on the same robe he'd worn the day before though Safala's golden and pink dust had infiltrated every fiber. He ran his hands through tousled hair, and slowly descended the marble steps with dread and hunger arguing in his stomach.

As he reached the fish pond in the main hallway, the front door swung open; a slightly built man with a pointed, inscrutable face and dressed in a robe of muted brown, slipped quietly inside. His bright eyes flickered over Ambro but before either of them could speak, Lord Tafari strode forward, his bright purple robe billowing and the kiffa circlet around his forehead catching the early sun that slid through skylights overhead.

"In here," he said, motioning the slight figure toward a small room off to one side of the hall. It was the room, Ambro knew, where visitors awaited Lord Tafari's attention. The stranger motioned toward Ambro, and Lord Tafari turned to see him for the first time that morning. His expression betrayed nothing; in fact, for a moment, Ambro wondered if the lord even remembered the events of the previous evening. Perhaps they could all be forgotten as though they had never occurred; even as he thought this, Ambro knew that it was a childish hope. Lord Tafari was unlikely to forget an event as painful as a boy being robbed of his birthright.

"Ambro, you may join us. After all, this matter has concerned you in the past."

Puzzled, suspicious, Ambro crossed the pink-veined floor and entered the small room; Lord Tafari lounged in a carved chair with his elegant legs crossed but the other man stood with his back to the narrow window. Now, coming closer to this stranger, Ambro saw that, although his eyes were tawny, the wisps of hair escaping around the base of his turban were brown. He was of mixed blood, Ambro thought, or else a foreigner; the kind of person who could slip through a crowd and leave no memory of his passing because his emotionless expression and drab clothing were so unremarkable. Something that had tensed in Ambro, when the stranger came through the door, relaxed. A man such as this could have no news of his family for good or ill; although then why, Ambro wondered, had Lord Tafari said that the matter concerned him?

"Be seated," Lord Tafari said, his glance flicking commandingly over both Ambro and the stranger. "Now, Dabu, what news do you bring of my horses, of Dune Dancer and Sun Runner, stolen away by those hyenas, those shugra dung, in the Dunes of Enlon?"

"My lord, I have heard rumors of a man who rides like the wind, who slips away like a shadow before the noon sun, who shoots across the desert night like a comet. This man has two horses the color of old ivory, with golden stripes across their hind quarters. It is said that he has family in the area of Omo, and that his father died behind a Kiffa chariot for his insubordination and insolence. The son of such a father might be the one, my lord, to attack your caravan and steal away your cherished horses."

Lord Tafari's eyes never left Dabu's face as he spoke, and they kindled with a fierce light.

"This is true?" he asked. "How do you know all this?"

"My lord," said Dabu plaintively, "have I ever misinformed you? My sources are well paid from the generosity of your treasury; my information is always accurate."

Lord Tafari nodded consideringly, his gleaming eyes fixed on the carpet at his feet.

The horses! Ambro thought and remembered how he had first seen them waiting, hitched to the lord's chariot, on the harbor wall in the port of Jaffa; remembered their glossy shoulders gleaming in the dusky light; remembered their fiery eyes and flaring nostrils lined with pink and their hooves ringing on the stones and echoing against the mosaic walls of the kiffa temple. And he remembered Lord Tafari's story, related as they crossed the desert, as the red tassels swung on the horses' harnesses and their striped haunches bunched and strained on either side of the chariot shaft; remembered how the first kiffa had punished the first horse for its pride by chasing it through salt pan and corda groves, over dune and rock to leap at last and rake it with mighty claws so that every desert horse since that beginning time had borne the marks of the kiffa's touch. Remembered how the kiffa was then king in the desert.

But after the telling of this story, the bandits had poured over the dunes, their black plaited hair wound around their heads, their orange and tawny tunics blending with the desert, their swords upraised. And later on again, after the attack, "I will help you be avenged," Ambro had vowed, standing beside the chariot's empty shaft, when Lord Tafari's sword had rattled impotently into its scabbard and he'd cursed the bandits.

Now, an idea nudged Ambro's mind. "My lord," he said impulsively, and immediately both pairs of eyes in the room turned toward him. "My Lord Tafari, let me go to this place, Omo, and find your horses and bring them back."

A lazy smile crossed Lord Tafari's golden face, although his eyes remained fierce and intent. "You, Ambro? You don't know the desert; you are a child of the seashore, of tides and waves. And are you unhappy here in Safala, in our beautiful rose-red city?"

"No, my lord. Only—I haven't found my family and—and, I have no home to live in, and I thought I would join the army. But perhaps first I could find your horses and bring them back to Safala so they could pull your chariot again. Since I have nothing else to do, I mean. I could perhaps be of use to you." He stopped abruptly, aware that his voice had taken on a pleading quality. He cleared his throat and folded his lips in a firm line, and stared reprovingly at Dabu, challenging him to display even a hint of amusement. But Dabu's narrow face remained impassive.

Lord Tafari recrossed his legs negligently and smoothed his golden moustache. "It is true that to have my horses returned is my heart's dearest desire. And that Dabu's information is rarely false for he is a master spy with a network as spreading and complicated as the ropes in a hunting net used to catch antelope. And you, Ambro, you would like to be of use to someone so that they might provide you with a home...am I right?"

Ambro flushed to the roots of his hair but his gaze did not flicker. "I am offering my help because I love the horses and want to see them with their rightful owner," he said, which was true but only the partial truth. A sense of honesty compelled him to add, "And because I want a home."

Lord Tafari smiled. "Well spoken. I am too young to be a father. Nonetheless, I could perhaps be an uncle to you, if you returned to Safala with my fleet and fiery horses. I could have your name added to my family's records of lineage; I could find you a place in my trading empire."

Ambro strove hard to maintain a face as impassive as Dabu's, but a singing happiness was rising inside him so that he wanted to jump on the spot and shout. He felt his face split into a grin that stretched his cheeks and sparkled in his eyes. He bowed low to Lord Tafari in the Kiffa-walker style, and then he let out a whoop of pleasure that he knew immediately was undignified—but he didn't care, in that moment, about dignity. His singing, hopeful pleasure superseded all other feelings.

"So, it is settled," Lord Tafari said. "Ambro, I charge you with this Hunting. Kneel."

Ambro knelt on the crimson and green rug at Lord Tafari's feet and tilted his face upward as Lord Tafari unscrewed the lid of an alabaster pot and dipped his finger into the cinnamon-colored mineral paste that filled it. The paste felt smooth and cool on Ambro's skin as Lord Tafari applied it across his cheeks in three straight diagonal lines.

"Do you accept this Hunting, Ambro d'Monti? Will you travel afar in good courage and return with my horses?"

"I will," Ambro said with fervent resolve. He had never felt more sure of anything in his life than he felt now of the rightness of this Hunting.

"You will leave this morning with Dabu and some of my household guard. You will take my chariot with brown ponies harnessed to the shaft; you will return with Dune Dancer and Sun Runner. I will be proud to have such a nephew, who succeeds in a Hunting, numbered amongst my household."

"Yes! Oh, yes!" Ambro said and leaped up, then bowed deeply to Lord Tafari and even, in his enthusiasm, to Dabu.

"You will need food," Lord Tafari said with a smile and Ambro spun on one heel and ran down the hall to the kitchen to tell the cooks to begin packing for the journey: flasks of water, dried gazelle meat, figs and dates and apricots, nub nubs roasted over a slow fire into dry crumbling sweetness. In his room, after he leapt up the stairs, he found fresh clothes spread upon his bed in the hot sunshine, and when he and Dabu swung out through the front door, six soldiers waited at the bottom of the steps, beside a golden chariot, with their faces stern beneath their leather helmets.

Lord Tafari handed a bag of chinking coins to Dabu. Ambro bowed again, and bowed even lower to Lady Tafari who stood at the lord's side with her face floating above its column of golden rings, and her tawny eyes smiling amongst the golden lines painted on her cheeks. "May Kiffa hunt with you, Ambro," she said kindly, and handed him a parting gift of a pair of earrings—star sapphires and pearls from Lontano. He bowed once more with happiness spreading in his chest, its warm glow making him feel light and invincible. Already, he thought, she is treating me like a nephew, like a member of this family.

He sprang lightly down the steps; the previous evening, when he had toiled up them in such gloom, seemed to have receded far away, as far away as his memories of Verde were in this moment. Eagerly, he jumped into the chariot where Dabu held the reins in callused hands. A hooded falcon rode at his feet in a wicker basket. The soldiers mounted their fidgeting ponies and the chariot wheels began to roll. Ambro glanced back once, craning his neck; high overhead, in the doorway in the cliff, Lord Tafari leaned elegantly at ease in his billowing purple robe, and watched them depart. Ambro waved and the lord waved back, then stepped inside and swung the door shut. Ambro turned to look ahead over the ponies' stiff bristly manes and tossing heads; the streets of Safala were already growing busy and Dabu edged the ponies skillfully along, past women carrying baskets of lemons and tangerines, past carpet sellers hanging their wares up on poles for display, past simmering urns of cinni and braziers where nub nubs roasted, past heaps of green melons and hot red peppers becoming wizened in the sun.

At last, the ponies trotted down the long passageway that led to Safala's mighty gate covered with sheets of embossed metal, and Ambro strained his eyes for the first sight of the valley of Nini. Now they approached the gate and the guards silhouetted there; several of them were assassini, Ambro noticed, but today, swaying along high in the chariot, he hardly gave them more than a glance. The brutti dogs leapt forward, snarling, and the ponies shied and snorted, their eyes rolling in terror. Dabu's hands were unyielding on the reins and the ponies shot ahead. The brilliant green of the valley of Nini filled Ambro's vision as they exited the passageway and rolled into bright sunlight.

Ahead, the road swooped down into the valley and across it; Ambro followed its dusty lines with his eyes and saw the towering cliffs on the opposite side of the valley, then found the slender thread of path as it ascended those cliffs, climbing toward the sky. And at the top, Ambro knew, the desert began. He was filled with longing for its harsh beauty, its windswept emptiness; something in him that had felt constrained in the city began to unknot. Already, he imagined, beyond Nini's scent of fresh water and young growing things, he could smell the desert's alkaline blue smell; the scent of freedom. And he was on a Hunting now; a challenge, an adventure, a chance to prove himself. I will find those horses; he vowed to himself. Once, I helped to banish a sea dragon so surely I will succeed in this Hunting. I will return across this road in the valley with the horses running like comets. I will sweep past the assassini and the guards in triumph; Lord Tafari will embrace me and welcome me home.

Ambro felt almost giddy with hope; he whooped at the brown ponies and they broke into a canter, their small hooves pounding a staccato rhythm on the road so that women carrying baskets of green onions and bundles of bean vines had to scurry aside. Dabu let the ponies canter for several minutes before reining them in. "They have many miles ahead of them; the morning is young," he said.

"May I learn to drive them?" Ambro asked, for in his vision of returning across this valley, it was he himself who drove the desert horses.

Dabu stepped aside in the chariot and handed Ambro the reins; he straddled his weight on both feet to balance to the jouncing rhythm and felt the eclectic current of energy running up from the horses into his arms. Sunshine lay warm across his shoulders, and sparkled on the star sapphires clipped to his ears. He felt, rolling across the valley of Nini toward the cliffs and the desert's expanses of wind and sunshine, as though he was master of the world. He began to sing something that Mia had taught him on the beaches of Verde while the tides surged between the twenty-two islands of the pirati archipelago.

The ponies flicked back their ears as Ambro sang, and as they strained at the chariot shaft, pulling it up out of the valley toward the lip of the desert. As the path steepened, Ambro and Dabu climbed from the chariot to walk, leading the ponies, and Ambro sang softly into their flickering ears. "Come, brothers," he urged them. "You can do it," and the ponies bent their necks and dug their hooves into the dusty grit, hauling the chariot around the corner of a rock face so that when Ambro glanced back, the city of Safala had vanished and even the valley of Nini seemed insignificant, five hundred feet below and obscured by the knot of soldiers and ponies that followed the chariot.

At last, they reached the top; the soldiers remounted. Ambro gazed outward across the desert and breathed in deeply, filling his lungs with wind and emptiness; he felt supremely happy as they turned south along the track and headed toward Omo. For five days they traveled; growing dustier, and burned by sun and wind. The ponies' thin coats darkened with sweat but they were tough and trotted onward willingly, their scrubby tails limp in the heat. Ambro scanned the path ahead, and the desert to each side. He noted the hoof prints of gazelle, and the place where a wild warti hoggi had rooted for nub nubs beneath a grove of corda trees; he helped the soldiers pick aloba leaves to brew into bitter-sweet amber tea at the evening campfire; he recognized the hohoba shrub with its prickly spines. Everything that Lord Tafari had told him about the desert, as they traveled from Jaffa to Safala, remained clear and sharp in his memory.

From Dabu, he learned more: how to stew the bark of the jobi shrub to make ink; how to mash the leaves of the succulent ghubi plant into a green paste that could be spread on foreheads for heatstroke. Together, they hunted with the falcon, sending it aloft to swoop upon songbirds like a shooting star; they roasted the birds on spits over the evening fire and picked the tender flesh from the tiny bones. At night, after the fire had died to a feeble glow of embers and the sleeping soldiers snored amongst the hobbled ponies, Ambro lay on his back and stared at the stars. He named the constellations as the hermit in the archipelago had taught him to: Sirena's Dolphin, the Sea Horse Twins, the Horn of the Corno d'Oro, the Cracked Pot. His muscles ached but the sand was warm beneath him, and the sky was a vast bowl above. Space stretched out all around him; a space that was rolling and filled with life, like the sea of Verde, and for which he felt a deep affinity.

Uncle, he thought. Aunt. He imagined saying these words aloud. "My home," he imagined saying to other Kiffa-walker boys whom he would meet and befriend in Safala. "Would you like to come home with me for a meal?" he would ask, and proudly but nonchalantly he would lead them up the hewn stairs and into the marble hall with its brilliant tapestries and pool of orange fish. And what role would Lord Tafari assign him in his trading empire? Perhaps, if he proved himself with this Hunting, he might be given a doda train to oversee. He imagined riding at the head of a caravan into the port of Jaffa and how the eyes of Markos Dulah would bulge in his plump face when Ambro knocked at his door, holding the reins of chariot horses carelessly in one hand, come to barter and trade, to dictate line after line of goods to a scribbling scribe. And returning to Safala, the caravan would be attacked by bandits intending to pillage the barrels and sacks and chests strapped to the dodas, but Ambro would lead a swift counterattack and the bandits would be forced to withdraw in shame so that the caravan might pass unscathed and bring its treasures through the city gate. Lord Tafari would clap him on the back with admiration and gratitude. "My nephew," he would say with fond pride as he introduced Ambro to traders, translators, and army captains.

Later, as the moon rode higher, Ambro smiled in his sleep and dreamed that he was on the back of a dolphin, soaring over the waves of dunes.

When they reached Omo, Dabu left them. He wouldn't say where he was going, only that there were people he needed to talk to. He would not take Ambro with him, and when Ambro asked the soldiers if they knew what Dabu was doing, they laid their fingers along their noses. "Tightening his net," one said with a wink. For two days, Ambro and the soldiers camped in the village square amongst bleating goats and clucking hens. The soldiers carved little wooden toys for the children, or played nam nam beneath an acacia tree, and Ambro joined them and began to learn the rules of the game, scooping the glass balls from hollow to hollow on the carved board. Impatiently, between games, he paced the compound and stood in the gateway, staring out into shimmering mirages and wondering where Dabu was and where the horses were.

Over and over he imagined that moment when he would drive them across the valley of Nini, with the red tassels on their harness swaying in the wind and their bright bits gleaming, with their arrogant scooped faces tossing and their fiery eyes holding mid-summer sky. He imagined himself high in the chariot, his robe billowing in the wind of his passing, his hands strong and skilled upon the reins. Lord Tafari would come running down the steps in the mountain to embrace him, to welcome him home to his family; his face would be alight with pleasure as he stroked his hands over the horses' necks and led them into their stable in the base of the mountain, to feed them the plumpest of grain.

This image was a star sapphire in Ambro's mind, gleaming and precious.

On the second evening, Dabu returned, his face impassive, his dusty clothes making him less conspicuous than ever. Ambro jumped up and ran to meet him.

"Well?" he asked impatiently. "Where are the horses? Can we get them tonight?"

"They have left," Dabu said in his usual expressionless monotone. "I am told they have headed north with two riders. We will set out after them tomorrow morning."

"Can't we leave now?"

"The tracker asks for daylight."

Ambro stared past Dabu to see a tall thin man in a yellow shawl and conical straw hat. In the shade cast by the hat, the man's blue eyes shifted uneasily to and fro and would not meet Ambro's curious gaze. Ambro noted the pitted scars that ran across one cheek, and the left hand that dangled uselessly from a crooked wrist.

"Is he any good?" Ambro muttered to Dabu.

"He will betray his mother for gold. He was a Wanderer; now he licks my shadow. He says he knows the ancient wind-ways of the desert."

Ambro glanced again at the tracker, feeling startled, but the man's gaze remained averted. All night long, Ambro tossed and turned, feeling the fleet desert horses moving farther away, and his chances of success dwindling. He sprang up at the first hint of grey dawn and roused the soldiers by shaking their shoulders. "Dabu," he said, "let us go now. Let the men eat as we travel."

Dabu nodded impassively and went to harness the ponies to the chariot; they rolled out the village gate before the sun had risen and the landscape lay before them in tones of blue and grey without definition or depth. It was like moving in a dream, Ambro thought. The tracker walked ahead of the chariot, casting around on the ground for any trace of hoof prints. His yellow dog, its ribs barring its torso, ran beside him, its nose to the ground and its tongue hanging limply from its mouth as the sun rose and the heat gathered.

All that day and the next, they followed the tracker and his dog; they marched across a mineral plain in white dust that coated their faces, they manhandled the chariot down into a tiny crack of valley and stared at the remains of a fire and the holes in the ground where tents of shugra hide had been pegged down. The valley was filled with the cleft hoof marks of the shugra and with piles of their dry dung. Dabu and the soldiers waited for hours while the tracker roamed up and down the valley, looking for any sign that horses had passed. Ambro roamed beside him, learning to read the palm of the desert and to understand its lines. Finally, on the second afternoon, they came to a narrow gulley that angled up the valley's steep sides amongst hard dark rocks. The tracker bent over the ground; the dog sniffed the rocks and suddenly both man and dog tensed. Ambro knew immediately that they had found something.

"Fetch your men," the tracker told Ambro, and soon they were all scrambling up the gulley and following the tracker across the grassy plain that lay beyond and where the passage of the horses was easy to read in the bent stems of grass. Beyond the plain, the trail doubled back; again the soldiers waited while Ambro and the tracker and his dog cast around for the trail. It took them a day to find it; then, after a few miles, they lost it again as it entered a trickling stream that was evaporating in the heat and receding from its clay banks to become only a memory of moisture. For miles the tracker worked the banks, looking for hoof marks to emerge and at last he found them and the party continued traveling north. They lost the track again that afternoon, but Ambro insisted they press onward, and the next morning they came across a goat boy herding his flock. He stared at them suspiciously, surrounded by his bleating animals with dangling ears and green glassy eyes.

"Have desert horses passed here?" Ambro asked. "Colored like ivory, ridden like the wind?"

The boy shrugged and Dabu opened a pack and pulled out a string of beads and a bolt of bright cloth that Ambro held aloft. "Have you seen anything in the desert passing north?"

The boy nodded. "Two riders, a boy and a girl, on desert horses," and he held out his hand for the bribe. As they rode on, Ambro looked back to see the boy wrapping the fabric around his waist in a bright pleated skirt that seemed incongruous against the tawny desert and amongst the brown and black speckled goats.

Now they rode on fast, the tracker often running. The man seemed tireless for even in the heat he could run for hours, a thin twig of a man in the yellow shawl, his conical hat casting a pyramidal shadow. Ambro rode in the chariot, its swaying motion so familiar that he balanced without conscious effort; the reins so familiar in his hands that he managed the ponies without thought, simply felt their movements and responded to them. Dabu rode in silence, his narrow face closed around many secrets.

On the edge of the empty quarter, on a sheet of rock, they lost the tracks again and though they spent hours searching for them, they had at last to admit defeat. It was as though the horses had vanished like mirages. "I do not know the wind-ways in the empty quarter," the tracker muttered sullenly, and flinched when Dabu's shadow fell across his face.

Slouched against the chariot rim as they headed toward a spine of jagged rock to seek a camp for the night, Ambro tried to recall the joy he had felt crossing the valley of Nini and the triumphant return he had envisioned, but his mind was blank and heavy. He felt overwhelmed by the desert's vastness; in its expanses, his Hunting seemed futile and impossible. Wearily he conferred with Dabu as to the best site in which to pitch camp; he trudged around amongst the soldiers, overseeing them as they hobbled the ponies and gathered dried cacti for a fire. He knew, with painful awareness, that the soldiers did not need his supervision; that throughout the journey they had probably been laughing at him, a boy of sixteen from a salty world, giving orders to them, hardened veterans of Terre's heat and dryness. It is only because they are in Lord Tafari's employ, he thought, that they pay any attention to me at all. I would never be given command of a doda caravan; I am too young and inexperienced.

He wandered away from the soldiers to stare over the plain below and to the mountain that Dabu had said was called Lalibela. Its massive flanks of rock glowed red in the setting sun, scored with harsh black shadows in gullies and crevices. When he turned back to the encampment, he saw that a pot of stew was simmering over the fire, and he sighed and went to receive his portion.

"We should turn back tomorrow," Dabu said at his shoulder, as he gazed into the flames. "The trail has grown cold."

"No!" Ambro exclaimed.

"I have spent long enough on this; I have other tasks to attend to at home."

"No!" Ambro said more forcefully. "I have not completed my Hunting; we cannot turn back."

Dabu's expression remained as inscrutable as ever. Ambro stared at him fiercely, willing Dabu to obey his wishes and aware that the soldiers, gathered around the fire, were watching with unconcealed curiosity.

"We cannot turn back. We will continue northward tomorrow and hope to pick the trail up again," Ambro ordered, knowing even as he said it that he could not order men much older than himself and expect to be obeyed. He clenched his jaw.

The yellow dog whined uneasily at their feet, and the tracker shrugged, shadows rippling in the folds of his shawl, and the whites of his eyes pale in his dark face. "I am turning back," he said.

"We will go on without him," Ambro insisted, glaring at Dabu. He too shrugged but made no reply before joining the soldiers and holding out a bowl for a ladle of broth. Ambro stood alone with his arms folded over his chest, feeling foolish and conspicuous. Later, lying on his bed roll, he stared unseeingly at the stars. I will avenge you, he had promised Lord Tafari. But I have failed, he thought. I had faith in the tracker and his yellow dog. I believed they would find the horses for me.

Vividly, one last time, Ambro imagined hitching Sun Runner and Dune Dancer to the chariot shaft and how it would spring forward beneath his feet as the horses thundered toward Safala and the man who would become his uncle.

But not now.

I will return in shame, he thought, and the lord's face will darken and set with disappointment, and I will slink away to enlist in the army, an orphan with no home. But why? Why do I look like a Kiffa-walker if I am not one? And why do I love the desert so, if it is not my home? Is there no place that I belong?

He slept fitfully at last, his forehead creased in a frown as his thoughts worried at themselves like a dog chasing its own fleas.

At dawn, he gave up trying to sleep and went to stare out over the plain; its expanse of hard minerals, its scrubby bushes. Mount Lalibela loomed on the horizon, soaring from its spine of jagged rock. The land lay empty and silent. How beautiful it is, Ambro thought. I will not leave it to return to Verde even though I have found no family here. He sighed and turned back to the camp where the soldiers were stirring and Dabu was distributing portions of dried figs and water to them.

"We will travel on northward," Ambro said, repeating his orders of the previous night, but Dabu shook his head.

"Then I will go alone!" Ambro blazed out.

Dabu shrugged. "You will be vulture meat very soon. We don't have enough food to spare you much, nor water. We need to leave this empty quarter and find an oasis. Lord Tafari will not think more highly of you for dying on this Hunting, for taking also the life of one of his ponies. At the first oasis, you may buy yourself supplies and continue alone if you wish. I have other matters to attend to."

Ambro ground the toe of his boot into the sand in frustration but he knew that he had no choice but to accept Dabu's counsel. He strode toward the chariot ponies, avoiding the eyes of the soldiers, afraid that they would contain secret mirth at his helplessness.

As the sun rose, they saddled the ponies and turned the chariot around. "We will head for the nearest caravan route and follow it home through the village of Dahki," Dabu ordered. With a heavy heart, Ambro climbed into the chariot and stared southward, the mountain at his back; the morning sun illuminating the desert, his hopes quenched yet cold and heavy in his gut. His head ached from lack of sleep. The tracker left them and began to lope southward toward his home, the skinny dog ranging alongside and their thin shadows gliding over the ground.

"A little fresh meat for lunch would be pleasant," Dabu observed, and bent to lift the falcon from its wicker cage. The bird perched on his leather wrist band and when Dabu removed the hood, Ambro saw the bird's eyes glinting in the rising sun. Suddenly it was airborne, soaring above them on outspread wings, sun tipping its feathers.

Ambro squinted upward, watching the falcon cutting through yellow sky. Suddenly the bird plunged, a magnificent rushing force that knocked a small bird from the air and sent another one twirling and fluttering. The falcon seized the first bird in its hooked yellow beak and swept downward to land on Dabu's outstretched arm; the ponies snorted nervously as it passed over their heads.

Dabu removed the rock-rose from the falcon's grasp and turned it over in the palm of his hand. The little bird was dead and lay limply, its barred feathers ruffled and its wrinkled lids half-closed over dull eyes.

"There's something on its leg!" Ambro observed, and Dabu removed the scrap of parchment.

"We near the sacred place," he read, the orange ink clear in the strengthening light.

"What does it mean?" Ambro asked.

Dabu turned the scrap of parchment over but the reverse side was blank. With a peremptory shout, he summoned a soldier and sent him riding after the tracker to bring him back. When he arrived, the tracker looked at the stiffening rock-rose and the scrap of parchment. He shrugged and scuffled his feet in the sand as his eyes darted to and fro.

"What do you know?" Dabu asked.

The tracker muttered, "Nothing, nothing."

"Look at me!" Dabu roared. "Choose your words carefully. Remember what price I can extract from you! What do you know?"

The tracker's face twitched spasmodically, wrinkling the scars on one cheek. His left hand spasmed on its crooked wrist. "The nearest sacred place is Mount Lalibela," he muttered. "Though I have never been there."

Dabu nodded in silence, deep in thought. Then he had the chariots turned around and the whole party returned to the rocky spine where they had encamped the previous night and which Ambro had not expected to see again. "Use your spyglass," Dabu said, and Ambro nodded. He didn't want his hopes to rise again, only to be dashed. There was no reason that he could think of why a bandit with desert horses would be making a pilgrimage to the mountain; he thought crossly that Dabu was wasting all their time and that the day was growing fiercely hot. It would have been better if they had used the cooler morning to make southward progress toward Safala. Not that he cared whether he ever saw it again either. Maybe he would try and find a troop of soldiers somewhere along the way and simply join them.

He pulled himself up to the spine's ridge, then clambered onto a large flat rock and lay along it, resting his spyglass on a smaller rock and training it upon the plain. Shimmering white heat. Blue mirages. Scrubby hohoba bushes. The occasional clump of sword grass. He swept the spyglass around toward Mount Lalibela, stared at its craggy gullies, its dry crevices, its sheets of reflective red rock that were shining in the sun's direct rays. He swept the glass over a lone sand-pine teetering on the edge of a ridge, and watched a magpie fly into it and disappear among the limp needles. He lowered the glass down the mountain, down to the base where the jumble of red rocks lay.

Movement.

Ambro tensed, steadied the spyglass. There it was again, near the base of the mountain, amongst the jumbled rocks. Now the figures emerged on the path, winding up toward the ridge halfway up the peak.

Horses! Desert horses! Ambro's hand shook and the little figures swung and trembled in the spyglass's round eye. He took a deep breath and held the spyglass more firmly. Two desert horses, ivory in color, with stripes of amber across their quarters, were picking their way up the mountain behind two small human figures. Yes, there could be no doubt: they were Lord Tafari's stolen horses, Dune Dancer and Sun Runner. For one more moment Ambro squinted hungrily at them, feeling hope and happiness leap in his chest. He might return to Safala after all; he might sweep through the gates in style and receive a hero's welcome. He might yet have a family and a lineage to call his own. Yes!

Exultantly he leapt down and tore across the sparse grass to where Dabu waited, feeding morsels of rock-rose to his falcon. "It's them!" Ambro panted. "It's the horses we're after! They are being led up the mountain. If we fly, we can cut them off as they return to the plain! Hurry, Dabu, get the soldiers moving!"

Without betraying any emotion, Dabu pulled the hood over the falcon's eyes and placed it, flapping its wings in complaint, into the wicker basket. He shouted for the soldiers and when they had assembled, Ambro addressed them from the chariot. "We will follow the edge of the ridge and stay hidden amongst the rocks for as far as possible. Then we will make a dash across the open plain toward the base of the path ascending Lalibela!" His clear voice soared out over the men's heads, over their intent faces and upright spears, and he was gratified to see enthusiasm kindle in their eyes. Dabu swung the chariot around and as the ponies trotted out, Ambro clutched its rim with white knuckles. The horses! So close! He marveled at this; it seemed like a miracle granted after all hope was lost.

He tried to use his spyglass again but it was impossible in the swaying, jouncing chariot and presently he slid it back into an inner pocket of his robe against the narrow shaft of his flute, and stared ahead with his naked eye. It was impossible, at this distance, to see anything, and anxiety gnawed at him. Could the riders have turned back? Maybe they were already skirting the mountain and getting away! Maybe all that would be there when the chariot finally arrived would be hoof prints that vanished into thin air as they had so many times before. Ambro looked back to see the tracker loping alongside the soldiers, his thin weather-beaten face inscrutable under his conical hat.

Hurry, Ambro thought. Hurry!

As though sensing his anxiety, Dabu whipped the ponies into a canter and they pounded forward, the chariot lurching between hohoba shrubs and prickly vines bearing bitter gourds. It seemed as though the mountain receded away from them mockingly as the heat gathered; froth flew from the ponies' mouths to splatter Ambro's arm and he could smell their sweat.

Hurry, oh hurry! he thought, his eyes narrowed in creases of skin as he peered ahead.

And now the mountain loomed above them, closer at last. Now it was possible to see the individual rocks jumbled at the base in their purple shadows and now—Ambro gave a shout and pointed; Dabu whipped the ponies into a gallop and the soldiers around them thundered alongside, for the desert horses and their riders were plunging down the face of the mountain at breakneck speed. At any moment, Ambro expected to see the horses fall, their slender legs snapping, their bodies plunging and rolling down the mountainside to land in a mangled heap. But the horses did not falter and Ambro marveled at their flight, at the beauty of it and the magnificent daring courage.

"They will get away!" he yelled, and Dabu's whip sang out over the ponies so that their eyes rolled white.

The soldiers were in amongst the rocks now, and suddenly the desert horses arrived at the bottom of the path and plunged forward, fighting their way out through the soldiers. Ambro thought he had never seen anything as terrifying and beautiful as Sun Runner rearing and plunging, his long legs flashing like spears, or as Dune Dancer wheeling on her hind legs, eluding capture. But surely, at any moment, the horses would be caught; Ambro anticipated the touch of their smooth flanks as he harnessed them to the chariot. At any moment, victory would be his.

But now—no! It wasn't possible. The stallion's rider was being unseated by soldiers who dragged at his breeches and flaring tunic—and the stallion himself was soaring through the red capes and leather helmets of the soldiers like a fury, with the mare pressing behind him.

"Catch them!" Ambro yelled and he jumped impetuously from the chariot and flung himself into the fray, reckless for his own safety. He dodged wheeling ponies, flying hooves, flung spears, the buffeting shoulders of the men who had dismounted to struggle with their captive. Ambro thrust his way through and leaped toward the desert mare. Her haunches spun away beneath his outstretched hand; for a fraction of time he felt the glossy heat of her skin, but then she was gone from his touch. In that fleeting moment he saw the girl rider against the white hot sky: saw her smooth oval face, her wide terrified blue eyes, her streaming hair woven with cowry shells. Shock coursed through him as he recognized her—the girl from the temple in Safala—but it was followed quickly by desperation because he realized that the horses were escaping. "Catch them!" he shouted desperately at the soldiers but already it was too late; the horses were soaring clear, were breaking into a gallop; were racing away raising clouds of mineral dust. Ambro snatched at the trailing reins of a brown pony and flung himself onto its back to race after the desert horses; he knew that he had no hope of catching them but his anguish at their loss drove him on. He chased them around the base of the mountain, crouched over the pony's neck, until it was blowing and exhausted. The ivory horses were far ahead now and becoming smaller by the minute, the rhythm of their hoof beats dying into silence. Briefly they were silhouetted on a swell of land, then were gone. Ambro lay along the pony's drooping neck and felt tears of bitter disappointment burn through his closed eyelids and down his cheeks to evaporate quickly in the heat.

At last, he slid from the pony's back and spoke kindly words to it in a breaking voice, and then turned to lead it back over what seemed like miles of cracked mineral dirt. His mouth was so dry he couldn't swallow, and his swollen tongue pressed against the roof of his mouth.

When at last he rejoined the soldiers, he found Dabu sitting in the chariot chewing nub nubs, with a man roped to one wheel. Dabu asked nothing about the desert horses. "Put that pony in the shade and give it a little water," was all he said and then, when Ambro had followed his instructions, he gestured at the bound figure slumped against the chariot.

"What shall we do with him?"

Ambro turned to look at the captive and shock again coursed through him, as though he had been kicked in the stomach. He stood rigidly, glaring down. The bandit glared back unflinchingly, defiantly, with his brilliant blue eyes; the blue mineral paste on his cheekbones was smudged with sweat, blue beads glittered at his throat and his plaited hair shone like a crown on his head.

"You!" Ambro choked. "You are the one who knocked me down and who stole Lord Tafari's horses in the dunes of Enlon!"

"My own horses!" the bandit said with cool disdain.

"You webbie scum!" Ambro blazed. "Don't you know better than to drag valuable horses into the empty quarter? And now they've escaped! You have cost me a family!"

The bandit shrugged insultingly. "You have cost my people many families, many mothers, many fathers, many brothers and sisters—all gone into the dark."

For a moment something flickered in Ambro's mind, some uncertainty linked to his memory of the brutto attacking the child in Safala, but then his angry grief blotted it out before he had time to examine it.

Dabu moved at his shoulder. "There are slavers in the village of Mandi to our south," he said. "Shall we sell him?"

"Do whatever you wish," Ambro muttered through clenched teeth. Reeling with fatigue, he stalked off to sit in the shade under a large gritty rock, and bent his aching head into his arms. In the darkness behind his closed lids the horses kept running, farther and farther away, trailing white dust, the light streaking along them, their great legs eating up the horizon. Disappointment and thwarted desire burned in his chest.

"Eat," a solider said with rough kindness, thrusting a handful of figs into his palm. Ambro shoved them into a pocket for he was not hungry for food, and raised his head to see the webbie bandit being marched away between two soldiers with his wrists bound at his back and a rope around his neck. One soldier yanked on the rope and Ambro saw it tighten around the bandit's dark throat; his beads had already been taken from him. The figures moved away across the shimmering plain, the soldiers mounted on ponies but the bandit walking, and became tiny dark things distorted and wavering in the heat. Ambro watched them without really seeing them for his thoughts remained fixed upon the escaping horses. And the girl—what was *she* doing here? Could she possibly be the girl from the temple or was he imaging things in the ferocious heat? If she was traveling in company with the bandit to Lalibela, did this mean that she was a Wind-wanderer?

"Dabu," he called. "When the men and ponies have rested and the heat has abated, we will track the horses."

But Dabu shook his head. "There are no oases in that direction for many miles, and we haven't enough food and water. We will retreat to Dahki as planned."

The soldiers dozed in the mountain's shade, their breastplates and helmets lying beside them, their sweaty faces slack, and the ponies dozed with their lower lips hanging and their tails whisking at flies. But Ambro stalked over to the edge of the plain and stood squinting along the lines of hoof prints leading north and felt a great tug of longing. He stood there for a long time, at the point where the tracks leading north and south diverged. All his attention was riveted to the image of Dune Dancer and Sun Runner hurtling north over the ridge from his sight, and he gave no thought to the southward-leading tracks of two ponies flanking a man who walked with a rope around his throat.

CHAPTER TWELVE

"WE HAVE BEEN HERE long enough," Ambro announced to the men lounging in the harsh, sword-shaped shadows cast by the fronds of nuga palms in the oasis of Dahki. Soldiers glanced up as he spoke but none of them moved, and one man continued to shake a pair of dice within the palm of his hand and let them fall, with a tiny clatter, onto the board of a bahwa game. A rainbird gave its cry, like a shriek of laughter, overhead.

Ambro spoke more loudly, in the commanding tone that he had heard Lord Tafari use when he strode through his marble hallways, demanding supper to be served on the terrace, or when visited by scribes from his treasury or the captains of his caravans. "We are leaving for Mount Lalibela, before the sun climbs higher and the heat increases. Gather your possessions and saddle the ponies."

"A loud roar for a young cub," one man muttered and a snicker ran through the men. Ambro felt a flush rise into his cheeks and the back of his neck burned.

"I am returning south," Dabu said, materializing silently at his shoulder in his drab robe and dusty boots.

"You are in the lord's employ," Ambro protested. "And so are these men. And I have been given command over all of you for my Hunting, which I have not yet completed."

Dabu shrugged laconically and adjusted his turban. "I have other matters to attend to in the lord's employ. You may follow the hoof prints northward from the mountain if you wish, but the tracker has returned to his village."

A momentary pang shot through Ambro as he thought of the tracker's indefatigable energy and the keen nose of his loping yellow dog, for he might have need of them; then he became aware of Dabu drifting away, blending with the shadows beneath the palms.

"Who will come with me?" he cried suddenly in a clear, ringing voice. "Who is man enough to face the desert—or shall I go alone? Shall I tell Lord Tafari, who pays you in gold, that you would rather lounge around the well and play games than track with me? Shall I tell him this is how his gold is spent, on beads for village girls, and bowls of goats' milk, and bets placed upon nam nam and bahwa?"

The men stirred uneasily and glanced up to meet the level, challenging glare of Ambro's tawny eyes. After a moment's silence, in which goats bleated in the distance and women laughed softly around the well as they heaved skin containers of water onto their heads, a soldier named Manni rose to his feet and looked around at the other men in a considering fashion before turning his gaze to Ambro. "I will come north with you through the empty quarter," he stated firmly.

"And so will I," agreed another man.

"And I."

Ambro nodded with satisfaction at them; Manni, Dabali and Bohra were all young men with fierce eyes, and golden moustaches that Ambro secretly envied; they were all sinewy and strong, and rode their tough ponies with consummate ease.

"We are returning to Safala with Dabu," spoke a man leaning against a nuga trunk, and the remainder of the men nodded in agreement. Ambro ignored them and spoke to those men who stood awaiting his orders. "Let's saddle up. I will take a pony to ride and the chariot can return to Safala."

He had struggled with this decision, knowing that a pony was more practical in the empty quarter's rugged territory, and yet clinging to his vision of returning to Safala with the desert horses hitched to the chariot and thundering toward the gate with him swaying above them. With a sigh he let the vision go, and turned away from the well to find himself a pony; the young soldiers who were to accompany him folded up their nam nam board, and paid the bets they had lost. They strapped on their leather breastplates and picked up their helmets from where they lay amongst the pile of saddles and bridles.

As they set off from Dahki, Ambro's pony tossed its head eagerly and broke into a dancing trot as though infected with Ambro's own tension. He reined the pony in so that it sidestepped beneath him, its small hooves churning up the sand. "Easy, easy," Ambro said, "We have many miles yet to go." He strained his eyes toward the horizon that retreated away from him into its shimmering mysterious distance, and felt that tug of longing for the horses. Where were they in all that infinity of space at this very moment: standing quietly in the shade of a corda grove with their heads hanging and the fires banked in their purple eyes? Or were they drifting across the desert at an easy lope, their tails floating behind them as they moved farther away from him and became invisible again?

"Is it the horses you're after—or the girl?" Manni teased, his lips smiling beneath his golden moustache.

"She could ride, that one. I don't know if Ambro could handle her," Bohra said.

"He wouldn't want her—she was a dust-eater," Dabali argued. "They smell like shugras, those women. And they dress like men. Ambro wouldn't know what to do with her."

Laughter ran through the soldiers and their ponies snorted and shied beneath them. A southeast wind lifted their sparse tails and played amongst the stiff tufts of their manes.

"It's the Ismata, the wind from the Moon Mountains," Dabali called to Ambro. "It blows in mid-summer for days on end."

Ambro nodded, lifting his nose into the eddying currents; they smelled sweet and fresh as though they had blown through the bright greenness of ferns and cascades of hanging flowers and over beds of fragrant mint; they swept the harsh alkaline scent of the dust before them like water flowing into a dry river bed. Ambro took a deep breath, sucking in the sweetness of the Ismata, and tried to imagine the place from which it had come: the mysterious mountains that men spoke of but that no one seemed to have traveled to.

"Does no one live in the mountains?" he asked.

"No," Manni replied. "There is nothing there but forest and monkeys; they say panthers stalk amongst the trees and a man might hang himself on the great vines that wrap the forest or be swept away in torrential rivers or might disappear into the smothering mists and never walk out again. There is nothing in the mountains of any value for trade or commerce, with the exception of mahogany wood that is cut by a tribe of men called FahFahs, who flicker through the forest like shadows and live on wild honey. But in the high mountains themselves, no man goes and no roads traverse the steep slopes."

"There is a power there as old as the stars, an ancient magic," Dabali added, jerking nervously at his pony's mouth so that the animal flung up its head and rolled the whites of its eyes.

"What kind of power?" Ambro asked, but Dabali made the sign of spread fingers to ward off evil, and shook his head.

"They say the spirit of some ancient female deity walks there with her beasts, their horns shine golden in the light of the moon," Bohra said in a low voice, and he too spread his fingers.

"It is old crone's talk," Manni declared too loudly, and the men kicked the ponies into a canter, spreading out across the desert so that conversation became impossible.

All that day and the next they rode, skirting dunes that drifted across the narrow track, climbing in and out of dry river beds where the ponies' hooves grated on smooth round pebbles the color of amber, stripping the leaves from aloba bushes to brew into tea. Late on the second afternoon, as the sun lowered and cast distorted shadows away from the ponies' feet, Ambro gave an exultant shout." The mountain! We will camp there tonight!"

Lalibela glowed red on the horizon, a pimple of rock on a thread of dark ridge; they rode hard toward it in tired silence, the men's faces taut and intent and the ponies trotting in dogged fashion with their heads low. Darkness nipped at their heels, chasing them ahead of it as the light faded and the mountain blended into the purple sky with its long streamers of gauzy clouds that glowed brilliantly even after the sun had disappeared over a ridge crowned with jobi bushes. When at last they picked a path in amongst the jumbled rocks at Lalibela's base, Ambro was almost too tired to talk. He slumped by the small fire of dried cactus and stared out into the darkness; he could feel the proximity of the northward track with its twin set of hoof prints.

In the morning, at first light, we will begin to follow them, he promised himself. We won't give up this Hunting until I have achieved success, until I have proven to Lord Tafari that I am a Kiffa-walker even though my father's name is lost. He will acknowledge that I am a child of Terre; that I can command men and persevere through difficulties. He will reward me with a place in his trading empire. Although I am too young to command a doda train yet I might train in one, learning from some older man, and perhaps by the time that I can grow a golden moustache I will be desert hardened and knowledgeable enough to lead the gold and salt through the desert and bring it safely to ports and treasuries. Or perhaps Lord Tafari will send me to sea on a merchant ship, for I have already proven to him that I have skill with waves and tides.

A new image eddied into Ambro's mind: he saw himself astride Sun Runner, with Dune Dancer led alongside on a crimson rein, racing across the valley of Nini toward the dark mouth of the city gate. He imagined how the farmers would straighten up from stooping over onions and tender bean vines, how they would shade their eyes to watch him gallop past with hoof beats ringing in the still air; imagined how women on the road would stand to one side with their baskets of wheat and sorghum balanced on their heads; and how the guards would peer toward him as he approached trailing a cloud of dust.

He imagined again Lord Tafari's noble face shining with delight, as he draped an elegant arm over Ambro's shoulders and welcomed him home.

"He's thinking about that girl," Dabali observed, digging Ambro in the ribs with an elbow, and the other men shot appraising glances at Ambro where he sat, drowsy eyed in the firelight with a smile tugging at the corners of his firm, wide mouth.

Ambro shook his head and laughed. "It's only the horses I want."

He slept soundly that night but awoke with a start to sit up and peer around. The soldiers were dim mounds on the ground nearby, wrapped in their red capes, and a thread of pale grey light rimmed the eastern horizon. Mount Lalibela loomed at his back, a solid dense mass of rock that still radiated a slight heat from the previous afternoon. No sound broke the deep silence.

He rose and shook Manni's shoulder. "Morning. We're tracking horses today!"

"Hmmph. You need to switch to girls, Ambro. More fun when you catch them."

Ambro ignored this and shook Dabali and Bohra in turn; they stretched and their wind-burned faces split into luxuriant yawns.

"Eat as you ride," Ambro commanded, untying the hobbles on the ponies' front legs as the men, still yawning, lugged saddles and bridles to them. "Hurry, hurry," muttered Bohra without malice, as he slipped the bit into his pony's mouth and pulled its forelock free of the brow band. "This young kiffa is always in a hurry, always hungry for the hunt."

"Places to go, horses to catch. A family to win," Dabali agreed.

Ambro, tightening the girth on his own pony's saddle, wondered how the men knew that he was trying to win a family, a place in Lord Tafari's household. Perhaps Dabu had told them. He swung onto the pony; a high tight tension hummed in him as he trotted over to the tracks left by the desert horses. On the salty mineral plain, the hoof marks were quite clear, and for hours they followed them as they angled northwestward toward the blue cresting wave of the plateau lands. Ambro thought anxiously of what he'd heard of that rugged place—the ramparts of the Moon Mountains, serrated by deep canyons where hidden rivers ran at the foot of golden cliffs—and hoped that the desert horses had not taken refuge there for he might never find them. But how would that girl, the one from the seclusion of the forgotten temple in Safala's narrow alleys, know the way to the plateau lands? And who was she anyway? Her startled eyes, and swinging black hair woven with cowries, teased at the edges of his mind. How had she learned to ride desert horses when she had seemed to be only an acolyte of Sirena, goddess of salty waves and frolicking dolphins? And if she was a Wind-wanderer, what had she to do with the pirati goddess in the first place? She seemed as mysterious, to Ambro, as the Moon Mountains that reared into misty shrouds somewhere far to the east, beyond the plateau lands.

Ambro wrenched his thoughts away from the girl and kicked his pony on, fretting at the delay that had been caused by returning to the oasis of Dahki for food and water. If only he could have followed the tracks while they were still fresh, while the horses were only hours ahead of him!

By the middle of the afternoon, the summer sun was a burning ball lodged between their shoulder blades and even the Ismata had died to a wispy breath of sweet air that gusted occasionally through the smells of dust and alkali and the tang of resinous sap that oozed from the hohoba plants to drip into the sand. Sweat trickled down Ambro's chest and his hands were slippery on the reins. The men rode in silence, enduring the long hours until dusk when the Ismata would pour more strongly over them, chasing away the heat with its blue minty smells.

The ponies climbed doggedly to the rim of a hill and suddenly the ground fell away to reveal a bowl of land holding in its centre a pool of glittering water as round and bright as the eye of Ambro's spyglass.

"A spring!" Dabali crowed. "A swim!"

"You can't swim, you'll sink like a stone and blow bubbles!"

"Last one in is shugra dung!"

Manni whooped exultantly, a sound that flushed a single magpie from a nearby shrub to scatter across the sky in a flurry of black and white feathers. The ponies whickered in anticipation of the fresh water, and sprang down the slope eagerly in plumes of sand as the men kicked them on.

Ambro reined his own pony back and remained on the rim of the hollow. Mesmerized, he stared at the pool: a fallen scrap of midsummer sky. Despite its beauty, a premonition of disaster shivered through him. His sweaty skin rose in goose bumps. Hair stiffened on the nape of his neck. He opened his mouth to shout but the heat sucked all moisture from it and fear locked his jaw. He swallowed with difficulty as the pony fretted beneath him; he tightened the reins with effort in stiff fingers. He had to act, had to avert what loomed ahead, only moments away. He would wrench his safety from the fate that had brought him here.

"We have no time for this!" he yelled. "Let the ponies have a short drink and then keep going!"

The men gave no sign of having heard him as their ponies splashed into the shallows of the pool and bent their heads, concentric ripples spreading from their muzzles and the gusty breath of their nostrils. The men slid from their backs, ankle deep in water, stripping off their red capes and leather helmets to toss onto the sandy shore, and pulling boots over well muscled legs.

"Stop! I command you! We haven't time for this!" Ambro yelled again, forcing the words out past the weight pressing on his chest and the constriction in his throat. A fresh wave of cold tingled through him.

Still the men ignored him. Manni was naked now, his torso oddly pale golden in contrast to the wind-burned skin on his arms and face. He plunged deeper into the pool, shattering its placid surface and shouting incomprehensibly, his face alight with laughter. Sheets of water sprayed from him and seemed to hang, sparkling, in the perfectly still air for the Ismata gusted softly high overhead, above the rim of the surrounding hills.

Dabali, already stripped naked, paused to lead the ponies away from the water, lest they bloat themselves, and tied them to a hohoba shrub.

"Get out of the water! We ride on!" Ambro shouted.

Dabali squinted at him, poised on the ridge against the cauldron of sky, and waved him toward the pool. "Come on!" he yelled. "Last one in is a dust-eater!"

He tied the final knot in the reins and turned to run after Bohra; fresh sheets of water sprayed up as the two men plunged in and began to chase Manni who was already in the centre of the pool, swimming lazily on his back with light flashing on his long arms as they cut arcs above the surface.

Go! shouted a voice in Ambro's mind. Save yourself! Get far away from here!

He tried to shout one last time at the men but fear stiffened his face into immobility. His heart thundered in his ears and chills shook him. He kicked the pony forward, around the rim of the hollow. As it fought to run downhill toward the water, he wrestled desperately with it, turning its head away, the reins bunched in his hands, and thumping it with his heels. It gave a shrill whinny of anger and the men glanced up from the pool.

"Ambro's escaping!" Dabali yelled.

"He's afraid of the water!"

"He's afraid of getting clean; he wants to smell like a webbie!"

"So the webbie girl will like him and give him the horses!"

Bantering, laughing, the men splashed through the shallows and ran after Ambro, their bodies glistening in the sun and their dark golden hair plastered to their heads; even their golden eyebrows were saturated and sparkled with beads of moisture.

"Come for a swim Ambro!"

"We won't let you sink!"

Ambro kicked the pony on but it crabbed sideways beneath him, its jaw locked around the bit and its neck twisting toward the lure of the water and the thin shade where the other ponies dozed, satiated and peaceful. The men's bare feet thudded closer. Despair flooded over Ambro; already, he could feel the moment slipping beyond his control and plummeting toward disaster.

Manni caught the pony's bridle and dragged it to a plunging standstill.

"Let go!" Ambro shouted and pummeled Manni's shoulders, fear dancing in his vision so that it swung dizzily, filled with glimpses of blue water, blue sky, pony's rolling eyes, Manni's sleek wet shoulders, Dabali's golden arms reaching for him, Bohra's grinning face and white teeth.

"Let me go!" he shouted angrily as the men dragged him from the pony; it lunged away, leaving strands of wiry mane in Ambro's clutching fists, and ran down to the pool to drop its muzzle and suck water thirstily.

"Leave me alone!" he shouted, lashing out with his feet and flailing with his fists, but the men were sinewy and strong, hardened by the rigors of the desert, and there were three of them. They hauled Ambro downhill, laughing, teasing. Sand gritted between his teeth; a kaleidoscope of light and shadow whirled in his vision. He was as cold now as though drenched by deep ocean, as though drowning. His muscles felt slow and stiff with the coldness of his fear, and his voice died in his throat. In silence, as they reached the wet sand rimming the pool and as the smell of the water filled his nose, he began to struggle harder; the men threw themselves on top of him and wrestled, still laughing.

"A big kiffa we have caught!" Dabali yelled.

"He fights like a fiend!"

Ambro's foot, lashing out, caught Manni in the stomach and he doubled over, a shadow of annoyance crossing his face and dimming the laughter in his eyes. "Pull off his boots before we throw him in," he commanded.

Ambro writhed beneath Debali's grip but couldn't throw him off. Bohra and Manni caught him by one leg and began to drag off his dusty Kiffa-walker boot of fine grained leather with a fleecy rolled top. Ambro felt the boot slide down his cold, sweating leg.

For a moment, time paused. The Ismata held its breath. The surface of the pool became perfectly calm, a mirage of sky and azure light. The ponies stood unmoving by the hohoba shrubs, their hocks bent in rest. Shadows stopped slipping away across the sand as the sun hung in the limitless dome of sky. A blue lizard draped on a rock, its thin scaly feet still and even its beady eyes fixed motionless in their sockets. Ambro went limp, like a small animal in the jaws of a predator, when it accepts that its fate has brought it to the door of death.

Time began to move again. Ambro's boot slipped over his heel, and Dabali gave a shout of triumph. "Into the water! Heave him in!"

"Aiiiyeee!" Bohra's shout of incredulous horror cut the air like the edge of a serrated knife that leaves a jagged wound. A gust of Ismata swirled downhill and ripples scudded before it across the pool. The magpie tumbled overhead, crying harshly.

Ambro flinched, struggling to pull his foot away, but the men held it in burning grips, and Ambro knew that he could not avert his fate after all.

CHAPTER THIRTEEN

AGAINST THE SKY, THE MEN'S faces hung in Ambro's line of vision, contorted with rage, disgust, amazement, contempt.

"Webs! He has *webs* between his toes!"

"Shit of the kiffa!"

"He's a webbie bastard!"

Ambro struggled to sit up. "I am a Kiffa-walker!" he yelled. "Open your eyes and look at me! Lord Tafari, who pays you, knows that I am a Kiffa—ask him!"

"We do not need to ask! We have eyes of our own!"

"We see your webs!"

"No Kiffa has webs!"

"Have you shown them to Lord Tafari? What would he say if he knew?"

"He would not want you for a nephew then!"

Their jeering voices beat at Ambro; sounds that seemed to ricochet in his skull as though it were an empty space, as though fear had emptied his brains out. His chest shook with the hammering of his heart.

"Please," he begged, "we have traveled together. We have enjoyed ourselves."

He looked beseechingly at the men but their faces were set in hard lines of disapproval and their lips curled in scorn.

"You can travel alone from now on, dust scum," Dabali said.

"Take his stuff, take his pony. Let him walk!"

Ambro lunged onto the balls of his feet and grabbed at his boots and his tunic of green Barbari silk where they lay on the sand, but the men tore them away. He ran toward his pony, tethered among the hohoba shrubs, but feet thudded behind him and the weight of a torso knocked him to the ground. Air whooshed from his lungs and dark spots danced before his eyes. His diaphragm filled with a huge pain that swallowed him into itself. He writhed on the ground, struggling for breath, as rope bit savagely into his wrists and ankles, tying them together.

He lay still as the men moved away, his cheek against the hot sand. Feet tramped to and fro in his line of vision, at first bare, but then booted. Ponies' legs shifted and stamped. The ends of reins and ropes swung to and fro. Boots sprang upward as the men mounted the ponies.

"Lord Tafari will hear of this! He will send you into the gutters!" Ambro cried defiantly.

Dabali laughed with contempt. "It will be a long time before anyone hears anything from you!"

"Cut the ropes."

Bohra's boots moved closer; Ambro could smell the water of the pool on the man's arms as they reached down with a knife. The tip of the blade swung menacingly, mockingly, before Ambro's face and then was removed; there was a tug as the ropes were cut and fell slack. Ambro thrashed, loosening their coils and hearing the hoof beats of ponies quickening into a trot. He yanked the last clinging strand of rope from his ankles and began to run after the soldiers as they surged up the far side of the hollow toward the open sky and the rolling land that lay beyond.

"Bring back my pony! You have no right to him!" Ambro yelled, panting as he struggled up through shifting sand and loose rock that fractured into thin shining sheets, but the men kicked the ponies into a canter. Ambro doubled his fists and ran harder, heat and rage and grief surging through him so that he felt like a shimmering thing, a mirage of a boy struggling toward a place he never reached. His bare webbed toes gripped at the sand, speeding him upward, but the ponies were already too far ahead when he first began to run. He knew, but would not yet admit, that he had no hope of catching up to them. They topped the rise of land and broke into a gallop. Ambro stood and watched them dwindle away, his chest heaving. The soldier's red capes billowed behind them in the rising Ismata; the peaks of their burnished leather helmets shone like tiny eyes in the light; they balanced perfectly to the rhythm of the ponies' running. Ambro's own pony raced beside them on a lead rope; the stirrups on its saddles swung emptily. Smaller and smaller they dwindled into the blinding blue distance, the tattoo of hoof beats and the shouts of the men fading into silence.

For a long time Ambro remained standing on the hilltop, staring south after them. Tears prickled in his eyes but he willed them not to fall. Offal of jackals, he thought. Hyenas. Cuttle fish. High tide scum. But behind these names that he hurled into the listening desert, he was aware of his memories of the men's faces as they had joked with him along their journey; a sense of loss gnawed at his anger because their camaraderie was broken and their rough friendship withdrawn. He would miss them, cuttle fish though they might be; miss their long legs clamped around sturdy ponies, their wind burned faces, their easy laconic acceptance of danger and their readiness for adventure.

At last he became aware of himself and his predicament, and of how tiny and alone he was in the vast silence. He swiveled on his heels, searching the face of the land with his spyglass that he'd pulled out from a small cloth bag still slung at his waist. Everything lay empty, silent, unmoving. In every direction, heat shimmered in waves and rocks threw back blinding reflections of the light. Cacti and jobi shrank inward, preserving the remnants of moisture in their cores, enduring the height of the summer.

Ambro trudged back down to the pool to see if the men had left him anything at all, and found only a full water flask lying beneath the hohoba bushes, amongst the trampled sand. There was no food left for him, and his silk robe and boots were gone. At least I still have my flute, he thought, and the earrings that Lady Tafari gave me; it was fortunate these were in my cloth bag with my spyglass. And, he realized, I am still wearing my golden bracelets which must be worth something.

Considering, he continued to stare around. The marks of his fight were clear; the sand sprayed and scuffled into lines and ridges. Ambro traced the marks with his bare toes; his horrible, disgusting toes. They had ruined his fine dreams. As he stared down at them, shaken by grief and anger, a plan formed in his mind.

I will head to the plateau lands, he thought. I will hide there in a canyon, by a river, and I will deal with my problem where no man can spy on me, where there will be time and space set apart for me. Later, I will search again for the desert horses and bring them home to Lord Tafari. No man will be able to say then that I am not worthy to be his nephew.

He strode to the edge of the pool and waded in; the water seemed deserted and forlorn now that the men had left with their banter and laughter. Ambro dove under the surface and pulled himself strongly through the pool's dark depths; water sang in his ears and fine bubbles trailed from his mouth. He broke upward into the bright air and felt the water shining on his cheekbones, along the golden mineral lines of his Hunting. He rolled over and began to swim to and fro across the width of the pond. It was easy swimming here; he had learned to swim in the swirling tidal currents of the pirati archipelago with its trailing weeds and coral reefs where bright fish darted and where surf boomed overhead, lifting swimmers in its surge and flow—a place where his webbed toes had made him swifter and more powerful than anyone else. There had been struggle and joyousness in such swimming but now, in the still eye of the pool, Ambro swam only to forget, to wash himself clean of the men's contempt, their sneering eyes that bored into his skull, their mocking voices that rang in his ears. He swam to wipe away his memory of that moment when his boot slipped over his heel and revealed his foot. He dove and plunged to wash away the words that clung to his skin: dust, scum, webbie—they had seeped into his pores, into his bones. He let the water take him into its depths, into its still darkness so that he might rise to the surface at last, cleansed, gasping for air.

Exhausted, he staggered onto the shore and lay down in the hohoba shade to wait for darkness and the moon. When jackals laughed along the horizon, he rose and picked up the flask, its leather sides tepid and water gurgling softly as he moved it. He slung it over his shoulder and began to walk up the eastern slope of the hollow, barefoot and wearing only the green silk leggings that he had worn previously under the Barbari tunic, and with the small knife that Lord Tafari had given him still strapped to his waist, and with his spyglass and his flute in a cloth bag. On the ridge, he cast around for tracks. The hooves of the ponies had obscured the tracks of the horses; all the animals and men seemed to have continued heading eastward. For the first time, it occurred to Ambro that the soldiers would hunt for the horses without him. The men will catch the horses and take them back to Lord Tafari, he thought despairingly. He'll give them each extra pay; they'll tell him about my toes. My toes!

His jaw clenched. He stopped uncertainly and stared eastward along the trampled line of tracks, then southward toward Safala. Was there any point in going to the plateau lands, if the men were going to catch the horses? What of his plan? For several minutes he stood undecided, then turned eastward and began following the tracks again. Moonlight illuminated his way, lying ghostly over rocks and scrub, and a steely resolve lent Ambro strength. Bravely, boldly, he strode across the desert as it rolled and heaved toward the wall of the plateau lands like the swell of deep ocean approaching a high shoreline of cliffs and rocks.

As he walked, he thought of the soldiers sleeping somewhere around a small fire and wondered whether anything disturbed their dreams, or if they thought of him with any regret. And he thought of Lord Tafari waiting for word of his Hunting, and of

Dabu arriving at the gates of Safala and slipping inconspicuously through the crowded streets. He thought of the tracker loping into his village compound with his yellow dog. Once or twice, the image of the girl crouched in Dune Dancer's flurry of mane slipped through his mind: her wide blue eyes, her dark high cheeks lined with blue paste. He wondered if Mia was safe and happy, with food in her belly, in some market plaza.

We are all scattered over the land like spilled beads, he thought. There is no sense to the patterns we make. His feet felt suddenly heavy and slow; sand dragged at them. Then he shook his head and focused again on the moment, on the broken tracks like a line that was reeling him in, on the scrape of rock against rock, and the sharp scratch of thorns against his arms.

Hour after hour he strode on boldly, not faltering even when a kiffa roared far off in the darkness and the high cackles of hyenas sounded to the north. Occasionally, he allowed himself a tiny sip from the flask; the water tasted like rocks and sand. The moon set behind his back, and his long shadow wavered eastward at his feet. His hair lifted and stirred in the breath of the Ismata as it poured toward him from the mysterious, far off Moon Mountains and he wondered about the panthers and vines and secret waterfalls and the trackless slopes of that distant place. The suspended crest of the plateau lands loomed higher before him; dawn seeped over them in a wash of pale grey that changed imperceptibly to pink.

Fatigue dragged at Ambro, and again he felt his resolve faltering. Was his plan so wise? Perhaps he should turn back, find his way to Jaffa, buy himself another pair of rope soled shoes and embark on a ship for Verde. Or Lontano or Angoli or Mombasso. It didn't matter where he went. He would forget about the Kiffa-walkers, the lost father he might never trace, the hope of a lineage and a family. He would be a wanderer across the oceans of the world, his toes hidden in his shoes, his face pressed into the wind.

A shred of hope and longing struggled weakly with his faltering courage. He remembered his promise to avenge Lord Tafari; remembered the moment when he had first climbed into the lord's chariot and felt the splendor of being a Kiffa-walker with a billow-ing silk robe and a sense of certainty and purpose.

Wearily he dragged himself into a jumble of rocks, his weakening resolve and his thin thread of hope tangled within him. He needed something to spur him on in his intended purpose, and he thought of the kiffa's roar that he'd heard in the night. If I could just see it again, he thought, I'd be brave enough to carry out my plan.

Perching on a flat rock and taking out his flute from his cloth bag, he began to play the song of the desert that is high and pure, filled with wind and space and loneliness. He played his anguish and grief, coaxing the animals in close. A lizard ran over his bare ankle and rested with its toes gripping the hem of his silk leggings. A spotted desert cat crept forward on its belly and crouched beneath a jobi shrub, its eyes narrowed to green slits. A vulture spiraled from the sky and strutted around, its wattles glowing pink. A blue and red snake slithered across the sand and coiled by Ambro's webbed toes; he did not move them so much as an inch. A jackal slunk into the circle of animals and listened to the flute with its head cocked and its mouth open to reveal pointed teeth.

On and on Ambro played, but the kiffa didn't appear.

At last, Ambro laid the flute in his lap and the animals drifted away into the sand and the sky. I will have to continue without the kiffa's blessing, Ambro thought. Maybe it was too far off to hear my flute. Maybe this too is a test of my courage; maybe I am meant to struggle alone. He rose to his feet, ignoring the stirrings of doubt in his heart, and toiled on toward the plateau, toward the line of blue shadows at its base, with the sun dazzling his eyes and heat burning into his bare back.

In the late afternoon, he rested in a corda grove, in a patch of ramba grass that released its distinctive peppery odor as he crushed it beneath his body. The thin, twisting trunks of the trees cast waver-ing shadows across him; for two hours he slept and then he rose again, swigged water from the flask, and continued to follow the tracks of the ponies. It was dusk when he came in amongst the first rocks jumbled at the base of the cliffs. Abruptly, he lost the tracks.

He cast about, left, right, backward—and found a place where the ponies had milled around. He imagined the soldiers arguing together. Of the horses' tracks there was no sign—both Ambro and the soldiers had lost them. Doggedly, Ambro searched but found only the tracks of three ponies heading south; then the tracks of another pony zigzagging to and fro along the edge of the cliff. Two men had decided to leave for Safala but the third still searched for the desert horses, Ambro thought. He trailed the tracks of the single pony for an hour or more, until finally it too turned southward and disappeared into the desert.

I am alone, Ambro thought, and didn't know whether he felt relief or sadness.

Despondently, he wandered into the mouth of a narrow canyon. The air grew cooler as he continued farther in, below the golden cliffs, where grasses starred with white flowers grew underfoot. He came to the bed of a stream but it lay dry and empty, and he hefted the flask anxiously in one hand and felt its lightness.

Darkness fell suddenly, the ribbon of sky dimming overhead, and he built a small fire from sticks washed downstream and left to bleach in the dry riverbed. His stomach growled and his head felt light with hunger and fatigue. The flames flared dizzily in his vision.

Later, I will find food, he promised himself. I will look for nub nubs to dig up. But first: my task, my plan. This is more important now than the horses, or than the stories the soldiers are carrying south. My plan is all that matters now.

Then he drew his knife from its sheath and held the small glittering blade into the flames to clean it. He spread the toes of his left foot; the webs between each one shone pale and semi-translucent, a rosy pink in the firelight. Firmly, deliberately, his lower lip caught between his teeth, he began to cut out the web from between the two smallest toes on his left foot. The sharp blade sliced cleanly through his flesh. Blood welled around it, dripping on the rounded pebbles strewn by the river in spring flood.

The scrap of skin dropped to the ground like the limp, furled petal of a dying flower.

Pain and a black horror flooded Ambro. His head swam.

I am not afraid, he told himself. I am a Kiffa, and I am not afraid.

Yet horror crawled up his neck, seized his heart and bludgeoned it against his ribs, darkened his eyes. He blinked, waited for his vision to clear, and began to cut the web from between the two smallest toes on his right foot. Again, blood dripped onto pebbles. The fire crackled and snapped, flaring with a strange blue light.

Ambro dropped the web onto the sand and stared at his hand on the hilt of the knife; watched a trickle of blood run from his fingers down his wrist and amongst the golden hairs on his forearm.

The blue eyes of the girl in the temple flickered across his vision, reflecting his terror. He tried to blot it out with the memory of the kiffa that had come to the sound of his flute when he sat by Lord Tafari's fire. How powerful its elegant frame had been; how confident the gaze of its tawny eyes!

I can do this, Ambro thought. I am not afraid. The kiffa is with me.

Yet his grasp slackened on the knife and it slipped to the ground with scarcely a sound. Ambro bowed his head over his feet, feeling their throbbing pain run up his legs so that they shook, feeling it knot in his throat so that it constricted around his breath.

Pain does not deter me, he thought.

But something larger than pain seemed alive in the night; a terrible darkness into which he was falling, losing himself, forgetting the joy he had felt in Verde when the sun rose over the salt pines and the dolphins leapt through the waves, forgetting the slippery chuckle of the water against his body when he swam to the reefs; forgetting the laughter of the sea urchins around beach fires as planets winked into yellow light overhead. He was losing the joy he had felt in the infinity and heat of the desert; the mysterious dark beauty of his mother's smile; the songs that Mia had taught him and the moments he'd danced to her hurdy-gurdy with his entire being awake with joy.

With every dark drop that fell from his mutilated toes to wet the pebbles, he was losing himself.

"No!" he cried aloud. "I cannot!"

Sobs shook him. This is the final failure, the final loss, he thought. I cannot be a Kiffa, I cannot return to Lord Tafari. I will never ride a desert horse, I will never travel with a doda caravan seeking adventure across the sea of sand. I renounce my father, whoever he was. I leave his name to oblivion.

I have failed.

There is nothing for me now.

Spent, shaken, exhausted, he slid the knife back into the sheath without cleaning the blade, and curled up beside the fire, forgetful of his hunger, forgetful of the pain still coursing up his legs. He pulled his knees against his ribs and plunged into the deep sleep of total exhaustion.

At dawn, he woke groggily. The fire was a small pile of ash. The white starry flowers on the grasses were opening as the first light touched them. Memory and pain throbbed through him; a desperate loneliness filled his mind. He pulled his flute from the cloth bag at his waist and ran his fingertip along the faded golden lettering: Ambro d'Monti. My namesake, he thought. A man far away, in another time, in another land. A man who made things of beauty. Though he never knew of me and we will never meet, I am unworthy of him. What name is left to me?

He put his lips to the flute and began to play a thread of sound, a weak mournful tune in a minor key.

The furry brown animal hopped falteringly, hesitantly, out from the bushes and across the pebbles of the river bank. It was a round animal with a soft fine coat and upright ears that glowed translucent pink in the rising sun; it was larger than any rabbit that Ambro had ever seen in Verde. Its face was long and shy, and it had huge dark eyes above extraordinary whiskers that fanned outward in delicate drooping lines and were so long that their tips almost brushed the shingle. Slowly it came closer to Ambro and he saw that it favored one large hind foot, limping slightly. As it came closer still, he saw there was a deep cut across the side of the foot, extending into the fur of the sole. He waited until the animal was close enough to touch, its whiskers grazing the top of his knees, and then he laid down the flute with slow caution and spoke softly to the creature. With the dark, blood stained blade of his knife, he cut a strip of cloth from the hem of his leggings, and poured a little of the last water in his flask onto the cloth. Gently he lifted the animal's foot and wiped the wound clean before binding it with a second strip of cloth. When he had finished, the animal gazed at him intently with kindness in its eyes before it hopped clumsily away into the bushes again, as silently as it had arrived.

The sun was higher now, beating onto Ambro's exposed head. He thought again of nub nubs, and gazed vaguely around at the surrounding riverbank but saw no plants that he recognized; a stupor of heat and fatigue throbbed in his head. He crawled to the edge of the bushes and curled up again on his side.

Presently, the animals came shyly and silently from the clumps of grass that grew thickly against the canyon walls, beneath little trees that gripped the rocks with thin twisted roots. Their soft brown coats blended into the rocks and the drying grasses. They gathered around Ambro in a semi-circle; through half-closed eyes, he observed that they were even larger than the wounded one that he had helped earlier that morning and he assumed that it had been a young one. These adults had the same huge dark eyes and extraordinary whiskers with tips almost brushing the ground. They held their small front paws at belly level as they sat up on their strong hind feet. With a kind courteous attention they watched Ambro and the pain gripping him abated somewhat under their gentle scrutiny.

His head began to swim and the animals slipped in and out of focus. He closed his eyes; the memory of his shame and outcast state welled up again and his belly growled with hunger and grief. After a long while of heat and silence, he opened his eyes to find that the animals had slipped away and he was once more completely alone. Dry sobs shook him.

Something soft as Mombasso velvet nudged his face. He opened his eyes and stared at the face of a new animal. Its short fur was as purple as a perfectly ripe aubergine and patterned with brown markings; its soft eyes were fringed with curling purple lashes, and small knobs of horns grew from its forehead and were covered in purple velvet. Ambro's eye traveled onward, seeing a long neck and impossibly long spindly legs with knobby knees. The entire animal towered over him, as strange as a dream.

It's a magrazzi, he thought in amazement. Once, in Verde, he'd been told about these creatures by a pirati boy called Giovanni who claimed he'd ridden one imported from Terre, which was the creatures' indigenous land.

Gently the magrazzi nudged his face again, and he noticed that beyond it, the small round animals with the huge clumps of whiskers had gathered. He rolled over and sat up, his head swimming, and a sharp pain shot up his legs from his cut toes. The magrazzi knelt beside him, folding its delicate legs and lowering its long neck in a graceful curve. It pressed against Ambro and he knew that it wanted him to climb onto its back. He stared at the long spine, too tired to think clearly

Why did it want him on its back? Could he trust it? Why had the whiskered animals returned to watch?

Then the thought of their eyes, filled with calm and gentleness, reassured him and he grasped a handful of purple mane and pulled himself, breathless with the effort, onto the magrazzi's back. When he was astride, it rose swaying to its feet; the ground fell away below so that Ambro was looking down on the tops of the whiskered animals' heads. The magrazzi began to pick its way out of the canyon's mouth, its cleft hooves swinging between shrubs with easy confidence. The whiskered animals bounded alongside, their ears glowing translucent pink when the sun shone through them.

At the mouth of the canyon, the animals began to climb up to the plateau, following a route that they seemed to know of but that Ambro couldn't see. He clung to the magrazzi's mane; often his eyes closed against the harsh glare and he saw nothing, simply swayed with the creature's long stride and let his mind go blank. Higher and higher they climbed to the top of the plateau, where

Ambro opened his eyes to see acres of grass that swayed in the Ismata's cool breath, and dotted with spreading trees that cast huge circles of shade and in whose branches bright birds fluttered and warbled. Now the magrazzi began to trot, its long purple legs sweeping through the green waves of grass, its head bobbing. Lost, confused, amazed, Ambro watched the landscape pass like a dream, it brightness and airy space seeping into his dark thoughts.

All day the animals moved across the plateau, skirting the lips of deep canyons in which Ambro heard the sound of water running and the chorus of birds. At dusk, they began to descend into one such canyon, again following some route that was invisible to Ambro but that they followed with sure footed certainty, dodging rocks and skirting crevices to arrive at the base of the cliff, on the banks of a rushing river that gleamed with a silky sheen in the last light. The magrazzi kneeled and Ambro slid from its back to stagger to the water. When his legs buckled, he fell forward, flinging his arms out to save himself. Then he scooped water into his mouth and felt its sweet coldness flood his senses and run over his swollen tongue and down his parched throat. He splashed water onto his face, and felt it wash away his dizziness. He flung it over his bare shoulders and it cooled the heat of his sunburn. Kneeling back into the flowers and patches of fragrant mint he stared around, looking for something to eat and wondering what would happen next.

The furry animals loped in close and touched his face with their quivering whiskers and their flat noses; a sensation as delicate and brief as the touch of butterfly wings. The magrazzi bent its long purple legs again, and Ambro mounted to be carried deeper and deeper into the canyon with sheer cliffs of dry golden rock soaring on each side and the voice of the river growing louder. Willows leaned over the water, their trailing leaves creating ripples. The shoreline of the river narrowed until the animals followed a thin thread of bank and passed beneath the trees that clung to the cliff face and reached out with twisting branches; their small tender leaves brushed across Ambro's bare back and their scent, tart like lemons, drifted into the still air.

Deeper and deeper the animals forged into the canyon, the land rising around now in high blue slopes that merged into the falling darkness and became indistinguishable.

Ambro dozed, his eyes drooping, his legs aching against the magrazzi's ribcage, the pain throbbing still in his feet.

Suddenly the animals stopped and Ambro opened his eyes to see that their way was blocked by a set of massive doors. It was the first thing made by humans that he had seen for days, and its unexpected presence here in the heart of the plateau lands shocked him. He sat bolt upright on the magrazzi's back in amazement. The door completely filled the bank between the river's rushing water and the dark rise of the cliff. It was surrounded by a frame of great timbers of black wood that shone in the light of the rising moon with a dull gleam; they were so large than Ambro could not imagine how they had been moved here to this remote place and set upright. Or by what means they were fastened together. He had never seen timbers as mighty. The door itself appeared to be formed of two pieces of the same solid wood; they were of equal dimensions and met in the centre along a very thin dark line. There was no handle nor lock nor bolt anywhere upon the door that Ambro could see. He waited, wondering what would happen, and then the magrazzi again folded its long legs and Ambro slid off and began to limp toward the door. The round furry animals formed a circle before it, blocking his way, and then nudged him to the side of the path, against the base of the cliff, where they lay down amongst clumps of grass. Ambro lay down too and the animals cuddled in against him; he felt the silkiness of their fur and the tickle of their sweeping whiskers. The magrazzi bent its long neck and brushed its lips across his cheek, then turned and trotted away into the night, heading down river in the direction from which they had traveled.

In the morning, Ambro thought drowsily before he fell asleep, in the morning I will find a way to open the door and discover what lies beyond it.

CHAPTER FOURTEEN

Sunlight slid across Ambro's cheek and he awoke with a sneeze. The furry animals were grazing nearby amongst the riverbank grasses, and Ambro tried to rise and go down to drink. He discovered that he could only hobble for fiery red lines ran upward from his wounded toes and his feet throbbed with pain. Was the morning exceptionally hot, he wondered, shading his eyes, or was the heat of fever in him? He staggered to the river and bent to splash water over his face and cup it in his hands.

Then he limped over to the massive doors that had shone in the moonlight the previous night. He ran his hands over the dark wood; it had a short swirling grain and was as smooth as metal to the touch; worn, perhaps, by many years of wind and sun. Again Ambro searched for a handle or bolt but found none; instead, he noticed that the doors were carved with borders of flowers and animals—panthers, wombos, moon wrens, magrazzi, and the whiskered animals themselves—and with sickle moons and rayed suns. He pressed upon the doors with his palms but they did not move even a fraction. He shoved against them with his shoulders, ramming them with increasing force, but again no fraction of movement occurred. Baffled, he slumped against them as the throbbing in his feet spread into his chest, his shoulders, his head.

The whiskered animals moved toward the doors and sat before it, gazing at the towering surfaces. Their eyes held an intent, faraway look and their ears stood straight up. It was as though, Ambro thought, they were listening to something that lay beyond the doors. Suddenly, he felt movement beneath his shoulders and in shock he stepped back to watch as the doors, in utter silence, swung wide open of their own volition. Awestruck, he stared at them but the whiskered animals bounded through and paused to look back at him; he gathered his courage and followed them under the hard bar of shadow that lay beneath the massive framework high overhead. The doors swung shut as mysteriously as they had opened and although Ambro looked for any person or animal that might have opened them from the inside, or for any mechanism or handle, he again saw nothing.

Shaking his head in perplexity, he turned to hobble after the whiskered animals that alternately bounded ahead or stopped to nibble at leaves and grasses. His vision danced with hunger, and fever throbbed in his head. With each step that he took, pain shot through his feet and up into his legs and lower back. Stumbling, lightheaded, he followed the animals deeper into the canyon.

Despite his wretched state, he recognized that it was the most beautiful place that he had ever seen. On each side, high above the river and the shady path that Ambro followed, the cliffs soared five hundred feet into blue sky, their dry golden strata reflecting the heat, their crevices sprouting twisted trees with delicate fans of lemon-scented foliage. The river, its water clear as crystal and a bright aqua green, tumbled rambunctiously over shining amber rocks in flurries of white water, or swirled slowly in deep mysterious pools beneath the banks. Fish hung motionless in the eddying currents or flickered away beneath the overhanging banks, and a gauzy mist rose from the water's surface into the perfectly still air. Huge trees with pale green bark mottled with orange, and with massive gnarled trunks, flanked the river and spread thick horizontal limbs over both the path that Ambro followed and the water itself; they were so mighty, and each one was so distinctive, that Ambro felt awed by their presences. Here and there, he imagined, wrinkled faces watched his halting progress from among the swirls and gnarls of the trunks. The leaves of the trees were a pure tender green, so dazzling that they flickered and burned like fire amongst the branches. In the mottled sunlight beneath the ancient trees grew smaller bushes, flowering vines, pink orchids, waist-high ferns with a downy fuzz upon their stems and a spicy-sweet fragrance, pungent herbs with narrow grey leaves, and soft green grass with blue flowers as tiny as raindrops; all the foliage shone and sparkled in the light, and dew licked Ambro's bare feet. The air was cool and pure, filled with the fragrance from blossoming trees that swayed in white clouds, and rippling with bird song. Ambro sucked the air greedily into his burning lungs.

I have entered an enchanted place, he thought. And it was strong magic that opened the doors. He moved forward as though in a dream, the canyon's essence of power and beauty stronger even than his feverish pain.

As the sun rose higher, the dew dried on the grasses; the mist evaporated and the river ran silkily between the banks. Now the canyon grew steeper, and Ambro's breath came in short gasps. Sweat sprang out on his forehead and back; his vision blurred and heat seemed to roar through his head like a fire and consume his thoughts. The furry animals came in close around him and nudged him on gently with their noses against his legs and dangling hands, for they were as tall as his knees. He staggered between them, around rocks and up steep stretches where the path became thin and tortuous. A dull roaring filled his ears.

At last, the path flattened out and Ambro saw before him a steep cliff blocking their way and a high plume of waterfall; its roar was louder here, and it fell into a swirling pool between yellow rocks. Too tired to proceed farther, and thinking that this was the end of the path, he watched as the animals skirted the pool and then, to his astonishment, they scrambled along a ledge that led toward the falls, and disappeared into its rush of white water. After a few minutes, his curiosity stronger than his fatigue, and with the very last of his strength flaring in him, he scrambled along the same ledge. The rocks grew slippery and wet beneath his feet; the water's roar filled his ears and its spray coated him with a fine mist. He edged in behind the wall of water to discover a high, dim tunnel of dry rock. Staring down it, he saw that it opened into a high chamber, like a cave, but dry and lit brightly by sunlight entering from some aperture overhead in the rocks, and he hobbled toward it and leaned, his head swimming, against the rocks at the entrance.

The smooth, striated walls of the space—golden and pink and terra cotta—were decorated in ochre paint with running horses and singing birds and magrazzi, with vines and leaves and flowers, with flying cranes and rayed suns and sickle moons, with human hand prints. Beneath the paintings, the walls were lined with wide rock ledges and on these the whiskered animals were stretched out with their pale stomach hair showing, or were curled asleep in round nests woven of dried grasses. Higher on the walls, small golden birds, barred with pink, crooned in crevices.

"Welcome, traveler." The voice was deep and resonant; its music seemed to fill the airy, golden space and lap against the stone walls. A huge woman in a green gown sat behind a tiny fire that gave off only a pale glow, a translucent shimmer of heat, in the sunlight of the cave. River pearls hung from her ears and circled her forehead, and a multitude of twining strands hung from her neck along with precious stones of amber and aquamarine, carved in the shapes of leaves and stars.

The woman's impressive presence filled the cave; Ambro felt the strength of her magic encircle him; in its presence he was awestruck and stood perfectly still, simply looking. Her strong, plump arms were folded across the rolling folds of her massive body. In her dark face, her black eyes glinted unfathomably with ancient knowledge. Though he looked long into her eyes and at the generous curves of her face, Ambro could not say whether she was young or old; her face seemed to change as the light from sun and fire moved across it for at moments it appeared as smooth as the face of a girl but at others it was hollowed and creased with years. And, Ambro noticed, her loose flowing gown and the cape hanging from her shoulders also changed as the light moved across them; swirls like water or clouds appeared and disappeared; shapes like fish or birds flickered. There were moments when Ambro thought he glimpsed leaves or flowers in the fabric but then they too were lost to view as the color transmuted from tender green to silvery blue to a tawny orange like the rocks of the cave walls.

The woman herself did not stir beneath Ambro's searching gaze; she seemed as immovable and permanent as the mighty spreading trees that Ambro had walked beneath; her power seemed to pour and flow over Ambro like the river; her eyes glinted like starry flowers or dew on grasses. He sensed that from her flowed the canyon's enchanted beauty; and that she and the place were one indivisible whole.

He bent his head, pounding with fever, and kneeled before her.

"Help me," he said although he had not planned to say this.

The woman rose with a graceful sway. Her smooth brown toes padded silently across the floor. When she laid her palm upon his forehead, he felt it drawing away pain. She led him to a bed of sweet grass against the wall of the cave, and as he lay there she gathered leaves from the bundles of herbs that hung overhead; crushed, they released a swirling medley of odors into the cave. She stirred them over the fire in a small pot, and spread the warm paste upon Ambro's toes.

"Who are you?" he asked faintly.

"I am the mugwawa, the Keeper of Stories."

"Are you a Kiffa or a Wanderer? Have you always lived here?"

"I am neither Kiffa nor Wanderer, I am the mugwawa, and there has always been a mugwawa living in this place. Only the desperate of heart, and those with a high purpose, find this place, and hear the stories that we tell."

Ambro subsided into the heavy swells of his pain and fever, and fell into a restless sleep. For a time out of time he tossed and turned on the sweet grass. Sometimes when he opened his eyes it was night and the mugwawa's fire glowed soft orange, comforting and constant, in the cave's darkness and he saw the woman's shape, solid as a mountain, silhouetted against the glow as she sat by him throughout the night. The waterfall at the mouth of the tunnel filled the cave with a soft roar that soothed Ambro back to sleep. At other times, he awoke to see sunlight sliding across the walls, dappled and dancing, illuminating the flying cranes, the human hands and running horses painted there in haphazard fashion. The images swung and wavered in his feverish vision, and the pain from his feet roared within his chest. He slept again; woke; slept. The mugwawa's face hung over him, sometimes worn with time, creased and granular as the surrounding cliffs, but at other times as fresh and smooth as washed river stones; her gown swirled and shimmered with changing colors and patterns, her cape quivered with constellations. Her river pearls hung above him like drops of rain; her leaves of precious stones shook as though wind passed through them. He fell into the unfathomable depths of her dark eyes; abandoned himself into the cool touch of her palms that sent a tingle of power running through him, and to the smooth feel of the paste being spread upon his toes, and the taste of the vegetable broths that she fed him with a wooden spoon. The whiskered animals lay in their nests and chuckled to each other in bubbling voices, and the golden birds peeped in their crevices.

At last, one morning, Ambro awoke to feel coolness and stillness in his body, and knew that the fever had passed. He struggled to sit up, weakness shaking in him, and saw that the red streaks coming from his feet had disappeared and that the wounds between his toes were healing, growing new pink skin, growing—webs again! He looked at them in disbelief and frustration. No matter what I try, he thought, my plans are thwarted.

"Ambro d'Monti," the mugwawa said in her deep musical voice that resonated in the cave and became one with the roar of the river falling down the cliff into the magic canyon.

"How do you know my name?'

"The ponies knew it, and the rock-roses brought news of your coming across the desert. The hareenas told me that they found a boy by a dry river bed, playing with a small knife as sharp as the claw of a kiffa. They saw that this boy had a heart containing both kindness and music, although his face was filled with grief, and they fetched a magrazzi from the high plateau and asked permission to bring the boy into my canyon."

"You opened the doors for me."

The mugwawa inclined her head, the waving tresses of her dark hair filled with tiny plaits, with pearls and beads, with blue and golden feathers. Cranes flew across the dusky purple shoulders of her cape and vanished into a shimmer of orange patterned with handprints.

"I have restored your loss," she said, and Ambro stared again at his toes and the new webs growing there.

"Thank you," he said in a low voice and was startled when a chuckle as deep and musical as bells undulated the swelling stomach and great breasts of the mugwawa. "You do not know what you thank me for, you are not sure whether or not you even feel grateful. But I have given you that for which you asked."

Ambro remembered his plea for help when he arrived in the cave, wracked with grief and fever, and he flushed with shame.

"I do thank you," he said sincerely, "for your healing—even though it has helped to bring my previous plan to nought." Biting his lip, he tilted his chin and stared unflinchingly at the mugwawa, his gratitude and his frustration struggling against each other.

Magrazzi drifted across the mugwawa's gown, through a green bright as plateau grass, and disappeared as the fabric changed to black. The mugwawa's face became craggy and furrowed; her impenetrable eyes looked consideringly at Ambro, and he remembered the horror of that night beside the fire when he had tried to change his toes; his skin crawled with the memory of that deep abyss of blackness he had sensed himself teetering along the edge of.

Then light slid across the mugwawa's shoulders and her grown changed to bright blue where fish flickered. The light touched her cheeks and Ambro saw them plump and rounded with smooth curves of flesh, and the memory of the canyon's fragrant beauty filled his mind and removed his horror.

"Although your heart is torn in different directions, I think that I do not need to ask for your knife," she said.

"No," he agreed fervently.

"And for what story are you seeking, young Ambro; what story impels you across Terre's empty quarter to the mugwawa's cave?"

"I don't know. I don't think I am seeking a story."

"It is always a story that brings travelers to my cave."

The mugwawa turned to the small ashy heap of her fire and looked intently at it; it flared up in orange flame and sticks crackled in its heart, although a moment before Ambro had seen no sticks, only burned embers. The mugwawa lifted a pot onto the fire and held her hands over it; although Ambro had seen nothing in them, tiny yams and wild leeks and twisted roots whose names he didn't know fell from them into the pot. Presently, it began to steam and release a fine aroma. Ambro's mouth watered.

When the mugwawa turned back to him, sunlight flowed across her waving hair; her gown changed to yellow and sprays of flowers sprang up in its folds. "Think," she commanded him. "You must know what story it is that you seek, for I will only give you the story that you most desire or that you need most dreadfully."

Ambro shrugged; he still felt weak and his thoughts seemed to eddy slowly through his mind. "I was not searching for a story in the empty quarter. I was tracking desert horses that a Wanderer bandit had stolen from Lord Tafari, a Kiffa-walker."

"And what story lay in the tracks of these horses?" asked the mugwawa, and the feathers in her hair changed to green and orange, and finches flew across her cape.

"I don't know about stories in their tracks. They were noble horses; they bore the marks of the kiffa. And—there was a story!"

He suddenly recalled it with delight for it seemed to belong to a faraway time, when he had been filled with innocence and hope, crossing the country from Jaffa in the lord's swaying chariot and falling giddily in love with the desert and with his destiny as a Kiffa-walker. "There was a story that the lord told me about the horses, how the first horse had been chased by the first kiffa and clawed for its pride, and how the claw marks are born by every horse in the desert to remind them that the kiffa is king."

The mugwawa turned to her fire and lifted off the pot to pour the contents into a bowl which she handed to Ambro. He tilted it to his mouth and slurped greedily at the broth, burning his tongue in his haste.

"An old story, that of first kiffa and first horse, very old," the mugwawa said, her face worn into inscrutable lines, as timeless as the rocks on the cave walls. "But a story twisted in the retelling, Ambro. For what you heard was a Kiffa-walker version and not the true telling of it, not the telling of it kept safe under the mugwawas' tongues for many centuries of sand and rock, of river and cloud. Listen to this story, young Ambro, for it is the story that has driven you to me in desperate need—and I will only tell it once. This is the true telling of the story of first kiffa and first horse."

Ambro drained the contents of the broth and set it on the floor, then folded his legs under him and prepared to listen to the mugwawa's story. Memories of Lord Tafari's fine golden chariot and tall elegant figure, of his mighty doda caravan and silky billowing robes floated through Ambro's mind; he did not see how the mugwawa could tell this story any better than had the lord.

Against the mysterious indigo of the mugwawa's gown, her river pearls glowed with a strange pale light and those twined around her forehead gleamed against her smooth dark skin. It seemed to Ambro that a shimmer of blue light surrounded her massive form and that he felt her power tingle on the surface of his skin. Moon wrens and sickle moons shone on her cape, and her deep eyes glowed so that Ambro felt as though they were pulling him in, transporting him through time and space until he had left himself many eons behind, until he had flown through strata of pink and golden rock and many risings of sun and moon to arrive at the first dawn that ever sent light over the continent of Terre.

"This is a tale of the far-off days, when the kiffa and the horse and the other desert creatures had scarcely any form or shape, when they were not as they appear now, when they were weak and dusty creatures just beginning to be formed. In those days, there was a horse, which did not look much the way a horse looks today but more like a cloud of soft dust blowing in the wind. This horse, who was skittish and thirsty, came down to drink at a watering hole early in the morning, when the kiffa was there drinking. Now the kiffa did not look as he looks today either, but was a small thin creature, like the shadow of a thorn bush. The kiffa, disturbed as he drank, looked up to see the horse trotting closer kicking up sprays of sand in the morning sun. And because he was a proud creature, the kiffa snarled at the horse, "You must wait your fill. I am the king here, and no animal may drink in the mornings before I do." The horse tossed her head playfully, and rolled her wild eyes haughtily. "I am as much a child of the desert as you," she said. "I shall drink whenever I am thirsty."

"Hearing these words, the kiffa sprang at the horse to drive her away and teach her a lesson. So it began. The kiffa chased the horse through morning's calm, through afternoon's deep heat, through evening's lilac shadows. He chased the horse up the sides of sand dunes and over rippled plains; he chased her amongst jumbles of rocks and past salt-licks and through scattering antelope. He twisted after the horse amongst the tough trunks of corda trees, and galloped across cakes of cracked mud, and splashed through water holes and mirages of water holes and the smell of minerals. The chase continued through the desert for many, many days—"

"But I know this story," Ambro interrupted with rash impetuosity. "It is as Lord Tafari told it to me."

Swirling dark shapes, menacing and formless as storm clouds, rushed across the mugwawa's gown and the aura of blue light around her crackled and fizzed. Her eyes and her river pearls glowed with an eerie light. Ambro clamped his tongue between his teeth and shrank down into himself with his heart thudding.

"This is the true telling, before the Kiffa-walkers twisted it for their own ends," the mugwawa said, and her voice rolled and echoed in the cave louder than the sound of the waterfall. The fire flared and leaped with strange blue flames and their light shivered over the cave walls. "Listen, young Ambro, though you be as bold and impetuous as a kiffa, for this is the story that you have traveled in search of, though you did not recognize its calling."

Ambro nodded meekly and the mugwawa continued with the story.

"As they ran, the kiffa became burnished by the sun and glowed red as the desert rock. His thin legs thickened and strengthened and he grew splendid paws that ran silently across dunes. His teeth grew longer, sharpening themselves on his anger and his hunger. His skinny chest swelled around his new and mighty lungs as he sucked in air. Yet always the horse ran just ahead, out of reach.

"So the chase continued. The kiffa chased the horse over brittle salt pans and over sheets of polished amber, through sword grass and groves of bay trees, through sunrise and sunset. As she ran, the horse's legs stretched longer and more elegant; they ate up the horizon. Her hooves became tough and durable; they pounded over sand and mineral pan, and filled the air with their rhythm; the first drumbeat of the desert. Her eyes held the light of the moon and grew dark and mysterious, and her tail floated on the wind and became silky as a banner.

"At last, with a mighty spring, the kiffa flung himself off a rock and onto the horse. In that moment he was assured of success for his leap was straight and true; he anticipated the horse staggering and falling beneath him. But at that very moment, when victory sang in his ears, a brilliant silver light dazzled his eyes so that he was blinded and faltered in midair. Instead of landing on top of the horse and throwing her to the sand, he fell short and only the tips of his claws raked across the horse's hind quarters; in that moment the kiffa was filled with shame and despair for he had chased the horse so far in order to show her that he was king in the desert.

"Then a voice spoke from the midst of the silver light, and the kiffa and the horse paused, flanks trembling, chests heaving, and looked up to see Luna the moon goddess standing before them.

"'My children, she said, you are both magnificent; both fleet of foot and wild with freedom, and you must live together in the desert in peace. You, horse, will bear through all generations the mark of the kiffa's claws, that you might remember he is your brother and must be treated respectfully. But I will give to you another mark also.' Then she kissed the palm of her hand and placed it upon the horse's forehead, and where her hand had touched the horse there appeared the mark of a sickle moon. 'You will bear this mark for all generations. And you, kiffa, when you look upon the moon mark, will remember that the horse has been touched by the goddess, and that she is your sister and must be treated with respect. In the desert, you shall both be noble and free.'

"And so, Ambro, from that day to this, the desert horses are striped on their hindquarters with the marks of the kiffa's claws, whether their coats be ivory or amber, cinnamon or lilac gray. And every desert horse bears, on its forehead, the pattern of a crescent moon. And when the horses run through the desert, the kiffas watch respectfully from their rocks and do not give chase, but when the kiffas roar at the water holes, the horses wait respectfully for their turn to drink."

Ambro listened with eyes half closed as the mugwawa's voice reverberated through his very bones, through the timeless space in which her story existed and to which he had been transported. Gradually he became aware of his present surroundings, of the hareenas rustling in their grass, smoothing their exuberant whiskers with their tiny forepaws, and of the empty bowl lying at his feet.

"But what does the story mean?" he asked, as the echoes of her voice died into the silence of the cave that was not silence, but a warm bright space filled with water's roar and fire's crackle.

"I tell only the stories in their true telling; it is for the listener to find the meaning they have come seeking."

The mugwawa's gown swam with silvery shades filled with white clouds and fluttering moths, and her eyes seemed to float in pools of pale light. Her skin looked washed and fine grained; it gleamed beneath her headband of river pearls and Ambro had to look away, his eyes dazzled with her strange and sudden beauty. When he looked back, she was herself again, neither young nor old, but simply there like a stone or a mountain, immutable and ancient.

"Perhaps the one who sleeps can tell you more about the desert horses that you hunt, though it was their *story* that you needed and that was your true Hunting," the mugwawa said, gesturing toward the ledges of rock around the cave's perimeter. Ambro glanced in that direction and noticed for the first time that a person lay along one ledge, in the shadows, amongst a huddle of sleeping hareenas. Intrigued, he rose and crossed the cave on shaky legs, but was grateful to find that there was no pain in his feet or his new pink webs. He bent over the sleeping figure—then started back in shock.

"Here! Again!" he whispered, and the girl opened her brilliant eyes. Instantly, terror flooded her dusky face and she bolted upright, rigid with shock. The cowry shells swirled in her cloud of black hair, and her crumpled ochre tunic fell open over a grubby ivory top.

"You! Again!" she gasped.

"What are you doing here? Do you have the horses with you?"

"What do you know about horses?"

"I am tracking Sun Runner and Dune Dancer; they were stolen from Lord Tafari by a bandit and I am trying to return them to him. It is my Hunting."

The girl's face went blank, then horror filled it. In that instant, Ambro realized that she had not seen him in the fray at the base of Mount Lalibela, that when he had seen her silhouetted against the sky, her eyes had not been turned in his direction. But now he had given himself away.

"You were there? With the soldiers?" she asked.

He nodded uncertainly, feeling but not understanding the anguish that burned in her eyes.

"Where is Hasani? What have you done with him?"

"Hasani?"

"You took him captive!" she cried. "The soldiers pulled him from his horse."

"Oh, the bandit. They took him away to sell to slavers in Mandi."

She bent over as though he had hit her, and when she straightened a terrible light filled her face though her lips trembled.

"May the moon turn her dark face upon you," she cursed. "May the kiffa piss on your grave."

Tears streaked her cheeks and she rushed past him and down the dim tunnel to step onto the lip of rock that skirted the waterfall's rush. For a moment she hung against the white and blue streaked light, a graceful figure, and then she vanished from view. On their ledges, the hareenas sat very still, their paws folded and mournful expressions upon their long faces.

"What?" Ambro cried, turning away from them. "What have I done?"

"There are many balances that tremble," the mugwawa said enigmatically. "Many cuts that need to heal. Many stories that need untwisting." Her fire had died to a dusty glow and her gown had faded to a pale sandy color. Her face was lined and inscrutable, closed around her many stories.

Ambro stood uncertainly before her but she stared down over the folds of her belly and ignored him. After some time, he walked weakly down the tunnel and felt the rushing water spray its minty breath upon his face and wet him with its fine spray. "I will go and find her!" he called back to the mugwawa, and he sidled out along the ledge, trying to ignore the dizzying plunge of the water on one side.

In the canyon, birds sang with piercing sweetness amidst white blossoms. Balanced at the edge of the falls, Ambro stared over the treetops, scanned the golden cliffs and the banks of the aqua river, stared into patches of fern and flowering grasses. But though he squinted into the brightness and swung the eye of his spyglass around in all directions, he saw no sign anywhere of the girl from the temple in Safala.

CHAPTER FIFTEEN

NOLEENA LAY AMONG THE waist-high ferns, in the nest that she had built for herself beneath the spreading sycama trees, and waited for her thundering heart to quiet. Shock coursed through her.

That boy—that same boy who had talked to her father—was here! And, though she had not noticed him in the melee at the base of Mount Lalibela, it seemed he had also been there with the soldiers.

She had felt safe since coming to the mugwawa's canyon, as completely safe as she used to feel as a child, in the temple at the end of its twisting alley. When the desert horses had brought her to the mugwawa's mighty black doors, and they swung shut behind her, she felt as though the dangerous world that Terre had become was being closed out and she had been filled with relief. She wished to simply stay in the enchanted canyon, eating wild honey, sleeping on the rock ledges with the wise and gentle hareenas, wading in the river.

But now it seemed, she thought, that there was nowhere safe anymore, and no place of sanctuary. What was the boy doing here?

Was he hunting her, chasing her across the desert? Had he been following her ever since that night when he had invaded the temple and startled her from sleep beneath Luna's statue? But why?

Noleena laid her face onto her arms and wept. Leave me alone! she cried at the Kiffa-walker boy in her thoughts. Go away and leave this place—it is mine! You are a person who spoils everything! You have no right to be here with your Kiffa pride and your cruel ways!

Images of Hasani taken into slavery seared her imagination like red hot coals—ropes at his wrists, a whip lashing his back and laying skin open in painful weals, a burning brand imprinting the letter M onto his shoulders—along with images of him as she had known him: free and magnificent, riding through the desert with the blue marks of her Seeking decorating his cheekbones. She remembered the afternoon when they had swum in the hidden pool, how the water had sparkled as they flung it at each other, how his face had shone with laughter.

She lifted a finger and touched the corners of her lips.

Hasani, Hasani. Where are you now in this moment? she wondered. Are you alive or dead, your bones scattered in the sand? Her throat ached with loneliness, with longing for him.

"I warned my dear one to beware of wandering out so far, so far, so far away across the sea of sorrow."

The words rose into her mouth and broke there into pieces; she could not sing them. It was said that those taken captive by Kiffas were never given their freedom; were never seen again by those who loved them.

She had tried to return to find Hasani after the ambush at Mount Lalibela but the desert horses had carried her for many hours through the empty quarter's barren hills; though she tried to turn them, they wouldn't turn. They had carried her into the night. When at last they stopped to drink and rest, she had slid from Dune Dancer's back and begun to walk southward to Mount Lalibela. Then the horses blocked her path, shoved her with their shoulders, nipped her with their teeth. At last, as she persevered, Sun Runner had reared in front of her, towering up and up against the stars, his mane whipped by the Ismata into a stormy cloud. An imperious neigh rang from him; she saw the starlight fiercely shining in his eyes as he struck out at the night sky in warning. She had admitted defeat and slumped wearily in the sand to sleep. The next morning, the horses had carried her on, heading toward the blue crest of the plateau lands, swept with wind and swaying grasses, and to the mugwawa's cave.

And later, after meeting the mugwawa and resting for several days, Noleena had forced herself to attempt to leave the canyon and search for Hasani. Yet no matter how far she walked, she could not again find the great dark doors; the canyon seemed to stretch on forever, shimmering with patches of red and blue flowers along its riverbanks. Noleena could find no landmark that she recognized from the afternoon when the horses had brought her there. Each night a fresh wave of grief lulled her to a restless sleep.

Now, Noleena dried her tears and pondered the mugwawa. She had mainly been avoiding this ancient being, for although the mugwawa had offered to tell her the story that she needed most to hear, Noleena had replied that she was not ready for the telling. She didn't want some new understanding, some deeper knowledge, to disturb the peace and security that she felt in the canyon. She didn't want to be reminded of her Seeking, of her failure and her continuing responsibility. She wanted only to be left undisturbed and safe, like a small creature that has found shelter after arduous flight from danger. This was wrong, she knew; it was a weakness. She was a Wind-wanderer princess and an acolyte of Luna and now, in this time of grave and pressing distress, she should have been aiding her people instead of hiding away. It was fear that held her captive in the canyon; she spent hours each day trying to outwalk her guilt, to ignore it and imagine it away. But it followed her tenaciously, reminding her that while she turned her back on Terre, the evil Maldici queen in the red-walled palace of Safala was casting her net of darkness across the land, pulling it tighter, ensnaring all who lived there, and scheming—as had her father before her—to conquer all lands around the Middle Sea.

A yellow finch with a blue crest flew overhead and presently Noleena heard it warbling in a nearby tree. Dappled shadows fled across her brown arms and legs, and shone on the moon in her pierced bellybutton. A wild bee buzzed amongst the ferns and darted off, a golden comet, toward its nest in the cliffs.

Why did I decide to go and sleep in the mugwawa's cave for once? Noleena asked herself. I was trying to raise enough courage to hear my story, but I probably wouldn't have anyway. I am too weak and frightened. If I had stayed away from the cave, the boy would not have seen me. If only I hadn't fallen asleep on the rock ledge. Did the mugwawa cast a spell over me? If I come out from the ferns, where will I go? Will the boy still be here? How long will he stay for? How long must I remain hidden?

Sun slid across her shoulders, and her belly rumbled hungrily. Thirst puckered her mouth. At last, in the sleepy heat and dreamy silence of mid-afternoon, she slipped cautiously from the ferns and followed a thread of track through the flowering grasses to the riverbank to drink. She hung her feet into the water and felt its playful swirl and tug. She thought that perhaps the horses would know, in their mysterious way, what to do. Perhaps they would know that it was time to leave this canyon, to find another hiding place, and perhaps they would be able to find the dark doors. She rose and began to walk through the massive sycama trees, keeping to the thickest foliage beneath the horizontal limbs that were like ribs overhead. Warily, she glanced around as she moved but saw no sign of the Kiffa boy.

Perhaps the mugwawa had sent him away. But, Noleena thought, he will know where this place is now. Even if he goes away, he might return. He might even bring other Kiffas with him. I will never feel safe here again.

She arrived at the edge of a clearing, where the river curved away from the base of the cliffs and across to the opposite side of the canyon. She paused before stepping out into the sunlight of the clearing where the horses grazed. Nothing moved in her vision except the horses themselves, walking slowly as they grazed, their teeth making a faint ripping sound. She began to step forward.

Suddenly, she froze. With infinite slowness she edged backward until she again merged into the shadows of the trees. She crouched under a bush, holding her breath, wishing herself to be invisible.

The Kiffa boy entered the clearing from the opposite side, clothed as he had been in the mugwawa's cave in nothing but tattered green leggings and with a small knife and a cloth bag hanging from his waist. Barefoot he walked across the clearing and she saw suddenly that he carried ropes woven from vines in one hand, and realized that he was going to catch the horses, Hasani's horses—and all that she had left of him.

Her fear of losing the horses overpowered her fear of the boy.

"No!" she shouted, bounding from her hiding place into the sunlight. She flew across the meadow with hair streaming and feet pounding the grass. The horses flung up their heads, snorting and startled, and the boy lunged toward Dune Dancer and flung his coil of vine rope. It slithered over the mare's shoulders and she broke into a gallop. The boy spun on his heels, his golden hair a burning brightness, and flung the rope toward Sun Runner. The stallion reared up, as Noleena had seen him do in the desert, his mouth open and teeth bared, his hooves slicing the air and his eyes rolling white. He plunged toward the boy but the boy stood his ground—even through her anger and the rush of her running, Noleena noted his courage. The stallion's front hooves struck the ground a foot away from the boy and he let out a wild whinny but the boy remained unflinchingly still, rooted to the spot.

When Noleena reached the boy, she hurled herself toward him; a tiny part of her mind registered astonishment at her own daring.

She grabbed the vine rope and tried to wrench it from his grasp. "No!" she yelled. "You can't have the horses! They are Hasani's. You cannot have them!"

They reeled on the trampled grass, tugging and wrestling with the rope as the boy's tawny eyes flared with surprise. Suddenly, he let the vines go and Noleena staggered, panting and glaring at the boy as the horses trotted away into the trees and were lost from sight.

"They are Lord Tafari's horses," the boy said, his face puzzled. "To return them to him is my Hunting."

"They are not any lord's horses!" Noleena retorted passionately. "They were bred in the valley of Engedi by the Wind-wanderer people; they were stolen away by the Kiffas. Hasani owns them—he captured them back because they are his! Hasani's father was the guardian of the ancient book of horses' lineage in the valley of Engedi, before the Kiffas tried to take it away. When he would not give it to them, they tied him behind a chariot and dragged him until he died, suffocated on sand and shredded by rocks and thorny scrub."

The Kiffa boy shook his head slowly from side to side; then he swayed suddenly, as though with weakness, before sinking to his knees. Noleena turned away from him but remained standing nearby, panting. Now that the moment of struggle had passed and the horses were safe, her courage had deserted her. She wanted to run far away and hide in the ferns again, but her legs were shaking so much that she could barely stand.

The boy made a movement in the periphery of her vision and she tensed. But he was merely shifting to sit with his chin on his knees, clasping his arms around his legs. Noleena's gaze ran down their sinewy length to the torn hems of his leggings where silky threads dangled, to the golden hairs on his ankles and their fine strong bones, to the arch of his bare feet, to his toes.

Her eyes widened and the boy, glancing up, caught her look. He jerked his legs back and sat upon his feet.

"You have webs," Noleena said wonderingly; just for a moment she forgot her fear of him. She stared at the smooth, hard lines of the boy's golden face. "Who are you?"

"I am Ambro d'Monti, and I am a Kiffa-walker of Lord Tafari's household."

"You are not a Kiffa if you have webs."

Something flickered in the boy's tawny gaze—a shadow of sorrow and longing—and he bent his head suddenly and fiddled with the knife at his belt.

"Then what?" he muttered. "If I am not a Kiffa, what am I?" He flashed a miserable glace at Noleena and she saw that his face had reddened.

"Who were your parents?" Noleena asked, still standing, her muscles tensed for flight.

"I am told that my father was a Kiffa called Dawit Jaser but the record keeper of that family denies that such a man existed. I don't know my mother's name; she drowned along with my father when I was very young. I remember only her smile…"

Noleena folded her arms across her chest and suppressed any stirring of sympathy; she reminded herself that this boy was part of the Maldici's dark net, whether he was a Kiffa or not. She scowled down at him; when he squinted back, his own expression was puzzled.

"Why are you angry at me?" he asked.

Outrage and disbelief struggled in her. Was he so stupid that he didn't know the evil that his kind was inflicting upon Terre, with their red-caped soldiers, whips and brutti dogs? Words rolled over each other in her mouth.

"Why?" the boy asked again.

"Why do you hate us?" she blazed out, fresh courage leaping within her. "Why do you hunt us through the desert like rodents, and tear apart our families? Why do you whip us and brand us and send us down into the dark from which we will never emerge again into the wind, into light of moon and sun? Why do you steal our horses? Why do you wear our fine-grained boots of shugra leather, the golden jewelry that we have forged, and sit upon the carpets we have woven—but treat us like dung? Brown skin, gold skin—why is one any better than the other? Blue eyes, tawny eyes—the seeing is the same! Jewelry in your ears, jewelry in your bellybutton—who judges which is more fitting?

"You think that the Kiffas are important because they build temples and navy ships, because they have an army filled with their sons and with foreign mercenaries, because they trade and bustle around as if they run the world. But who digs the gold mines, who cures the leather, who grows the desert nub nubs, who weaves the carpets and finds the precious amber in the desert cliffs, and brings the salt above ground for the doda caravans to carry away? Who? The Wanderers, Ambro d'Monti, that's who!"

Noleena stopped to draw breath; her uncharacteristic anger had taken her by surprise, like a fire bursting out in dry scrub in the heat of mid-summer, consuming all that lies around it. She must have been storing this anger up ever since the priestess in Safala had told her about the Maldici queen. Since then, she thought she had always been afraid but perhaps, deep under the fear, there had been a cellar where she had stored up every particle of outrage at the cruelty being done to her people.

The boy looked dazed. Noleena placed one foot beside his in the grass and spread her toes. "Webs," she said. "I have them, you have them too. So what? Do they make me disgusting, scum, a dust-eater? Am I less human because of them? Should I be ashamed? You—you are the one who should be ashamed! You, with your soldiers and your cruel arrogance, and your lust for power! Hasani's blood will be upon your head!"

"It wasn't me—I wasn't thinking—I didn't send him to Mandi," the boy stammered.

"You were there at Mount Lalibela; did you do anything to stop the soldiers from taking him?"

The boy shook his head and she turned away, feeling her face contorted with pain. The Kiffa boy would not see her tears. She strode across the grass, willing her shaky legs to carry her to the refuge of shadows beneath the sycama trees. At the edge of the forest she paused and glanced back; the boy slouched in the grass where she had left him with his head drooping over his bent knees. "You will never catch the horses!" she shouted with the last ounce of her courage. "They are too smart for you! They will not go anywhere with you!"

She plunged into the shrubbery, trampling past pink orchids with spotted throats where bees hung. Sun Runner and Dune Dancer moved toward her through the shadows and she laid her face against their soft muzzles and waited for her heart beat to slow. Gradually, she felt resolve forming within herself.

It is time, she thought. I must go to the mugwawa for my story.

The horses shadowed her as she made her way up the canyon, and when they reached the pool at the base of the waterfall they bent their heads to drink, then lay down in the shade. Noleena balanced along the rocky ledge, the roar of water thrumming in her ears, and entered the dim tunnel. Beyond it the cave lay quiet, bathed in shifting golden light. The mugwawa sat, mountainous, unmoving, before her small fire.

Noleena felt her courage falter as the mugwawa raised her eyes and contemplated her; felt herself falling into ancient depths of inscrutable knowledge. She paused at the cave's mouth, fear biting her belly. Stars and the ghostly fleeting shapes of horses streamed across the mugwawa's cape; the river pearls glowed around her forehead and her face transformed into smooth plump lines. Noleena took a deep breath and stepped forward. She bent her head in a gesture of respect and kneeled before the fire, beneath the ochre colored paintings on the cave walls.

"I have come for my story, for its true telling, please." Her voice quivered as the weight of her Seeking pressed upon her.

The mugwawa's gaze remained steady and impenetrable; the feathers in her hair became white with blue streaks, her cape swirled with moon wrens, and a silver panther walked across her gown leaving paw prints that dissolved into clouds flying across a crescent moon.

Suddenly, without warning, the mugwawa began to speak and her deep resonant voice rolled around the cave, lapping at the painted walls, flowing down the tunnel to merge with the water's roar. "This is the telling that you have come here for," she said.

Noleena held very still, waiting for the knowledge of her fate to be cast upon her: a snare that she could not hope to escape from but must live and act within.

"Over its mountains the Blue Moon
Hangs like a baited hook;
At the moment that the great fish leaps
Stand in the sacred gate and look
For Luna's wisdom that will safely keep
A balance in the tides of Terre."

When the mugwawa's voice fell into silence, Noleena stared at her incredulously. "That's my story?" she asked. "That's all? But I have heard this already, in the temple in Safala!"

The mugwawa's eyes were black craters in the silver light that swirled about her; the contours of her face shifted within it like a landscape lying in the path of a storm: harsh angle of cheek and forehead, high contour of brow, fierce bend of nose, dark valley of mouth.

"All?" boomed the mugwawa's voice. "If you can understand and act upon this story, it will be all that any mortal could do. What more do you wish for, Wind-wanderer? You have been given an ancient story, a verse preserved beneath mugwawa tongues for you alone and for this moment of greatest sorrow. In this verse lies a riddle that no one has ever solved, and that no one has ever acted upon. In this verse lies your destiny, perhaps your death. You wish for more?"

Noleena bent her head again beneath the mugwawa's consuming gaze; she felt power flickering and pouring over her. Her scalp and the nape of her neck tingled; bumps rose on her bare arms and she shivered in the cave's warmth. Her heart beat fluttered erratically in her ears.

"Thank you for this true telling," she whispered, and the cave sank back into stillness; the air that had seemed charged with swirling power grew peaceful once more. Noleena became aware of the rock-roses rustling in their nests, cheeping softly, and of the chattering of the hareenas on their ledges.

"Now, your mark shall join the mark of all who have been brought or driven to this canyon for their story," the mugwawa said, and Noleena saw that she held a small terracotta pot containing a paste of ochre pigment that she stirred with a peeled stick.

Gracefully the mugwawa rose and swayed across the cave, gesturing for Noleena to follow. Then the mugwawa took Noleena's hand in her own, which was smooth and dry and warm, and pressed it upon the cave wall. Noleena watched in amazement as the mugwawa tipped the terra cotta pot to her lips and took a mouthful of the thin ochre pigment; it sprayed out around Noleena's hand, coating the surface of her skin. When she removed her hand from the cave wall she saw its outline, her own mark, there upon the gritty rose and golden strata. She felt a tingle of delight and awe, knowing that it would remain there for time out of mind; that wherever her Seeking took her, a small part of her would always remain in the dim golden warmth of the mugwawa's cave.

"Now find the boy, Ambro," the mugwawa said. "He too must make his mark."

"I don't think—are you sure?" Noleena asked. "He's not—he's a Kiffa."

"Can you see his burden or live his story?" thundered the mugwawa. "It is not for you to say who shall have a true telling and leave their handprints here upon the walls. If you had the vision you need, you would see that Ambro is a thread in your own weaving. Who is to judge the colors of one's story?"

A gust of Ismata whirled down from overhead, where the aperture in the cave roof let sunlight stream in, and seemed to push Noleena across the floor and into the dim tunnel. She rushed down it and along the ledge, bursting out into the valley where the horses waited. As they followed her, brushing through the shrubs, clouds of tiny insects with green eyes and lacy wings rose glittering into the air. The horses' manes became starred with flowers sifting from the chestnut trees, and with winged seeds that fell from the sycama. Their tails brushed the flowering grasses, releasing a fragrance like jasmine.

Although she looked around her as she walked, Noleena saw no sign of the boy, Ambro, and reached her cave in the cliff without meeting him. Climbing upward, she perched on a lip of rock as hot and crumbling as bread crust, and rested her head on her knees. Why had the mugwawa given her a story that she had heard already? She felt cheated somehow; for days she had been afraid to ask for her true telling and yet all along she had known the verse; it was nothing new. Why come all this way to be told something she had already heard? It seemed ridiculous. Perhaps the mugwawa was not as wise as she seemed. Noleena retracted this thought hastily, with a superstitious fear that the very rocks and trees might understand her doubts and then, in some mysterious magical fashion, convey them to the mugwawa.

I do believe in her power, Noleena amended herself. And I did believe in the wisdom of the priestess when she told me the verse in Safala and said that it was all she knew about the star gate from whence Luna returned to the heavens from the Moon Mountains that lie eastward, beyond the plateau lands. And I did not understand the verse on the first telling; perhaps this is why I needed to hear it again. If I am to seek help from Luna, and failed at Mount Lalibela,…perhaps it is my Seeking to find the star gate and beseech the goddess there for wisdom or a sign, for some power with which to fight the net of evil that the Maldici queen is casting over Terre and my people. But what does the verse mean? How am I to Seek if all I have is a riddle?

Her head ached and she felt drained by all the emotions of the day: the fear that kept her captive in the canyon and the guilt that accompanied this; the surprising flare of anger directed at the boy; the doubts she felt about the mugwawa; the puzzlement over the verse. She stared out over the canyon; it was dusky with shadows. The horses ripped peacefully at grass amongst the trees below her, their coats a dull gleam. The smell of the minty river water drifted up the canyon walls. Then she noticed the boy, Ambro, sitting on a fallen log near the horses. Her muscles tensed. Was he trying to catch them again with his vine rope? Had he seen her in her cave?

She remained rigid, watching him, but he simply sat upon his log and stared into the trees. There was a brooding stillness about him as though his mind were churning with thoughts.

He is a thread in your weaving, the mugwawa had said. What did she mean? And, Noleena remembered with a guilty start, I have not yet given him the message about going to the cave and making his hand mark. If I sit here and stay quiet, he may go away without even noticing me. Sooner or later, he will leave the canyon. My mark will be on the cave wall but his will not; his mark does not deserve to be here in this sacred place. He is not part of this beauty.

Again, she had the strange feeling that the whole valley was listening to her thoughts, that the trees and leaves were absorbing them in like rain water or sunlight and conveying them to the mugwawa. I suppose I must tell the boy the message, she thought with a sigh, and she clambered silently down the rocks. As she crossed the grass, the boy rose and came to meet her, walking with a kind of hesitant caution. Her heart drubbed in her chest, as though she were approaching a fierce unpredictable animal.

"The mugwawa would like to see you again before you leave the canyon," she said, her gaze skittering timidly over the boy's shoulders toward the darkening trees.

"I don't know when I am leaving, where to go," the boy responded. "If I cannot return to Lord Tafari with the horses, I have nowhere to go. Was it true, what you said about the bandit being the horses' true owner?"

His beseeching tone caught her attention; she did not think he was a boy who very often beseeched anyone for anything. She flicked her eyes across his briefly, feeling a momentary pang of compassion. He sounded as lost as she had often felt since embarking on her Seeking.

"It's true," she replied. "The Wanderers bred the horses in the valley of Engedi. You Kiffas are all the same; blinded to the truth by the evil spells of that Queen Maldici who has taken over our country through cunning and sorcery."

"I don't know very much about Terre, not really. I only arrived from Verde a few months ago. I was looking for my family."

Again, Noleena felt a momentary spasm of sympathy and again she suppressed it. "You should learn more about a country before you go rushing around, being so important, hurting people."

The boy nodded, flushing. "Who are you? Why are you traveling through the desert?"

"I am on a Seeking, to find help from Luna and bring aid to my people."

"Luna? It was in Sirena's temple that I first saw you. I know Sirena, she is the dolphin goddess of the pirati people in Verde."

"No, you are wrong. That was Luna's shrine in Safala."

"In Verde, Luna is the moon goddess. She doesn't have dolphins cavorting at her feet."

"Here we have only Luna, with both moon and dolphins. Perhaps Luna and Sirena are one and the same," Noleena suggested. "We believe that Luna will guide us through the sea of sand, through the currents and storms of our lives, and through the dark water that lies beyond. The moon controls the tides; they are inseparable."

The boy nodded. Darkness was thick in the valley now, like a purple mist. A moon wren, perched overhead in a sycama tree, gave a liquid warbling trill. As the dew fell, the smell of damp earth and grass, of night blooming lilies and of minty water seeped mysteriously through the still air, and a diaphanous mist rose from the river.

The boy shivered. "I'm going to light a fire."

Noleena thought of the dry shelter of her cave but said nothing. It was her place, secret and private, and nothing to do with the boy. She turned to move away, anxious to be alone again, but the boy called, "Wait! Please wait!" and she halted, tense and with her back to him.

"Please—stay and talk to me. I haven't had anyone to talk to for a long time."

Noleena remained rigid, her desire to escape struggling within her.

"Please," the boy repeated. "I won't hurt you."

"You've already hurt me," she muttered breathlessly.

"Then help me to make things better. I've been making a mess of everything since coming to Terre."

Grudgingly, Noleena perched on a log as the boy moved around, rustling through shrubbery and collecting wood. Presently he struck a spark with a flint he pulled from one pocket of his ragged green silk leggings, and a petal of flame curled up through the sticks.

When he came and sat on Noleena's log, she shifted away from him. Even if he was lost and alone, even if he had webbed toes like hers, there was too much Kiffa in him; she watched him carefully from the corner of her eye. His golden hair flared in the firelight and his skin was smooth and golden over the straight planes of his face. Soon he would grow a drooping moustache and hide his toes again in Kiffa-walker boots with rolled tops, made of shugra leather that her people had cured.

"You could join the army now that you have had to abandon your Hunting," she said, her anger flickering bravely into life again.

The boy shrugged. "I don't know…everything is so muddled. Lord Tafari told me the story of the first kiffa and first horse, and how the kiffa taught the horse a lesson in respect and how after that he was king of the desert. But the mugwawa told me another version—the true telling, she said—and in her story the moon goddess saved the horse and set her mark upon it and told both beasts they must live as brother and sister, as children of the desert and equals. I don't know what to think."

"That is an easy enough telling to understand," Noleena said. "The Wanderers are the people of the horse, and the Kiffa-walkers are people of the kiffa. We have always lived peaceably together in Terre, trading and existing in harmony. It was only after the king in Safala died, and his son was ensnared in the sorcery of that foreign Queen Maldici, that our two peoples began to live in enmity and cruelty. It is my Seeking to adjust the balance and restore harmony. Though how I am to do this, I don't understand…"

There was silence for several minutes, then Noleena whistled low and soft and waited for the horses to come in close, their forelocks sweeping their dark eyes. "Look," she commanded the boy, and she lifted the long hair aside. Gently the boy traced the mark of the crescent moon that whorled in the hair of the horses' foreheads, and his face was wondering. "The story was true."

Noleena nodded and perched back on her log.

"I have something we could eat." Ambro pulled a handful of tiny yams from one pocket and held them out to Noleena; she took one and chewed its nutty orange flesh.

"What story were you told?"

She shrugged defensively. "It was for my ears only."

"You're still angry with me."

An image of Hasani hung before her; across the leaping firelight, his blue eyes gleamed beneath his plaited crown of iridescent hair. His smile crossed time and distance to flicker across her; she felt an instant's warm pleasure followed by pain. She jumped to her feet and when she replied to the boy, her rising voice disturbed an owl that flapped ponderously overhead.

"I will never trust you! You have sent Hasani to his grave. I will never forgive you!"

"Never is a long time," Ambro said, pain tightening his voice. "I am sorry about Hasani. Truly. I wasn't thinking straight; I was obsessed with the horses and my own Hunting. I didn't come to Terre to hurt anyone. Perhaps I could find Hasani and rescue him from the mines."

"A rescue takes planning, but you are a person who acts without thinking. You have said so yourself."

He stared uncomfortably at his bare feet and made no reply as she paced around at the edge of the firelight.

"Please sit down again," he said at last. "I don't even know your name. We are both lost; both failing in our purpose. Couldn't we help one another?"

Noleena shrugged again but perched on the very end of the log. "My name is Noleena. And I am not failing in my Seeking, I am just resting here."

She wished this were true; wished that fear was not rising in her again as she sent her thoughts up over the golden cliffs, across windswept miles of empty plateau lands, toward the looming peaks of the forest-clad and mist-shrouded and impenetrable Moon Mountains. For surely that was where the star gate would be—but what did a star gate look like and how would she recognize it if she found it? She clenched her white knuckled hands in her lap and stared unseeingly into the darkness under the sycama trees, feeling wave upon wave of fear lift and toss her heart.

The fire died into embers and a breath of Ismata spilled over the canyon walls and rustled through the trees, sending almond blossoms flying through the darkness like pale moths.

"I will go and see what the mugwawa wants me for," Ambro said at last, rising to his feet and stretching. "Will I see you tomorrow?"

"I will have left on my Seeking," Noleena replied, her voice deliberately distant and cool—although she did not think it likely that she would have found the courage to leave. "I don't think we have anything else to say to one another, Ambro d'Monti."

The boy shrugged and averted his face; she glimpsed a pinch of hurt around his lips. An apology rose to her mouth but she bit it back. The Kiffa boy, or whatever he was, did not deserve to feel happy in this enchanted place—or in any other. He had caused his own misery and would have to endure it, as Hasani had to endure the fate that this boy had brought upon him. And as her father had to endure his lonely enclosed life within Safala; her father, a prince of the desert, of the valley of Engedi where once horses had danced for him.

After the boy moved away, Noleena waited until she was sure that he had gone, and then she climbed to her bed in the cliff and curled on its willow wands and sweet grass. A hareena cuddled against her, its whiskers tickling her shoulders. Behind her closed lids, horses and moon wrens surged across the mugwawa's cape; forest vines ascended into massive trees. *Over its mountains the Blue Moon hangs like a baited hook...*

CHAPTER SIXTEEN

W HEN NOLEENA AWOKE THE next morning, with sun creeping over her face, she lay still and considered the events of the previous day. *I was horrible to the boy,* she thought. *I have never before been like that with anyone, so angry and so bold; usually I am timid and shy. The boy must think I am a terrible person.*

But what does it matter what he thinks?

When I first lived, Noleena, after Tekle cut me from the cross and nursed me in his tent, my hatred for the Kiffa-walkers was like a wild beast within me. Her father's voice spoke in her head, and she remembered in vivid detail the morning when she had sat in the alcove outside the temple; saw again her father's seamed and rugged face, the leather strap tied across his blinded eyes. What else had he said, then, about his feelings for the Kiffa-walkers? Something about sending away your enemies' animal, Noleena thought, her memory worrying around the image of her father's face. *If you wish to stay alive amongst your enemies, Noleena, you must be careful not to let their animal create a lair in your own heart. To keep the kiffa out—though he paces circles around me—I practice forgiveness in every moment.*

Did this apply to the boy? Noleena wondered. He wasn't entirely a Kiffa, and she couldn't tell whether he was exactly an enemy; nonetheless, she had said that she would never forgive him. She squirmed uncomfortably on her bed of springy willow when she remembered saying this; yet another, stronger part of her clung tenaciously to the feeling. How could she forgive someone who had brought harm to Hasani? Never mind, she had more important things to think about, like finding the stargate.

And how could she forgive herself if she didn't pursue the meaning of the mugwawa's riddle, and attempt to find the stargate and seek Luna's aid? I will leave this very morning, she resolved. I must not stay here, hiding. I will ask the mugwawa to lift her enchantment and let the horses and me go from this canyon. She rose, brushing grass seeds from her top, pulling on her ochre tunic, and went to stand in the cave door and survey the valley. A circle of animals were gathered below her: the horses standing still, the hareenas sitting up on their long back legs with sun shining through their upright ears, the rock-roses pecking at seeds. Were they waiting for her? Did they in some mysterious manner know of her new resolve? When she scrambled down to touch the horses' muzzles, Dune Dancer bent her knees and lowered her head in invitation to mount, and the hareenas crowded against Noleena's legs, their long whiskers shimmering and quivering, so that she moved toward the mare's back. Obediently she mounted and Dune Dancer surged to her feet.

It is indeed time to leave this place of peace, Noleena thought with mingled trepidation and excitement. I will not have to worry anymore about the Kiffa boy; the horses will take me away from here. We will travel to the Moon Mountains. We will seek the meaning of the riddle.

Unhurriedly, calmly, the horses moved down the valley with the hareenas bounding alongside and suddenly, rounding a shoulder of cliff, Noleena saw before them the massive doors looking just as they had when she first came to the mugwawa's canyon, their soaring frames blocking out sky, their smooth surfaces shining and dark.

"But I came here before—I searched this far, and never saw them!" Noleena said aloud in amazement. At the sound of her voice in the still air, something moved at the base of the doors. The boy, Ambro, who had been sitting in the grass amongst a cluster of hareenas, rose to his feet. Noleena's heart bounded.

"What are you doing here?"

"The hareenas took me to the mugwawa this morning. The mugwawa said that the hareenas would show me the way to the gates. And she gave me these." He hoisted aloft a light wicker cage containing the huddled shapes of a rock-rose and a grey dove that cooed softly at the sudden movement. "She said that we might need them."

"What do you mean? We?" Noleena's voice faltered.

"You are going to the Moon Mountains on your Seeking, aren't you? My true telling from the mugwawa, that you explained to me yesterday, showed me that Kiffa and Wanderer must work together to save Terre. So I am coming to help with your Seeking."

Panic beat in Noleena's chest. "I didn't ask you to come…and how do you know where I am going? How—you can't just decide to go on my Seeking like this—so casually!"

"This is not casual, Noleena. I have lain awake thinking about it all night. I cannot complete my Hunting for Lord Tafari so I am free to join another cause."

"This is not just any cause! It's something serious and of grave importance. You have to take an oath; you have to wear the right patterns on your face. Anyway, you're not even a real Kiffa so all that stuff about Kiffa and Wanderer working together doesn't matter! To you or me!"

Beneath her, Dune Dancer snorted and Sun Runner jostled against her legs and gave her a warning nip on the thigh. The hareenas' bubbling voices moaned softly at the horses' feet, and the boy Ambro still stood there infuriatingly in her path, holding his wicker cage and challenging her with his level stare.

"I can take an oath," he said. "Tell me what to say."

Memories of Hasani kissing his palm and placing it upon her forehead, and of his musical voice flowing over the old and sacred words of the Wanderer oath, filled her head. She bit her lip and averted her face.

This is too hard! she thought. I cannot do this! It is hard enough to go alone into the Moon Mountains, but why should it be made harder still because of this boy? His Kiffa looks frighten me. What if he has soldiers waiting somewhere to intercept us? What if this is all a trick? The mugwawa had no right to tell him where I was going!

She looked up and sighed. The hareenas pressed against Ambro's legs, and stared at her reproachfully.

I suppose I will have to let the boy come with me, she thought, since the animals and the mugwawa will it. I am resolved to go to the mountains and finish this! I will not let the boy stop me. But I cannot forgive him or trust him

"Make your oath then," she said through gritted teeth.

Ambro bent on his knees and inclined his golden head gracefully. "I accept your Seeking as my own; I swear my loyalty to it. Should I prove unfaithful, may the west wind send its waves to drown me; may the north wind freeze the marrow of my bones; may the east wind carry me away beyond the Middle Sea; may the south wind unleash its torrential rains upon me."

He glanced up into her face. "I don't really know any other oaths. Will that one do? It is an oath spoken on the coastlines of Verde."

"It will have to do then," Noleena muttered uneasily.

Ambro's grin of response lit his face with such brightness that she felt startled; she had never seen his flashing smile until this moment. Sun Runner kneeled before him; wonder and delight illuminated the boy's face as he understood the stallion's invitation and as he mounted. When the stallion had risen to his feet, Ambro looked across at Noleena. "I have waited a long time for this moment," he said, and his hand caressed the stallion's shoulder and flowing mane.

"Just don't think you're going to take him back to Safala."

She nudged the mare forward to the doors; as before, they swung mysteriously and silently open and beyond them Noleena was amazed to see, not the canyon snaking onward, but a windswept plateau rising to the foot of the Moon Mountains not more than a day's ride away. All that day, as the sun climbed higher to illuminate the grasslands with shimmering brightness and cast pools of shadow beneath the spreading trees, where herds of magrazzi dozed, Ambro and Noleena rode toward the mountains. For the most part they rode in silence, deep in their own thoughts, but Noleena kept the boy in the periphery of her vision constantly. He did not ride very well, she noted; he bounced around like a sack of nub nubs when trotting, and clung to the stallion's mane at a canter. Unlike Hasani, she thought. And unlike me; I was able to ride well from the first time because my father bequeathed me this gift in my blood. But, countered a stern voice in her head, Ambro is brave to climb upon a stallion as fiery as Sun Runner when he has no previous experience—for what could a boy of salty water know of desert horses? Yes, Noleena agreed grudgingly to this voice, he is brave.

Brave, but like a wild animal. I will have to watch him all the time, she thought, because I don't know what to expect next, and because I don't understand why he is coming with me. What concealed purpose might he be pursuing?

Her thoughts also circled constantly around the riddle told to her by the priestess and repeated by the mugwawa. The Moon Mountains must be the location of the star gate, she thought, and a Blue Moon is the moon that rises on the tenth night of the last month of summer; that is several weeks from now, so we have a little time in which to find the star gate. But what is the great fish that leaps? Will we find a pool or a river near the star gate? And why would the moon be like a baited hook? She had never fished and had only the vaguest of ideas about hooks and bait. She wondered if the mugwawa had given the riddle's information to Ambro and once or twice, as they rode, she opened her mouth to ask him but each time she held her silence. The mugwawa had said that each person would only be given their own story, so surely she would not have shared Noleena's telling with Ambro. And it might not be safe to trust Ambro with the information; perhaps then he might be able to betray her to Kiffa soldiers. And if she asked him—who would surely know—about baits and hooks, then in return he would want to know why she asked.

They camped that evening at the base of the mountains, their slopes swelling upward into the mist that writhed around the forested higher slopes. Watching darkness slide into ravines and gullies and the last light illuminate the mountain flanks, Noleena shivered. She had never met anyone who had been to these mountains, but even in Safala she had heard tales muttered about them: cautionary tales about rushing rivers and snakes as large around as a man's thigh, about vines that strangled trees and sucked the life from them and black pools filled with oozing mud into which an unwary travel might sink to his death.

The next morning, after sleeping in a grove of small trees, Noleena awoke thinking of Hasani. How could she turn her back on the plateau and the desert westward of it, where Hasani was alone somewhere, to ride into the mountains? Wasn't this a chance to go and find him and, hopefully, to rescue him? Experimentally, she tried to head Dune Dancer westward after mounting but the mare pranced uneasily beneath her, flinging up her head and neighing shrilly in protest. Sun Runner snorted and came swiftly across the grass with the boy, Ambro, clinging ungracefully to his mane, and stood before Dune Dancer to block her way. He bared his teeth at Noleena, his eyes rolling wildly.

"What's happening—what's the matter?" Ambro called.

"Nothing." She turned her face toward the mountains as the horses wheeled around and began to climb the slope. Your destiny is to help your people, her father's voice said in her head. You are a Wind-wanderer princess and an acolyte of Luna.

She didn't see though, how Hasani could ever forgive her for abandoning him to his fate and heading eastward with his horses. Not that this mattered, she thought bitterly, since she was unlikely to ever see Hasani again.

The lush grass of the plateau lands changed into a springy tufted grass and trees advanced down the slopes to meet them like the first outriders of the great massed army of trees that awaited them higher in the mountains. By late afternoon, they had climbed to the edge of the forest. In awe and amazement, Noleena stared at the wall of trees, at their massive soaring trunks covered in red, black or golden bark; at their canopies of leaves far overhead that undulated gently in the Ismata and that were woven through with the brilliant flowers of vines whose long lianas wrapped themselves through the branches. Beneath the trees, the air was dim and very still; the horses stared into the depths of the forest with breath snorting softly through their nostrils. Noleena felt as fragile as a sapling, and as easily crushed.

"Now this is an adventure," Ambro said and Noleena saw that his face was alight again, his wide mouth grinning, his eyes bright with eagerness. For a moment she felt irritation and opened her own mouth to reply that a Seeking was not an adventure. But then she bit the words back and instead felt glad, suddenly and for the first time, that he was with her and for the dependability of his courage. Nervously she followed him into the forest and felt its shadows fall across her shoulders. She glanced back and saw the mountain falling away with sunlight pouring over it and out onto the flat blue distances of the plateau lands. The scattered trees there, that had seemed so spreading and large, were now mere dots. How high we have climbed already, Noleena thought. Then, as they penetrated farther into the forest, the plateau lands were lost to view and they became surrounded entirely by shrubbery and the soaring columns of trees. The air grew damper and cooler as they climbed, and a cloak of silence fell upon them for the birds were far overhead in the canopy and their songs were only faintly heard.

Noleena began to find the silence oppressive; her nape prickled and she kept glancing uneasily about with the feeling that they were being followed through the silence by something unknown and dangerous. But the horses moved steadily upward, and Ambro picked a pink flower from a towering rhododendron bush and tossed it to Noleena. It gave off a delicate perfume and Noleena tucked the stem through a buttonhole in her tunic and rode on feeling slightly comforted.

That night, they lit a small fire using enormous dried leaves and dead vines. Delicate green moths swooped overhead and hunting bats flitted past with squeaking cries. Noleena stared upward; the light from the fire illuminated only the bases of the tree trunks and above that they soared into darkness like the pillars of a mammoth temple.

"The mugwawa didn't say anything about what we—you—were coming here for," Ambro said, giving Noleena his level, challenging stare across the fire. "Am I allowed to know?"

Noleena shrugged uncomfortably. As always, when Ambro turned his attention directly upon her, her heart lurched. But perhaps, she thought now, if she were to tell Ambro the verse, he might be able to help her—and it seemed only fair to tell him, since he had made the effort to travel all these miles with her. Yet she did not trust him, and neither had she forgiven him for Hasani's capture; the memory of that melee beneath Mount Lalibela was a hardness lodged in her mind, like a stone that cut raw sores every time her thoughts handled it. So now she lifted her eyes from the flames and replied, "My Seeking is my responsibly; I will take care of it myself."

"As you wish," Ambro replied.

For some time they sat in silence. Noleena closed her eyes, feeling the fire's heat flicker over her lids, and thought longingly of the days she had spent with Hasani. She thought too of the priestess with her silvery voice and wished for her wise guidance. Like Hasani, she was probably dead by now.

When Noleena's eyes drifted open at last, she saw that Ambro had stretched his feet to the fire and was staring at his toes; their webs were pink in the light. The boy's face wore an expression of grief, but when he felt Noleena's gaze upon him, his tawny eyes flashed haughtily so she closed her own eyes again and said nothing.

Onward they traveled, penetrating farther east into the depths of the mountains as days passed. Often their progress was impeded by ravines, their cliff faces hung with moss and trees, and their green bellies noisy with torrential rushing rivers. Once Sun Runner tripped on a sprawling vine and Ambro shot forward over the stallion's shoulder to land at the base of a tree. The rhododendrons and azaleas grew to great heights, covered in flowers of brilliant pink, deep crimson, creamy white and soft purple.

Noleena grew increasingly concerned as time passed for, though she tried to choose routes that would lead them up into the mountain peaks where she thought the star gate might be, the mountains themselves seemed intent on thwarting her. Time after time, she and Ambro had to turn downhill due to deep chasms, or ridges so thin and sharp that it was unsafe to climb them, or strange swamps filled with warm thick mud. For hours, they struggled through vines that Ambro slashed at valiantly with his knife, the blade becoming notched and dull. At other times, just when it seemed that they might finally make upward progress, their vision would be obscured by impenetrable blankets of mist that swirled down over them from the peaks and through which it was dangerous to travel. Crouched beneath dripping trees, with the horses mere ghostly shapes only feet away, Noleena and Ambro would peel roots and berries in disconsolate silence.

"Is it true?" Ambro asked on one such occasion. "What you said in the mugwawa's canyon about the Wanderers tanning the leather, weaving the carpets, and breeding the horses?"

"Yes, it's true." Then Noleena described for him the intricate designs that the women wove into their carpets, of cranes and flowers and wrens, and explained that the fleecy rolled tops on Kiffa boots were made from the hair of shugras. She told him of the valley of Engedi where the horses danced on the spring-nourished grass. She recited the story of her father hanging upon the cross of corda wood while the Kiffas ate roasted shugra and waited for him to die, and of how they blinded him in their impatience.

She felt choked with grief by the end of her telling, and glared at Ambro's shocked expression without sympathy. He was silent for many hours afterward, appearing deep in thought. She wondered what it was that he thought of but she didn't ask. Surely soon the star gate would be found and then she would know what she must do next; then Ambro would be freed from his oath and they could part ways. She wouldn't have to wonder, then, whether or not he was trustworthy and of what he thought—nor be pricked with guilt over her lack of forgiveness, nor be reminded simply by his presence of the events at Lalibela. It would be a relief, she imagined, to ride away from Ambro with the two horses. Perhaps she would have to again find her people camped in the desert; she could not take Ambro to them with his golden Kiffa hair and skin.

On another occasion, as they waited beneath trees for the mist to clear, Ambro asked hesitantly, "That bandit—Hasani—who you were with at Lalibela...who was he?"

"He is the son and grandson of my father's friends. He is brave and kind, and had dedicated himself to my Seeking."

She caught her lip between her teeth and bit it, trying to stop the flush from spreading across her cheeks.

"I do not fill his place," Ambro said soberly.

"No!" She turned abruptly away and strode into the mist to sit behind a clump of shrubbery and wait for the tightness in her chest to abate.

As they journeyed, the mountains seemed unchanging; each day brought deep ravines with minty water; towering shrubbery and even higher canopies of trees. Every day they heard the hoots of monkeys high above, and the sharp distinctive cry of white birds with yellow beaks that flitted through the foliage. Nowhere, in all this tangle of vines and flowers and steeply contoured land wrapped in streamers of mist, did Noleena see anything out of the ordinary, anything that might be a star gate. Time was running out. The Blue Moon would rise one evening, the moon she could not see through the thick canopy, and she would still be laboring along blindly and stupidly, buried in the forest. The moment would pass; the Maldici queen would tighten her net more powerfully over Terre while Noleena, confused and ridiculously ineffective, would continue to struggle amongst the rhododendron bushes and wonder what it was that she searched for. She fretted over whether or not Ambro could be trusted. He is kind, she thought one afternoon, watching as he stroked the stallion's neck and spoke softly to him. But he is still more Kiffa than Wanderer, and he did nothing to help Hasani. She clamped her mouth around her plea for help, and rode on in silence.

But finally, as they set out into the mist one morning, she could bear her worries alone no longer. "I don't really know what we are looking for," she confessed hesitantly.

Ambro shot her a surprised glanced from Sun Runner's back. "Didn't the mugwawa tell you?"

"She gave me a riddle. Listen."

The horses stood still as Noleena recited the verse; the Ismata swirled gently around them, stirred the foliage, made flowers toss on boughs as though they floated on water.

"The mountains in the verse are the Moon Mountains?" Ambro asked, and Noleena nodded.

"That's the easy part. And the sacred place, I think, is the star gate: the place where Luna departed the earth and returned to the heavens, and the place where I must be in order to seek help against the Maldici on behalf of my people. But I don't know about the great fish or the baited hook, and I don't know what a star gate looks like. Do you?"

Ambro shook his head and stared out over the infinity of the mountains through a break in the trees. "So much forest," he said slowly. "How will we ever find it?"

"Every day here seems exactly the same; the forest seems endless." Noleena shook her head disconsolately. "We should be climbing to the peaks because they're closer to the stars, but we never seem able to make headway."

"I noticed you were struggling upward and being turned back."

"I am failing again," she said in a small voice, her throat closing around the words. "Just as I failed at Mount Lalibela."

Ambro flushed. "You were there seeking help?"

"From the goddess, but her statue was desecrated by Kiffas."

"I had not been to the temple," Ambro said earnestly. "Noleena, it was not us—my soldiers and I—who desecrated the statue. I wouldn't do such a thing. In Verde, Sirena was our protector at sea and I have swum with her dolphins."

Noleena looked up. "Truly? You have swum with the dolphins? I have always dreamed of this." She sighed, remembering the statue in the temple in Safala and how she had loved to slide her fingers over the smooth marble backs of the carved dolphins frolicking at the goddess' feet; remembered how she had always wondered what they were like in the flesh. Such childish, wondering innocence seemed long ago; here in the forest everything was infinitely more complicated, as tortuous and tangled as the giant lianas themselves. She was well aware that, although she had shared her problems with Ambro, she had not forgiven him. She was also aware that she had relaxed her vigilant watching and that sometimes whole hours passed when she forgot to worry about ambushes, betrayal or red-caped soldiers. Perhaps, she thought, I trust him a tiny bit—but this is not the same as forgiveness.

She nudged the mare on with her heels and the stallion fell into step behind as they navigated their way through the endless trees and down the treacherous incline of another ravine. The horses slipped and slid on the damp leaves underfoot. In the belly of the ravine ran another nameless river, still high and fast even at this time of year, its water clear and green. The horses whickered happily and dipped their noses into the swirling currents to drink. Noleena slid from Dune Dancer's back and cupped her hands into the water. The stallion stepped out into the river, snorting, his hooves sliding on rocks. Ambro sat astride gripping a handful of mane, and beginning to search, as he always did, for the best place in which to cross.

"This river is deeper than most," he said. "And faster; I think we—"

At that moment a family of grey ruffed monkeys with yellow tails burst from the forest behind them and onto the shoreline, giving their raucous hooting cries and running silently on their bent knuckles. The horses leapt forward. The stallion was swept off his feet, afloat and swimming, striking out for the far shore with his long pale legs.

The mare plunged into the river after the stallion and Noleena, washing her face, was just in time to catch hold of the mare's mane as she surged past. She felt the cool depths of the water snatch at her as the mare surged out deeper; felt the mare's energy and power as she began to swim, her head high and nostrils flaring; felt her hands slipping from the mare's mane. The water pulled harder on her, insistent, powerful. Her grip was not strong enough. The water tore her away from the mare and sucked her in, rolling and tossing her. She yelled but the mare was already feet away. Rocks bashed against Noleena's legs. Water filled her mouth as her head went under and she was momentarily blinded as water filled her eyes. In panic she thrashed against the churning currents.

I can't swim, she thought. I can't swim!

The water washed her against the solidity of a boulder and pinned her there. White wavelets streamed from her shoulders and around the rock. She clawed at the granular surface, finger-nails scrabbling. Resisting the water's swirl and tug, she heaved herself onto the boulder's surface and squatted there, shaking in every limb and gasping for breath. Water poured from her forehead, into her eyes and mouth. She wiped it away, her vision clearing so that the world was no longer a kaleidoscope of blue and green light.

In that instant, she saw the mare reach the far shore and join the stallion waiting with Ambro still astride his back. They are all together and I am here alone, Noleena thought. Ambro will take the horses and leave me. This is the moment that he has been waiting for and that I have been dreading: the reason he came on this journey with me. He can return to Lord Tafari with the horses, earning a welcome and a home as well as laying claim to all that the Kiffas possess.

She felt paralyzed with fear, trapped and isolated on her rock as water washed over her feet and her wet hair clung to her back. Her heart floundered painfully. She stared across the rushing torrent and waited for Ambro to wheel away into the trees on Sun Runner, for the mare to follow, for the forest to swallow them up.

But Ambro was edging Sun Runner along the shoreline, looking for a safe place to reenter the water. He had unslung the bird cage from his back and left it on the rocks. Now the horse was in chest deep and the boy's intent face, his bright tawny eyes, were turned toward her. "Don't worry!" he shouted. "We'll come for you!"

Now the stallion was afloat, mane pouring out sideways like a curtain in the water. Now he reached the place where the white wavelets poured around the boulder and he swung there in the current, fighting against it. Ambro stretched out an arm and pulled Noleena onto the stallion's back behind him.

"Hold on!" he shouted and she wrapped her arms around the cool, slippery skin of his bare waist and clung as the stallion, snorting with effort, turned in midstream, fighting the current that carried him downward. He struggled back to the far shore to heave out at last, dripping and blown, a quarter of a mile downstream from where the mare waited, neighing anxiously.

Noleena slid to the ground and her knees buckled. She staggered to the nearest rock and dropped onto it, still trembling.

"You see, not every day is exactly the same here," Ambro teased. "Some days are more exciting than others."

She stared up into his infectious smile; his eyes sparkled with humor. Water had splashed onto his hair, darkening the bright highlights, and it was plastered across his forehead. In that moment she became aware that the rock, carried within herself over many miles, began to soften around its edges.

She bent over, suddenly shy, and wrung water from her hair, the cowry shells smooth against her palms, and then stood and removed her tunic and wrung water from it too. The stones at her feet, pale green and silvery blue like all Moon Mountain rocks they had encountered, became splattered with water in strange random patterns.

"Thank you, Ambro," she said as she straightened. "I am sorry not to have trusted you."

"I wouldn't trust me either after how stupid I've been. But you know how it is—webbed toes must be good in rivers so I never worry about water." He held out one foot from the stallion's heaving sides as he spoke, and spread his toes so that his webs shone pink in the sunlight, and he grinned depreciatingly, inviting her response. Noleena felt her face softening into a smile; perhaps the first true and unconstrained smile that she had ever given this boy who was neither wholly Kiffa nor wholly of her people, and for a moment they were simply still, sharing that smile. Then the mare nudged Noleena in the small of her back and began to scramble up the side of the ravine with Noleena following. Ambro slid from Sun Runner and they too began to scramble upward.

Did I mean it? she wondered as they climbed. Am I sorry? And if I am, does this mean that I trust him now? Just because he pulled me from the water? Does his swift action balance out his rash pursuit of fame and reward that caused Hasani to be enslaved? Conflicting emotions and images tussled within her mind so that she rode without noticing the surrounding trees, or even the place where they grew sparser as the mist too thinned. It was the suddenness of brilliant sunshine that finally captured her attention and caused her to look around.

A long swath of grass and herbs stretched out in both directions like a ribbon laid down through the forest. "Have men been here cutting trees?" Noleena asked, but looking around neither she nor Ambro saw any sign of disturbance and concluded that the grass swath must be natural. Beyond it, the forest appeared less dense and chips of blue sky were visible, like mosaic tiles flung randomly amongst the spreading limbs.

"Can we rest here and let the horses graze?" Noleena asked, and slid from the mare's back to lie in the fragrant grass. She fell into a doze as her clothes, still damp from the river, dried into stiffness against her skin.

Suddenly Dune Dancer snorted; Noleena sat up and gazed sleepily around. "Someone is coming," she whispered urgently and Ambro, who had been dozing nearby, jerked upright rubbing his eyes. They both stared at the distant figure.

The boy was slightly built but lithe; as he ran steadily toward them through the grass, Noleena had the impression that he would be able to maintain his steady flowing lope for many miles. He flickered through the shadows of trees, disappearing in the dimness where his very dark skin provided perfect camouflage, for he was naked but for a loin cloth. When he stopped before Noleena and

Ambro, the boy nodded his head of tight dark curls; his breathing was even and slow, his ribs barely lifting the clay and bone amulets hung around his neck on a leather thong.

"Greetings," he said mildly in a soft voice that reminded Noleena of the Ismata stirring the foliage of the rhododendron bushes.

"I am Rafa—a FahFah Runner, from a village a little to the south."

"Where are you running to?" Ambro asked.

"Another village, northward from here. I will Run anywhere that a message must be taken; if a village is too far away to hear the voice of our drums, we send messages by Runners. I have been Running for days, along the High Running at the edge of the Sky Meadows, through cloud play and leaf dance."

"The Sky Meadows?" Noleena asked.

The boy waved one arm; it was like a branch from a sapling of the black-barked forest trees: thin, but almost impossible to break. "Beyond those trees you see ahead, lie the meadows where the Corno d'Oro used to run and Ismati, the moon goddess, blessed all creatures of the night: the moon wrens, the gentle wombos, the spotted panthers, the silver bats. Even now, the star lilies bloom where she walked. The meadows are a sacred place of great power; only our Elder Witch would ever wander there." And the FahFah boy touched the little circle of blue mineral paste that was painted on his chest, just over his heart, in a gesture that seemed to indicate respect.

"We call her Luna, but I think Ismati must be another name for her," Noleena said.

"The Ismata is her wind, blowing from the mountains," Rafa replied.

"Do you know about a star gate?" Noleena asked but the boy shook his head, his curls quivering.

"I do not know about the things of Sky Meadow magic," he said and he touched the blue circle again, more fearfully this time, as though seeking protection. "I must continue now until my Running is completed."

He bowed his head and sprang away to lope through the grass, his amulets rattling like seedpods. Shortly his figure was swallowed by shadows and blue distances, still moving swiftly and smoothly along. It was as though he had simply been absorbed into the landscape.

"Do you think the Sky Meadows are what you seek?" Ambro asked, and Noleena nodded, feeling hope quicken within her.

"We should press on to them before dark," she said with sudden energy, and called to the horses. As they moved into the last fringe of forest, riding through elongated shadows, Noleena's gaze was fixed over the mare's pricked ears. She waited anxiously for her first glimpse of a place that even the FahFahs, children of the mountains, would not venture into.

CHAPTER SEVENTEEN

FOR THREE DAYS THEY CAMPED in the meadows, surrounded by sweeping vistas of distant mountains that receded wave upon wave into blue haze; their slopes cloaked in towering trees with black, golden or red bark, and with spreading canopies. The meadows themselves were covered in tall grass of a pale silvery blue that rippled and ran like swells of water in the Ismata's breath, and was strewn with white lilies. The air was perfumed by their fragrance. Noleena had never been anywhere as wonderful, for this place was even more magical than the mugwawa's canyon. The first morning she ran through the swaying grass while the Ismata tangled her hair and filled her lungs; her whole body felt light and free, and her skin tingled. Small bent trees opened pink and white buds every morning; by midday they were clouds of pale blossoms; at dusk the petals drifted from the trees and fluttered through the air amongst the pale blue moths that flew at that hour. The horses rolled on their backs and frolicked like foals, kicking up their heels, and Noleena thought how her father would have loved to see them dance on this high and sacred roof of the world.

But after one day of this giddiness, this abandonment to freedom, Noleena began to search systematically for the star gate, riding out each morning in a different direction from the camp that she and Ambro had made beneath a weathered pile of silvery-blue rocks. Ambro asked if she wanted his company but she did not; she still harbored an obscure suspicion that he might somehow sabotage her quest at its most important moment if he found out where the star gate was located.

One evening, Noleena sat down upon their campsite rock and calculated on her fingers the number of days left until the appearance of the Blue Moon. In all her riding through meadows she had seen nothing but grass and tiny rivulets of sweet water that were the tributaries of the rushing rivers in the forest ravines below. Though she kneeled amongst the grasses, grasping her father's amulet in one hand, and begged Luna for guidance, she saw no sign.

Now, when she had finished her calculations, she became rigid with shock. I must have made a mistake, she thought. I will stay calm and calculate again. After a few minutes, she let out a gasp. "Tonight!" she exclaimed, and stared aghast at Ambro who sat nearby on the flat rock, feeding seeds to the birds in his wicker basket.

"What is tonight?"

"The Blue Moon rises for the first time, Ambro. And I haven't found the star gate."

Panic flooded her. "How can we have come so far and not found anything?" she wailed. "Luna has deserted her people; the days of the Wind-wanderers are numbered. The Kiffas will soon possess all of Terre, her desert spaces, her fleet horses, her amber and salt and gold, her rosy dawns and golden sunsets. All is lost...lost for my people! Lost forever!"

She bent her head over her knees and rocked to and fro in sorrow as the first stars pricked into faint points of yellow, green, and silver high overhead in the vast bowl of sky where the light was draining into the west and a stain of indigo seeped. The sky grew increasingly black, velvety and dense, until the stars seemed to hang close overhead, just beyond the reach of an arm, throbbing and burning with their cold magnificent fires.

Ambro moved across the rock to Noleena's side and patted her shoulders in comfort but she ignored him; she was so consumed with guilt and sorrow that she barely noticed the warmth of his palm on her shoulder blades. Her thoughts were on the corda groves with their crooked nets of shadow, and of how the Kiffas would chop them all down one after the other to use for firewood in the gold smelters; and on the valley of Engedi where the Kiffas would stride possessively in their bright flowing robes, renaming the horses; and on the temples to Luna scattered throughout Terre, that would decline into crumbling ruins where nothing moved but striped lizards; the chanting of the priestesses would be forgotten and absorbed into silence. Lost, all lost, the voices of her people.

Finally, Ambro lay on his back on the rock. "There is the Cracked Pot," he said, pointing up at a constellation. "And there are the Sea Horse Twins. Which ones do you know, Noleena?"

"What?' she asked; although she had been aware of Ambro's voice at her side, she had not been paying any attention to his words.

"Which constellations do you know?"

She lifted her head from her arms and stared upward. "The Gazelle Twins," she muttered in a heavy voice. "And Old Woman's Knee."

"In Verde we call that one Olive Branch. And there is the Hunting Gufo, and there, Sirena's Dolphin. See it?"

Ambro pointed and Noleena, in an effort to return his friendliness, squinted along his arm. "That is part of the constellation we in Terre call the Kiffa's Paw."

"No, no!" Ambro was laughing. "Anyone can see it is a great fish leaping. Look! You make a line between that yellow star there, and on to the green one, and then over to the west to that one there…"

His arm sliced across the sky, drawing its imaginary line.

"Sirena's Dolphin? A great fish leaping?" Noleena asked slowly, and she saw the shine of Ambro's eyes as his gaze swiveled toward her; she knew instantly from the tension in his shoulders that he had understood her.

"A great fish leaping....I did say that, didn't I?"

"*Over its mountains the Blue Moon hangs like a baited hook; at the moment that the great fish leaps, stand in the sacred place and look,*" Noleena quoted softly. "So this constellation that we have forgotten in Terre, but that you in Verde call Sirena's Dolphin, is the great fish leaping?"

"And here is the moon!" Ambro exclaimed, and Noleena looked to the eastern horizon of rumpled mountain peaks to see the Blue Moon, the first moon of the tenth night in the last month of summer, swinging curved and thin into the sky. "It is the shape of a fish hook, like the ones I fished with off the reefs of Verde," Ambro explained.

Noleena jumped to her feet and stared at it. "But we are not in the sacred place!" she cried. "This is the time of which the riddle speaks but we are not in the star gate!"

She leaped from the rock and began to run through the waist high grass, wildly, impelled with longing and the weight of her Seeking. It seemed as though she ran for hours, staring up at the sky, where the thin moon rose higher; straining her eyes around her in the meadows, longing to see something, anything, that might mark the star gate. At last, when the moon was high overhead, she turned and wearily retraced her steps toward the rock where she had left Ambro sitting. She heard the delicate sound of his flute before she came within sight of him. The flute's haunting melody was as clear as mountain water, as sweet as lilies. The stars seemed to hang lower as though listening, and when Noleena parted the grass around the rock she saw the animals: the moon wrens that had fluttered to Ambro's feet, the sleepy wombos that had climbed the rock to his side, the silver bats that flitted overhead. She stared in amazement, for what manner of magic did the boy possess that could entice the animals? Climbing onto the rock, she sat beside Ambro; with legs folded, she let the flute's melody pour into her.

The spotted panther padded toward them silently, a magnificent creature with flowing limbs and velvety paws, with a silver coat patterned with ghostly dark markings like clouds that gleamed in the faint light. Its eyes were pools of green fire above its wiry silver whiskers. Noleena stopped breathing; she felt power tingle over her arms and up her spine, for this was a creature as old as the reign of the moon goddess, and one that she had blessed. Never, in all her life, had Noleena ever expected to see a spotted leopard, a beast so rare that it was spoken of like a myth in the taverns and courtyards of Safala. Closer and closer the leopard padded toward the sound of Ambro's flute and Noleena heard his fingers falter for a moment.

The great beast mounted the rock in one sinuous flowing leap and padded toward Noleena. Every hair on her body rose, prickling with awe. Then the leopard laid one great paw upon her arm with its razor sharp claws retracted; the pads were smooth and soft as newly tanned leather. The green eyes burned into her own and stars and sickle moon flared across her vision and for a moment she heard her name being called in a woman's strong clear voice. Then the great cat leaped into the sea of dark waving grass and paused, looking back over its shoulder at Noleena and waving its elegant tail.

"I think it wants me to follow it," she whispered.

"Shall I come?" Ambro asked, taking his lips momentarily from the flute, but she shook her head for it was not for a Kiffa to follow the creatures of Luna.

She stared at the cat's fiery eyes, and at the dark wilderness of waving grass that lay beyond, and her throat constricted with fear. The leopard began to move away, its back silvered by moonlight and the grass parting around it like water parting around a great ship; at the last moment, just as its tail disappeared into the grass, Noleena found the strength to scramble to her feet and snatch up her pack.

"I must go!" she whispered to herself, aware of her voice squeezed thin with fright.

"Go!" Ambro urged.

Noleena jumped down into the grass and ran after the leopard along the trail it had parted; as she caught up to it, the great animal glanced back over one silver shoulder and flicked the black-striped end of its tail into her hand. Noleena caught hold of it gently, amazed at her own audacity, and the cat led her on across the High Meadows, star lilies glowing with an unearthly light around her in the darkness. Time out of time she followed the beast, as though they swam across the sky, across the waving rippling sea of grass. A delicate mist rose from the ground and swirled about them; it too glowed with a pale unearthly luminescence. Blue moths and white petals drifted through the mist. The stars seemed to hang lower and lower, pulsing and throbbing in the mist until they were all around Noleena and the leopard, until she was wading or perhaps floating amongst them. Were her feet even touching the ground anymore? She could not be sure. Nothing seemed real except the firm warm tip of the leopard's tail clasped in one hand.

Finally, swelling above the mist, there appeared a high knoll of land crowned with black rocks. Noleena followed the cat up the flanks of the knoll, her feet slipping on the springy short grass; her nostrils filled with the scents of fragrant herbs. As they climbed, the mist rose around them; within it, the stars seemed to pulse and sway. A high unearthly music, sweeter and clearer than anything Noleena had ever heard, filled the air. Cool blue light shivered over the surface of her skin; she could not tell whether it was starlight or something else. The Ismata stirred in the mist and Noleena imagined that she heard it whispering her name, calling her, coaxing her onward to the top of the knoll, toward the highest point of Terre, the one small place that the desert and the plateau lands and the Moon Mountains rose toward, upward and upward to lift at last into the wheeling stars. As Noleena reached the crest, the leopard stopped still; she saw its whiskers glinting in the moonlight. Stars swirled around her head; her eyes were dazzled with their silver and blue, green and yellow light. Still the high sweet music rang in her ears. Looking ahead, Noleena saw that the rocks crowning the knoll stood upright in a circle. Darkness, utter and absolute, lay inside it. Noleena stared into it, her skin crawling with fear and her heart leaping into her throat.

The leopard swung its great head toward her; she saw the smooth dome of the skull, the fire in its eyes, the soft muzzle pierced by silver whiskers and lying over fearsome teeth. Her legs shook. The animal swung its head against her legs and nudged her toward the darkness inside the huge standing stones. Like a dreamer, she moved. The shadows of the stones fell across her shoulders. She put out a hand and touched the nearest stone for support; felt its rough surface, saw it veined with blue where the moonlight fell upon it.

When she reached the centre of the ring of stones, she was alone. She kneeled upon the grass and waited, shaking in every limb.

Overhead, the stones contained a perfect circle of night sky. It was utterly black. Gradually, the hook of moon rose into this dark pool; its light tipped the standing stones with blue fire. Then, a star appeared, the first star of a constellation that wheeled gradually into position as Noleena waited, holding herself still on the short grass and chanting everything that she had ever learned in the temple in Safala. The words flowed away from her; she hardly knew what it was that she spoke. The Ismata sighed and whispered against her skin, eddying around the cornices of black rocks. When she peered through the cracks between them she could see nothing but luminescent mist and throbbing starlight: no leopard, no grasslands. It was as though the circle of stones existed somewhere out of time and space.

Now the constellation in the dark pool of sky overhead moved higher so that Noleena was able to see its entirety. "The great fish!" she whispered, and saw how it leapt toward the hook of the moon.

Brighter and brighter blazed the moon's light until it was a dazzling amulet of silver fire hanging above Noleena; the rocks around her glowed in the brilliance. Noleena stared in awe, dazzled, overwhelmed. Now, in the centre of the light, the face of a woman took shape. It was as pale and smooth as the moon itself, surrounded by a mass of streaming hair like stormy clouds and with eyes as brilliant as blue stars. For a moment it drifted through the brilliance, then the light became unbearably bright and Noleena closed her eyes. The Ismata ran softly across her brow and over her arms, and she heard its sibilant whisper all around her. It sighed across her skin, poured into her ears. Words swirled around the rocks, chased each other through the grass.

Daughter...daughter of the moon...moon...I hear the cries of my people...I send you forth...I hear...I send you with power...courage and power...take my gift...set my people free...free...take my gift...

The breath of the Ismata died and the air grew still. The light began to fade. The brilliant blue sheen of the encircling rocks transformed into blackness. Once more, Noleena glimpsed the pearly outline of the woman's face with tender blue eyes and serene lips, then her dark hair swirled across it. Noleena blinked. The hair had become clouds that drifted over the hook of the moon, now a tiny thing high above and casting only a pale glow. The constellation named Sirena's Dolphin was already moving away, leaping across the heavens and out of the circle of sky pooled in the rocks' embrace.

Noleena shook her head, like a sleeper awakening. Stiffly she climbed to her feet and stared around. All seemed ordinary on the knoll now: the air was sweet and still, the stars and moon far overhead. The shadows cast by the rocks had shifted position since she had entered their circle; what had previously been shrouded in darkness now held the moon's pale glimmer. The box sat in the light. Noleena's glance swept over it, then darted back. Surely it had not been there before; a square dark object small enough to hold in both hands. Or had shadow hidden it? Noleena stepped toward it slowly. Was it meant for her? Should she touch it?

She paused, staring down at it. It had a surface of black wood polished to a silvery sheen and inlaid with a white stone forming patterns of star lilies. The lid was embossed with a sickle moon and a rayed sun—the marks of the Corno d'Oro and the moon goddess, Noleena thought with a sharp intake of breath. Was this box the gift of which the goddess had spoken? But of what use was such a trinket against the spears of the Kiffa-walkers, the cruel whips of the assassini, the dark sorcery of the Maldici queen?

Noleena stooped and touched one fingertip to the lid of the box; a hot electric tingle swept up her arm and raised the hair on the nape of her neck. She snatched her finger away and stared at the box but nothing more happened. The lid, she saw, was hinged with silver and held closed with a silver clasp. Did the box contain something that would be of use against the oppressors?

Noleena pulled off her tunic and wrapped it around the box, then lifted it and cradled it reverently in her arms. No sound of contents shifting position came from within it, and it felt light as air in her arms. Cautiously she turned, then paused to see what might happen. She strained her ears, but no words slipped woven through the wind. Noleena turned to walk out between the great rocks. The leopard crouched outside on its belly. Noleena laid her palm gently upon its forehead and it rose to its feet; together they went down the knoll into the sea of mist and grass. The mist too seemed ordinary now, no longer filled with stars or blue luminescent light. It was simply mist, draped in scarves through the motionless grass.

For a long time Noleena waded through it, not knowing where she was but letting the leopard guide her, and at last she saw the dark outline of a flat rock, and heard the sweet melody of Ambro's flute. The leopard stayed with her until they reached the base of the rocks and then, with one last affectionate nudge at her leg, it turned and melted into the darkness. Noleena climbed onto the rock, amongst the circle of moths and wombos and bats that still listened to Ambro's music. She sat beside him, with the wrapped box on her lap, and waited until his music died away and he turned a questioning face to her.

"Wasn't I gone for—for a great length of time?" she asked. "You are still playing your flute."

He looked surprised. "You were gone for only a few minutes."

"Did you see the moon grow dazzling bright as Sirena's Dolphin leapt across the heavens toward it?"

"No, the moon is only a new one and gives only a small light. Look at it."

She looked and saw the tiny crescent hanging over the eastern horizon, barely shedding any light upon the swelling contours of the meadows and the peaks of distant mountains. And the stars, that had hung throbbing around her head, now seemed remote and infinitely small and far above.

"Was there a mist here?" she asked but Ambro shook his head.

Noleena lay flat on her back and gazed upward unseeingly. "I have been to the sacred place," she said in wonder. "The leopard took me there, your leopard that you magicked with your flute. The mugwawa was right, for she said that you were a thread in my weaving."

"But where did you go? It must have been close by because you were gone so short a time."

"I went to a knoll with a circle of tall stones. I don't know where it was; I had never seen it before. And I think that tomorrow I will not be able to find it again…I cannot describe it, Ambro. It was not—not real, like daily life is real. And yet, it was more real than anything else. It was all mist and stars and wind and beauty."

She did not speak of the face of Luna, for such a dazzling sight was more than a tongue could bear the weight of, and neither did she speak of the goddess's voice whispering in the Ismata for she lacked the words to describe such sacred speech. Despite her silence, Noleena felt an unfamiliar confidence rising in her like a tide; power tingled in every fiber of her being and she felt the tender regard of Luna's brilliant eyes. She is watching me, she thought. She is with me as I struggle through the darkness that ensnares Terre, and with her wisdom I shall prevail.

"And was your Seeking successful?" Ambro asked at last, after a long silence in which the animals slipped away into the night.

"I have a—a gift," she said. "In the morning, I will look at it and decide what to do next."

"I'll help if I can. Let me see the gift." He extended his hands, reaching for the box enfolded in Noleena's tunic. In that moment, in the faint moonlight, she saw the Kiffa bracelets on his arms shine as thin and golden as the strands of his hair. Her first memory of him, when he had woken her in Safala's temple, flashed through her.

She snatched the tunic and the box onto her lap. "You have fulfilled your oath; I release you from it. You can leave me now and follow your own paths."

Her formal words hung in the air between them, sounding stiffer than she had intended, and ungrateful. Already, her moment of irrational fear was fading. She swallowed with difficulty. He is not a Kiffa boy marauding a temple, she reminded herself; he is Ambro who I have begun to trust.

"I didn't mean—you may ride from the mountains with me, on the stallion, if you wish to and if we are going in the same direction," she amended. "I only meant that you were no longer bound by your oath…"

She faltered into uncomfortable silence as something hard and bright flared in Ambro's eyes.

His tone, when he spoke, was a stiff as her own had been. "You will be glad when I am gone. I am not Hasani. I am not even a true Wanderer, though the Kiffas disown me for my webs. So why would you need *me*—a mixed-blood orphan—to help *you*, Princess?"

"But I am grateful to you; I couldn't have reached this place without your help."

"My help?" he said bitterly. "Surely you would have traveled faster if you hadn't had to watch me all the time, to make sure that I wasn't about to fall off the stallion or run away with him."

"No, I don't think so…of course not—" The truth contained in his words silenced her, flushing.

"Be assured I will not stay with you much longer," he said. "If we travel from here to the FahFah village that the Runner came from, perhaps we can find you another traveling companion, and perhaps the FahFah can tell you of routes to wherever you wish to go. As for me, I have other matters to attend to." He jumped to his feet and gave her a mocking Kiffa-walker bow before turning away to spread his sleeping roll; shortly, he was prone upon it, a silent mound at which Noleena stared miserably from her own bedroll.

I have treated Ambro badly, she thought. I have treated him as though he had no feelings, as though his friendship and service were a burden to me; as though I was the only one whose ambitions mattered. This is the same treatment that the Kiffas have inflicted upon my own people and that I seek to free them from—yet I am guilty of it myself. In the morning, I must apologize and ask for Ambro's forgiveness. But perhaps he will not grant it. Why should he, when I have said I will never grant him mine?

All night, as the moon climbed higher and constellations wheeled, her dreams were filled with the whisper of the wind, its lily-scented sweetness, and with the fiery glow of the leopard's eyes. Sometimes, she dreamed of the moon; a ghostly face flickered in its brilliance but when she expected to see Luna's tender smile, black clouds rushed to cover the face, and the moonlight grew blue and cold so that her dream-self shivered, and in her sleep she moaned.

At dawn, she awoke tired to sit up stiffly and look around. Ambro still slept on the rock. The meadows were suffused with rosy light, and white buds were tiny embroidered knots on the bent trees. A flight of cranes passed high overhead, their wild thin cries whistling into the pale sky. I have work to do, Noleena told herself sternly, drawing from her pack the wrapped box. I have failed with Ambro but I must not fail my people. Her heart skipped a beat as she stared at the folds of tunic. Contained in them, perhaps, lay her future and that of her people and of the whole land of Terre: its rift valleys terraced with wheat and sorghum, its oases of nuga palms and flashing rainbirds, its shimmering high desert smelling of alkali dust, its splendid cities of fretted stone. Its children, playing Fox and Jackal in dusty streets or plunging their faces into slices of green melon in desert valleys, their blue and tawny eyes alight with innocent laughter.

The tunic fabric trembled in Noleena's fingers as she unwrapped the box. She turned it in her hands but the polished surfaces yielded no clues, and there was nothing to be seen that she hadn't already seen: the star lily inlay, the embossings of the Corno d'Oro hoof prints. How, how was this box going to save her people? Surely, she decided, it must *contain* the gift from Luna, the gift that would ensure freedom. Although Noleena didn't understand how such a small box could contain such a huge gift, she believed implicitly in that moment that such a thing was possible. Holding her breath, she bent to discover how the silver clasp worked. With infinite caution, she unfastened it and lifted the lid; its silver hinges yielded soundlessly.

The box was empty.

CHAPTER EIGHTEEN

Ambro tried to run as fluidly and smoothly as Rafa ran; a steady loping that he hoped he could maintain for hours. He had begun the day feeling rested, having spent the previous two days in the FahFah village with Noleena, lounging in the shade whilst waiting for Rafa to return from his previous Running. Loping into the village at last, with the evening sunlight glistening on his sweating chest, Rafa had agreed to guide Ambro out of the mountains. They had left the FahFah village in the morning when the sun was still a pale ball tangled in the white-cane.

Now the grass of the High Running swished against Ambro's knees. The birds cooed in their basket upon his back as the sun rose higher, soaring up into a shining sky. Sweat ran down Ambro's forehead and he blinked his eyes; the red trunks of forest trees flickered in the periphery of his vision. The energy of his resolve carried him for many miles before they stopped to rest beneath a flowering thorn where he hefted his flask and drank three mouthfuls of tepid water infused with mint. Rafa unslung a narrow tube of polished wood and took one sip only of whatever liquid it held.

Leaning against the tree, Ambro waited for his breathing to steady and the burn in his thigh muscles to ease. Now that his legs were still, sharp thoughts prickled his mind.

How could Noleena have spoken to him so, with coldness and stiffness, after all the miles he had ridden beside her, after he had saved her from the rock in the mountain torrent? Hadn't they forged trust between them, all those misty afternoons as they labored through rhododendron and lianas, all those warm nights when they had crouched by small fires beneath the black canopy where monkeys screeched? Yet she had snatched her moon gift, wrapped in her tunic, away from his reach two nights ago with such startled, wide blue eyes that he had been momentarily transported to Safala and the evening when he'd accidentally woken her in the temple. Although she had regretted her action almost immediately; he had seen the shadow cross her face as she realized what she'd done. And then, this morning, she had offered him the stallion for his journey; a generous gift indeed and one that it would cost her much to give, and one that he had once coveted with all his being.

That time of covetousness has passed, he thought. Now I will take my Kiffa strength and return to the desert where I belong. There is something that I must do that is more important than finding horses or even than helping Noleena; for many miles it has weighed my heart down and is my true Hunting at last—or perhaps my true Seeking. Which will it be? Am I Kiffa or Wanderer? The soldiers abandoned me because of my webs, yet all Noleena sees when she looks at me is my golden hair and tawny eyes. Can no one accept me for who I am? On this important Hunting and Seeking that I undertake now, he decided, I will be both tribes and neither; I will be only a human following the path of my heart.

With a swift, backward glance and a gesture indicating that Ambro should follow, Rafa began to move away again through the forest shadows. Ambro straightened beneath the thorn tree, tossed his hair back, twisted the golden Kiffa bracelets on his arms, and stared along the High Running with a narrowed, haughty gaze.

For a moment his wide mouth compressed into a line of determination, and then he too began to run again, his golden head shining in the light.

On and on they ran, southwestward through the forest, down and down, traversing ravines on spindly bridges of swinging knotted lianas; the water ran dark and fast far beneath Ambro's gripping toes, and his stomach heaved with the swing of the vines. Finally, again on the evening of the second day's journey, they reached the crest of a hill and saw, falling away below them, a thin strip of plateau lands and beyond it the shimmering golden-blue emptiness of the desert. Ambro's gaze swept across it with a surge of delight and he breathed in deeply, seeking the alkaline smell that he loved.

"Run safely, brother," Rafa said solemnly, bobbing his head of dark curls, and he lifted an amulet of carved hoggi tusk from around his own neck and placed it over Ambro's head. Ambro clasped his hand in thanks and then began to run slowly, for he was tired, down the hill into the plateau grass with the amulet bouncing against his breastbone and the desert calling to him like a distant lover.

For three days Ambro traveled across the desert eating the honeycomb and dried anbara fruit that Rafa had given to him, until he reached the village of Mandi where Hasani had been led with a rope around his throat like a dog being taken away to a new master. Here, Ambro sold a bracelet to a woman at a stall, and used a portion of the money to buy a new pair of Kiffa boots of soft leather with fleecy rolled tops, and a robe of azure blue with pearly clasps, and a pair of violet colored leggings to replace the ragged remains of his green silk pair. Then he paid for a room at a mud-brick inn where he slept for twelve hours, and rose to eat gazelle casserole and flat bread rolled around chick peas, and where he found a dark-haired woman with blue eyes and a brand on her shoulder serving behind the bar.

He pulled her aside and bent his head close to hers, and whispered to her for several minutes as her eyes grew wider and he thought with a momentary pang of Noleena. Then he sat at the bar drinking cinni tea and watching the comings and goings of travelers with his haughty Kiffa gaze. He waited several hours before the woman behind the bar nudged his elbow and whispered, "It's them," and Ambro looked up with a lurch in his chest to see two men enter the dimness. The folds of their robes, and their golden moustaches, were soft with dust and the planes of their faces were hard as rock. They swaggered across to the bar and sat beside Ambro who nodded in greeting. "May Kiffa keep you," he said smoothly, and the men directed their flat gazes across him.

"You look tired, brothers," Ambro continued. "Let me buy you a drink," and he spilled some of the coins, remaining from the sale of the bracelet, onto the bar's surface of scratched ceramic tiles and the branded woman brought three tall glasses of fermented nuga sap to them. The men raised their glasses to Ambro. "Death to webbies," they toasted, and Ambro bent back his long golden neck and swallowed, the nuga sap burning a path into his belly and filling his chest with desert heat, with anger, with pride. The men ordered nuts and dates which they shared with Ambro and presently, as they drank, their hard faces softened and their blank fierce stares grew unfocused and their tongues loosened. Ambro nodded and questioned. He laughed at their cruel stories; men begging on their knees for mercy and receiving a kick in the stomach instead; small children tied onto slaver's doda in bundles of five like kindling; and of one man brought in from Mount Lalibela who, when branded, had fought so hard it took three men to truss him up and how then, in punishment, he had been dragged behind a doda's bare pink legs all the way to the gold mine at Kalifa.

As darkness fell, the woman behind the bar lit lanterns of shugra oil and the slavers called for more nuga sap and for apricot fire-juice; in the lantern's flicker their crooked teeth gleamed and their stories grew more cruel, and Ambro found himself clutching at Rafa's warti hoggi amulet as though for protection. He slipped it quickly into the folds of his azure Kiffa robe and yawned with feigned indifference though his heart drummed in his ears.

"Brothers,' he said at last, "I must travel on early in the morning on my Lord Tafari's business. I bid you goodnight; sleep beneath Kiffa's gaze."

He slipped out, pressing his last remaining coin into the palm of the dark-haired Wanderer serving behind the bar, and then he walked through Mandi to the enclosures where animals were bought and sold; in the light of palm flares, he peered at a milling collection of shugras, ponies, goats, and pacing doda. For a second bracelet he purchased a pony with a rolling eye and a loud snort, which tried to kick him when he approached but which the seller insisted was young and very strong. Ambro and the pony circled each other warily until finally Ambro sprang on, with the birds strapped to his back, grasping a handful of wiry mane and wrapping his legs tightly around the pony's sides. The seller swung the enclosure gate open and the pony surged out, writhing like an eel, with Ambro hauling on the reins to turn its head southward. For miles the pony rocketed along, snorting and rolling his eyes; his small hooves rang sharply on the flinty path that led through Kadah and Swilia and Ankha and finally to the gold mines of Kalifa.

By the time they reached Kalifa three days later, the pony had ceased bucking and settled into a docile trot but Ambro ached in every bone and felt as though dust covered even his eyeballs. In the mining town he took off another bracelet and sold it to a gold merchant for a bag of coins; he stabled the pony behind another mud-brick inn and went into the bar to drink cinni and ponder things over. He wondered about Noleena, about what the moon-gift had been and if she knew how to use it and whether she was out of the mountains by now. But I don't care where she is, he thought, with a flicker of wounded pride. He wondered whether she would have the courage and ability to turn back the tide of darkness that was washing through Terre, rising higher every hour with a rushing force that swept away men's lives like flotsam. He didn't see how anything could be done, especially by her with her wide timid gaze and her soft voice.

And I can only do one thing myself, he thought. It's a small thing, but it is my Hunting now. I vow to do it, even if I die.

And he raised his glass of cinni in Kalifa's bar, and threw back his golden hair and drained the liquid from the glass in one long gulping swallow, trying to blot out the fear in his belly. It was possible, he knew, that he would indeed die on this Hunting to which he had now dedicated himself. This was not a Hunting for horses and honor, nor to help a girl, but a Hunting where life, precious and irreplaceable, lay at stake—though treated as cheaply as a handful of glass beads.

And if I die on this Hunting, Ambro thought, it is perhaps only just and fair. My life for Hasani's. Perhaps it was for this end that I climbed aboard a Kiffa trading ship off the pirati archipelago, and crossed the water to this rolling desert land with its harsh beauty. Perhaps it was not to find a family that I came, but to save one life.

So be it; I have vowed.

And he strode out, holding his back straight, into the marketplace where he bought scrolls of paper, a small sharp knife, a quill pen, and a ceramic pot of blue dye made from the inner bark of the sheena tree. Back at his room in the inn, he sat up late into the night carving Lord Tafari's seal, a rainbird superimposed upon a kiffa's paw and surrounded by fronds of desert saw grass, into a piece of wood. Shavings fell onto his azure robe. Then he spread the paper flat upon the table and dipped a quill into a pot of jobi ink and wrote a brief message in a sweeping hand; his tongue was clenched between his teeth in an agony of concentration. One blot, one misspelled word, and the parchment would be ruined. He signed it with a final flourish and left it to dry whilst he mixed the blue dye with the beeswax from Rafa's honeycomb. When the wax and dye had melted by the fire, he folded the parchment into three, and sealed the edges with the wax, into which he pressed Lord Tafari's seal. It left a clear imprint; with a pang Ambro remembered seeing Lord Tafari's long clever fingers break this seal open to read reports from his treasuries, his overseers of doda trains, and his masters of slaves at gold mines. It had been pleasant, in those days, to hope to be Lord Tafari's nephew instead of his enemy. But those days had passed away, and now was the time for Ambro to put aside dreams and become a man for as much time as he had left to be alive.

In the morning, Ambro haggled in the animal market until eventually he'd traded his wild pony for a larger, sleeker one and a red harness with tassels that bobbed as the pony trotted through Kalifa with Ambro's azure robe blowing across its back. They passed the workshops of leather engravers and potters, passed the community bread ovens and the aqueduct bringing Moon Mountain water to the well where women waited in chattering lines, passed the mud-brick fort where sentries paced the battlements beneath the Kiffa's tawny flag, and trotted down the valley toward the dusty cloud that hung above the gold mines, trapped in the still air between Kalifa's hills.

Closer and closer they approached; the pony's flanks a sheen of sweat, and Ambro's star sapphire earrings—retrieved from his cloth bag—glinting in his ear lobes in the hot light. He clenched his jaw, and felt for the reassuring dry sheaf of parchment tucked inside his robe.

The mine workings were encircled by a deep ditch, on the outer perimeter of which a continuous row of sharpened stakes pointed inward. It would be impossible, Ambro thought as he rode closer and studied them, for any man to climb up the sheer wall of the ditch and then get out through that line of stakes. Besides which, sentries paced along the inside of the ditch; some, Ambro noted, were assassini with brutti trotting beside their hairy, booted legs. There was one gap in this perimeter enclosure and here Ambro was stopped by the knot of guards who clustered around him with fierce suspicious gazes. He swallowed, sitting tall on his pony, and regarded the soldiers with a haughty stare.

"I demand to see your captain," he said in his cool, clear voice, and then ignored the soldiers as he waited for the captain's arrival, sitting firmly upon his fidgeting pony and regarding the soaring wheel of vultures over the mine encampment as though it were of no interest at all. When the captain arrived, Ambro withdrew the parchment from his robe. "I am on Lord Tafari's business," he said. "He sends his greetings and hopes that his interests in the mine here prosper. I am being trained in his household and have been sent to Kalifa to learn how the gold is extracted and then sent by caravan to Lord Tafari's treasuries. This is my Permission of Passage," and he held out the parchment with an unflinching stare. The captain held the wax seal to the light and studied it. The pony fidgeted. Ambro fixed his gaze on the dry ridge of hills above Kalifa and willed himself to breathe quietly.

The captain, seemingly satisfied, broke the seal and unfolded the parchment to read the letter that Ambro had penned, in Lord Tafari's hand, at the inn table.

"Fine," the captain said suddenly, refolding the parchment and slipping it inside his leather vest with its embossed, snarling kiffa. "This man will be your guide for the day," and he gestured to a nearby soldier who stepped forward with a bow.

"I wish to see every aspect of the mining process," Ambro commanded imperiously. "I will ride."

The soldier fell in beside the pony as Ambro rode through the gap in the ditch with its wicked spine of stakes; the pony shied as a brutto trotted past, its drool spattering the churned dust. Drool that kills if I'm bitten, Ambro thought, and a chill rippled through his hot robe and clenched around his ribs.

"The gold lies in the quartz," the soldier explained, "and the digging follows the quartz veins."

Ambro followed the direction of the man's pointing arm to see a series of trenches snaking up from the valley on diagonal lines into the hard dry hills. As they approached closer, he was able to see the Wanderer children staggering from the trenches beneath heavy pieces of jagged quartz that glittered like white fire. The children's shoulders were laced with scars and smeared with fresh blood; the edges of the quartz were sharp as glass. Ambro halted the pony and watched in pity; saw the children's small legs strain beneath the weight of rock, and their callused feet walking painfully through dust and debris; saw the blank pools of their eyes. They passed him without a glance, without awareness, like ghosts walking forever in their own misery. Dust coated even their eyelashes, and lay thick on their heads of shorn dark hair. Beside them the overseers cracked their whips and shouted hoarse commands.

"Who cuts the rock from the trenches?" Ambro asked.

"Men do. And then men crush it, and the older men and the women mill it. Do you wish to continue?"

Ambro nodded curtly and nudged the pony forward. In the valley bottom, below the mine trenches, he watched as the procession of children dropped their rock loads and returned doggedly to the trenches for more. Men seized the quartz as the children delivered it, and swung at it with huge hammers. Their backs rose and fell, rose and fell in the dust and blinding heat, backs slick with sweat and laid open with whips; every shoulder, Ambro noticed, was branded with the M for Maldici. His stomach churned and he swallowed heavily and willed himself to be still on the pony's back. A man cried out as a shard of quartz flew into his eye; an overseer dragged him away yelling. Whips flickered through the cauldron of white dust like the tongues of enormous snakes. The ringing of the hammers was deafening and relentless. It was impossible, Ambro thought, that men could perform such work in such heat and not die quickly of it. He saw how the men's eyes were glazed with fatigue, how their ribs strained at their skin.

Hasani, Ambro thought with a clutch of dread. Perhaps he is already dead. Perhaps I will never have a chance to redeem the great wrong I have done to him.

"You have seen enough?" the soldier asked and Ambro nodded, although he had not seen Hasani though his eyes strained in every direction amongst the whips and pacing brutti, amongst the rise and fall of bloodied backs.

"Next, the milling," the soldier commented. He led Ambro farther down the valley to where older men, and Wanderer women dressed only in the tattered remains of their breeches and with scarred breasts, ground the fragments of hammered quartz into powder in rock mills.

"After this, it is washed," the soldier explained, and Ambro watched as baskets of powder were dumped onto sloping boards and then saw how the powder was washed down through sieves of shugra hair where the gold, extracted at last from its bed of quartz, glittered and clung in the darkness of the hair. The water itself ran on downhill into tailing ponds, beyond which the ground was wet with seepage, and reedy, and deserted. Apparently, the sentries didn't patrol the lower reaches of the valley with much diligence, choosing instead to muster around the washing boards. There, at the final stage of the gold mining process, the assassini were most in abundance and the brutti ran loose and wild, snarling and snapping at the Kiffa soldiers as they bagged the gold dust, as they weighed it and tallied it, as they passed it into the hands of the caravaners to load on the doda preening themselves as they waited.

And once I dreamed, Ambro thought, of leading such a caravan; the animals loaded with gold and human misery, with the great burden of human lives. Shame burned in him, and a mounting urgency to find Hasani.

"I have not seen into the trenches," he said to the soldier, and they turned and made their way back up the slope of the hills to where the trenches were gouging into the rock; here too, men's backs rose and fell as they hacked at the quartz. A slab fell suddenly, landing on a man's foot, and when the slaves working beside him rolled the slab away, Ambro saw that the foot was crushed beyond saving. An overseer's whip sent the slaves back to work, and the injured man was dragged away, screaming in agony, by an assassini. "What will happen to him?" Ambro asked, and the soldier beside the pony shrugged. "He will be vulture food tonight," he replied indifferently.

Ambro quelled a shudder, and willed himself to continue riding along the lip of the trench, willed himself to recognize Hasani's back; that strong, straight, broad back that Ambro had last seen as the bandit walked south between the slavers. Yet I barely looked at him when he left, Ambro thought, so how would I recognize him in this inferno of misery? Despair washed over him and his sweat was cold beneath the hot folds of his robe; he wiped his clammy brow and stared along the line of the trench. They are digging their own graves, he thought. They will all die here—and he remembered, in a flash, the wild fierce freedom of the bandits as they had swooped upon Lord Tafari's caravan in the dunes of Enlon. Now, in this moment, he at last understood their ferocity, their freedom, and the passion of their wild charge. It was their own deaths they were riding out against.

How ignorant I was, Ambro thought miserably. How foolish.

He pulled on the reins, turning the pony's head away from the trenches.

"There is more to see?" he asked, and the soldier shrugged. "The vulture pile for the sick, below the tailing ponds," he said. "Nothing more. The men who survive the pile return to work, the others feed the birds."

Ambro nodded and, suddenly sickened beyond endurance, kicked the pony into a trot without saying goodbye to his guide, and continued at a trot out through the one gap in the perimeter defenses, and along the valley to Kalifa's town. Here he returned to his room at the inn and lay within its hot mud walls, listening to lizards scuttling in the roof and feeling desperate with stupidity. The little birds shuffled in their wicker basket and presently the rock-rose began to chortle softly.

Ambro, who had fallen into a doze, opened his eyes and grew intent. An idea flickered in his mind like heat lightning. He swung his feet off the bed and bent to open the cage. "These are my birds," the mugwawa had said to him, "and they will fly to any person you name in Terre. The rock-rose will carry a message; the dove will lay eggs so filled with nourishment that a man may live off them alone for weeks."

Now, Ambro gently lifted the birds from the cage; they perched upon the end of the bed and cooed and fluttered their wings while Ambro cut a thin strip of parchment with his knife and dipped his quill into the jobi ink. *Noleena sends her love*, he wrote in a tiny script. *Speak my name, Ambro, and follow the birds to me at the hour of the evening star.*

He rolled the parchment around the rock-rose's delicate leg and fastened it with an azure thread pulled from the hem of his robe. Then he lay down to wait for dusk, whilst the birds tucked their heads beneath their wings and slept peacefully.

In the coolness after sunset, Ambro placed the birds in their basket and strapped it on his back. He rode the pony out along the eastern fringes of Kalifa, and came in a roundabout fashion to the lower end of the mining enclosure, below the tailing ponds. Tethering the pony in a grove of corda trees, Ambro removed his clothes and rubbed himself all over with damp clay so that his body blended into the desert's fading colors. Then he tied his bag with its spyglass and flute around his shoulders, and slung a piece of rope, bought that afternoon in Kalifa, around his back.

On his belly, and dragging the bird cage beside himself, he crawled cautiously over the ground until he came within sight of the ditch and its bristle of stakes. The evening star glimmered in the tailing ponds' flat surfaces. Ambro lay still and listened; faintly, in the still air, he heard the moans of the dying tossed on the vulture pile. If Hasani were still alive, he must surely be there. Ambro watched for some time, until he was sure that all sentries were as far away as they would move on their assigned routes, then he lifted the rock-rose from the cage and crooned Hasani's name to it over and over before tossing it skyward. For a moment it circled overhead, then flew across the stakes and over the tailing ponds and disappeared.

Ambro crawled to the edge of the ditch and, uncoiling his rope, tied it to the base of a stake. Then he crawled back to the pony, tied the cage to its side and tied the other end of the rope, padded with his clothes, around the pony's chest and urged it forward. It strained and heaved, sweat breaking out on its shoulders, until Ambro despaired that anything would happen. His plan was going to fail. He whacked the pony across the haunches and urged it on; in the silence its heaving breath and scrabbling hooves moved him with pity. Finally he went to its head and let it rest; it stood with drooping neck. He left it to crawl toward the ditch where he lay still with the earth tepid beneath his chest and one eye pressed to the spyglass. The sentry passed once, then twice. Ambro felt around the base of the stake but it seemed not to have moved at all in its bed of sand, despite all the pony's efforts. Ambro slithered back into the corda grove and sat with his head in his hands, thinking. The plan that came to him was reckless, but he didn't fear it. He placed his flute to his lips and began to play a night song of the desert, an ancient, rustling, moonlit, secret song.

The blue lizard entered the corda grove from the north. Its great dark head, craggy with spines, was raised high on its long swiveling neck and the starlight shone in its hooded, reptilian eyes. Ambro suppressed a shudder of horror and delight; he had heard of this huge blue lizard that lived in the valley of Kalifa though it was rare indeed to see one for they were ancient creatures, old as the desert, and wily and fierce. It was said that some of them were man-eaters. It was this creature that Ambro had called to with his flute, pulling it to him with the force of his longing.

Ambro continued to play and the lizard moved closer, its long clawed toes shuffling aside fallen corda leaves, its scaly back glistening with a metallic sheen and as hard as rock. It was magnificent.

Ambro played until the lizard was beside him, its massive shoulder like a buttress, then with infinite caution and still playing his flute, he moved alongside its muscular tail. The lizard's head, with massive jaw, swiveled slowly, following his movement. Quick as a flash, he dropped the flute and lashed the end of his rope around the tail. It swung beneath his grip, knocking him off his feet so that pain exploded in one leg, then lashing him across the face so that his nose gushed blood. He rolled away, covering his head with his arms protectively, waiting for the lizard's teeth to pierce his spine. But the lizard, hissing with outrage, surged from the grove. The rope held taut for only an instant until the stake to which its other end was attached yanked free from the sand. The stake flew past

Ambro, knocking against his legs with a blow that left him dizzy with pain. He lay still, breathing in gasps, then at last stood up shakily and grinned. His plan had worked. He wiped the blood streaming from his nose and tried to quiet the alarmed pony.

Once more dropping to his belly, he crawled back to the ditch and found, with great satisfaction, that not only had one stake been pulled out but that a second one was half over. He waited until the sentry's torch was far off up the valley and then began to dig feverishly at the base of this dislodged stake, pushing it further over and widening the gap. Then he crawled back to the pony and removed a rein from its bridle and returned to the ditch once more.

He waited.

An ant crawled up one leg, tickling.

His wounded leg throbbed, bleeding into the sand.

He swung the glass but the mining enclosure had fallen into darkness save for the occasional flare of a passing sentry's torch.

A gossamer mist began to rise from the ponds.

The moans from the vulture pile fell into silence.

Far off, in the desert, a jackal called to the evening star.

A small bird flew into Ambro's circular lens. Then a man appeared, crawling on his belly beneath the bird. Ambro clenched his jaw in excited disbelief. Hasani? It had to be Hasani! Into no other man's hands would the rock-rose have flown with its message.

The sentry's torch began to descend the valley. Hasani dropped flat against the ground and the bird circled above him. Would the missing stake be noticed? Ambro wondered. Would Hasani himself be noticed? Ambro held his breath and continued to wait. The sentry passed Hasani lying just outside the palm flare's light without noticing him, and came on toward the palisade of stakes. Closer and closer the light came, splashing like water down into the ditch, spraying up over the long dark lines of stakes with their gleaming sharpened points; five stakes away from Ambro's hole, four stakes, three. He's going to find it, Ambro realized. He'll raise the alarm. And Hasani is still inside, behind him.

He placed his flute to his lips and played; the flare swung and light poured over Ambro where he lay on his belly with his flute in his muddy hands. The sentry loosed a volley of shouts; dimly, Ambro heard them returned from much higher up the valley but then the lizard's blasting hiss filled Ambro's ears as the great reptile surged out of the darkness at such speed that he brushed past Ambro, knocking him aside, and through the hole in the stake defenses. The lizard's momentum carried it across the open ditch and onto the sentry; there was a stifled yell as the man fell. The flare landed in the sand, sputtering, smoking, and went out. Ambro heard the crunch of bones as the reptile bit into the fallen man. After some time, there was silence except for the shuffling of the lizard moving away up the valley. Ambro raised his head cautiously, and spat sand from his mouth.

"Hasani?" he called, and presently he heard the flutter of a bird above his head and saw the silhouette of the bandit on the opposite side of the ditch.

"Drop down," he called softly. "I'll pull you out on this side."

Hasani rolled and dropped into the earth with a thud whilst Ambro dangled the pony's rein into the ditch. He wrapped the other end around a stake and began to pull; Hasani's feet scrabbled weakly inside the ditch as Ambro hauled him up the side and then out through the gap in the stakes.

Loud yelling broke out higher up the valley, beyond the tailing ponds. Flares began to descend. Ambro pulled Hasani to his feet and steadied him with one arm when he staggered. "Come," he urged. "I have a pony in the trees."

Together they stumbled into the corda grove and Ambro boosted Hasani onto the pony and untied it. He thought that he would hold onto the one remaining rein and run alongside the pony, if his wounded leg would allow him to do so. Pain seemed to be robbing the leg of all its strength, so that even standing by the pony was an effort. Still, he would have to try.

Then, suddenly, just as he wrapped a hand around the rein, he heard the dry susurration of sand and leaves at his back. Instantly, he dropped the rein. Only the pony, carrying one person on its back, would be fast enough to escape. "Ride!" he shouted at Hasani, slapping the pony's haunches so that it shot forward into the empty desert beyond the corda grove.

Then he turned, scrabbling desperately over the dark ground for his flute. Somewhere it lay amongst the dried leaves, invisible. The lizard's enraged hiss filled his ears as his wounded leg buckled beneath him and he went down.

CHAPTER NINETEEN

"AN EMPTY BOX, FROM A STONE RING, in the High Meadows of the moon goddess," the FahFah Elder Witch mused solemnly in the tongue of Terre so that Noleena might understand him. He had not touched the box since Noleena laid it at his wrinkled brown feet with their long toenails, had only stared for a long time in silence at the box's silvery sheen and its embossings of sun and moon, its inlay of lilies.

With Ambro, who remained uncharacteristically withdrawn despite her apology, Noleena had ridden along the High Running all the previous day, arriving at dusk at the FahFah village: a strange collection of grass huts with conical roofs where blue lizards basked in the heat from cooking-fire smoke that rose through the peak of each roof. Spotted dogs ran to meet them, yelping, and tiny warti hoggies, with sagging bellies and yellow tusks, milled squealing around their feet. Naked children tussled amongst the dogs and hoggies, and presently adult FahFahs drifted from their supper pots to investigate the commotion.

Sliding from Dune Runner's back, Noleena had been assailed by shouting children and scruffy dogs; through the din that arose, she'd been amazed to pick out the strains of a hurdy-gurdy and the beat of a drum. Surely it couldn't be...? She peered into the dusk, ignoring the children who jostled against the horses' legs. Then, around the curve of a hut wall had come a strange procession and one that she recognized instantly: the sand fleas cavorting and somersaulting, led by the twins in their flared pantaloons whilst Mia danced and played in their midst.

"But what are you doing here?" Noleena had cried as the troupe circled around her.

"We have been wandering," replied one of the twins simply. "We met the FahFahs selling mahogany at the edge of the desert, and followed them back to this village."

"They give us the most delicious honeycomb to eat!" cried Mia, her fingers idly plucking the strings of her hurdy-gurdy with one hand and rubbing her stomach with the other.

"Mia!" Noleena cried, delighted and comforted at the same time.

"Mia?" Ambro said, sounding surprised.

"You know Mia?" Noleena asked, and Ambro nodded and explained that she'd come to Terre with him.

Noleena stared at Mia; the girl wore a tattered skirt of grass and leaves that rustled against her thighs as she danced. Amulets swung from her skinny neck, and green whorled patterns swirled over her dark cheeks. Even her hair seemed somehow different; was it beginning to curl? When she invited Noleena and Ambro to share the troupe's supper and their sleeping spot beneath a cluster of white cane, the two accepted gratefully.

Now it was morning again, and Ambro had departed on foot and in the company of Rafa who was going to guide him back to the desert. "Do you want to take Sun Runner?" Noleena had asked, still trying to make amends for her previous ungraciousness, but Ambro shook his head. "I have a task that I will do best alone," he said, tilting his golden chin with a look both determined and haughty. After a moment, he softened it with a smile and gripped

Noleena's hands in farewell. "Princess, may you find your power in this time of greatest need," he said kindly, and bowed without mockery before turning to lope after Rafa who was already disappearing down the mountain trail.

After this, Mia had brought Noleena to the hut of the Elder Witch to ask him about the box. Sitting at his feet, Noleena tried to wait patiently. She had refrained from asking any questions, and had struggled not to stare around; nevertheless, in the periphery of her vision, she was aware of the interior of the Elder Witch's conical grass hut with its dangling bunches of herbs, dried roots, twisted animal skins, tiny skulls, carved amulets, and dark limbs of misshapen trees. She stared at the whorled green patterns running up the Elder Witch's withered legs to the fringe of his grass skirt; even dared to stare fleetingly at the deep fissures of his face dotted with white paste and green tattoos, and at the rheumy darkness of his eyes in their pouches of sagging skin.

Now, his first movement alerted her back to full attention. He stretched out a long skinny arm and touched the tip of one finger to the box. A sibilant hiss pursed his lips. He ran his tapering nails across the embossings, and muttered words in the FahFah tongue that ran through the mouth like wind in grass and was not spoken anywhere else in Terre. His arms waved like sticks over the box; his twiggy fingers signed gestures of which Noleena didn't know the meaning. His eyes grew flat and expressionless, as though his mind were traveling far off along the roads of his secret knowledge. Indeed, Noleena had the impression that his whole spirit was moving away from her and from its own body, as though it were a runner simply slipping away into leaf dance and cloud shadow. She glanced at Mia. The girl's face seemed, for a fleeting moment, so old and grave that Noleena was reminded of the mugwawa and gazed at her in shock. In that moment, the whorls on Mia's face seemed to turn into leaves and branches and vines, and the girl's dark eyes peered out from this screen of forest like the eyes of a secret watcher. Noleena blinked and the illusion was broken; she saw nothing but Mia's familiar face painted with patterns. As though sensing Noleena's uneasiness, Mia laid a palm upon her knee; comfort seemed to flow through it and Noleena's heartbeat steadied.

She became aware that the light was fading; was it dusk already? For how long had she sat here cross-legged on a straw mat, waiting for advice on how to use an empty box against the sorceress in Safala?

She jumped in surprise as suddenly a fire flared up, spitting colored sparks, amongst a ring of stones. The Elder Witch's shadow, growing mysteriously huge, swung against the roof of the hut and paced panther-like across the golden walls of woven grass. His incantations rose and fell, weaving a strange rhythm that seemed to take possession of Noleena's thoughts; spittle flew from the corners of his mouth and flames danced in his eyes. The twisted limbs seemed to stir and rustle on the walls, and a gust of wind eddied in the open door of the hut so that the flames streamed sideways before clawing higher.

Noleena swayed dizzily on her mat, the nape of her neck crawling, and clung to Mia's hand.

Now the Elder Witch flung the leaves and stems of dried plants into the fire so that an acrid smoke billowed through the hut; moon moths and the ghostly shapes of lilies ascended in it. The Elder's limbs twitched and flailed in the strange light as he pranced around the fire, and light gleamed along his bones so that he resembled an ancient tree riven by storm. Seed pods rattled around his wrists and ankles, and in his hair as wild and coarse as tree moss. His incantations rose to a shout; his body convulsed in a frenzy of energy so that its own shadow seemed to devour it.

The hut plunged into darkness as the fire extinguished without warning. Noleena whimpered, then felt the grip of Mia's fingers around her own. Noleena could not hear a single sound from the village outside and it seemed preposterous to believe that the village even existed with its chattering children, clucking hens, and barking dogs. The space inside the Elder Witch's hut, she felt, had become somehow separated from the village and existed in another dimension of time or space; a place, she knew, that she would not be able to find on another day just as she would not be able to find the stone circle in the High Meadows again.

As the Elder's chanting rose and fell, Noleena fancied that she heard the sound of the box's lid being opened and closed, the roar of wind or perhaps of water, the cries of animals, the clatter of rocks falling.

Then, gradually, the Elder Witch's chanting died to a mumble. Noleena became aware of the tiny creaking of crickets, the peep of tree frogs. A finger of pale light crept over the doorsill of the hut and when she glanced over her shoulder at the doorway itself, she saw that the village stood outside cloaked in afternoon sunshine. A young hoggi stuck its snout around the edge of the door, then leaped away as though terrified and rushed off squealing.

Noleena stared around the hut. Cold ashes filled the fire pit and the air in the hut was clear, holding no trace of smoke or herbal fragrances. The twisted limbs and tiny skulls hung motionless upon the grass walls, through which slivers of sunlight penetrated to lay intricate horizontal patterns upon the Elder Witch lying on his back on a sleeping mat. The silvery box was clasped to his chest. His mouth gaped in a soft snore, and his gnarled walking stick lay against his side.

"Come," Mia demanded, tugging at Noleena's hand in a child-like gesture. "Let's find something to eat; I'm starving."

"I need the box," Noleena said.

"Leave it for now. Come."

But as Noleena rose to her feet, the Elder Witch stirred his long legs and opened his rheumy eyes. After a moment, he sat upright and extended the box to her.

"It is a box that only moon and shell can fill, wind and dark, storm and rock, tide and calm," he said. "You must fill it with the powers of Terre, and not open the lid again until you need those powers."

"What...?" Noleena began to ask, but the Elder Witch had lain back and instantly recommenced snoring, as though he had never spoken. Gingerly, Noleena held the box and scrutinized it but it seemed unchanged, unmarked, and with the lid closed as before.

"Come," repeated Mia and Noleena followed her outside into the long light where women were pounding tubers into sticky paste in stone mortars, and either smiled at her cheerfully or cast her suspicious glances. I'm wasting my time here, Noleena thought. And time is precious; with every minute that passes, another child is taken into slavery, another laboring back is laid open with an assassini whip. What am I doing here, clutching this box about which I still know nothing, in a village of strangers in grass skirts, who are probably ignorant of Terre's grief? Panic fluttered in her at the thought of how far she was from Safala, and how much time she'd wasted since her father sent her forth to find aid for her people.

To Mia she said urgently, "I must ride. I must go to Safala and confront the sorceress." A tremble ran through her as she spoke, for the box upon which she'd pinned her hopes now seemed useless. She hadn't understood the Elder Witch's words regarding it, and how was she to confront the evil Maldici queen without help, without a source of power? Nonetheless, the conviction that she must do so rose in her with a rush of reckless courage, and she turned away from Mia and the women and strode to where Dune Dancer and Sun Runner were tethered in the shade beneath a towering tree.

"No need to be so hasty," Mia panted, running up as Noleena swung onto Dune Dancer with the box stowed in her pack. "Would you like my company or do you prefer to roam alone, alone-o?"

Noleena paused to glance down at Mia, and the sight of the girl's face—familiar despite its green whorls—filled her with comfort. "Please come," she agreed.

As the stallion moved after the mare, Mia took a flying leap with her legs drawn up almost to her chin, so that for a moment she resembled an actual sand flea, and gripped the stallion's back as she landed on it. Sun Runner snorted and tossed his head, then followed Noleena and the mare down the steeply sloping trail that wound from the village across a gulley and over the farther slope, amongst clumps of flowering white-cane.

"Turn south!" Mia yelled as the trail forked, and Noleena swung the mare's head toward the southern horizon of mountain slopes that basked in the late afternoon light. For hours, they rode through the call of crickets and the shrieks of unseen forest birds with the horses' hooves pounding lightly on the trail that they followed down deep ravines and along the banks of rushing streams. Noleena scarcely felt the thick lianas brushing her arms. A great dread filled her as she thought of what she was rushing toward: those impregnable palace walls, that malignant power against which her people were helpless. She imagined the Maldici sorceress as Ambro had described her in the words of a lemon seller he'd once met; a foreign exotic beauty with a curtain of red hair, and flashing hawk eyes.

Noleena felt unable to muster a plan or any rational thoughts as to what she might try to accomplish in Safala; how did she think she would even make her way past the guards ranged at the palace gates? She had no weapon, no money for bribes; she'd lost both Hasani and Ambro with their bright fierce courage. Only Mia accompanied her, clinging to the stallion's back without grace or style and yet grinning—Noleena saw when she glanced back—as though she'd just been thrown a large coin in the marketplace.

Easy enough for *her* to grin, Noleena thought in distraction: she has nothing to worry about. She is not going to Safala to fail, to die, to plunge her people into darkness. The hope of Terre doesn't rest upon her skinny shoulders.

Noleena pressed her heels into the mare's sides and rode her fast down the winding trail as monkeys whooped overhead and the sun set in a fiery ball behind tangled trees.

"Supper time?" Mia called hopefully, but Noleena shook her head.

"I must ride on!" she cried back.

"The horses need to rest! We can't ride all night without resting!"

Grudgingly Noleena admitted the truth of this and brought the mare to a halt on the crest of a ridge, the land falling steeply away into mysterious blue shadows and the smell of ripe banya fruit scenting the air. Bats flitted through the twilight. She slid to the ground and felt the box, stowed in her pack, nudge her between the shoulder blades. What had the Elder Witch meant? she wondered as she shrugged the pack from her shoulders. What powers of Terre could possibly fit into this small container?

She laid the pack under a tree and glanced around to see that Mia was already scrambling, agile as a lizard, up the sloping trunk of a nearby banya tree toward the clusters of yellow fruit, encased in soft husks, that hung from the topmost limbs.

"Catch!" she yelled gleefully, flinging fruit down, and Noleena stretched out her arms just in time. They ate seated cross-legged on a rock; Noleena was so consumed with worry that she scarcely paid attention to the fruit's pulpy sweetness or the trickle of juice that ran down her chin. Beside her, Mia spat out the black seeds with amazing precision, hitting the flowers on a nearby clump of white-cane so that they swung like tassels.

The Ismata, still all day, began to rise as they ate. It eddied through the dusk like a soft breath that lifted Mia's black hair in tendrils, and the forelocks of the grazing horses. It ran over Noleena's hot forehead, and the cold sweat in the small of her back. Becoming stronger, it sighed through the banya trees, stirring their long limbs so that the clusters of fruit trembled and swung; it rushed up the side of the ridge where the girls sat, and buffeted their shoulders.

What had the Elder Witch meant? Noleena asked herself fretfully again. Of what use was the box, stowed in her pack? Maybe it wasn't a gift from Luna after all, she thought, just because I found it in the stone circle. Maybe it was just some old, lost thing that I happened to find for no particular reason. But even as she thought this, she knew it to be untrue. There was power amongst the stones, and she had heard the voice of Luna murmuring in the wind, in the same wind that eddied and sighed against her now, that lifted the bats aloft and carried their shrill squeaking cries over the forest; the same wind that caressed every leaf, every vine, every flower of the Moon Mountains. The Ismata, a power of Terre.

A power of Terre! Noleena thought. The words seemed to run through her with electrifying force. Perhaps, after all, there was a way to gather the land's power for the task that lay ahead of her, for wasn't she the Wind-wanderer princess, and heir to those powers? Noleena scrambled to her feet with such haste that Mia almost swallowed a seed that she'd been preparing to spit at a caterpillar inching its way up a grass stem three feet away. Unfastening her pack, Noleena carefully extracted the box, running her fingers over the closed lid, feelings its sheen even though, in the deep velvety twilight, she couldn't see its patterns.

"You must ask the goddess to fill it," the Elder Witch had said. Could so small a box hold the powers of the land of Terre? Noleena felt determined to try. She walked to the edge of the rocks, where the Ismata swirled up the slope from the ravine below, and opened the lid silently on its silver hinges. Then she held it up at arm's length and cried aloud in the old tongue that she'd learned in the temple in Safala. "Luna, have mercy upon us, send us aid. Fill this box with the power of your land. Luna, I beg you, give me power against the Maldici queen and aid me in this darkness she has brought upon your people."

The wind poured over Noleena; she felt it whip her tunic about her thighs and run over her arms and fling her hair around so that the cowry shells tinkled against one another. Every cell in her body seemed to breathe in that wind so that she felt saturated by it, as though she were immersed in water instead of air. Despite its rush, the lid of the box remained open and the wind licked into its dark interior and sighed around the silver hinges and slid across the embossing of lilies. Noleena held the box aloft into the wind's surge until her arms shook; she gritted her teeth and forced herself to hold the box still. Stronger and stronger the wind blew until Noleena felt herself quivering on the edge of the ridge; it seemed possible that at any moment she would become airborne and sail into the twilight sky as light and flimsy as a bat. The smell of mint poured through her, stretching her lungs, making her mind feel sharp and light. Mixed with the mint was the alkaline smell of the desert far to their west, and Noleena fancied that she felt the sting of wind-blown sand upon her cheeks. She narrowed her eyes against the blast, and felt sand grit between her teeth. Harder and harder she shook, her feet clinging to the edge.

Mist eddied on the wind, rising in curtains from the ravine, billowing about her arms and the open box. The air darkened over the forest, blotting out the first stars. A squall of rain pattered upon Noleena's shoulders and head; the drops were heavy and warm, making the leaves of the banya and the white-cane gleam in the mist's pearly light. The Moon Mountain rain trickled through Noleena's eyelashes, wet her lips with a taste of ferns and rhododendron blossoms, dripped from her chin. With a rush and a roar, the rain increased in intensity until Noleena felt as though she were standing beneath a waterfall, until it seemed that sky and earth, air and water, had all merged into one surging element in which she was immersed, lost, absorbed. Her tattered Wanderer tunic and breeches clung, saturated, to her chest and thighs.

Mia grabbed one sleeve. "Perhaps you should close the box now!" she yelled into the blast of the Ismata and the roar of the rain, and Noleena brought the box down against her chest and closed the lid. The wind sank to a murmur amongst the banya trees, died to a sigh in the shadows that lengthened into purple darkness. The din of rain hushed to a patter, then to the soft percussion of drops falling from the tree canopy.

Noleena's shoulders slumped with fatigue. The wild exultant hope that she had felt, holding the box above her head, was departing. A box could not hold the wind, any more than it could contain dark or calm or tide or any of those other things that the Elder Witch had muttered about. Noleena stowed the box into her pack, ate the last of her banya fruit, and then trudged over to Dune Dancer. "We must ride now," she said tenaciously, summoning her resolve.

When she looked around for Mia, she saw the girl standing very still beneath the deep shadows of the banya trees. There was a tension in her, like the tension in an animal alerted to the presence of a predator.

"What is it?" Noleena whispered, and Mia motioned for her to come closer, into the shadows. They clustered there, the two girls and the two horses. Noleena strained her ears but heard nothing except the occasional call of a monkey, and the muffled thump of an over-ripe fruit plummeting to the ground.

"I thought we were being followed," Mia whispered. "I felt it. I felt eyes in the forest."

Noleena pressed against the mare's flanks and shivered. It was inky black now; though she strained her eyes, she could not see even the clump of white-cane growing ten feet from their hiding place. "Stay here," Mia commanded and, before Noleena could prevent her, she'd slipped away into the night and vanished. Noleena waited for what seemed an endless time; when Mia reappeared, a breath at her elbow, she jumped nervously.

"Nothing," Mia said, but her voice sounded uneasy. In silence they mounted and headed the horses down the trail that led on, faint in the light of the rising moon.

They rode all that night and for several days, winding down across the plateau lands where spreading trees shaded sleeping magrazzi, their elegant necks bowed. Often as they rode, Mia glanced sharply behind them or to one side, as though sensing a presence. Her lips thinned and her eyes grew wary and suspicious, but when Noleena questioned her she said that she saw no one, only felt eyes on her back.

Noleena scarcely glanced around at all as she rode. A sense of urgency gnawed at her, consuming her thoughts, filling her stomach with churning dread. Nothing, she felt, could stop her now. She must reach the palace in Safala and then battle the fate that awaited. If she died in the attempt, at least she had tried. She no longer puzzled over the box, no longer wondered about that moment on the mountain when the Ismata had swirled about the opened lid. She had, she felt, only herself left now; only what courage she could muster; only some destiny reeling her in as overpowered as a fish on a line. Perhaps it was the power of her own determination, or perhaps the power of the sorceress, reeling her in across the northern slopes of Terre, making the mare's feet pound through the sweeping waves of grass, making Noleena lean forward into blowing mane while a vision of Safala filled her eyes:

its red stone archways and passages, its fretted balconies, its rosy towers encircled by wheeling doves, its secret aqueducts rushing with Moon Mountain water. Noleena felt herself straining toward this vision so that it seemed weightier and more real than the cloud shadows chasing across the plateau lands, or the finches singing in the trees. She seldom thought even of Mia, riding at her side, her callused hands twisted in the stallion's mane, for of what use was a street urchin on such a mission, and against such power as awaited Noleena in the great red palace in Safala?

When they rode down the tortuous trail that clung to the last cliff and deposited them onto the floor of the desert, Noleena stared across its sweeping emptiness through eyes that watered with fatigue. For one moment she felt overwhelmed by the desert's immensity, then she remembered traveling through it with Hasani; recalled the names that he had taught her of plants and animals, and the delicate patterns of cranes flying overhead in a clear sky. For a fleeting instant, she imagined that she heard Hasani's laughter and his deep melodious voice calling her name. She leaned over Dune Dancer's neck and ran her palm across its glossy sheen. "To Safala, by the wind-ways," she murmured and the mare flicked back her ears to listen and, at her side, the stallion snorted and tossed his head.

The horses began to skirt the base of the plateau lands, beneath the golden cliffs with their gnarled trees, then suddenly turned and headed into the desert, their nostrils sucking in air, their eyes alert and bright. For days they carried the girls southward, never passing through villages, never meeting goat herders with unruly flocks grazing the thin grass of rift valleys. Every morning and evening they brought the girls to hidden springs amongst rocks, or to tiny pools hidden by sedges, where they filled their water flasks as the horses bowed their necks to drink. Mile after mile the horses trotted, sure footed, the sun burning in their glossy manes, the moon rising in their eyes. Sometimes they broke into a canter for no apparent reason, or sidled and snorted as though something was making them anxious. At these times, Mia craned her neck and searched the landscape through narrowed eyes. "What do you see?" Noleena asked, but Mia always shrugged and replied, "Nothing."

The hours passed Noleena like mirages: shimmering, timeless, devoid of meaning. Despite the heat, she grew colder and colder with fear; in the very centre of her cold heart, she felt her resolve as hard and implacable as a rock.

"We are not alone, I am sure of it," Mia muttered on the fourth day. "You wait at the next waterhole with the horses and I'll circle back."

"You shouldn't go alone into the desert!" Noleena protested but when, at dusk, they reached a trickle of water issuing from a rocky cleft before soaking into the sand, Mia slid from the stallion and slipped away, circling a dune and disappearing. Noleena cupped her hands in the water and sucked it into her parched mouth, before standing aside so that the horses could drink. Usually they rested then, lying on the sand with their heads bowed over their forelegs, but this evening they shifted restlessly, their ears fluttering and eyes rolling. The stallion stamped a foreleg uneasily. The sense that something out in the desert was watching them, crawled beneath Noleena's skin. She twisted her hands in the mare's mane and leaned onto her warmth, trying to calm herself. How far will Mia go? she wondered. How will I know if she needs help? Darkness deepened and time dragged past until Noleena felt her nerves stretched thin as wire. She swung onto the mare, determined to track Mia and find her, but just as she nudged her heels into the mare's flanks, Mia reappeared, scrambling over the lip of the dune.

She caught Noleena by one sleeve. "I found tracks," she hissed. "We must ride hard."

"Whose tracks?" Noleena asked, as Mia caught the stallion's mane and leaped onto his back.

"Tracks that change between one patch of sand and the next," Mia said. "The most secret power of the FahFah is to shape-shift, Noleena. Someone has followed us from the mountains."

Noleena gripped the mare as she plunged forward; briefly she saw Mia's crouched form silhouetted against the moon as the stallion moved away. Questions bunched in her mouth but it was impossible now to speak to Mia and all she could do was trust the mare's surging power, her hoof beats drumming the skin of the desert. Countless times, Noleena swiveled her head to stare backward but saw nothing; only shadowy dunes, the dark patches of corda groves, the sheen of moonlight on slabs of wind-abraded rock. But there! Did she see something? Or was it merely a cactus moving in the wind? And there! That movement in the periphery of her eye; what was it? Perhaps a rock falling from an overhanging ledge above a dry riverbed; perhaps a small animal leaping. Once, off to her left, Noleena was convinced that she saw the stooped outline of an elderly woman, but as she opened her mouth to shout at Mia, the outline became the bent stems of a jobi shrub growing twisted on a steep slope. Once too, she thought she saw a snake winding its way across her path; the mare half-reared and snorted in alarm, but it was merely a twisted stick that lay before them on the gravel.

"We should rest the horses!" Noleena cried, when the moon was high in the blanket of stars, but the horses refused to be halted and cantered on, the whites of their eyes gleaming.

The night seemed vast and endless, a great plain over which they rode toward a horizon that receded like an outgoing tide. Terror stalked them; Noleena felt eyes on the small of her back, on the nape of her neck, so that her skin crawled and her heart drubbed in rhythm with the mare's running hoof beats. Would they never reach Safala? Would the sun never rise and shed some light and hope upon them? Was it the Elder Witch that followed them? Noleena thought of his rheumy eyes gazing far off down his own roads, and of the green whorls on his skinny legs, and shivered. What did he want with them? What powers did he command, and for what purpose might he use them? Would he help her, perhaps, to use the box stowed in her pack, or did he travel to Safala for some dark reasons of his own? If it were even he who followed...

At last, straining her eyes, Noleena saw the almost imperceptible stain of light above the horizon to the east. Like milk, it seeped heavenward, laid its pale light along the stems of cacti and the rocky spines of bare ridges. Now Noleena could see the mare's mane shining in the first sun, the gleam on the stallion's haunches ahead of her. She stared all around and behind them, but saw nothing suspicious; no tracks, no slinking animals, no shadowy figures. All was ordinary in the light and her anxiety began to subside. Perhaps Mia was wrong about the tracks, or about the powers of the FahFah. Anyway, why would a FahFah bother with them or their journey to Safala, when it was common knowledge that the mountain tribe kept to itself and lived for wild honey and for dancing around fires to the beat of hoggi-skin drums? The only dealings that the FahFah had with the other peoples of Terre was when they sold mahogany trees, felled deep in the forest with bone-handled axes and dragged out lashed together with ropes made from the bark of anbara trees. No, the FahFah were not interested in traveling from their cloud shadows and leaf dances into the desert.

The mare's pace slowed. Noleena came out of her reverie to see that the horses were picking their way into a ravine that sloped steeply between walls of striated rock. More and more narrow the ravine grew until it was little more than a cleft twisting between the cliffs; Noleena's toes brushed against the walls on either side and she pressed her knees tight against the mare. Suddenly, the ravine opened out onto a flat pan of rock; an expanse of blue sky filled Noleena's line of vision. The horses paced slowly to the lip of the rock pan, and Noleena gazed downward to see that a fan of rocky scree fell away below them; her eyes widened in amazement as she saw, far below the scree, the towers and rooftops and balconies of Safala. Beyond them lay the valley of Nini with its nuga palms, its terraces of beans and wheat, its huddled villages tiny in the brilliant morning light.

"The horses have brought us a secret way," she breathed, and Mia nodded.

"The back door to Safala," she agreed, her face creasing in a satisfied urchin grin. Then, suddenly, she jerked around at the sound of movement behind them.

"Look!"

Noleena followed the line of Mia's arm to see a wild hoggi, its brown hide covered in sparse grey bristles and its snout gleaming, burst from the ravine and onto the rock pan with its cleft hooves scrabbling for purchase. Its small eyes gleamed malevolently in their creases of thick hide. The horses leapt sideways in alarm. Sun Runner plunged toward the hoggi, almost unseating Mia, and lashed out at the creature with his forelegs, giving a high-pitched angry squeal. The hoggi darted away, sprang onto a rock and then—Noleena stared at it in astonished confusion and rubbed her eyes. The outline of the hoggi blurred and writhed; for a fraction of time Noleena thought she saw within the twisting form the arm and face of an old woman, then this was lost in a flurry of feathers. Her mouth gaped open as the bird, a small black-barred hawk from the Moon Mountains, lifted off the rock that the hoggi had sprung onto and swooped downward. Mia shouted something in a tone of command and a tongue that Noleena didn't recognize; for a second the hawk faltered in midair, its wings feathering as it slipped sideways. Then it regained its balance and continued its downward flight; at Noleena's side, Mia stamped a foot in frustration.

"That old hag!" she spat.

"What?" Noleena asked, narrowing her eyes as the hawk dwindled to a speck that soared over the rooftops of Safala and was lost to view amongst the city's towers.

"It is she who has been following us all these days…the Elder Witch's sister. It must be her. Why didn't I realize sooner? She has a daughter who lives in the red palace."

"She—the hoggi—what?" Noleena asked incoherently.

Mia reached from the stallion's back and gripped Noleena's arm to give it a hard shake. "Listen," she commanded fiercely. "The FahFah Elder has a sister who tried to usurp his powers and use them against another villager with whom she had a feud. Blood was spilled. The villagers outcast her and she lives in a grove of anbara trees outside the village and practices small, mean magic; villagers sneak to her at night with payments of rooster and wild game. She casts the cruel eye on people for these payments. But she has deeper magic that she dare not use whilst her brother is still Elder Witch, and she hankers for power, and grows bitter and twisted in her longing for it. She has a daughter who she sent away, and who lives in Safala, in the red palace of the Maldici queen; it must be to her daughter that she has flown in her guise of a hawk. The daughter is a nursemaid to the Maldici's young son. Perhaps the old hag has gone to seek her daughter—but what purpose does she pursue?"

Noleena stared first at Mia's worried face, then downward again, down and down through hundreds of feet of air that was beginning to shimmer as the sun warmed the cliffs and they reflected the heat, down past the first red balconies, the first towers of Safala. She searched for a glimpse of the palace, or of the sloping roof of her old sanctuary in the temple at the end of its twisting alley, but neither building was visible from this vantage point. The hawk did not reappear.

"We must ride on," she said.

"We'll have to leave the horses and scramble down on foot."

"No!" Noleena cried; it seemed unthinkable to part from the rushing power, the sleek solid heat, of Dune Dancer and Sun Runner with their wise eyes and their knowledge of the desert's secret paths. They had been steadfast through so many miles.

"The slope is too steep for them," Mia argued, "and they would attract too much attention in the city. Anyway, they brought us to this lip of rock, so they must intend for us to enter the city by this route. Noleena, you can see the slope is too steep for them."

Noleena nodded, though tears blurred her vision. Sliding from Dune Dancer's back, she pressed her cheeks against the mare's face and inhaled her familiar, comforting scent of sweat and dust.

"May your paths lead to Engedi; may you dance by the springs; may your foals dance beside you," she whispered, and the mare breathed softly over her shoulders and ran her velvety nose down Noleena's arm in parting. Together, Mia and Noleena stood on the lip of the cliff and watched the horses wheel about and begin to pick their way up through the ravine's tortuous trail; after a minute, they rounded a bend and their shining haunches and floating tails were lost to view. A sob shook Noleena, for they were Hasani's horses and now the last thread that bound her to him had snapped like a thread stretched too tight on the loom and torn from the weaving.

Mia stepped in front of her and grasped her hand with both of her own. "Princess," she said, "your people wait for deliverance. You must walk on."

Noleena nodded and wiped her eyes with chapped knuckles, and pushed back her hair with its weaving of cowry shells as she had done once before, long ago now it seemed, when Hasani had stood waiting for her at the base of another slope of scree. For a moment the memory of him flared up in her; something shining and bright that lent her strength. She stooped, and lowered herself over the lip of the cliff onto the scree slope, and began to traverse it on a diagonal line as rocks slid and clattered away from her, falling and falling toward the rooftops of Safala like a hard rain.

CHAPTER TWENTY

THE LIZARD'S HEAVY JAWS SWUNG above the boy thrashing amongst the leaves. Its spiny head was a silhouette against the moon. Ambro groaned and rolled behind a tree but the lizard, amazingly swift despite its bulk, surged around the opposite side of the tree and cut off Ambro's escape. Overhead, limbs were smashed off by the lizard's scaly spine and fell in a tangle into the clearing. The creature's blunt snout battered into the boy's ribs and he cried out, then deftly jack-knifed away behind another tree. For a moment the lizard became entangled in the shattered limbs and paused to wrestle its claws free. The boy rolled farther away, hands scrabbling at the ground.

There, suddenly, beneath his fingers Ambro felt the familiar smooth length of his flute. He snatched it up and rolled into a sitting position as the lizard rushed toward him, light gleaming on its teeth. A smell of decay filled the clearing. Ambro lurched to his feet, pain exploding through him and fresh blood gushing from his leg and nose. He stood in the lizard's path and, as it advanced upon him, began to play. With all his might he thought of the desert; he allowed it to fill him and pour through him. He was no longer a thing of pain and trembling, panic and gut-wrenching fear; he was transformed into the desert's song: the clear sky of cold evenings, the wheel of hawks, the dance of gazelles on dunes, the maze of cracks in mineral pans, the wind lifting curtains of glittering sand.

As he played, the lizard sank to its haunches and listened, only feet away. Its dark chest reared before Ambro like a prison wall. Its jaw hung slack; its hiss died to a sibilant whisper.

Hasani is free, Ambro thought. I have accomplished my Hunting. If I die here, I have finally accomplished a thing that I vowed.

His legs shook and he sagged against the tree trunk at his back. The lizard shifted closer, and terror ran through Ambro so that his fingers faltered on the flute. He drew a ragged breath and forced himself, with all his might, to think of Moon Mountain water running over amber stones in the canyons of the plateau lands. He thought of rainbirds nesting after storms, and of the jobi shrubs sprouting new green shoots, and of oases as blue as summer sky.

Closer the lizard shifted, listening, settling its weight on its talon-like claws. Its eyes glittered malevolently. Ambro closed his own eyes to shut out the fearsome sight, and he played of first kiffa and first horse running through the desert, and of the beauty of Dune Dancer fleeing from Mount Lalibela, and of the soft down on the breast of a rock-rose.

Now the lizard's blue jaws were only inches from him; he felt its hiss run up his arms so that the hairs stood on end.

Fatigue coursed through him. He shook like a leaf, and the taste of blood coated his tongue. I can't play for much longer, he thought. How will this end? He knew that if he stopped playing, even for an instant, the lizard's teeth would close around his arms and break them like tree limbs. I must play, he thought. I must play so that I live, and Hasani has time to escape. He forced himself to think of the rock strata of Safala, rosy in evening sun; of the flicker of tiny yellow lizards, and the dust of dry stream beds. His flute sang to the lizard as the stars wheeled, as the moon set, as he passed beyond fatigue into a strange world where he floated above the corda grove and, as though from a great distance, beheld himself: a sagging form at the nose of a man-eater, playing a thin thread of sound to ward off death. Then even this vision faded and he was a husk, a shell, merely the shape of a boy lost at the horizon of his own mind.

The first light tickled the tree leaves. It slid up the lizard's blue back so that its scales gleamed; its warmth soaked into the reptile. Its hooded eyes winked sleepily, for it was a night hunter and by day it escaped from the heat into its rocky burrow dug in the hills above Kalifa.

Slowly, the lizard withdrew from Ambro's side, sliding backward through the dead leaves and broken tree limbs. It swung around ponderously, and paused to survey the desert, then with a last surge of speed it shot out across the sand and up the hillside, its claws scrabbling at rocks that rolled away with a clatter. In a trance, Ambro watched the lizard disappear. And, as though still in a trance, he continued to play for several minutes until at last the flute slid from his grasp and he keeled over in slow motion to lie on the warm ground. His eyes closed immediately. His head throbbed and darkness closed around him like a fist.

After an eternity, he felt liquid dribbling into his mouth. Horror at the thought of the lizard rushed through him and he struggled convulsively, but a hand restrained his shoulders. "Be still. I've come to help you," a deep, soft voice muttered at his ear and he let himself go slack again. Heat and pain roared in his mind. "Drink," the voice said and he opened his lips and let the tepid water run down his throat. "Can you stand?"

Ambro opened his eyes and saw bare webbed toes, covered in cuts and gashes, and thin dark legs. He rolled over slowly and painfully to stare at the boy standing beside him; saw the defiant stance, the high cheekbones and brilliant eyes, and the iridescent hair—once long and braided in a crown—now hacked off and blowing across the boy's shoulders in a ragged mane.

"Hasani?" he croaked.

Hasani bent his head in a graceful gesture of assent; then his eyes grew hard and narrow with suspicion. "You were in the dunes of Enlon? You were at Mount Lalibela? Yet you rescued me last night?"

Ambro nodded but it all seemed too complicated to explain. Instead he simply stretched out one foot and spread his toes; the bandit's eyes widened as he saw the webs.

"You know Noleena," he muttered. His eyes flared, burning fiercely at Ambro. "Is she safe?"

"She was the last time I saw her. She has been to the Moon Mountains to seek help," Ambro replied, and the fierceness faded from Hasani's eyes.

"There is much here I don't understand," he said. "But now is not the time for more; we must ride before the sentries find us. Can you stand?"

Ambro lurched to his feet, feeling Hasani's arms supporting him. Dried blood cracked open on his wounded leg. Before him, the pony, the trees, and the dunes beyond swung in sickening circles. He retched with fatigue, doubled over his empty stomach, then staggered forward against the pony as Hasani guided him.

"You were supposed to escape," he muttered.

"I did escape but I didn't know, in the dark, who you were. I thought perhaps you were one of my tribe come to rescue me and that you'd join up with me later. But after I'd waited all night in the hills to the west, I grew worried and circled back. I found you lying on the ground; I saw the marks of the lizard's feet. Now, get on this pony."

Ambro scrabbled his way upward with Hasani's help; he dimly noticed that his own clothes were draped across the saddle. "My flute?" he asked, and Hasani nodded. "I put it in the pocket of your robe."

The pony began to move into the shimmering waves of heat; in Ambro's swinging vision the tall dark frame of Hasani rippled alongside with the birds, safe in their basket, strapped to his back. Ambro was too weak to ask where they were going, and simply allowed the boy and the pony to convey him away from the mining camp's misery, away from the nightmare of the blue lizard, and into the desert stretching westward from the valley of Kalifa like a great sea of silence. Hour after hour they toiled along; sometimes Ambro became conscious of the smell of sweat rising from the pony, or of the ragged breathing of Hasani at his side. Once he suggested that Hasani should ride the pony, but the bandit refused and Ambro continued to sway along, the pain of his wounded leg filling his consciousness.

At dusk, they reached a craggy ridge of rock thrusting up from the sand and rising into a pillar of red basalt. Hasani led the pony through the boulders at the base and then tethered it in the shade where thin grass grew.

"Come," he said to Ambro, and pulled him off the pony's back into his arms. Staggering, they wound their way upward through the rocks, their breath rasping in their throats, until they reached an alcove about two-thirds of the way to the top. Ambro slumped into the space, against a hard bone of rock, and closed his eyes. Sleep descended over him almost instantly.

When Ambro woke, it was already morning; he could feel heat radiating from the surrounding rocks although he himself lay in the shade. He raised his head to look around. Hasani lay nearby, still sleeping, and Ambro studied him and noticed for the first time how thin the bandit had become in his time as a gold miner. The M branded upon one shoulder was a ragged wound that had not healed; it oozed a yellow liquid and the shoulder surrounding it was an angry red. Hasani's face was taut even in sleep, the skin stretched over the cheekbones. With a terrible pang, Ambro remembered Hasani as he'd seen him before with his crown of braided hair, with the mineral patterns across his face and the blue beads at his throat.

As though aware of Ambro's scrutiny, Hasani's eyes opened, fully alert like the eyes of a wild animal that wakes when danger stirs its secret senses. Ambro held the fierce gaze. For a moment their mutual pride battled in the air between them like crossed swords.

"Who are you?" Hasani demanded, sitting upright.

It was hard to know where to begin explaining his muddled story, so Ambro began at what seemed very long ago on that stormy night when he and the sea urchins had rowed out to help the trading ship bearing down upon the reef like a pelican in flight. He told of Lord Tafari, and of the stolen horses, of his own hunger for a family, of his Hunting to bring the horses back to the stable carved in the rocks of Safala, and of the girl in the temple who wore a blue gown and had cowry shells in her cloud of black hair. He was aware of Hasani tensing as he spoke of Noleena and for a moment he faltered in his narrative; then he plunged on to tell of the events at Mount Lalibela and in the mugwawa's canyon and the journey through the Moon Mountains to the star gate.

"I left her there in a FahFah village," he confessed.

"She is stronger than she appears," Hasani said staunchly. "She will accomplish her Seeking for her people. But why did you leave her since you had dedicated yourself to helping her?"

Ambro shrugged uncomfortably. "I stayed with her until she reached the star gate, and had the sand fleas and our friend Mia to keep her company. She never trusted me; I grew...tired of it. And I wanted to make one thing right in all the muddle of my life. I wanted to save you from slavery in Kalifa."

For a long moment, Hasani held Ambro in his piercing blue stare; anger and a haughty contempt flickered through his eyes. Then his gaze softened and his shoulders relaxed. "For rescuing me, I forgive you all else," he said, his musical voice flowing over the words with such grace that Ambro felt as though he'd been granted a blessing, or at least a truce.

"Noleena has spoken to me of Mia," mused Hasani. "They traveled together when they were searching for me near Omo. Perhaps now they travel onward together again. We must find them after we've rested here and regained our strength."

"Your shoulder?"

"Infected," Hasani said tersely. "It will not heal." He rose to his feet, still graceful despite his protruding ribs and the scars on his legs, and moved to the bird cage. Opening the wicker door, he slipped a hand inside; after a moment, he brought an egg over to where Ambro lay. "From the dove," he explained, and Ambro cracked the warm, pale shell on a rock and tipped his head back to let the contents fill his mouth. He thought that he had never before tasted anything as wonderful; the white of the egg was sweet as nuga sap and the yolk seemed filled with buttery richness.

For three days they rested amongst the rocks, keeping themselves alive on dove's eggs and waiting for their strength to return. Each morning, Hasani scrambled down to check on the pony and to fetch water from a spring near the base of the rocks. Each evening he paced around the tiny space where they rested, staring out over the surrounding desert as the setting sun stained its sand to pinkness.

"Tomorrow, we must ride," he said each evening, but each morning found them too weak to stir. The liquid draining from the brand on Hasani's shoulder became thicker and gave off a foul smell; the wound on Ambro's leg throbbed as red streaks spread up his thigh. A sense of desperation began to gnaw at him. What was the use of rescuing Hasani? he wondered. What was the use of surviving the lizard? What does it matter whether we keep ourselves alive on dove's eggs? We are imprisoned here in this fortress of rock and we'll die here; I should tell Hasani to untie the pony and let it escape.

Still, he ate the next egg that the dove laid, and drank the alkaline water that Hasani carried from the spring. On the morning of the fourth day, watching Hasani pace around the edge of the rocky alcove, Ambro had an idea. He crawled over to the bird cage, for his leg was now so painful and weak that he couldn't stand upon it, and lifted the rock-rose from inside. Slowly, fumbling in his pain, he wrote a message on a scrap of parchment taken from the pocket of his robe: *Hasani and I are wounded; please help us.* He tied it to the rock-rose's leg and then held the tiny bird at eye level; it cocked its head and regarded him with its bright eye as he crooned the mugwawa's name. Then he threw the bird over the edge of the cliff and watched it catch air under its wings, lifting itself from a plummeting descent into a fast climb. It circled once above their prison of rocks and then began winging north, its tiny shadow slipping over dunes like a wind-blown leaf.

All that day Ambro lay feverish, wondering how long it would take for the bird to reach the mugwawa's cave behind its screen of waterfall in the hidden canyon, and whether she would send them any help. But she helped me before, when I asked, he thought stubbornly. She healed my severed webs. All day, and for the two that followed, in his feverish imagination he watched the fall of almond petals and smelled the minty breath of the Ismata as it poured down the mugwawa's canyon. A sense of peace eddied gradually into his turbulent thoughts and in mid-afternoon on the third day he fell into a peaceful sleep from which he was woken at dusk by the cooing of a rock-rose. He opened his eyes to see Hasani holding out one arm for the bird to alight upon.

"What does it say?" Ambro asked, as Hasani unfurled the message wrapped around the bird's leg.

"Infuse in water to wash wounds. I send the impossible thing," Hasani read aloud, his brow furrowing as he gazed around. Ambro followed his gaze but saw nothing out of the ordinary; only streaky sunset clouds, and lilac shadows stretching from the base of their rocky fortress.

"Birds," Hasani said suddenly, his sharp desert vision picking the specks out from the sky. Shortly, two more rock-roses fluttered down to land on the ground beside Ambro and he saw that each bird carried a sachet of silken cloth; when he removed them and opened them, a pungent smell of herbs rose into his nostrils. "Infuse in water to wash wounds," he repeated. "The mugwawa has sent us her healing."

Hasani crossed the ground swiftly, picking up the water flask, and they tipped the contents of the sachets into it since they had no other container. "Hold out your leg," Hasani commanded, and Ambro stretched it out, mottled with purple bruises from the impact with the lizard's tail and streaked with red around the wound. A fiery pain consumed the leg as Hasani trickled the flask's contents over it and swabbed it with a piece of cloth torn from his breeches. Sweat broke out on Ambro's forehead and he gritted his teeth until gradually the pain subsided to be replaced by coolness.

"Your shoulder," Ambro said, and Hasani kneeled beside him. Ambro poured the remaining contents of the flask onto the brand, sluicing its ragged lips and charred skin, washing away the foul ooze. The bandit's face, Ambro noted admiringly, remained immobile despite the pain he surely felt.

"It is because I did nothing that this happened to you," he muttered in remorse.

"You have done something now," Hasani said. "So it's lucky that I didn't slit your throat when I found you lying amongst the tracks of the blue lizard."

"Did you consider it?"

"For a moment. I recognized you from Mount Lalibela and so it was hard to believe that you might also be my rescuer. You had separated me from Noleena."

"So why didn't you then?" Ambro asked. "Why didn't you kill me?"

"The Ismata eddied through the trees as I stood watching you. It cooled my anger. I thought of Noleena and remembered that her Seeking is to wipe evil from the land, to restore harmony between Wanderers and Kiffas. How could I come to her again if I had taken a life? Even the life of a kiffa," he added with sudden ferocity, "those jackal offal who torture my people in the mines."

"Noleena will be happy to see you once more. She spoke of you often."

Something shining and bright flashed through Hasani's eyes, then he bent his head over the water flask with his ragged hair falling forward. After a moment he asked, "What about the rest of the mugwawa's message? What impossible thing is she sending us?"

"I don't understand that part; I don't know."

"She speaks to all animals of the land of Terre," Hasani mused. "Perhaps she sends us some kind of beast?" After a moment's contemplation, he said in a surprised tone, "The song! The song was a prophecy!"

"What song?"

"This is nothing to do with the mugwawa, though it has beasts in it. There is a song that is sung in the slave lines, and that Mia taught to Noleena as they wandered in the desert. Listen." And Hasani began to sing a mournful tune in a minor key, a song of sending one's love a rosy bird, a tender word, a kiffa cub, a cooing dove, a lizard blue.

"Don't you see?" Hasani asked in excitement after the third verse. "You are the kiffa cub, Ambro. You rescued me at the time of the evening star, you called the lizard, you brought the birds; and in your message tied to the rock-rose's leg, you sent Noleena's love."

A rush of hot amazement swept through Ambro. It was a strange feeling, to have been sung of in the slave lines, and suddenly all the pain and confusion of his time in Terre seemed worth what it had cost him, and to have been given meaning and simplicity. He could feel his incredulous grin stretching his face wide, and saw his pleasure mirrored in Hasani's answering smile. In that moment, the last vestiges of suspicion and anger fell away from between them; Ambro felt it passing like a physical weight removed from his shoulders.

"But who wrote the song?" he asked. "How could there be a song about me?"

Hasani's face fell back into contemplation. "That I cannot even guess. These are strange times, Ambro. Much swings in the balance and I don't know what roles you and I play. But we must heal; we must find Noleena." A steely determination tightened his face and he flexed his leg muscles in impatience.

"Perhaps in the morning," Ambro encouraged, "after the herbs have taken affect."

"We must," Hasani repeated, pacing restlessly until finally settling himself into a shallow depression in the hard soil and closing his eyes. Ambro drifted off slowly; it was a relief to find the pain in his leg easing as the herbs soaked into the wound. He woke at dawn to Hasani's urgent whisper, and shook back his tousled hair to find Hasani's face only inches from his own.

"What's the matter?" he mumbled.

"There's a—a creature above us on the rocks. Get up! Slowly!" Still fighting sleep, Ambro stood cautiously and gazed upward to where the topmost pinnacle of basalt rose like a finger against the sky. For a moment, he was distracted by the red flare of stormy light in the clouds, and by the rising wind that swirled around the rocks and buffeted his back.

Then he saw what Hasani had already noticed. An exclamation of disbelief burst from him; Hasani clamped a hand over his mouth to cut it off.

The great beast perched motionless and regarded them with a piercing blue gaze.

Ambro had never seen anything of such majesty, such power. His knees quivered. He tried to speak but words failed him.

"It is the impossible thing," Hasani breathed in his ear. "It is the Sky Strider of which myth tells but no man has seen in Terre in living memory. It is both kiffa and desert horse. It walks the path of storm."

Ambro nodded without taking his eyes from the beast. It balanced on the basalt with its huge soft kiffa paws, and with golden claws extended in a steely grip. The wild light shone along the smooth shafts of its wings, folded in against its horse's body covered in tawny hair, and along the crest of its proud neck ending—not in a horse's head—but in the sculptured face of a kiffa with black eye stripes.

"The impossible thing," Hasani breathed reverently again.

"Greetings from the mugwawa," the creature spoke, with its deep, resonant voice rising above the eddying wind. The sound reverberated in Ambro's chest. He felt his eyes bulge and fine hair rise on his spine.

Beside him, Hasani made a croaking sound, then answered in a voice that trembled only a little: "We thank you for bringing her greetings."

"The great storm of Terre rises, the wind runs the old roads," the beast continued. "The goddess sends her breath over the desert and breaks the shackles of her people. The Maldici witch weaves her treacherous webs in the red palace of Safala. Who can say what devastation this storm will wreak upon all peoples? Who can say when the powers of the earth god and the moon goddess will unite and bring peace?"

Ambro glanced at Hasani wondering if he, with more knowledge of this land, understood the Sky Strider's words but Hasani's face betrayed nothing except a mesmerized intent.

"Your pony has broken free, and your birds have flown," the Sky Strider continued. "Now you will ride the storm with me. May your lives be spared; may your fates be favorably cast in lights of sun and moon."

Ride? Ambro thought. Ride that awesome being, into the wind-torn sky? A great pit of fear opened in his stomach and he swooped down into it, falling, falling like a seed pod from a high tree. Hasani gripped his arm. "We will be honored," Hasani answered firmly, and Ambro became aware of solid ground yet beneath his feet. He gripped his courage and nodded.

"Honored," he agreed in his clear voice, and the creature's gaze focused narrowly upon him for a moment.

"Young Ambro d'Monti, another impossible thing," the Sky Strider said. "A kiffa with webbed toes. Come, both of you, climb up to me for the desert rises to meet the sky."

Glancing down for an instant, Ambro saw that indeed the wind was lifting curtains of fine sand from the crests of dunes, as it might lift salt spray from the crests of waves. The sand rose, swirling toward where the boys clung amongst the rocks, and Ambro felt its sharp sting against his cheeks. The Ismata's minty aroma rose with the wind, more pungent, sharp and clear than he had ever before smelled it: a fierce wild smell that seemed to scour the inside of his nostrils.

Following Hasani, he scrambled upward, clinging to crevices amongst the rocks, his azure robe whipping his thighs. His leg, he realized suddenly, had regained its full strength for the mug-wawa's herbs had wrought their healing. He squinted against the sky's tumult and saw that Hasani's branded shoulder had healed smooth and clean; only a faint silvery M remained visible like a very old scar.

Hasani disappeared over a lip of rock and after a moment, Ambro hauled himself up to join him and found that they were at the very feet of the Sky Strider. Each claw was the length of Ambro's arm, and the massive furred feet filled his line of vision. He craned his neck, staring at the great jut of shoulder and sweep of belly towering over them, and for a moment the pit of fear yawned in his stomach again. He glanced downward, down and down to where jobi bushes, mere specks on the ground, flailed in the Ismata's roar. I can't do this, he thought. He gritted his teeth, resisting the impulse to slither to the ground and wedge himself into some sheltering crevice, to hide from the vast expanse of open sky.

The Sky Strider unfolded the great length of its wings. The shafts of the feathers were longer than the height of a man; every tawny barb lay straight and precisely aligned; the vanes were sharp edged as the blade of a sword.

The beast crouched over the boys. "Climb onto my back," it commanded, and together they pulled themselves up the wing extended toward them, and onto the base of the neck, grabbing handfuls of the pale golden mane that whipped in the rising storm. For a moment the creature clung to the basalt, quivering in the updraught; then with a great thrust it launched into the wind and soared upward. Wind tore Ambro's breath from his mouth and flattened his eyes. A thrill of terror and joy surged through him and he shouted aloud incoherently. Sky poured over him like a flood tide. Beneath him, Terre stretched and fell away, ochre, amber, red, and smoking with driven sand. Rocks and gullies flattened into insignificance as the Sky Strider wheeled ever higher. Now the plateau lands came into view far off on the eastern horizon, and beyond them the pale blue smudge of the Moon Mountains. Towering storm clouds, dark as aubergines, boiled heavenward to the south, riven with flickering tongues of lightning brighter than flame, and smoldering in the veiled red eye of the rising sun.

"Safala!" Hasani shouted into his ears, gazing toward the writhing turmoil of lightning and cloud, and Ambro remembered what the Strider had said about the witch in the red palace. Across great sweeps of blue sky the Strider soared, faster and faster, riding the gale. Wind plucked at Ambro's robe and hair. He wrapped the Strider's mane around his arms like ropes and pressed his face against the beast's thick neck. Cloud enveloped them; the wind rose to a shrieking roar that blasted all conscious thought from Ambro's mind. The smell of mint was so strong now that it seemed to fill his entire skull. Sand whirled about them, rising higher and higher in a choking cloud against which the boys closed their eyes and breathed through their sleeves until the Strider lifted them higher yet above it into bright sunshine.

Gradually, after some immeasurable space of time, Ambro became aware that they were descending and he opened his eyes into slits and peered downward to see, ghostly amongst the blowing sand, the rectangular outlines of mud buildings; after a moment, he realized that they were flying above Kalifa. The Strider swept down the valley, barely beating its wings, merely feathering the tips of each vane as turbulent eddies swirled between the dry hills that rushed past.

"The camp!" Ambro shouted, and Hasani nodded, staring intently downward as the shadowy lines of mining trenches, and the great ring of stakes, came into view. Around the main gate a cluster of people milled in ant-like activity; the guards were out in full force, Ambro thought. Then, as the Strider continued to descend, he realized that it was the Wanderers themselves who clogged the main gate and streamed away, in ragged lines, toward the hills and the open desert with their dark shoulders hunched against the wind and their clothing flying from their bodies like telltales. As they reached the slope of a dry gulley, they began to run with the wind at their backs pushing them along, their webbed toes speeding them across the slopes of flying sand.

"They are going to the wind-ways, the old roads," the Strider said, speaking for the first time since becoming airborne. "The land is calling them home."

"But the guards?" Ambro asked, and the Strider wheeled in a great circle above the camp so that the boys could glimpse the Kiffa-walkers. They reeled in circles, buffeted by swirling funnels of wind, blinded by sand, deafened by the wind's wild cry. They staggered, fell to their knees, buried their faces in their arms, cried aloud for help. Sand enveloped them in glittering sheets. Yet here and there, assassini still ran through the encampment, cracking their whips and turning slaves away from the main gate. Tiny forked tongues of lightning flickered about the assassini, and wherever they ran the wind seemed to die and the dust to fall so that they ran in clear air with the brutti howling at their feet. There was some power working to help them, Ambro thought, that he didn't understand.

He glanced at Hasani as the Strider began to ascend higher into the sky, the mining camp fading to a speck and then becoming invisible in the clouds of blowing sand, and saw a fierce exultation light Hasani's face. "It is Noleena!" he cried. "She has awoken the mercy of Luna and unleashed the storm; she is doing battle with the sorceress in Safala!"

"The webs of the Maldici are forged in darkness deeper than imagining," the Strider warned them, circling on an updraught. "This storm has not reached its height, though the wind rises ever faster. Pray that it has the strength to break the powers in the red palace."

Coldness soaked through Ambro like the drench of surf, and he saw how the sand billowed along the horizon in every direction so that they seemed to be flying over a bowl of swirling colors: grey and pink, red and ochre, tawny and lilac. In this maelstrom, all landmarks disappeared; even the peaks of the Moon Mountains were obliterated along the eastern skyline as the wind stirred Terre like a soup, and ululated in her valleys like a voice wailing for its dead. Only, above the driven landscape to the south, the massive dark clouds lifted, writhing in strange shapes; Ambro imagined that he saw holes like empty eye sockets, and great gaping maws like those of dragons gleaming with teeth, and the lashing tails of serpents; pillars of smoke and the continuous flicker of lightning parted the swirling images.

"We go to Safala," the Strider roared above the wind, and Ambro wrapped strands of mane tighter around his arms, so tight that his skin whitened, and closed his eyes against the shifting, tilting chaos of Terre, and fought against the fear that weakened even his breathing.

CHAPTER TWENTY-ONE

At the base of the scree, Noleena and Mia climbed over a wall and dropped on its far side into a deserted alleyway skirting the northernmost boundary of the city, where it abutted against solid cliffs.

Noleena paused. "I can't go wandering around like this," she said, gesturing at her Wind-wanderer clothing. "If I gave you some food, could you run out to a market stall and barter for some clothes for me?"

"Wait."

Mia unslung her pack and rummaged through it while Noleena squatted at the base of the wall and stared down the alley toward the rectangle of light marking where it joined a larger street. Figures flitted across the light in billowing robes: Kiffa-walker merchants in high rolled boots, and street vendors, and children chasing each other between the legs of doda, and jennets laden with bales of trade goods. For a moment, everything appeared so familiar that Noleena had difficulty remembering the gravity of her mission; for a fraction of time, it seemed that she could find her way through the city and simply return to her sanctuary in the temple, sweep her ragged broom across the blue cracked tiles with their patterns of waves and dolphins, and build a small fire for the sand fleas to cook their evening meal over. Wrenching her thoughts away from the image of the temple's cool shadows, she returned her attention to Mia.

"A bit crumpled, but it will have to do," Mia muttered, pulling a rose-pink Kiffa robe from her pack and holding it out to Noleena. "Put it on over your breeches; I don't have any Kiffa under-things with me."

Noleena removed her tunic, stained ochre with desert dust, and slid her arms into the tunic's silky sleeves while Mia pulled a pair of golden slippers from her pack and dropped them at Noleena's booted toes. Finally she produced a gossamer veil of a darker pink, which she flung over Noleena's head and drew across her face. "Can't do much about your eye color," she muttered. "Keep your head down."

Noleena nodded. "I've been trying to think of a way to get into the palace. But I have never been to it before so I—"

"Follow me."

Mia darted off before Noleena could respond, her skinny legs scissoring beneath the FahFah grass skirt that she still wore, her dark hair an unruly tangle on her shoulders as she dashed past a mangy dog and a flock of scratching chickens that scattered at her approach. Noleena hurried after her. At the mouth of the alley they slowed their pace and merged decorously with the crowds of traders and shoppers. Noleena felt suddenly frighteningly exposed, as though the gazes of the Kiffa were hot knives tickling their blades across her shoulders, slicing through her flimsy disguise, reminding her that what awaited her at the red palace was likely her own death. She drew the veil closer against her cheeks and kept her head bent and her eyes focused only on Mia's brown ankles flashing along a foot ahead of her own in the tight unfamiliar straps of the golden slippers. The soles of her feet and the palms of her hands grew slick with anxious sweat as she followed Mia between stalls selling sapphires from Lontano, gourds and peppers and piles of cinni spice; with great care, they wended their way between preening doda and shouting fruit vendors and the click of weights being added to scales.

It seemed to Noleena as though they spent hours traversing the thoroughfares of Safala while the sun rose higher, shortening the shadows beneath man and beast, gleaming on the golden rings stacked between collar bone and chin of haughty Kiffa women with golden eye paste, and slave girls scurrying at their sides. Everything seemed too hot, too rushed, too bright: a whirling kaleidoscope through which Noleena moved in a daze of dread.

Suddenly Mia darted off down another small alleyway that twisted and turned between dark doorways and bleating goats, that bored its path through high cliffs of striated rock and the heat's growing intensity and ran at last into the shadows beneath a towering red wall, blank save for a few windows cross-hatched with iron bars.

"Up there," Mia said, pointing. "That's my way in."

Noleena lifted her eyes from the ground and stared upward to see, forty feet overhead, the graceful span of a narrow bridge; reached by a flight of steps carved into the cliff, the bridge arced from the cliff itself across to a doorway in the red wall. Beside the door Noleena glimpsed, before ducking her head again, the dark figure of a Kiffa guard erect in his red cape and snarling breastplate, and holding a spear.

"Is this the palace?" she whispered.

"It's the back door," Mia explained. "Lucky for us the old hag arrived as a hawk and entered over the battlements. Now I am going to get past the guard with a gift to my daughter, my lovely FahFah daughter for whom I bring wild honey. Then, I am going to lower a rope to you and pull you in through a window."

"But you—what—you—?" Nervousness and heat seemed to suck the air from Noleena's lungs. Her face blanched.

"You need to get inside, don't you?" Mia asked. "I can do this. Watch me!" And before Noleena could say another thing, Mia yanked a shawl, coarsely woven from the leaf fibers of the white-cane, over her head and shoulders, and began to move toward the stairs. Involuntarily Noleena started after her.

"Stay out of view until I let down a rope!" Mia hissed.

Noleena drew back into the shadows, pressing herself small in a cleft of rock.

Has Mia gone mad? Noleena wondered. How can she possibly pretend to be an old FahFah witch visiting her daughter? Anyone can see that she's a child, a scrappy little urchin sand flea.

But as Mia approached the stairs, she seemed to change; Noleena's eyes burned from the intensity with which she stared at Mia, trying to understand what was happening. Mia's jaunty swagger became a hobbling shuffle; a stick had appeared in one hand and she leaned on this as though for support. Her shoulders bent like those of an old woman who has spent years grinding yam paste in stone mortars, who has carried firewood up mountain slopes in all weathers. More and more slowly Mia shuffled along, bent and arthritic, her arms taking on the crooked appearance and hard sheen of tree limbs. As she crossed the stone bridge, Noleena glimpsed her profile, saw how long lines pulled her cheeks downward amongst the swirling green FahFah patterns; saw how her dark, mischievous eyes had acquired a flat, rheumy stare. Noleena rubbed her own eyes incredulously.

Now Mia had reached the guard; his stiff stance altered slightly as he bent his head as though listening. Noleena squinted against the glare of mid-morning sky, where doves wheeled like blossoms above the alley, and saw Mia pull a large chunk of honeycomb, wrapped in leaves, from inside her pack and hold it up for the guard's inspection. Then she pulled something else, too small for Noleena to discern, from her bag and slipped it into the guard's hand. The guard turned and swung the heavy wooden door, hinged and reinforced with steel, partially open. Noleena craned her neck, but saw only Mia slip inside and be swallowed by darkness. Of what lay behind the door, she saw nothing. The door thudded shut, withholding its secrets, and Noleena slumped against the rock behind her.

I am all alone, she thought.

The red palace seemed to stretch taller above her, its massive weight of rock pressing down upon her; radiant heat beating her back from its expanse; its narrow windows like glaring eyes; its guards and archers waiting to discover her and kill her; its brutti dogs sharpening their teeth on their hatred for her. And somewhere, in its labyrinth of rooms, at the ends of echoing hallways, at the head of flights of stairs, the Maldici queen awaited her, with a power and cruelty beyond Noleena's ability to imagine.

I am all alone, Noleena thought again.

I have nothing. Except an empty box, probably useless. And my huge fear.

Quivers shook her body.

With an effort, she straightened her spine and sucked the burning heat deep into her lungs. Thrusting herself away from the cliff pressed against her back, she balanced her weight on the balls of her feet and lifted her chin, staring at the palace with her wide blue Wanderer eyes. For my people, she thought, I will do this. I will enter this palace; I will hunt through its hallways and bring the power of Luna to the Maldici queen. I will do this for Hasani, lost to the slow death of the mines, and for my father with his blind eyes and the scars of a corda cross in the palms of his hands. I will do it for the children dancing around a fire in a rift valley and too young to be quenched with the horrors of slavery. I will do it for the priestess who raised me with kindness and who was dragged away by the hair, screaming. I will enter this place, that I dread more than any other, for the sake of my mother, killed at her loom's bright weaving in her tent doorway.

Noleena lifted the edge of the Kiffa robe and felt for the sickle moon hanging from her bellybutton. She gripped it between her fingers and swore an oath upon it, the same oath Hasani had used to dedicate himself to her Seeking:

"I swear by the breath of the desert, that is mother and father to us, and by the light of sun and moon; by the name of Luna and the power of the Corno d'Oro; and by the beating of my heart and the blood of my lineage, to dedicate myself to this Seeking."

Then she willed her heartbeat to steady, and her body to hold itself as erect and still as that of the guard forty feet overhead, as she waited for Mia's rope to snake down from a grilled window and for her fate to take her into its jaws.

At last, a twitch of motion beneath the bridge caught her attention. She tensed. A rusted grill swung open with a slight creak. After a moment, Mia's grin appeared in the dark hole that lay behind the grill, and she motioned for Noleena to join her. Noleena glanced up at the solitary guard and waited until his attention seemed to be elsewhere; she slipped off the golden slippers as she waited and carried them in one hand. Then she ran soundlessly into the shadow of the bridge, the straps of the slippers now clenched between her teeth, and grasped at the rope that dangled from the window ten feet above her head. The soles of her feet gripped the rock wall as Mia hauled her up, the rope wrapped around one iron bar. On the lip of the window, Noleena paused as her eyes adjusted to the gloom beyond.

"Store room," Mia hissed, and Noleena saw boxes and bales stacked to the high ceiling, and heard the scurry of a rodent along a far wall. A barrel had been rolled beneath the window and then upended; Noleena slid her toes toward it and then jumped to land with a hollow thud.

"Hurry!" Mia said, and Noleena jumped again to land on the cool floor. Mia, who seemed to have regained her normal appearance, gripped Noleena's hand and hustled her through a maze of passageways between the piled goods, and into the darkness of a stairwell beyond just as Noleena heard men's voices from the farther side of the storeroom.

"Where does this lead?" Noleena panted, climbing the spiraling stairs with one hand running along the abrasive rock wall to her left, and no sound but the rustle of Mia's grass skirt. Mia didn't reply and they continued to climb until Noleena's legs burned with pain and she struggled for breath. Just as she thought that she could climb no farther, the stairs ended on a small landing from which the girls exited through a door into a hallway lit dimly with burning tapers.

"Put your slippers back on," Mia muttered. "And leave your pack. You have to get through here looking like a Kiffa."

Obediently, Noleena slid her feet into the slippers, and then bent to her pack and extracted the embossed box; she did not know what use it was, but she had nothing else to carry against the power that awaited her.

"I must find the Maldici queen before I am caught here," she said, and was ashamed of the quiver in her voice.

Mia nodded; in place of her urchin grin, she wore an expression both grave and still. Grasping Noleena's hands, she said, "Princess, power is yours for Luna has spoken to you. With a great yearning, Terre longs for this moment when you will set her people free from treachery and greed, from cruelty and a lust for riches. All is in your hands. You will not fail for even the lands around the Middle Sea need your intervention before the queen's darkness is unleashed upon them." Her lips, kissing Noleena on each cheek, were soft and dry, and quick as the touch of a bird's wing.

"But—you're coming with me?"

"As far as I can," Mia agreed. "If we are separated, you must find the queen alone; I do not know where—"

The brutto's snarl cut off Mia's words. Noleena turned in time to see its dark bulk hurtling toward them, and the leaping shadow of the assassini that followed close on its heels, a serrated knife gripped in one misshapen hand.

"Run! Go!" Mia yelled, shoving Noleena hard in the small of her back. She sprang forward, grasping the box, her heart drumming in her throat. But Mia—she could not leave her! She whirled back, in time to see Mia dart into the stairwell, slamming the door. The brutto howled in frustration, a ululating crescendo of sound that raised shivers on Noleena's skin. The brutto's attention shifted suddenly to her; she felt the malevolent gleam of its eyes. "Stand where you are! Answer for yourself!" the assassini shouted, his leaping strides bringing him level with the brutto.

For one second Noleena's head swam with terror; deformed man, howling dog, and grotesque shadows melded into one whirling vision. Then she leapt away and began to run blindly, with the helpless desperation of an animal that knows a predator far swifter and stronger than itself is giving chase; ran for her life and had little hope of saving it. The golden sandals pounded the stone floor. The brutto's panting grew louder. She expected at any moment to be knocked forward by its heavy chest, to hear her neck bones crack in its jaws. Flares and rock walls rushed past in her peripheral vision.

Beneath the desperate grip of her bloodless fingers, the lid of the box shifted. Suddenly, as though they knew what to do, her fingers unclenched and fumbled the box open; the smell of mint seared her nostrils and her vision steadied and cleared. She stopped and swung to face her opponents; stood still in the centre of the passageway as the brutto and the assassini pounded closer.

In hands suddenly strong, she lifted up the open box.

"I call forth the powers of Terre; I call forth the—the sand!" Noleena cried, the words ringing against the stone walls. There was no time then to wonder where those words had come from, how she had come to cry them in a sure, clear voice that was barely recognizable as being her own.

Nothing happened.

The lid fell shut noiselessly on its finely crafted hinges. The shadows of brutto and assassini merged with her own; the sickly smell of carrion enveloped her; spittle from the dog's mouth flecked her arm and burned like alkaline. She saw the creature's drooling nose and its lips furrowed in a snarl; saw the dark M branded upon the assassini's hairy forehead, and the mad, blood-lust gleam burning in his eyes.

This is how it all ends—so soon, she thought.

The brutto launched itself into the air and seized her robe. The fabric tore with a loud ripping sound.

The sand lifted from the bare floor in a curtain and hung shimmering in the flaring light. The assassini flung out his knife arm as though to ward off the sand but it fell upon him soundlessly, cloaking him. He pitched forward, the knife clattering to the floor and one hand grasping his own throat as he struggled for air. The brutto's snarls choked into silence and the creature fell over sideways, legs thrashing. Within the waves of sand, Noleena could dimly see the outlines of both bodies as they sobbed and gagged for breath as they writhed within the sand's stinging embrace. Like tidal waves, the sand lifted and fell, heaping itself over the bodies; masking their thrashing struggles.

Noleena backed away, staring in horror. Turning, she fled down the passage with the box wedged against her chest and the pink robe flapping in tatters about her knees. The passage seemed endless, carrying her deeper and deeper into the red castle. She darted glances behind herself, momentarily expecting the brutto's snarling form to spring for her back and bring her to the ground, but neither it nor the assassini reappeared.

When she finally reached the first bend, she leaned against the wall and bent over the box, gasping for breath. Then she peered around the corner to see a high doorway that led into a broad corridor lined with narrow windows through which sun fell in slanting lines. Kiffa guards squatted on the far side of the door, playing nam nam on a board laid upon the floor.

Noleena jerked her head back and stepped deeper into shadow.

What had just happened? And what would happen next? Had she really called sand out from the embossed box, the gift from Luna?

I did not imagine it, she thought. I did not imagine the bodies choking in that undulating desert sand. The power of Luna's land has filled the box and is mine to command for this moment! She has sent me aid at last!

Her fingers smoothed the lip of the lid, and over the silver clasp.

Can I call forth sand again? she wondered. Or can I only call each power once? Shall I step around this corner and advance boldly down the passageway toward the guards, waiting until they see me before I summon the box's power? But what if I call and nothing comes to aid me? The guards will seize me; I shall be dragged in chains, broken and battered, before the sorceress. But if I don't try, I will never know. All Terre yearns for this moment, she reminded herself; longs for freedom.

She pulled a long breath into her lungs and then opened the lid of the box. "I call forth the twilight!" she whispered in a commanding tone. There was again a brief pause, then Noleena became aware of the air immediately around her shimmering; it thickened like a soup and took on the dusky purple hue of mountain twilight. Noleena waited for a long moment to see if anything else would happen; she stretched one foot far out from her body and saw sunlight, slicing through the guard's door, touch the tip of her toes. She withdrew her foot hastily and saw how dusky air shrouded it. Did the box's twilight cover her like a shawl? Would the guards be able to see her inside it? Could she slip through their doorway and into the halls beyond?

For what seemed an eternity she trembled behind the corner, trying to gather enough courage to step out. Finally, she made a first tentative move, sliding her feet along the floor so as not to make any noise. No guard looked up. She took another step, then another. Closer and closer she approached the guards until she could see the coarse hair of their golden moustaches, the sparkle of a ring on one finger as a man threw the dice, the gleam on their embossed leather breastplates, the Kiffa tattoo on a man's arm. She stopped and swallowed heavily. At any moment now, a man would glance up; his tawny gaze would sharpen at the sight of her; the men would leap to their feet with a rattle of spears, their golden hair flung back from their arrogant faces.

Fear froze her to the spot and for long moments she watched the game as though mesmerized, and listened to the clatter of the dice as they rolled and fell.

Then she began to move again with infinite caution, her breath held in the back of her throat, her sandals sliding over the floor. She slipped behind a guard's shoulder.

Now she was so close to the men that she could smell their sweat; could have touched the tunic falling from the closest guard's shoulders.

She stepped past him. Her foot came down on a cracked tile and she stumbled; air whooshed through her mouth. The guard nearest to her swiveled sharply, glaring over his shoulder with hard, alert eyes. A puzzled expression crept across his face and he rubbed a hand over his eyes. Noleena held very still, then rushed forward into the corridor, avoiding the slanting bars of sunlight and scurrying along the wall farthest from the windows. The guard, she saw when she glanced back, had half-risen from his squatting position on the floor and was staring after her still looking puzzled. Then his companions called to him and there was boisterous laughter; the man sank slowly to his former position and picked up the dice.

Noleena hurried on, beneath high walls painted with intricate murals, past tapestries and baskets of hanging flowers, and small pools with splashing fountains. She tried not to think about Mia or to wonder what had happened to her. Where, in all this city of rooms, would she find the Maldici queen? She hurried forward through the castle's brooding shadows, past other guards standing stiffly attentive outside heavy mahogany doors, past the timid scuttle of young serving girls and the blank stares of Wanderer slaves, and the occasional, strangely garbed merchant from a foreign land. As she climbed, the corridors grew ever more lavish; tiled with exotic rose marble where red lines writhed; lit with a thousand candles in glittering chandeliers; carpeted with rugs so thick that Noleena's feet sank into them as though she waded through sand.

Now she saw a party of Kiffa women in Mombasso silk and golden neck rings hurrying toward her. She pressed herself back against a tapestry and held very still as the women grew closer, their faces agitated and their voices rising in sharp dissent.

"—her orders!" one asserted in a high-pitched tone.

"I don't think—" contradicted another, sounding equally forceful.

"You're not paid to think; just follow orders!"

"Who will help us once we arrive in Shoa?" asked a third woman.

"We are to find—"

"The Guardians will accompany us!"

Now the women were close enough that Noleena could hear the watery swoosh of their robes upon the marble tiles and see that, in the centre of the group, one woman carried a young child bundled in a blanket of Angoli wool as soft as thistledown. The child's golden lashes fluttered sleepily and his pudgy cheek rested upon the woman's shoulder; his head of red hair lolled upon a slender golden neck.

Red hair, Noleena thought.

As the group of women drew level with where Noleena held herself still in her cloak of twilight, the woman carrying the child came to an abrupt halt and turned her head to stare directly at Noleena. Something flared in her eyes, and Noleena saw that, although she was dressed like the other women in brilliant Kiffa robes, her narrow face was patterned with the green whorls of a FahFah. Perhaps she was the old hag's daughter, Noleena thought, remembering Mia's words. The woman flung back her head, her face tense, her eyes darting along the walls, her narrow nostrils fluttering as though she was trying to catch Noleena's scent. The other woman milled around her in exasperation.

"Come on! We cannot stop!" one cried imperiously.

"What is wrong?" asked another, tugging on the FahFah woman's arm. The child's eyes opened and his mouth puckered, his wide soft lips turning downward at the corners and then opening to release a lusty wail.

The FahFah woman ran her narrow hand, with its long tapering nails, across the back of the child's head to soothe him but continued staring at the place where Noleena stood, and her brow puckered with frown lines. "Some power is present here," she muttered, but now the child's first wail rose to the outraged bellow of a toddler waking in unaccustomed circumstances, and the other women crowded close around him, pushing and pulling the FahFah woman along.

"We cannot linger!" one hissed, and the whole group swept away along the corridor, flickering in and out of sunlight like a school of fish, the child's wails growing fainter, and the FahFah woman snatching backward glances toward where Noleena cowered. After several minutes, the group disappeared around a corner and the child's cries faded into silence.

Noleena turned and hurried on, her legs shaking with tension. Surely, surely she must soon reach the queen's quarters. A flight of ivory stairs opened on her right; they gleamed with a yellow patina of age, and were inlaid on each step with patterns of kiffa and stars. Noleena grasped the curving handrail of polished fragranti wood, and began to ascend; the stairs wheeled up through the heart of the palace in dizzying swoops and Noleena arrived at the final landing with dots dancing before her eyes. A tall, slender, arched doorway lay ahead, filled with sunlight and giving Noleena a glimpse of a balcony with ivory balustrades. The amber frame of the door itself was carved with all the creatures of Terre; Noleena saw kiffa and moon wrens, lizards and gazelles and horses. She remembered that, before this palace was usurped by the Maldici, the Kiffa king had considered himself a brother to the Wanderer king—to her father. All peoples of Terre had known and revered the same animals. She ran a finger over the carvings; they had been crafted with skill and loving detail.

"Approach!" cried a high, imperious voice from the balcony that lay beyond the doorway; the air seemed to part and shiver around the voice. Noleena's skin crawled as though snakes were wrapping themselves about her. Her fingers fell from the carvings. A surge of weakness brought her to her knees; the embossed box slipped from her lap onto the rosy marble tiles.

There was a wild laugh of derision from outside and the shadow of a woman fell across the doorsill. Craning her neck back, fighting to stay conscious, Noleena focused with difficulty on the woman's silhouette centered in the arched doorway: a dark waterfall of silk as red as pomegranates, a wild mane of hair burning with a nimbus of afternoon sun. Red hair. Noleena closed her eyes and fought for breath. Waves of panic surged through her; her blood seemed to flee before it, rushing to and fro, leaving limbs dangling uselessly or filling her head with hot dark oblivion. Blood poured in and out of her heart so that it pounded wildly or flopped into her stomach with life draining from it.

I will not give in, a voice—tiny and steely as the tip of a knife—insisted inside Noleena's head. *I will master this weakness.*

I—will—master—this.

She fumbled blindly for the box, closed her fingers around its smooth sides, pressed them against the star lilies. Her vision cleared and her heart steadied. With immense effort, pushing back the waves of malignant power that streamed from the crimson-gowned woman on the balcony, Noleena stood to her feet with the box in her hands. Her toes gripped the ground. Her knees steadied beneath her though the skin on her thighs quivered. She stepped out over the doorsill into Safala's searing afternoon air, and heard the swish of fabric as the woman outside took two steps away from her.

Noleena lifted her head, her lips compressed to still their trembling.

She was high up, she saw in an instant; beyond the balcony railing lay only an immensity of space and shimmering blue air. The rooftops of Safala, jutting between rocks and carved from the cliffs, fell away far below; beyond them again, the Valley of Nini was a distant, wavering mirage. Hawks, riding updraughts, circled hundreds of feet beneath the balcony. Above it rose only, on one side, the topmost battlements of the red palace with pacing sentries and, on another side, the towering bastion of cliffs that protected Safala from the high desert beyond.

Against the void of space at her back, the Maldici sorceress regarded Noleena with eyes of hard, brilliant gold that pierced Noleena's cloak of twilight. Indeed, Noleena realized, her whole body seemed bathed in a light of such harsh clarity that even tiny stitches hemming the cuffs of her sleeves were each clear and plain. It was a magic light, she thought suddenly; a light that pierced any deception, any secret, and from which nothing could remain safe or hidden. In this light, it seemed that for a moment Noleena could do nothing; like a night bird blinded by a taper, she could only stare at the sorceress.

The Maldici's hair, decorated with ivory combs, lifted in the wind and swirled about the planes of her face with a thin electric crackle; white sparks flew from it and disappeared into the brilliant light. Rings of precious stones glittered on her long pale fingers; and her pomegranate robes, embroidered with golden lines forked as lightning and snakes' tongues, swirled and eddied about her with a harsh gleam. Against the balcony's fretted ivory balustrades she shifted and flickered like a column of flame. Even the air around her seemed to swirl and crackle with the heat and distortion of her power.

Her pouting red lips parted over her sharp white teeth. "A Wanderer! Dust dressed like a Kiffa!" The Maldici laughed derisively and doves, nesting in the cliffs, tumbled into the sky in a flurry of alarm; Noleena tried to ignore the hawk that swooped amongst them, and the plummeting fall of one tiny white bird.

"Have you lost your way, young girl? If you wish to work in the kitchens, they lie far below. If you wish to work in the desert, it can easily be arranged. You might feel more at home there."

Darkness filled Noleena's eyes again, and her head rang with the agonized cries of her people dying in the mines, tortured in dark shafts, falling beaten beneath whips. She staggered as the volume of sound grew to a crescendo inside her skull.

A cruel, knowing smile twisted the queen's mouth.

Noleena regained her balance and tightened her grip on the box; as the queen's glance fell upon it her eyes narrowed.

"Ah," she said playfully, maliciously, "there is a reason for your trespass. You come bearing a gift."

Through the roaring in her head, Noleena felt the queen's power crackling in her, disrupting her concentration, prying deep into her mind, jarring the rhythm of her breathing, sending pain shooting through her nerves. Her knees weakened; they shook and began to bend.

"You are ready to present your gift? Though what you might bring that I couldn't take for myself, I cannot imagine. There is nothing that Wanderers have to offer me except their miserable lives."

Dimly through a haze, and fighting to remain standing, Noleena saw the witch's jeweled hands reach for the embossed box. Her own grasp upon it slackened. She fought to tighten her fingers again but they remained as limp as though broken.

The box began to slip.

When the Maldici touched it, a jolt of such pain and terror surged through Noleena that she pitched forward, her head cracking against the balcony's marble tiles. The witch's mocking laughter shivered and echoed through the void inside her head; the empty void where even the small voice of resistance had died into silence. Blackness closed over her.

CHAPTER TWENTY-TWO

IT WAS THE PAIN OF THE BOX, digging into her ribs as she fell across it, that jarred Noleena back into consciousness. Although her vision swam and her head spun, she realized that her fall had knocked the witch's fingers from the box and that it was still in her own possession, albeit lodged beneath her. She lay still for a moment, wishing with all her might to be anywhere but where she was, lying alone at the feet of the Maldici queen on a high balcony of the red palace. She squeezed her eyes shut. When she reopened them, her vision had cleared and she saw that the witch's feet were only inches from her face; anklets of golden snakes, their eyes inlaid with Mombasso rubies, leered menacingly at her.

Noleena rolled, grabbing the box from beneath her, then lunged to her feet with the box held against her chest. The Maldici laughed, a cruel mocking note that shivered against the cliffs; the air seemed to shatter around the sound like bright glass.

"A gift indeed," she said, her eyes piercing Noleena so that pains, sharp as needles, stabbed through her and she staggered on the marble tiles.

"A gift from the Sky Meadows, brought to me by a pathetic, frightened girl. How weak the powers of Luna have become in the world of Terre, that she can find no better messenger to carry her gift."

"I do not bring the box as a gift!" Noleena cried wildly. "Luna does not yield her power! I come to tell you that your evil is destroying all peoples of Terre: Kiffa-walkers as well as Wind-wanderers. You have no right to disrupt our ancient brotherhood, to usurp our traditions, to pillage and ravish our land, using its salt and gold and amber to feed your armies and build your navy ships. You are a foreigner and have no right here!"

The queen gave a twisted smile. "Right?" she asked, tilting her head. "But I am lawful queen, married to King Mhadi, and mother of the heir to the throne. I have every right to the wealth of Terre, to tunnel into her soil, to harvest her salt, to hire mercenaries, to launch ships into her harbors, to harness the power of her people to my will."

"Your harness is killing us!" Noleena protested, bracing herself against the pain in her chest, and the harsh glare of the light that rippled and shivered around the sorceress and that seemed to beat against Noleena with a power like an incoming tide. "If you were a true queen, you would nurture your people and nourish your land, not twist all to your greedy ends!"

"Enough words!" the queen spat, her smile replaced by taut anger.

She has only been playing with me, Noleena thought. Did I really think that I could stave off her power with words?

"Give me the box!"

Noleena shook her head. "I forbid you to take it, by the power of stars and sun and by the dark face of the moon! Do not touch me! I command you in the name of Luna!"

The witch halted suddenly in her forward rush as though meeting an invisible barrier, and her face contorted. A shower of sparks flew from her hair and she cried aloud commandingly in a strange tongue that seemed to bore into Noleena's skull and echo there, shattering her resolve and her courage. She turned away from the witch and reeled across the balcony toward the cliffs, then halted in shocked horror as movement flickered on the rocks' striated surface. From cracks and crannies in the granular surface, huge black spiders slithered soundlessly, their jointed legs, covered in black spines, propelling them with remarkable speed.

Tear-makers.

Noleena had never seen one before, though the creatures were reputed to live in the high desert and she had been warned of their deadly bite since early childhood. Now not one but a dozen, twenty, thirty, ran rapidly down the red cliffs and leapt from the base of the rocks onto the balcony's smooth surface; their feet, as they ran at Noleena and drove her back toward the queen, made tiny clicking sounds like twigs tapping on windows. Their bulbous eyes gleamed with a strange green luminosity.

Noleena held her ground for only a second before whirling to sprint for the narrow arched doorway by which she had entered the balcony from the spiral stair, but the queen stood before her, blocking her escape and holding out her hands for the embossed box. Noleena slid to a halt, whirled back to face the spiders advancing like a dark seething carpet.

Her fingers scrabbled at the clasp of the box as panic bubbled in her throat. She raised the box skyward. "I call forth the powers of Terre—I call the rocks!" she cried.

There are no rocks in my box, she thought. Only sand, and I have called that power already. This will never work.

Yet still she held the box aloft, her arms trembling as the mass of Tear-makers rushed closer.

The face of the cliff seemed to lift into the air in an explosion of red dust that hung suspended briefly before sifting down to coat the balcony railings, and plummet through space onto the rooftops of Safala. With a low roar, a rubble of rock and gravel fell upon the balcony, muffling the witch's angry shriek, obliterating the spiders, pelting Noleena's upraised arms with stinging particles and coating her tongue with the alkaline taste of the desert. The spiders' bony carapaces crushed with a brittle sound like a thousand tiny bones breaking; as the dust settled, Noleena saw that the entire mass had been covered, although around the perimeter of the rock fall, a few hairy black legs twitched feebly.

The queen lunged toward Noleena, her face contorted with fury, her red robe billowing, and her golden arm bands sparkling with their jeweled inlays, their precious stones.

"Give it to me!" she commanded; her will surged across the space that lay between Noleena and herself so that Noleena's blood ran thin and the box began to slip from her grasp once again. The witch's power seemed to be sucking the life from her; her vision whirled.

"I will not give it to you! The land belongs to Luna!" Her voice seemed to be flung back at her by the power streaming from the witch and by the solidity of the harsh bright light that flooded the balcony.

Still the witch advanced toward her, her arms outstretched. Noleena fumbled at her neck and pulled out, from beneath the Kiffa robe, the silver medallion engraved with sun and moon that her father had given her. She held it up into the light. "Do not touch me!" she cried.

The witch halted and stared at the medallion with narrowed eyes, then flung back her head and cried again in the dark tongue of the black book that her father had discovered, mildewed and ancient, in the library of Lord Morte, that first great sorcerer of Verde.

Noleena waited to see what would happen; briefly, she was deceived and thought that the witch's powers had failed.

Only, at the last moment, she heard a slight rasping sound behind her and whirled as the scorpion raised its stinger over its back in a tight arc, the serrated tip agleam and dripping venom. Noleena shrieked in pure terror; the creature was almost as large as herself and had advanced so closely to her that every detail of it was visible: the strange red sheen of the body marked with black banding, the quivering tension of energy coiled in the tail's arc, the pincer that reached toward the tattered hem of her pink robe. She jerked back but the pincer shot out and gripped her; she pulled away, struggling frantically, and lurched sideways just as the stinger on the tail drove forward. It glanced off her shoulder, a shallow wound that filled her muscles with a burning pain that quickly transformed to a weak numbness. Her arm dangled uselessly as the scorpion's venom spread, and she gripped the box tighter in her other hand.

"Let me go!" she cried, struggling in the pincer's grasp and hearing the silk of her robe tearing as the witch moved closer in the periphery of her vision. The Maldici's arm reached for the box.

I cannot hold it with one hand, Noleena thought.

With a great rending sound, the fabric of her robe tore from hem to armpit and she reeled free of the scorpion's grip, the box tilting in her one strong hand so that the lid fell open. Staggering across the balcony, aware of the rush of movement behind her as the creature and the witch both pursued her, she cried fiercely, "I call forth the mist."

In an instant, the air around her thickened and churned, became a milky boiling mass that obliterated her view of Safala, that dimmed the witch's hard shimmer of light, that brought the scorpion to a halt, snapping its jaws in frustration. Red cliffs, blue sky, wheeling doves and looming battlements were all obscured. Within the mist's moist coolness, Noleena felt the burning in her shoulder subside, and she rushed along the balcony's length.

I must hide while the mist lasts, she thought. I must climb up to where the scorpion cannot reach me.

She thudded, sobbing for breath, against the stone wall that rose at the end of the balcony, and scrambled up the narrow steps, cut into stone, that led from there onto the flat rooftop; this stretched into the mist and she fled across it as the witch's voice rose behind her in a ragged chant. As she climbed, scrabbling against the cliff that rose from the roof's farthest lip, the first gust of wind hit her in the back, pressing her against the cliff's rough surface and filling her head with a stench of carrion and sulphur. Her eyes watered and she retched; her lungs seemed to tighten as though fighting the entry of this foul air. The witch's wind tore the mist into streamers and curtains, shredded them ever smaller, cleared patches of air through which the Maldici's harsh light shone like a beam that reached to where Noleena clung one-handed to the face of the cliff. She wedged herself into a cranny and hung there, waiting.

The witch spun across the rooftop below in a column of wind that swept the mist clear and revealed Noleena, still holding the box. The witch raised her arms and the sky seemed to fill with wind; it howled and screamed across the rooftops and hit the cliffs with a blast that dislodged birds and gravel, that tore the breath from Noleena's throat, that loosened her grip on the rocks and made her hair and her robe stream upward. Like hands, the wind worked its way behind her back and pried her loose from the cliff. As she trembled on the lip of her cranny, in imminent danger of being swept onto the witch standing below, Noleena flung open the lid of the box once again and called forth the Ismata, the goddess's wind.

Its minty torrent pushed back the stench of the Maldici wind, and Noleena took a firmer grip on the rocks, wedging herself into her crevice. The winds battled each other, moaning and wailing, roaring up and down the faces of the cliffs, throwing the witch's hair first in one direction and then another as cascades of sparks streamed from it. The witch writhed as if possessed, her red gown swirling in the blast, her eyes gleaming golden in the light that seemed to flicker and shift as the winds tore to and fro, raising whirlwinds of red dust. Over and over the Ismata tossed the Maldici backward toward the edge of the rooftop where she reeled and shrieked; at the last possible moment, her own wind propelled her to safety at the base of the cliff.

At moments the stench of carrion threatened to suffocate Noleena as the witch's wind tore at her, prying her loose from her place of safety. Then a blast of Ismata would relieve her, pushing her back into the cliff's embrace and clearing her choking lungs of sulphur fumes. She felt giddy, blinded by rushing air, her mind swirling like the wind.

Behind the witch, great clouds began to boil up, rising higher and higher like bruises against the sky. Within the clouds, tongues of lightning flickered pure white, and Noleena felt the air crackle and tingle against her skin. Ominous shapes appeared in the clouds: dark holes like eye sockets, leering masks, writhing snakes. It was the witch's storm, called into being by her anger and her whirling wind, Noleena thought. She shuddered and bent her face before another blast.

Closer and closer the lightning approached, stabbing earthward, illuminating the valley of Nini in a wash of brilliance that made even distant, tiny nuga palms stand out in stark detail, washing over the rosy rooftops of Safala so that they glowed momentarily a blinding crimson; flickering upon the witch's shoulders and burning in her hair. Noleena stared at the Maldici queen in horror; she seemed to be dancing now inside a circle of pulsating light that rushed between her and the towering clouds. Within this light, the queen chanted and keened, her face lifted to the sky. Hair rose all over Noleena's body in the charged air, and when she moved one arm, sparks flew from the torn pink sleeve of her robe.

Around the witch's feet, lightning wove a pool of white light. Tongues of flame rippled out across the tiles, darting hither and yon. Suddenly, they coalesced and took on form; they became fiery snakes with open mouths and glowing eyes as red as rubies that broke free of the light around the witch and undulated across the rooftop toward the cliff where Noleena clung.

She stared at them incredulously. Were they real snakes that the witch had conjured from fire, or were they tricks of the light? Faster and faster they moved as she narrowed her eyes; they seemed pure lightning, but then she thought that within their blinding white outlines she glimpsed the golden and red banded vipers that lived in the dunes to the west of Safala and that lay covered in sand, waiting to lunge upward and sink their fangs into the hock of a passing shugra, or a scurrying child.

The snakes reached the bottom of the cliff. Noleena realized with a shock of pure horror that they were able to scale it, sliding toward her by following almost invisible crevices and crannies in the rock; perhaps following the same route by which she herself had ascended. Struggling to maintain her grasp upon it, Noleena lifted the box's lid one last time and cried for the water, for the rain that fell upon the Moon Mountains, filling the canyons of the plateau lands with cold, clear torrents.

The first snake lunged closer, its mouth gaping. Noleena saw its body writhe within its mantle of flame with muscular force, saw the bands of color shift and roll, saw the quiver of its fangs. She scrabbled at the cliff with her feet, dislodging gravel, forcing herself upward and backward, wedging herself into the rock. But there was nowhere else to go, for above her an overhang blocked her progress, and to each side of her the rock fell sheer and smooth to the rooftop of the palace where the witch still reeled to and fro in the battling winds, ranting in her foreign tongue as clouds and lightning roiled in the air behind her.

The narrow head of the snake slithered past Noleena's toes and lunged at the folds of her pink robe; she saw its fangs plunge in and out of the fabric. Flame caught at her hem and rippled upward as she flailed at the snake with her feet in a futile attempt to hold it off or to push herself higher up the crevice. At any moment, the fangs would pierce through the fabric and reach her skin. The flicker of flame rose higher on her robe, leaving a path like a gaping wound with scorched edges; it darted into her trailing hair and she smelled the stench of singeing. Madly she beat at her hair with one hand.

With a great roar, audible even above the shriek of the winds, the rain fell in a solid sheet. Instantly, the flames in Noleena's hair and gown were doused. To her left, an aqueduct of red brick that carried water to the palace, shattered open like a ripe melon dropped on the ground and spewed out water that sheeted across the rooftop and doused the flames at the queen's feet. A wall of water dashed against the base of the cliff and washed upward in a flurry of spume. Within it, the snakes hissed and smoked, flashes of flame darting from them as they struggled, their tails whipping around. One by one they were extinguished. Noleena drew back her toes as water surged over them and fell away again. The witch stood in the water, tinged red with dust, that churned and swirled over the rooftop, sweeping away her scorpion; that poured over the balcony below to rush down the walls of the red palace and wash guards from their feet; that joined with the torrents from scores of other bursting aqueducts and plunged into the thoroughfare before the palace, knocking assassini and brutti into its waves. Still it surged onward, carrying their bodies through the streets of the city and out between the gates into the valley of Nini.

The witch's wind rose to a shriek of such magnitude, filled with agonized cries, that Noleena involuntarily lifted both hands to cover her ears. Instantly, the wind snatched at the box. It plummeted down to smack into the water still streaming over the rooftop, swirled past the witch's feet, and plunged over the edge to be lost from view.

Noleena cried out.

The witch, struggling to maintain her footing, shook her arms in a gesture that could have indicated triumph; a darker, more menacing cloud towered into the sky with alarming rapidity and a fresh blast of wind hammered Noleena, tearing her fingers from the rock face, pulling her outward by the tattered remnants of her gown as though she were a jennet on a rope. She felt the moment when her shoulder blades came free of the rock against which they'd been pressed; felt clearly the moment when her toes lost their purchase, the moment when her balance shifted and her weight swung out into space.

If I fall, she thought, the Maldici will kill me and the tide of her darkness will devour Terre for only I can stand between her and her purpose. And there is nothing now to prevent her from killing me for the box's power is lost.

Then she pitched forward and was falling, falling through the wind's stinking rush, falling toward the Maldici's shrieking chant and the burning of her golden eyes. The Ismata swooped beneath her and bore her momentarily sideways along the cliff face but then a blast of the witch's wind sucked her downward again. The rooftop's foam-streaked, blood-red water seemed to rise to meet her.

She hit the water with a great smack that filled her with pain, then sank into its rushing coldness and was borne along blinded and choking, plunging down and down and down, an endless fall. Dizzy from suffocation, she lodged at last against something thin and hard. Her head broke the surface. She shook water from her eyes and saw that she had been swept off the rooftop and onto the balcony; it was the line of curved ivory railings that had saved her. She clung to them as water poured over and around her, and fell in a mighty waterfall toward the city below. Its thunderous roar filled her head.

Reaching up, she gripped the top of the railing and hauled herself half onto it, then lay there with the ivory a hard bar beneath her heaving ribs, and with her feet still dangling into the surge of water that poured away between the railings.

What now? Noleena wondered. She pulled scorched hair and blackened cowry shells from her eyes and glanced to her right to stare through the curtains of rain at the floodplain that was the balcony. It seemed unlikely that she could maintain her footing against such a torrent and navigate a path for herself away from the railings. Indeed, she saw, water was even pouring through the arched doorway itself to cascade down the stairs inside the palace. Noleena craned her head around to see that the witch had advanced to the edge of the rooftop above her and was still chanting and keening; she seemed able to maintain her footing though water surged and foamed about her legs. The crimson gown floated on the turbulent surface like a water flower.

Noleena lay across the balcony railing and stared at the mesmerizing plunge of water and the slick rooftops of Safala hundreds of feet below. The rain pummeled her shoulders and plastered the pink gown across her back.

I will not let the witch win! she thought fiercely. What powers of this land can I still call upon? Surely Luna will not desert me now! I refuse to give up whilst I still have breath in my body!

She struggled against the weight of her drenched gown and, flinging one leg over the railings, hauled herself up to straddle it and then climb perilously to her feet, balancing on its slick surface. Rooftops swooped giddily below her.

"The power of Luna dies in Terre!" the witch screamed on a sudden note of fierce exultation. "And you!" She pointed a long bejeweled finger at Noleena, "You who have defied me, will die too!"

Noleena looked up to see that the witch had conjured for herself a shimmering, fiery stairway in the air, and that she stepped onto it with regal arrogance, lifting the folds of her gown with one jeweled hand and descending to the balcony. The stairs carried her to the arched doorway, where she stood and chanted until the flood water was diverted and no longer flowed down the spiral stair but shot off into midair from the balcony and then vanished. Abruptly the rain thinned, slowed to a trickle, and ceased; the air cleared and sunshine stole across the valley of Nini and warmed the rosy stones of Safala. Beneath Noleena, the surge of water weakened; the water level fell until the balcony's marble tiles became visible and before Noleena's stunned gaze, they dried in the sunlight.

Suddenly the balcony railing upon which Noleena stood began to vibrate; before her horrified gaze, a section tore free with a loud, rending crack and plunged away to spiral over and over though space and crash at last, cartwheeling, across the slanting rooftop of a building far below. With another loud crack, another section, this time to Noleena's other side, tore free. Noleena struggled to leap down from the remaining portion of railing but some force seemed to hold her to the spot.

With a twisted mocking smile, the queen gripped the carved frame of the arched door.

The Maldici was returning to her palace, Noleena realized, and she herself was going to live for only a few more heartbeats of time, until the railing shattered beneath her—already she could feel it quivering—and plunge her to certain death. Convulsively she balanced as cracks ripped open the balcony tiles, zigzagging toward her like forked lightning. When the cracks reach me, the railing will give way and I'll plunge over, she thought desperately. The Maldici proved stronger even than Luna, stronger than the powers of Terre. Or maybe I lost the battle by letting go of the embossed box. I'll never know.

She pressed her eyes shut and thought of Hasani, of the mugwawa's hidden canyon and the laughter of Wanderer children. Of the animals, the rushing power of desert horses and the shyness of hareenas and the majesty of the moon goddess's leopard. Behind her closed eyelids the land's animals paraded past as though summoned by Ambro's flute.

Tilting her face to the sun, she inhaled deeply, feeling Terre's warm air fill her with its scent of sand and apricot blossom, and on a sudden rush of strength she lifted her arms to the sky, stretching herself taller and taller upon the railing even as it wobbled beneath her feet, and cried aloud in the old tongue. Her voice rang and echoed off the red cliffs, off the wheeling doves, and pinned the queen against the arched doorway like a butterfly to a board. Strong and sure Noleena's voice soared over Safala while the warm wind lifted her hair around her like a cloud.

"Luna, my moon sister, hear me
From the star roads and the wind-ways;
Think on Terre that was beloved of you
In the old times, in the first days
When you played amongst the lilies.

Luna, my star sister, hear me!
Think on Terre's beauty in this final hour
Of suffering—See her rivers weep!
Across her send once more your power:
Some beloved creature loyal to your heart!"

CHAPTER TWENTY-THREE

"OPEN YOUR EYES!" Hasani yelled into Ambro's ear. "Safala lies ahead!"

Ambro obeyed, squinting into the torrent of air that rushed over and around him, and in which the awesome span of the Sky Strider's wings quivered and tilted. Through watering eyes, Ambro saw a ribbon of green in the desert; after a moment's consideration, he realized that it was the valley of Nini reduced to such insignificance by the great height at which the Strider flew. To either side of the valley the red cliffs, that Ambro remembered toiling up laboriously on a rocky trail, were similarly reduced to no more than bright threads of color. On the far side of the valley, he glimpsed the tiny pile of stone that was Safala; it seemed to huddle beneath the boiling darkness of the sky. Great bolts of lightning, like streamers of brilliant cloth, unraveled through the clouds and converged upon the city. Their blinding white light flashed along the Sky Strider's wings, illuminating every feather and barb in harsh detail.

"How can we have come this far already?" Ambro yelled, pressing his mouth to Hasani's ear.

"It is the goddess's wind that carries the Sky Strider!" he replied, his ragged hair streaming in the rush of their flight.

"What will happen when we reach the city?"

Hasani shrugged and shook his head. "We will find out soon enough!"

The Sky Strider pitched sideways suddenly and plummeted through hundreds of feet of wind-torn space. Ambro's stomach dropped away and away from him; in its place his body seemed to fill with an expanding bubble of air that pressed his heart small and made it drum in rapid rhythm. Now a stench of carrion and sulfur washed over them so that Ambro's lungs burned. He gagged and retched as the Strider tipped so far off balance that the boys hung from its back into the air, with the land of Terre flashing past, aboil with dust, thousands of feet below their dangling boots. Only the lengths of mane that they had wrapped around their wrists prevented them from plunging to their deaths. Ambro felt the sockets in his arms stretching open, and the pain as tendons neared their tearing point. He cried out in terror, aware of the Strider's wings flapping wildly above him and the great creature's body rolling and plunging through the sky like that of a drowning horse.

Now the Strider rolled completely over, whipping the boys through the air so that Ambro's mind went dark and his ears rang with a terrible high-pitched screaming sound. The sulfur fumes crowded his throat and vomit trickled from his mouth, plastered against his cheeks by the wind. His body jerked and flailed on the end of its tether of Strider mane like a puppet whirled on the end of a string.

"Help!" he cried. "Help!"

The smell of mint filled his nostrils with a sudden sharp blast and he sucked it into his starving lungs; his vision cleared and the roaring in his ears died to a dull throb. Above him, the Strider righted itself and spread its wings wider, finding its balance again.

The Ismata lifted them upward through the sky; although turbulence still rocked them, the Strider seemed to fly with renewed strength, responding to each blast and buffet of the wind with a skillful manipulation of its huge feathers. Ambro hauled himself painfully upward on the long strands of golden mane, digging his toes into the Strider's broad shoulders covered in thick hair and aware, in the periphery of his vision, of Hasani doing the same. Together they struggled onto the creature's back again and clung there, wrapping more strands of mane around their arms. Hasani's face looked stretched with fear, and starkly pale, in the pulsating flicker of lightning from the clouds that reared above them.

Nervously, Ambro thought that the lightning was flickering down closer and closer to them but perhaps he was imagining it. But no! A great bolt, crackling and rending the air apart, snaked toward the Strider; Ambro saw its wings outlined in a nimbus of flame and saw the quiver of lightning run up his own arms, raising every hair. In one second, Ambro saw the whites of Hasani's eyes, and the sparks that flew from the bandit's ragged hair and that danced over his own golden armbands so that his skin burned beneath their grip; saw the gleam of lightning shiver through the Strider's mane so that the individual strands flew up, taut as golden wire and streaming sparks; smelled the hair burning.

With a cry, the beast veered away and swooped in a circle, losing altitude so rapidly that Ambro's ears popped and he opened his mouth wide, trying to suck in the air that seemed to be evading his lungs. Down and down the bird circled until Ambro could see the valley of Nini more clearly, with its clustered villages and groves of nuga palms, its terraced fields of wheat and beans, its dusty roads upon which he'd once walked. Safala loomed ahead, alternately flaring crimson in the lightning or plunging into obscurity against the face of the cliffs.

Now lightning pursued the Strider again, crackling and tearing open the air. Ambro clung on in terror and pressed himself flat against the great creature's back. Like a carpet of flame, the lightning bolts wove themselves across the sky between the Strider and the city, so that the creature once more veered away and began to rise, gaining altitude into the turbulence that roiled beneath the base of the dark clouds. Tatters of mist and vapor flew past them, blocking Ambro's view of the city.

"There is magic afoot," Hasani muttered tensely. "We are being prevented from reaching Safala. Where is Noleena?" And he clenched his fists in the Strider's mane and glared fiercely through the flying gloom and blinding light, his eyes a brilliant blue.

Again and again the Strider attempted to change direction toward Safala, flying first out over the high desert, then over the valley of Nini; now approaching from the north and now from the south and west. Each time, the curtains of shimmering lightning wove themselves across the sky, blocking the Strider's flight though it persevered in each course until small feathers burst aflame and it was forced to turn away once more. On the fourth attempt, a great bolt snapped from the clouds; for one fraction of time, Ambro saw the writhing clouds thrown into darkness, saw the Strider's noble head and flying mane starkly illuminated against this darkness, saw the great wings stretched taut. Then the bolt hit them and everything was obliterated into a molten void; Ambro squeezed his eyes shut and felt the flame beat upon his closed lids with ferocious intensity, smelled the burnt hair and flesh and the reek of burning fabric.

"We are alight!" Hasani cried in terror, and Ambro felt the Strider's wing beats falter and suddenly the magnificent beast began again to fall from the sky, plunging through the sulfurous blast. Ambro opened his eyes and beat at the flames licking in the Strider's mane, beat at his own thighs where his azure gown smoked and glowed; wildly he flailed at Hasani's burning back as the Strider fell and fell, and as the red swirling expanse of the high desert rushed up to meet them.

We will never see Safala again, or find Noleena, Ambro thought. We will all crash to the ground and be killed in an instant.

With greater and greater velocity the Strider seemed to fall, its wingtips streaming banners of white flame that flared against the bruised sky.

Then rain sheeted down like a solid wall of water, extinguishing every flame, roaring in their ears, drenching them to the skin in an instant, pounding on the tops of their heads. Within the rain's engulf, the air grew calmer and the Strider's wings spread outward, once again lifting them up. Hasani grinned at Ambro, his hair plastered to his brown cheeks and his teeth gleaming.

"Moon Mountain water!" he shouted. "Luna's powers unleashed!"

Ambro licked his streaming lips and tasted mint; remembered vividly the moment the animals had brought him to the mugwawa's canyon and he had lowered his burning face into its cold torrents. He felt a sudden flash of joy, and gripped Hasani's fist in his own as the Strider wheeled upward, the desert dropping away and the cliffs above Safala coming once more into view. Now Ambro could see tiled rooftops, individual towers containing bells that tolled clamorously in the swirling winds, hanging balconies and the arched doorways of treasuries. His eyes widened as the Strider soared over the city streets where torrents of water surged, sweeping away the rolling bodies of assassini and brutti, the merchants' scales and weights, the contents of a hundred treasuries awash in Moon Mountain floods.

"The Maldici palace!" Ambro shouted into Hasani's ears as the Strider veered to the north and the battlements and narrow slits of windows came into view. The tiny figures of archers let fly with arrows that were swept away uselessly in the raging winds, like straws flung into rushing streams.

The rain thinned, died to an intermittent patter on Ambro's shoulders, and ceased suddenly. Weak sunshine pierced the gloom and the city rooftops glowed pale pink. In the growing light, the woman in a crimson gown, her red hair lifting about her head, rose like a pillar of flame at the end of a pale balcony on the topmost floor of the red palace; the Strider dropped sharply toward this figure with air thrumming through its scorched feathers.

"Noleena!" Hasani shouted beside him on a high note of joy and terror; Ambro tore his gaze from the red haired woman to see Noleena's figure balancing on the balcony's shattered railing. Her arms were raised skyward, her eyes were closed, and the power of her chanting rushed up to meet the Strider; it seemed to Ambro that her voice crackled along his spine. Doves and moon moths circled the cloud of her hair, and at her tilted throat her blue beads shone like raindrops. Ambro stared downward in amazement; although her figure should have appeared foreshortened from the height of the Strider's back, it seemed to Ambro that she was much taller than when he had parted from her company in the High Meadows, and the dusky planes of her face seemed to shine with a pearly radiance.

"Watch out!" Hasani cried. Cracks rushed across the balcony's tiled surface as the Strider swept lower; the remaining railing lurched over the precipice, and Ambro too cried out Noleena's name as she swayed on tiptoe, her hair whirling. Still she chanted with face uplifted and eyes closed, and still the crimson-gowned woman stood in the doorway as though pinned in place. She is the Maldici, Ambro realized suddenly, remembering how a lemon seller had once described her to him in the thoroughfare outside the palace. The Strider's shadow swept along the balcony's length and its wings stirred the air into swirls of pink dust.

Sunlight burned in the Maldici's narrow golden eyes. A dark flashing of anger flew from her pouting mouth; the balcony railing broke loose with a tearing shriek and Noleena's body pitched forward over the yawning void of space. With a defiant whoop, Hasani leaped from the Strider's back and caught the girl in one arm; agile as a kiffa and fleet as a desert horse, he sprang across the tiles as they shattered beneath his feet. For one instant, the Strider's paws touched the balcony and in that instant Hasani flung Noleena upward to be caught beneath the arms by Ambro as Hasani jumped and grabbed at the trailing golden mane. The Strider's wings, that it had held outstretched, feathered the air again and it rose off the balcony, pursued by a shriek from the witch who moved away from the doorway and strode onto the balcony, ignoring the cracking tiles and crying a stream of dark invectives.

Ambro dragged his eyes away from her long enough to glance at Noleena but she was only a rounded shoulder in Hasani's arms;

their scorched ragged hair flew mingled in one black cloud around them as they pressed their faces together and kissed each other's dusty cheeks, burned with wind and blackened by smoke. Ambro turned away to look again at the woman raising her arms toward them, her golden armbands and jewels flaring in the light.

The Strider hovered in a torrent of minty air rising up the outside wall of the red palace as the woman below continued to chant her dark words that raised shivers across Ambro's skin. Noleena leaned forward, her brilliant eyes intense and filled with a burning confidence. "Catch her!" she spoke to the Strider in urgent tones. "Luna has sent you to deliver her to her death. Take her in your claws and hurl her down."

"Her words are weaving power against me; I cannot fly low again," the beast replied.

"I will intercede for you." Noleena tilted her face into the wind and began to chant; Ambro felt the words run across his skin and through his hair with a crackle like lightning. He felt that, all around them as they hovered in midair, the witch's words did battle with Noleena's words; the air swirled and shadows seemed to flee across Ambro's eyes although the sky was clear. Cold then warm, the air gusted over his skin.

Now the witch stood directly below the Strider, her flaming hair quenched by its shadow. The bird began to swoop down and for one terrible moment Ambro thought that her words were knocking it from the sky, that they were going to die after all upon the tiled rooftops of Safala far below.

Perhaps the witch believed the same, for she did not turn to flee until she was within reach of the Strider's outstretched paws, its golden claws as long as a man's arm and ending in points as sharp as sword blades. Then she wheeled in a flurry of gown and a swirl of hair, whirled too late for the shelter of the doorway leading to the spiral stair. The Strider, back feathering with both wings, caught her in its claws, the fabric of her gown pierced and torn, her net of hair wrapped and entangled, and lifted her writhing from the shattered balcony just as it gave way and slipped, in a rushing roar of debris and fragments, over the lip to fall into space.

Higher and higher the Strider wheeled, while Ambro, Hasani, and Noleena—now silent again but stroking the Strider's mane with one hand—peered over its sides to glimpse the witch's thrashing form; higher and higher on the steady updraught of the Ismata until the great bastion of the red palace was nothing more than a small rock far below.

Then the Strider's claws unloosed their grip, and Ambro saw the Maldici plummet away beneath them with her gown and hair streaming straight upward around the hard narrow planes of her face with its glaring eyes and screaming mouth. Straight as a flung spear, she fell toward the battlements of the red palace and her death; though she cried in the dark tongue for the protection of Morte's powers to save her, she was engulfed by the Ismata and no protection could reach her.

"May the dark face of the moon swallow you! May the pulled tide engulf you! May Luna's mighty wind sweep you away!" Noleena cursed as the witch fell.

Ambro watched until her body was a tiny speck, still plummeting toward the red palace; watched until the speck dwindled to a dot tiny as a mote of dust.

"With Luna to guide us, the grip of evil has been broken!" Noleena shouted to the sky, and buried her face in Hasani's chest; one arm reached out to grip Ambro and pull him into their embrace and they wrapped their arms around each other. Light glinted on Ambro's armbands of golden wire, and on the cowry shells in Noleena's hair, and in the fierce blue of Hasani's eyes.

"Is it truly over?" Ambro asked. "Is the Maldici witch dead now?"

"She is dead this very instant," the Strider said, "and no power on earth may raise her. This battle in Terre is ended, though not until the powers of the earth god unite with the moon goddess will peace truly dwell in the world. My children, you have all done very well. "

"But what of Terre now?" asked Hasani. "What of the Wanderers?"

"At the moment that the Maldici sorceress died," the Strider explained, "the balance was restored between the tribes. The Kiffa-walkers will wake as though from a troubled dream, and will begin to trade peacefully with their Wind-wanderer brothers. In tent doorways in the high desert, and in treasury rooms in Shoa and Safala and Jaffa, Wanderer and Kiffa will discuss their business over cinni spice and carpets, and no man shall consider one tribe better than the other. The powers that Noleena unleashed from her box did not only affect Safala, but were felt throughout the entire land. The Ismata stirred up a great storm in the port cities; the queen's navy ships were smashed and sunk. The desert sand rose and smothered the assassini and the brutti in the mining camps; the rain and the mountain water drowned the assassini and the brutti in the cities. All Terre is purged of their terror, their cruel mastery. Now, in the valley of Engedi, the horses will dance upon the spring-fed grass, and Hasani will record their lineages in the ancient book that his family has protected through many generations."

Ambro glanced at Hasani and saw how the planes of his face glowed with a flash of joy, how his brown arms gripped Noleena as though he would never again let her go. A spasm of envy flickered in Ambro. I am still without family, he thought, and this land of Terre is no more home to me, even after all this adventuring, than were the coastlines of Verde. Where shall I go now, and what shall I do? I will never return to Lord Tafari with his horses, nor lead his doda caravans, nor be his nephew. There will be no army in existence in this land for me to join. All my dreams have ended.

With a start, he realized that it was the death of the Maldici queen that had closed the final door on his dreams, such as they had been; did this mean that he had been as deceived as the Kiffa-walkers whom he had so desperately desired as kin? A spasm of guilt twisted within him.

"What...what will become of me?" he asked the Strider in a strangled voice.

For a moment the great creature did not respond; it swept in a wide circle over streets where the flood waters were still flowing, and disgorging a burden of bodies, shattered merchant stalls, broken armor and golden bars stamped with the Maldici mark, into the fields of the valley of Nini. Now the Strider's circle brought them over the rooftop of Noleena's temple at the end of its twisting alleyway; the alley itself was filled with water but the temple courtyard, being higher, lay dry and bare. Ambro saw, with a nostalgic pang, the pale columns of the temple pillars. Noleena leaned against his shoulder, peering eagerly downward upon her childhood sanctuary; the Strider drifted low enough that Ambro could see the apricot tree standing in its net of shadow, and the courtyard pool with its lining of blue tiles.

"What will become of you, Ambro?" the Strider repeated. "It is not in my power to foretell the future, yet I believe that the desert loves you and its paths will carry you wherever you wish to go."

Ambro shook his head; unsure whether this vague answer held enough comfort to sustain him. Noleena glanced at his miserable face and gripped his arm. "Ambro," she said softly, "I too will go to the valley of Engedi, for one of Luna's temples stands by the spring, beneath trees filled with rainbirds; I have heard that, early in the morning, the Wanderer horses drift to the temple steps with their foals skittering at their sides, and bend their heads to drink the Moon Mountain water. I will be the priestess in this temple, if the Wanderers wish it. You will always be welcome in the valley though you should come in storm or clear starlight. Dune Dancer and Sun Runner await us there. Hasani and I will help you search for your mother's people."

"My mother's people?" Ambro asked, startled for the second time in as many minutes.

"From whom else did you inherit your webbed toes?" Noleena asked gently. "Did you never consider this, Ambro?"

He shrugged in surprise. Perhaps he had considered it, but had not wanted to admit to it; had not wanted to give up his dream of striding through Safala's streets in a billowing robe and being acknowledged by Kiffa and foreign merchants alike as the nephew of Lord Tafari. His mother. In a flash of recognition, he retrieved his only memory of her: a dark mysterious smile, a smooth dark face haloed in long, waving black hair. His Wanderer mother who must have worn, in a cabin on the doomed *Jaffa Queen*, a sickle moon in her pierced bellybutton and who had bequeathed to him, not only the translucent webs between his toes, but his love for the desert, its sea of silence.

"You are a princess as well as a priestess," the Strider reminded Noleena, interrupting Ambro's thoughts. "Hidden in the waves of the future lies the moment when you must lead your people."

"Nonetheless, in the temple of Engedi I will wait until that moment arrives," Noleena replied with her new certainty. Ambro shot her a searching glance and saw how her wide blue eyes, that so often in the past had been filled with timidity and fright, now shone with beauty and confidence; saw how she grasped the Strider's mane with strong arms and how she tilted her head back against Hasani's chest and smiled as the wind wrapped her hair through his. The battle with the Maldici has changed her, Ambro thought. She will never again be the terrified girl whom I awoke at the base of the altar in the temple; she has left that girl far behind. And when she becomes queen of the Wanderers, Hasani will be king and together they will rule with love and wisdom.

"Where shall I carry you?" the Strider asked, its shadow sweeping across flooded market squares and alleyways awash in the last of the water; the burst aqueducts, Ambro noted as the Strider wheeled against the face of the cliffs above the city, had ceased to flow and already their broken bricks were drying in the sun.

"We must find my father in Safala—and Mia, too!" Noleena exclaimed, and the Strider began a final descent over the rooftops of the city and swooped down, folding its great wings at the last possible moment, into the courtyard of Noleena's temple. They all slid off to stand, windswept and shaken and suddenly greatly fatigued, beneath the apricot tree. Ambro's boots crunched in the charred remains of a small fire; perhaps sand fleas had cooked a meal here recently.

"The wandering ones return, on the wing! Now let's sing! Now let's dance and prance! The witch is dead; long live the king!"

Ambro spun on his heel to see Mia frolic down the temple steps in a robe of brilliant purple stitched all over with birds and magrazzi, and with a lilac scarf knotted around her head. Sprays of cliff-star flowers, tucked into the scarf, swayed around her head as she moved; her face was creased in its familiar impish grin.

"Mia!" Noleena cried. "I've been so worried about you! What happened in the palace after the assassini chased us?"

"I remembered I had urgent FahFah business to attend to at home; the guard who let me out enjoyed his honeycomb," Mia responded with a wink. "And then I came to find your father and bring him here, safe from the flood."

"My father?" Even as she asked this, Ambro saw an old man emerge from the shadows of the temple and reach for the support of a pillar. Some stirring of recognition moved in Ambro but he couldn't remember when or where he might have see this man before. At the slap of Noleena's feet on the tiles, as she rushed to him, the old man's lined face broke into a smile of such radiance that Ambro could only stare in amazement; for an instant, it was as though he was transformed into a young man, into the prince he'd been, walking in the valley of Engedi while the horses danced and a desert woman drifted to him over the grass to steal his heart.

"King Lebna," Hasani said with reverence and bent to his knees; Ambro hastily did likewise. When he raised his eyes again, the Wanderer king was grasping Noleena to his chest and the instant of transformation had passed; now Ambro noted the stained leather thong tied over the blind eye sockets, and the great furrows of grief that scored the king's cheeks on either side of his wide smile. Then the man bent his head into his daughter's cloud of hair and cowry shells, and gripped her to his chest as though, like Hasani, he would never again let her go.

"My princess," he said, "my brave princess, my desert daughter. You have done more than well. Your people will sing of you in the cool of the evening; the children will learn your name in their shugra blankets. Hasani will name a line of horses after you, Noleena, child of the moon."

Then the king moved forward, with Noleena on one arm, and laid his hand upon Hasani's bent head. "And you have done well, too," he praised. "Son of Teckle, you have brought honor to your father's memory. To you shall pass the ancient book of horse lineage; for you they shall dance in the meadows."

Ambro stared at the tattered hem of the king's tunic as it moved closer to him; the king's shadow fell across his shoulders and then he felt Lebna's hand, a firm warmth, pressing upon his own bent head.

"Welcome Ambro, child of city and of sand; child of an impossible love. All Terre shall welcome you; her streets and alleyways, her high plains and her rolling dunes; her splashing tiled fountains and her secret oases. Wanderer and Kiffa shall call you brother, cousin, uncle, father. You will never be alone in Terre again."

A burst of such belief and hope rushed through Ambro that he felt his shoulders quiver; perhaps Hasani was aware of this in some mysterious fashion for he leaned his own shoulder against Ambro and steadied him with his touch. "Brother," Hasani said softly, and Ambro bit his lip against the sudden prickle in his eyes.

Then the king's hand was withdrawn, and Hasani and Ambro rose to their feet. Behind them, the Strider spoke, spreading its wings. "I return to my blue shadows, my mystery, my mountain places from which no man may call me and to which no man may roam to find me; only Luna and the mugwawa may call forth the Strider to ride the Ismata when the great storms rise in Terre. Farewell, children of the desert. May your paths be lit by bright stars."

The great creature spread its golden wings, feathers flaring, and jumped upward on its huge kiffa paws, their claws sheathed. In an instant, it rose above the walls surrounding the temple courtyard; its shadows swept across the upturned faces below, soared over the temple's pale roof, swept over the red tiles that lay beyond. Higher it climbed, riding an updraught of warm minty air that rose against the cliffs, higher and higher until it was merely a speck that disappeared over the rim of the cliffs into the great dome of blue sky over the high desert. Ambro let out his breath in a long sigh as the Strider disappeared from view.

He glanced around the courtyard to see that the old king was shuffling inside the temple, leaning on a gnarled walking stick, and that Noleena and Hasani were beneath the apricot tree, holding hands and talking in a low murmur of sound that reminded Ambro of the sleepy cooing of doves in rock crevices in the heat of the afternoon. For a moment, he felt alone. Then Mia scrambled out of the central pool, where she'd been wading with her skirts bunched in one hand. She pulled a sprig of cliff-star from her scarf and stuck it behind Ambro's ear, then stared at him quizzically with her head on one side. "Cheer up," she teased. "You can always join the sand fleas now that the army is disbanded. Can you juggle, can you dance; like a pony can you prance? Can you sing, can you bring the people flocking to your ring, ring, ring?"

"You're not making sense," Ambro complained, his face breaking into a grin despite himself.

"Never mind," Mia said. "I can't rhyme on an empty stomach. Let's go and find some food."

She gripped Ambro by one hand and pulled him out through the courtyard and into the alley, which was still filled with two feet of water although the moist layers on the rock walls to either side showed that the water had previously been much higher and was receding rapidly. They splashed through the alley's narrow twisting passage and came out into a market square where vendors were already rebuilding their stalls; Ambro noticed that soldiers were helping too, their red capes discarded and their snarling breastplates tossed aside in piles.

"Look!" he pointed. "Wanderers!"

Mia glanced along his outstretched arm to where Kiffa merchants, still arrayed in brilliant robes, stood chatting on treasury steps with a group of Wanderers in ochre tunics; smiles flashed across faces and nearby, Ambro noticed with great pleasure, several Wanderer horses stood waiting patiently beneath the shade of an acacia tree, up to their hocks in water.

"The Strider was right," he muttered. "On the witch's death, a dark spell was destroyed and the brotherhoods of Terre have been restored. But Mia, how did King Lebna know all about everything that has happened? Who brought him news?"

"Well me, of course," Mia responded.

"And where's your hurdy-gurdy gone?"

"Gave it to a FahFah."

Ambro reached out and grabbed a handful of purple fabric in one hand, jerking Mia to a halt. "Who are you?" he demanded. "You're not really a sea urchin or a sand flea are you?"

"Of course I am," she responded, throwing him an indignant look. "Haven't you seen the coins they throw me in the market-places, the goat's milk, the nuga nuts?"

"Be serious," Ambro replied. "Mia, you came to Terre with me; give me a true answer."

For a moment, her changeable face became still; her dark deep eyes flat. Then she tilted her chin and gave him a level stare in which there lurked no mischief or any hint of laughter. "I am the seventh daughter of the seventh daughter, in the family of the beetleman in Verde," she said. "Ask me no more."

Then she whirled from him with a hop and a jump that broke his grip on her dress; she shot ahead of him across the market square, dodging between grumbling doda and a band of small boys having a water fight to the annoyance of passing merchants. Ambro waded after her, mulling over her reply and finding that somehow it did not surprise him. Although he had never met the beetleman of Verde, he had heard tales of the man and his troupe of puppeteers; they had organized a revolt of the country people against Lord Maldici. And even though I know little of magic, Ambro thought, I do know that the seventh daughter of a seventh daughter is not an ordinary girl.

When Ambro caught up to Mia again, she was standing at a crossroads where four ways met, and peering in each direction. Ambro too paused to look around. A crew of builders hurried past, their shoulders bent beneath the weight of bright new bricks on swaying boards, and heading toward a shattered aqueduct. A foreign merchant, leading three jennets tied together with rope and loaded with sacks of spices, strode by. A Kiffa woman in a damp robe and shining neck rings, hurried past, laughing and hand in hand with a Wanderer woman in a pale tunic, whose sickle moon flashed against her smooth brown belly. A seller of silk had unrolled his sodden bolts and strung the fabric to dry between balconies; the air billowed with clouds of shimmering colors so that the upturned faces of passersby were stained pink and azure and aquamarine and a green as pale as the wings of moon moths.

"You haven't happened to see a red haired child anywhere, have you?" Mia asked, jolting an elbow into Ambro's ribs. "One with a FafFah nursemaid?"

"What?' he asked, bringing his gaze down from the glorious dance of the silk fabric against the bright blue sky, and thinking that what he wanted to do most was to buy some and build a kite to fly in the valley. "A red haired child? No, nowhere."

"Pity," said Mia dismissively, then, "Let's go and find some food; we've missed lunch and pretty soon we shall have missed supper." She plunged on again, nimble and quick as any street performer, dodging rows of washing hung to dry, and the streams of water that women dumped out into the streets from open windows.

"Where are we going to find food?" Ambro yelled, running after her. She glanced back only once, quickly, with her familiar impish grin.

"At Lord Tafari's!" she cried. "I heard the cook there makes the best chicken and fennel dumplings. And besides, the Lady Tafari has been asking when you were going to come home!"

Ambro doubled his pace and sprinted, laughing aloud, through the streets of Safala while Moon Mountain water, splashing about his knees, filled the air with shimmering, iridescent colors.

THE END

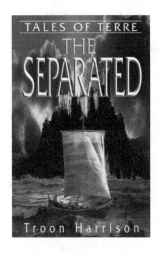

THE SEPARATED
The First Tale of Terre
by Troon Harrison

Chapter One

It was the first morning of the spring equinox when Vita came alone out of the mountains. She paused on a grassy slope above the waters of the Golfo d'Levanto. Shading her eyes, she stared towards the valley, hidden by a fold of the land, where her home waited. Already, she could see the smoke from village chimneys lifting straight into the still air like brush strokes of translucent gray. At this reminder of cooking fires and bread ovens, Vita's stomach rumbled hungrily. She had traveled light in the mountains for two days, eating only the figs and the goat's cheese that her aunt, Aunt Carmela, had packed into the sack that she carried slung over her thin shoulders.

I'm almost home, Vita thought. I should be happy.

She sighed and continued along the path as it wound downhill, her sandals beating softly in the dust. Her legs felt as heavy as though sand filled them, and a weight seemed to press on her shoulders along with the hot sunlight. She remembered how, when she was small, she had skipped down this path beside her mother, how she had picked wildflowers and sung simple tunes. It had been easy then, to be joyful. Today she felt old, much older than fifteen, and too miserable to sing. What was wrong with her?

She should have been satisfied, for yesterday she had completed the magic circle around the mountain realm of the Corno d'Oro. She had sung the ancient spells, drawn the sacred symbols with her fingertips on trunks of towering catalpa and fragrant acacia and gnarled olive and onto the backs of warm rocks. She had chanted the incantations over pools of water and rushing rivulets. Now the secret ways and places of the mythical Corno d'Oro were protected for the year's quarter—its paths invisible to the eye, its places of rest hidden behind the veil of magic she had created, its grazing meadows peaceful and secure.

When the next equinox drew near, she, the Keeper, would travel once more alone into the mountains, the villagers averting their eyes as she passed through their terraced gardens, their groves of nut trees. They had vowed to protect the Corno d'Oro from the evil that swept across the land, but only the Keeper could work the ancient magic and they didn't wish to spy on where she went or what she did when she climbed the slopes alone behind their houses, her eyes shining with old wisdom.

Now, leaving the path, Vita plunged abruptly downhill on a shortcut of her own. Around her, twisted olive trees cast a thin shade, their pale leaves fluttering above swathes of crimson poppies and of cyclamen in shades of white, pale rose, and deep crimson. Tiny butterflies of palest blue danced over the flowers. The trees quivered with bird song: the long warble of the olive thrush that was like water falling, the chitter of moon wrens, the sleepy hoot of a distant gufo.

Thick spring grass swished against Vita's bare legs, and the smell of the land filled her nose: the warmth of tilled earth, the aromatic whiff of rosemary and thyme, the tang of salt from the beaches below. She knew that she should have felt content in the midst of such beauty, not miserable. Moodily, she kicked a pebble down the path before glancing up to notice a plump girl of her own age seated nearby on a rock.

"Beatrice!" Vita shouted.

The potter's daughter turned and waved. Vita quickened her stride and climbed onto the flat rock beside her friend, who was rubbing dried clay from her fingers.

"You're back," Beatrice said, her cheeks dimpling as she smiled. "All is well?"

"All is well," Vita said shortly, but she didn't feel as though all was well. She felt as though a nest of snakes was uncoiling in her heart, restless and dangerous.

Beatrice stared at her for a moment. "I thought you might be hungry," she said, and held out a stack of almond cakes wrapped in a grape leaf.

"You're right," Vita agreed. She bit into a cake's crisp, golden edge. She munched through its soft centre, sticky with honey, and then silently ate a second one.

"Is something wrong?" Beatrice asked at last.

Vita shrugged. "No," she said. "Not really. Maybe. At least—it's me, Beatrice. There's something wrong with me."

"What do you mean?"

"I wish I wasn't the Keeper. At least, not yet. Other Keepers, in other generations, haven't had to be responsible at my age. I just wish I could do something else first. Travel. Have fun. See the inland plains and visit the cities. Buy from the merchant ships unloading treasure in the delta."

"But the Corno d'Oro's safety is in your hands," Beatrice pointed out. After a pause she asked shyly, "Have you ever seen him?"

Vita shook her head. "No. My mother said that if I ever see him, it will be at a time decided by him and not by me. And that, in the meantime, I see his spirit when the village children laugh, or the fish jump in the sea, or the wind and sun pass through the olive trees. But we know, Beatrice, what he looks like from the Keeper's Tale: wondrously beautiful, with purple-brown eyes, rippling mane and tail, a noble face and a tapering, spiral horn of pure gold growing from his forehead."

Beatrice sighed in awe, with lips parted and eyes gazing away down the slope. "You're lucky, to follow in your mother's steps," she said. "Since she was the Keeper, you must be the next one."

Vita swallowed, feeling tears close to the surface. She rested her elbows on her knees and bent her face into her hands, staring into the red darkness behind her eyelids.

"I wanted to grow up and be just like my mother—only not so soon," she said, forcing the words out. Beatrice's warm hand squeezed her arm. If only her mother had been more careful, eleven months ago, picking herbs on a mountain ledge. If only she hadn't fallen so far, landing on rocks below...Vita pushed away her grief, letting resentment take its place. Straightening, she rubbed a hand

across her lavender eyes and brushed away the strands of silver-blonde hair that had fallen across her face.

"Don't you ever wish you could wear a silk dress and eat food from faraway places?" she asked passionately, staring at Beatrice. "Don't you ever wonder what it would be like to live in a palazzo in Genovera? Don't you wonder about the parties they hold in the cities, with fireworks and exotic animals, games and street shows and dancing?"

Beatrice frowned, clasping her plump fingers together. "Not really," she said. "It's very beautiful here, Vita. I'm happy painting pots and living in the village. And I thought that being a Keeper was something special, a sacred trust—"

"Of course it's a sacred trust," Vita interrupted impatiently. "But I don't want it, at least, not yet. I want to—oh, I don't know. I want to be free first. This time, I almost didn't come home."

"What?" Beatrice sounded shocked.

"I could have walked down into the plain, on the other side of the mountains. There was no one to stop me."

Vita remembered how she had lingered on the eastern ridge of the mountains and gazed across miles of blue distance to where the plains shimmered. Restlessness had gnawed at her with a kind of hunger. She had longed for the freedom to walk down into the plains and explore the cities that spread by broad, shining rivers. In her imagination, she viewed the city's tall towers and huge squares, their cafes with bright awnings, their slender spires where bells tolled. She had heard about such sights from the wandering tale-spinners who occasionally passed through her coastal village. They talked about the nobili too, those rich merchants and princes who lived in the cities, riding on spirited red horses with hooves that struck sparks from the cobblestones. According to the tale-spinners, the nobili wore fabulous clothes of silk and velvet, ate from plates of gold, and could have whatever their hearts desired.

Balanced on her rocky outlook, Vita had fingered her own dress of coarse blue fabric with discontent. What would happen if she simply took the path winding down into the plains and journeyed to the nearest city instead of returning to her village? What an adventure that would be! And there was no one there to prevent her from going, or to see her leave. For what had felt like a long time, she'd lingered on the ridge and fought temptation while the breeze on her shoulders seemed to nudge her forward. As shadows lengthened, she had turned her back on the plains and her longings, and begun her journey westward towards the coast. For she was the Keeper, bound to the Corno d'Oro—and dreams of silk and dancing were not for her.

Although she knew that to be the Keeper was a great honor, lately she'd felt that it was a load that she carried, or a rope that bound her tight. She hadn't asked to be fulfilling the expectations of others: her dead mother and all the previous generations of Keepers, Aunt Carmela, the villagers.

"If you hadn't come home, there wouldn't have been anyone to tell the Keeper's Tale at the Feast of Dragomar this afternoon," Beatrice reminded her.

Vita followed Beatrice's gaze across the Golfo d'Levanto's wrinkled surface of water that stretched to the pale horizon. Two miles offshore, the rocky archipelago of twenty-two pirati islands floated on the surface of the sea.

"Another of my responsibilities," Vita sighed.

She would be expected on the largest of the islands, in the village of the pirati, to tell the Keeper's Tale before the feast. For most of the year, the pirati did not encourage mainland visitors to their islands, and the mainland villagers for their part preferred to keep to their mountain terraces and their small fields. But at the Feast of Dragomar, the Keeper always visited the islands to tell the Keeper's Tale because it was a story important to the pirati as well as to the villagers.

"Never mind," Beatrice said, poking Vita playfully in the ribs. "Giovanni will take you across the water."

Heat rose up Vita's neck when she thought of Giovanni's changeable sea eyes dancing over her face, of Giovanni's brown hand steady on the tiller, of his boat with its pale yellow sail and blue hull.

"Maybe there was something to come home for?" Beatrice teased, but Vita leapt to her feet and jumped down off the rock.

"Don't you have pots to paint?" she teased in return. "Let's go."

The Separated
by Troon Harrison

The evil Lord Maldici's powers are growing, and darkness looms over the magical land of Verde. Three sixteen-year-olds must discover their own strength and their magical abilities in time to win the battle for their land.

Are the magic spells of the Keeper, strong enough to keep the world in balance against the sorcery of evil Lord Maldici, who wants to conquer the land?

Can young Giovanni, the son of a pirate, fight the temptation of gold to vanquish a monstrous sea dragon?

Can Marina escape her powerful sea-witch mother and her own destiny as a witch to live on land, no longer a feared outcast?

Will the three, separately and together, save their world from certain disaster and slavery?

A brilliant, rainbow tapestry of war, flowering meadows, sea battles, witchcraft, exotic creatures, cruelty, and love.

ISBN: 9780976812616   368 pages, $12.95
Available from your bookseller.

What the reviewers say about
THE SEPARATED, The First Tale of Terre

Midwest Book Review, June, 2006

"A skillfully crafted novel of fantasy action/adventure, *The Separated* is very highly recommended for its creative and magical world and tangible vivid descriptions of battles of faith and revolution."

Curled up with a Good Book, August, 2006

"*The Separated* is a wonderful fantasy adventure set in the land of Verde in the world of Terre. This is the first book in Troon Harrison's 'Tales of Terre' series. A simple map is located near the front of the book for readers who want to follow the characters on their journeys.

Troon Harrison is one of the most pleasantly descriptive authors I have had the pleasure of reviewing. Use of physical reactions to stress, apprehension and fear were well done. In chapter five, on page 37, is one instance of an admirable use of words:

'In the pearly dawn, while the sea lay flat and the little waves barely licked the beaches, Vita and Giovanni slipped from his parents' house and walked down the cobbled alley to the harbor. ...The sails were indigo colored, dyed with pigment from the mullosks that clung to island rocks, and around the fabric's periphery stood other pirati, watching the scouts and talking about the assassini raid.'

While *The Separated* might have been written for a teen audience, it will certainly appeal to adults as well—after all, I am 37...and I have thoroughly enjoyed Harrison's latest fantasy novel. Readers may also be interested to know that the author has written 16 books (teen novels, junior chapter books, and picture books) which have been well-received by critics. She has been published internationally in five different languages and has received awards for her work, as well. Two of her children's books have been television shows on the YTV channel."

Reader Views, January, 2007

"…You can actually envision what is happening, and the story will come alive as you read it. The author's main point is to show that as these teenagers grow up, they change. As these teenagers change and mature, they gain freedoms and responsibilities that they have never experienced before, just as real teenagers might.

'The Separated' is for readers ages 12 and up, who enjoy fantasy or sailing. If you enjoy either of these topics, you will like 'The Separated.' In this book, three teenagers learn to appreciate what they have and find out where they truly belong. Troon Harrison expresses this in 'The Separated.' I'm looking forward to any future installments of the series 'Tales of Terre.'"

CM Magazine, September, 2006

"…a lengthy introduction to the world of Terre. The author uses vivid description, and flowing, often flowery language to paint a broad and very detailed word picture. Included in the book is a full page black and white map which allows the reader to follow the travels of the characters. In this story, we have sea battles, witchcraft, magic, several fantastic creatures, war, cruelty and romance. At the end of *The Separated*, there are sufficient unresolved crisis to allow the 'Tales of Terre' to continue.

This story will appeal to many fans of fantasy tales. While seemingly targeted toward the young adult market, (the main characters are sixteen), the book may also appeal to adult fantasy readers as well, especially those who love tales told in a style reminiscent of an Italian Medici mystery.
Recommended."

Finalist, Foreword Magazine Book of the Year Award 2007

Listed, Children's Book Council Summer Reading Extravaganza 2006